SLANT
OF LIGHT

A Novel of Utopian Dreams and Civil War

STEVE WIEGENSTEIN

Blank Slate Press
Saint Louis, MO 63110

Copyright © 2012 Steve Wiegenstein

For information, contact
Blank Slate Press at 3963 Flora Place, Saint Louis, MO 63110.

For information about special discounts or bulk purchases, please contact us at queries@blankslatepress.com.

Manufactured in the United States of America
Set in Adobe Garamond Pro
Cover Design by Kristina Blank Makansi & Jane Colvin

Library of Congress Control Number: 2012935148

ISBN-10: 0982880669
ISBN-13: 978-0-9828806-6-1

For My Mother and Father

Acknowledgment

I firmly believe that every human being is touched by inspiration—some often, some rarely. But we all have our moments when we have a big idea, a stroke of inspiration, or a moment of insight. Making those ideas reality is where the real struggle begins, and it's a struggle that cannot be waged alone. It's not enough to call on the Muse. The Muse has to answer and say, "You have my attention, and I am listening."

I have been fortunate throughout my life to have had people around me who have encouraged my bouts of creativity. My mother and father, Faye and Eugene Wiegenstein, supported every crazy idea I came up with as a kid, and the sense of empowerment they gave me went a long way toward making me the person I am today.

The good people at Blank Slate Press—Kristina Blank Makansi and Jamey Stegmaier, by name—have been extraordinarily helpful in getting this book in shape for publication, with ideas and information, thoughts on character development and plot structure, never settling for the "just okay" but always pushing toward the "just right." I am grateful for all they have done.

My wife, Sharon Buzzard, read every word of the manuscript more than once, and her suggestions and comments were always made with a keen literary sense and a belief in the power of storytelling. My gratitude for her contributions to the creation of this book is impossible to express.

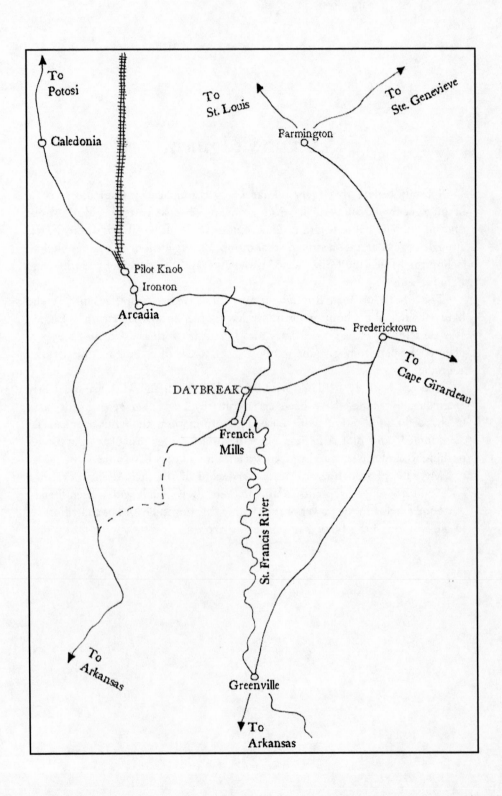

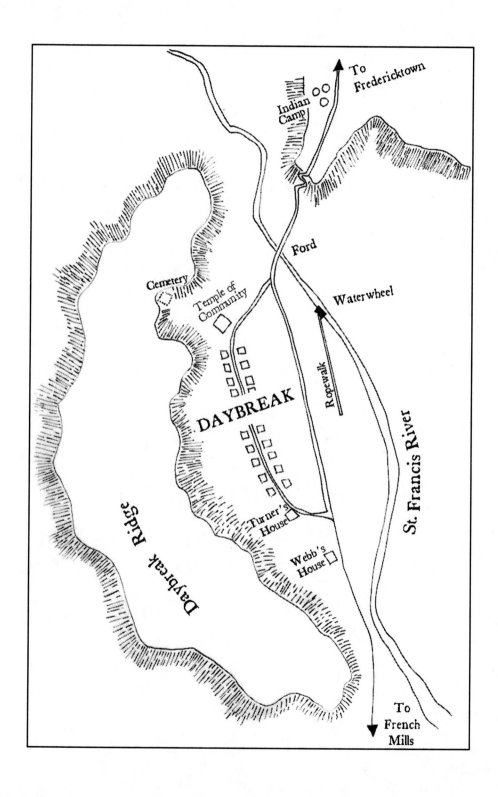

There's a certain slant of light,
On winter afternoons,
That oppresses, like the weight
Of cathedral tunes.

[...]

When it comes, the landscape listens,
Shadows hold their breath;
When it goes, 'tis like the distance
On the look of death.
-Emily Dickinson

Not in Utopia, — subterranean fields, —
Or some secreted island, Heaven knows where!
But in the very world, which is the world
Of all of us, — the place where in the end
We find our happiness, or not at all!

- William Wordsworth, The Prelude (1805 edition)

August 1857

Chapter I

The keelboat moved so slowly against the current that Turner sometimes wondered if they were moving at all. Keeping a steady rhythm, Pettibone and his son worked the poles on the quarter-sized boat they had built to ply the smaller rivers that fed the Mississippi. Whenever the current picked up, Turner took the spare pole and tried to help, but although he was tall and muscular, with a wide body that didn't narrow from shoulders to hips, poling a boat wasn't as simple as it looked. He pushed too soon, too late, missed the bottom, stuck the pole in the mud, all to the amusement of Pettibone's son, Charley. And with every stroke, Turner asked himself: *What in all creation am I doing here?*

"Limb," Pettibone called. They all ducked.

Turner had unloaded his cargo at a steamboat landing in Arkansas and come the rest of the way on the keelboat, winding through the tangle of bayous where the rivers met, the countryside flat and swampy, the loops of the river indistinguishable. Pettibone claimed he knew the channel of the St. Francis, so there was nothing to do but trust him.

Turner wondered now about the steamboat captain's advice to take a boat up the St. Francis instead of continuing to Cape Girardeau and traveling overland in whatever wagons he could rent or buy. Mosquitoes woke them before dawn and troubled them until the sun's heat drove them to the shade, then troubled them again as soon as the sun declined. To give more purchase to their poles, they hugged the bank, but that meant fighting through overhanging brush all day. In the center of the boat was a stumpy mast, a four-inch pole draped with a canvas sail, fixed with a series of shaky-looking braces. Pettibone was constantly adjusting it, but most of the time it just hung slack in the hot, wet air. At night they tied up on the few solid-looking humps of land and slept on the boat for fear of snakes, netting draped over their bodies to slow down the mosquitoes. Even then Turner could not sleep well, dreaming of fat water moccasins slithering onto the deck.

On the eighth day a long low rise appeared before them. "That there's Crowley's Ridge," said Pettibone. "Last piece of Arkansas you'll see."

"Thank God Almighty for that," Turner replied.

The ridge sat to their left like a humped cloud bank on the horizon, but the countryside didn't change. Arkansas on the left, Missouri on the right, it was all the same. Charley, a boy of thirteen, entertained himself by commenting aimlessly on everything he saw—turtles, herons, the stream of his pee into the river—until his father growled for silence.

The current strengthened as they rounded the ridge, and Turner had to wade ashore with a rope. At first he pulled directly on the boat, but Pettibone showed him how to snub the rope around a tree and keep it tight.

"Just take up the slack," he said. "You don't need to haul us upriver yourself."

Turner filed away this information, as he planned to file away every piece of knowledge he gained for the next few years. He had to; this new chapter of his life depended on it. He was no farmer and had thirty years' worth of experience to catch up on. But surely a man could pick up the tricks with attentiveness and study.

He didn't know what he had been born to become, but by God it was not a farmer. He'd seen them every day back in Illinois, clumping into the newspaper office on their trips into town to hear the gossip, to sit around the desk and spit, leaving the editor's boy—him—to clean up their misses. When he was small, he had disliked these men—their earthy smell, their beards, their ragged clothes. As he grew older, he saw that they were not dirty and ragged by choice, but by necessity, their lives swallowed up by their forty acres of ground, their debts, the prices handed to them by the local merchants and the railroad men. Of course they were ignorant of the larger world. Their world was no bigger than a quarter mile square, and that if they were lucky.

Even then, Turner knew he was not going to be a village editor like his father, listening with forced politeness to any son-of-a-bitch with a nickel, bowing to the county judges for the privilege of printing their legal notices. And now, if his father were alive, how he would laugh to see him on a keelboat, hauling a pile of tools and seeds into Missouri.

"Okay, jump on," Pettibone said. "We're crossing over."

Ahead, the ridge finally came down to meet the river, ending in some low chalk bluffs. A ferryboat was tethered on the Missouri side where a wagon track ended in a ramp of packed dirt.

The ferryman, thin and toothless, walked out of his shed as they poled by. He was shirtless but wore a battered hat. "Well, Pettibone," he called. "Come in and set. I got whiskey."

Pettibone cast a sideways glance but did not stop poling. "My customer here is in a hurry. I'll get you on the way back down."

The ferryman touched the brim of his hat to Turner. "You're welcome inside too, mister."

"No thanks. Not even noon yet."

"Where you headed?"

Pettibone interrupted. "Greenville, up by Greenville." They were almost out of talking range. "Save me some of that old tanglefoot for when I come back."

"I will, I will," the ferryman called out, and turned back to his cabin.

They poled in silence until they rounded the next bend.

"I tell you what," Pettibone said in a low voice. "That old bastard won't cut your throat for your goods, but he knows people who will."

By nightfall they had reached higher ground, and Pettibone's mood improved. Ahead of them Turner could see the Ozarks rising up in the distant dusk, so low and hazy that they seemed like an illusion, no mountains, hardly even hills from this distance, but surely more than he had grown up with on the Illinois prairie. As they poled toward an angle of bank to tie up for the night, Pettibone, in the bow, suddenly dropped to the deck and motioned for Turner and the boy to be quiet. The boat drifted on, and as they floated to the bank, a deer came into view about fifty yards ahead, drinking.

Crouched behind the pile of supplies, Pettibone quietly removed a rifle from a box beside him. He tamped the powder and ball, wadded the barrel, and rested it across some sacks of flour. As soon as the deer raised its head, he fired. The gun made a deafening roar and sent a cloud of smoke across the boat, but when it cleared they could see the deer, dead, half in the river and half on the bank. It was a small doe, about eighty pounds.

Within half an hour they had the deer dressed and hanging from a tree limb. Pettibone set to butchering while Turner and the boy gathered firewood. Soon they had a foreleg over the fire.

"We'll cook the rest tomorrow morning and take it with us," the boatman said. "Get to Greenville, I'll trade half of it for something. Full bellies tonight, boys."

They were waiting for the venison to cook, Pettibone and Charley resting against a log and Turner sitting on an upturned nail keg, when a man on horseback appeared out of the darkness on the other side of the fire. He arrived so quietly, he seemed to materialize out of the air. None of the three even had time to be surprised.

"I heard a shot," said the man.

Pettibone and his son sat stiffly against the log. There was an awkward pause. So Turner jumped to his feet. A quick mind and a firm handshake had gotten him this far.

"Yes, indeed," he said. "My friend here had some fine luck. Won't you join us? We have plenty."

The man glanced around the camp. He was tall and thin, with a narrow face and a long, bony nose. "Just you three?"

"Just us three." Turner took a step toward him. He was a young man in his twenties, with black hair and an attempt at a beard. From his saddle horn hung a rifle in a homemade canvas scabbard. A rope trailed from his saddle, and in the darkness behind him, Turner could hear the snuffles and snorts of hogs.

"Don't mind if I do," said the man. As he dismounted, his topcoat parted, and Turner saw the glint of firelight on the barrel of a revolver stuck in his belt. He guessed by their frozen expressions that Pettibone and Charley had seen it too.

"James Turner," he said, extending his hand.

The man shook it solemnly. "Sam Hildebrand." He glanced behind him. "I am taking some hogs to my cousin in Bloomfield. Hope you don't mind a hog."

"You are welcome," Turner said. "Hog, too."

They settled by the fire and carved off pieces of venison with a long knife Hildebrand produced from a saddlebag. Turner introduced him to Pettibone and the boy; Pettibone muttered a greeting and shook his hand, while the boy stood mute.

"You're a fine shot," said Hildebrand, eyeing the carcass of the deer.

"I had a rest," said Pettibone.

"You men afoot? I didn't see no horse pickets."

"We're aboat," Turner said. "Heading upriver."

"The piggies will go after those guts over there, if you don't mind," said Hildebrand.

Sure enough, in a moment three big sows followed by a cascade of piglets came into the clearing and took to the heap of entrails, shoving and squealing over the choicest parts. The sows were tied together with intricate loops of rope that wound around their necks, behind their forelegs, over their backs, and then to the next hog.

"That's quite an arrangement," Turner said.

"Ain't that so," said Hildebrand. "A hog does not like to be interfered with. That biggest one damn near cost me a finger, but I'll get her back come winter. Fortunately, a hog cannot go backward with any strength, so even a small man can hold them with a rope. If they ever figure out this stratagem and start coming at us, we humans are in trouble." His voice was soft, with an odd lilt, almost singing his words.

The sows had finished off the deer guts and settled on the ground to rest, the little ones tugging at their teats. The smallest of the three got up occasionally and snuffed among the leaves for a missed tidbit.

"Enough of hogs," Hildebrand said. He rubbed his hands on the grass to clean off the venison juices. "My curiosity is aroused. What brings you gents out here in the middle of creation on a boat?"

"I'm starting a settlement," Turner said. "I've been granted some land upriver, in Madison County."

"Granted? By the state?"

"No, a gentleman named George Webb."

Hildebrand lowered his head and spat thoughtfully between his legs. The meal finished, he plunged his knife into the dirt to clean it. Pettibone and his son had inched their way to the end of the log, their eyes on Hildebrand's revolver.

"I know who George Webb is. Good man. Never figured him for a town founder."

"It's not so much a town as a social experiment. I lecture on social reform, and Mr. Webb follows my ideas. All who come to join the community will own it together. All of our earnings will go to a common treasury, and we will decide democratically how to spend them."

Another long pause. "Free country, I guess," Hildebrand finally said. "Well, I better mount up. I can make another six, eight miles before bedding down." Then he spoke more softly to Turner. "A word with you, sir."

They walked to the riverbank, out of earshot. "You can read and write, then," Hildebrand said.

"Yes."

"Could I trouble you to write a letter for me?"

"Of course." They stepped onto the boat, where Turner fetched a pencil and his notebook from his bag. He saw Hildebrand cast an appraising glance over the mountain of goods. Turner sat on a stack of flour sacks and turned his notebook toward the firelight. "Go ahead."

Hildebrand paced back and forth in front of him, his voice low. "The address is Mrs. Rebecca Hildebrand, Desloge, Missouri." He cleared his throat. "Dear Mother, I hope you are well. I will reach cousin's by morning. The gentleman who is writing this for me will post it in Greenville." He paused. "You can, can't you?"

"My pleasure," said Turner.

Hildebrand nodded. "My travels have proceeded successfully and with no incident, although I am developing a dislike for hogs, or I should say one hog in particular. I believe my business may take me into Arkansas, Greene County or perhaps even farther. It may be more than a month before I return. Please give my fondest greeting to Father and brothers and keep a spot warm on the hearth for me. Your loving son, Samuel."

He stopped pacing and watched Turner finish the letter. "The art of the pen is something I never acquired," he said. "I do regret that at times."

Back at the fire, Hildebrand shook their hands again. "Best of luck to you on this venture," he said to Turner, and to Pettibone, "Thanks for the meat." He twitched the rope on his saddle to get the hogs to their feet.

"I bet you stole them hogs," Charley blurted out.

Hildebrand did not appear to move quickly; his motion seemed to Turner casual and deliberate. But it must have been quick, for in one moment he was twitching the rope and in the next moment he had his pistol out of his belt, leveled at Charley's chest, the hammer back. Turner stood in the sudden silence, his heart thumping.

Hildebrand held the pistol still. "You are a boy," he said after a long time, all the lilt gone from his voice. "A boy is likely to forget his manners. And this gentleman has done me a favor, so I will indulge your lack of manners this once."

Then as quietly as he had arrived, Hildebrand disappeared into the darkness. Turner, Pettibone, and the boy watched the spot where he had gone.

"I didn't—" Charley started to say.

Pettibone slapped his son across the cheek, hard. The sound echoed across the river. "Load up this meat," he said. "We are sleeping upstream and across. That fella may decide to come back, and I do not want to be here if he does." He kicked the chunks into the fire and walked to the boat without saying another word.

"Yessir," said Charley, rubbing his cheek.

They poled across the river by lantern light, feeling their way upstream in the darkness, until Pettibone found a campsite on a sandbar. "No fire tonight," Pettibone said. "Sorry you can't write your letter to your wife."

Turner squinted at the moon rising through the trees. "There may be enough light."

"Suit yourself," Pettibone said. "We'll hail Greenville by noon tomorrow and reach your place the next day."

Turner braced himself against his rolled-up blanket and angled his body so the moonlight fell on the notebook page. He'd made a practice of writing Charlotte every night since his departure and wasn't about to stop now.

My dear Charlotte—

But what to say? We were very nearly robbed and murdered today, and left on a riverbank for the crows? I have no idea what I am doing? Hardly. He imagined her response to such maunderings—quick, sympathetic, but level-headed. *What would you do? Turn around and go back?* Charlotte was a darling, but she was no coward, and no fool either. That was what had caught his notice the night they met, her wit and intelligence, the brightness in her eyes as she stepped into the conversation, as sharp as any man, and quick to dispose of any cant with a sweet smile and a firm rejoinder. *This is my match,* he had thought. *This is the woman who can be the stone to my blade, who can keep me sharp and true.*

His pencil hovered. There was no purpose served by giving her fears, and besides, his principle had always been that the idea preceded the action. If he pretended to know what he was doing, and pretended to be unafraid, then soon enough he would figure out what to do, and the fear would go away. He must act as if he had a clear purpose, and soon enough the purpose would emerge.

We had a most interesting encounter with one of the native folk today, a real woods ruffian, although his manner was gentlemanly. We are out of the swamps and into the hill country, and I believe I can detect a change in the air already—

He laid the notebook aside. He couldn't bring himself to write what was in his heart. *I am afraid. I feel a fool. I never meant for people to take my ideas so seriously. I wish I was with you, back in Kansas.*

He would have to finish the letter in the morning. As he rolled out his blanket on the rocky riverbank, Turner thought of the words his father-in-law had spoken to him before he left, trying to talk him out of this scheme: *Man is a wolf to man.*

Chapter 2

Three summers in Kansas, and Adam Cabot still had not adjusted. He started his mornings as he had in Boston, early and brisk, but by ten o'clock the sun had baked him dry. He rose early and campaigned hard, a foolish move, he knew, but an impulse he couldn't shake. Running for office meant visiting homes, shaking hands, arguing over ideas. He couldn't campaign from the safety of Lecompton; if he was going to be Leavenworth's representative to the constitutional convention, he needed to know the people of Leavenworth.

His friends warned him of the danger, but he'd been living with danger ever since he crossed into slave territory in the spring of '54 with fifty fellow abolitionists and a dozen wagons of supplies, each with a crate of Beecher's Bibles hidden under a false bottom. They'd stayed off the main roads through Missouri, crossing in the far north where the proslavery sentiment was not as strong.

Once in Kansas, most of the men headed toward the Free-Soil settlements farther south, but Cabot stayed in Leavenworth; the town was booming, and it felt like a place where a man could do some good. That was all he'd asked when the Anti-Slavery Society had called for volunteers to emigrate to Kansas, volunteers who would tip the scales against slavery by the simple weight of their bodies—to do some good. He had no skill with plow or ax. All he had was the freedom of youth, a college degree, and a desire to fight the great evil.

He had grown up in world where a certain amount of mild abolitionism was acceptable, even expected, as long as one kept it under control. It was fashionable to attend the lectures and to express one's outrage, but one stayed to the back of the hall and watched the loons try to shout each other down. One evening, though, Cabot had gone to see the famous William Lloyd Garrison, and something about the man's manner—his knife-edged precision of speech; his eyes, magnified by rimless spectacles, giving his gaze a strange, luminous, penetration; the curious contrast between his mild, intellectual appearance and the vehemence of his opinions—captured his imagination. He stayed after the speech to introduce himself.

"How can I help your cause?" he stammered.

Garrison's gaze flickered over him as if he were choosing fish at the market. "What are your capabilities, young man?"

Cabot was taken aback. "I can write. I can—" He stopped, uncertain.

A smile crossed the man's thin lips. "Harvard boy?"

"Yes, sir."

"Well, perhaps you can write, then. Do you have money?"

"Some," he said, blushing. "Not much."

"A Harvard boy with no money! You are a rarity."

"Some of my classmates are going into politics. Perhaps—"

Garrison interrupted him. "Politics! The art of compromise. How does one compromise? Make a man part slave? Perhaps only the right arm is enslaved, and the rest of the body free? No, my well-wishing friend, do not embrace politics. The Declaration of Independence is whistling wind, and the Constitution is the devil's document." He broke off abruptly, gathering his papers and turning to the door. "But you must excuse me. I speak at Uxbridge tomorrow."

Over his shoulder, he called, "Write something for *The Liberator*. We'll see if we can use you."

"What shall I write?"

Garrison paused, a look of amusement crossing his face. "Write an account of this lecture. I was planning to do it myself. We shall see whose is better."

The next week, it was Garrison's account of his lecture that appeared in *The Liberator's* pages, but by then Cabot was committed. Throughout his youth and college years, he had intended—what? He had never been sure. A career in the ministry, perhaps; or law, like his father; or a comfortable spot in business somewhere. But now he had a cause, something larger than himself, and devoting himself to it gave him a sense of meaning he had never known. He spent his days at *The Liberator* office and his nights at anti-slavery meetings. Old friends from parties and dances dropped away; new friends, earnest people with vigorous ideas and a penchant for argument, came into his life. And when the Kansas-Nebraska Act passed Congress, with its provision for popular sovereignty in the territories,

Steve Wiegenstein

Cabot saw a chance to act on his beliefs.

After the first territorial election, when Missourians swarmed across the border to send a slavery man to Congress, Cabot understood Garrison's words. Politics was a game for reasonable men, and Kansas was no place to be reasonable. Cabot did not have it in his nature to join the fighters, unlike those hollow-eyed fanatics he had come to the territory with, so he sought to be useful within the range of his talents. He wrote East for a Washington press and labored to learn typesetting, eking out pamphlets, broadsides, and a four-sheet newspaper when he could manage it. He filed for office and rode the trails west and north, encouraging the settlers to come out and vote for him. A quixotic move and likely dangerous, given the last election, but at least he saw himself as a part of the making of history rather than a bystander to its creation.

The road from Easton was stony and bare, and the lowering sun burned on his back. Sweat stung his eyes. With a full day of campaigning behind him, both he and his mare needed water and rest. He patted her flank and thought of the creek ford a couple of miles ahead, where the shade of a birch grove and hazel bushes offered a good place to pause and maybe even nap.

At the bottom of a small ravine, a man sat on the ground under a blanket draped over two sticks to keep off the sun, his horse tethered to a bush. He stood up as Cabot neared. The man didn't appear armed, but something about him made Cabot suspicious.

"Hello, friend," the man said.

"Trouble? Horse gone lame?"

The man was thin and bearded, dressed in a greasy linen shirt that had once been white and a pair of buckskin leggings that were down to a couple of strands of fringe. He gazed down the road where Cabot had come. "No," he said after a while. "I just stopped to think."

"I'll not disturb you, then."

"I was thinking about this road," the man continued. "How far you think this road goes?"

Then there was not one man but five, the others stepping out from the thicket on the other side of the road with leveled rifles. Cabot realized that no one in Kansas stopped to think on a summer afternoon.

"Get down," the man said, his voice suddenly hard. Cabot did as he was told. "What's your name, friend?"

"Charles Adams," Cabot said.

"Never heard of you. Ever hear of him, boys?"

No one answered.

Cabot's throat was parched. He could hear his heart beating in his ears.

"Where you from, Mr. Adams?"

"Leavenworth." Short answers—hide the Boston accent.

"No, before Leavenworth. Ain't nobody from Leavenworth to start with."

"Cincinnati." Anywhere but New England.

"You one of them seminary boys from Cincinnati? Jim Lane's seminary?"

Cabot tried to laugh, but his mouth was so dry it came out as a cough. "No seminary for me."

"Boys, let's toss this man in the wagon and take him up to the shed," the man said. "We'll see about this Cincinnati rooster."

"Alive or dead?" said one of the other men.

"Oh, alive," said the leader with a wave of his hand. "Tie him up and hand me them saddlebags."

Cabot found himself in a split-log shed a hundred yards off the road, blinking in the darkness as the men rifled through his possessions.

"How do you like Kansas, Mr.—what'd you say your name was?" the leader asked.

"Adams."

"Right."

"I'd like it better if I could travel in peace."

The man ignored him as he sorted Cabot's belongings. Bread, ham, coins, some notes on debts to be paid—and, Cabot recalled with a chill, his battered copy of Emerson, with a letter from his parents tucked in to save his place.

"Doff your hats, boys, we have a celebrated man among us," the man called out. "Our friend here is Adam Cabot, candidate for the constitutional convention—from the Free-Soil Party."

The men sent up a derisive cheer.

"I'll not be intimidated by violence and threats," Cabot choked out.

"Oh, we ain't going to intimidate you," the man said. "We're going to tar-and-feather you. Then we're going to take you down to the square in front of the Leavenworth House. And then we're going to hang you."

Chapter 3

Charlotte Turner lowered the lid of her trunk, then lifted it again to make sure that the fit was snug yet didn't crush the dried roses of her wedding bouquet, safely boxed among layers of clothing. She was ready.

She paused to listen for stirrings from her mother's room down the hall. Nothing. Mother liked for her to bring tea in the afternoon. Or at least Charlotte thought she did. Her arrival was rarely acknowledged, and often the tea would be sitting untouched and cold when she returned an hour later. But sometimes there would be a murmur of thanks, a few words exchanged. At least her mother was eating regularly now. For the first two weeks after Caroline's death she had taken no nourishment that anyone could detect, despite the entreaties of Charlotte and Colonel Sumner's wife. Things were still not good with Mother; she took her meals in her room, rarely changed out of her dressing gown, and spent most days in a chair by the window, writing long entries in her diary.

Charlotte walked downstairs to the kitchen, where the tea had been steeping. She bent over the pot and inhaled the aroma. How could anyone resist this fragrance, the smell of distant rain and exotic soils? It was hard travel from the slopes of India to this woodstove in Kansas, and she was determined to appreciate that journey. She poured herself a cup and sat on the sofa to listen to the wind.

Sometimes she still found it hard to believe that they had been transferred to Leavenworth after all those years at West Point. It was true, as Father had reminded them at the dining table, that an officer today was lucky to have a posting at all, what with Congress whittling on the Army every year, and some arguing that it was time to disband it altogether. "Thank heaven for the Indians," he said mildly as Caroline sniffled into her napkin. "Otherwise I might have to find respectable work at last, a barber or whatnot."

West Point had been a queer but pleasant existence, growing up one of the twin daughters of Captain Carr. From the time she and Caroline were twelve, cadets were a constant presence, looking for opportunities to serve. Was it her approval they were seeking, or his? Charlotte could never quite tell. Caroline was the prettier one, more vivacious; she knew how to talk to these lads. Charlotte was more inward and self-conscious. She had a strawberry birthmark on her neck and developed the habit of holding her hand over her chin to hide it. Holding a thoughtful pose all the time made everyone assume that she was pondering deep thoughts, and eventually she developed bookish habits that met their expectations.

Then the war broke out, and the shortage of officers threw her quiet, contented father from his classroom into the line of fire in Mexico. Some of the men he commanded were the same sleepy cadets to whom he had been lecturing about the properties of earth and metal a few months before. A year later, after the treaty had been signed, everything went back to normal, but of course it was not, could never be. The ones who had gone to war were scattered, some out on the frontier, some discharged, some dead. The new classes of cadets were seething, angry that their chances for glory had come so close but missed them. And her father walked along the cliffs in the evening, gazing out toward Constitution Island, his face turned away, always away.

When the orders came to report to Leavenworth, Charlotte almost welcomed the change. Mexico had cost her father so much of his humor, his equilibrium; he had commanded a battery at Chapultepec, an experience about which he never spoke. The newspaper accounts had been filled with praise for the heroes and their deeds, but when she asked him upon his return to tell her about the battle, he looked at her with the blankness of death in his eyes and simply said, "*Homo homini lupus.*" Man is a wolf to man.

That had been five years ago, when she was a girl of sixteen. The years since had been strained, with her father holding everyone at a remove and her mother, never strong of spirit, retreating into her own uninhabited territory of writing in her diary and gazing out the window. She and Caroline had been left to their own devices a good deal of the time—a child's dream, perhaps, but a loss as well. Caroline in particular turned into something of a coquette, in Charlotte's eyes, with a father who didn't notice and a mother who didn't mind. A posting on the frontier, she had imagined, might do them all some good. But that was before they had actually come here, and Caroline had married her lieutenant, and everything had gone bad.

But enough mooning. Charlotte was not one to sit and bemoan her fate. The tea was getting cold; she poured a cup and took it upstairs to her mother.

Father had left early, as usual, without a word, as usual. He retreated into duty as surely as her mother retreated into herself. Every day since the news had come, his uniform seemed to get stiffer, his manners more formal. The three of them moved through the house in silence, although at least Father had the respite of leaving every day to command his men. For Charlotte, relief came only in her occasional visits to town and in her correspondence.

She wrote to Turner every morning, when her strength was good and there was at least a hope of sounding cheerful and resolute. His letters were less regular, often brief, their penmanship marred by the jostling of the train where they were written, but they came, and they were welcome. She was re-reading Mr. Emerson at his suggestion, and they exchanged opinions. There were times when she found Emerson entirely too sanguine about hman possibility, too enraptured by the Great Eternals, insufficient in his account of the suffering and loss that accompanied it all; but then she remembered that he too had suffered a great loss and took comfort in the knowledge that somehow he had managed to overcome it and see beauty in the world again. As for herself, she had not reached that fortunate place—could not even see it in the distance.

So the world was cruel, and the wind whistled. She knocked quietly and placed the tea tray on the table by the chair. She had learned by now that if Mother wanted to speak, she would do so, and no prompting would make her if she did not.

Mother was gazing out the window as usual. "So dry and bare," she said. "And the wind."

"Yes." Charlotte knew what she was thinking about: the baked soil on the grave, the unbearable thought of weeds and animal tracks across the sacred, scalded plot. They knew the body felt neither heat nor cold, but there was something horrid about it nevertheless.

The news had come a year and a half ago, on a winter's day with snow spitting from a leaden sky. Charlotte and her father had ridden out to Fort Riley immediately, but by then Caroline and the baby had already been buried in the fort's graveyard, a crude wooden marker on the spot. The soldiers fidgeted nervously as Captain Carr stood at the foot of the grave.

"The woman done all she could," a sergeant said. "She's the wife of the trader.

She done all she could, she said."

Father heard it all without replying. The lieutenant, locked in his quarters wailing, would not see them, and they had not insisted.

"We'll be back in the spring with a better marker," he finally said, turning away. He climbed into the carriage.

Charlotte had not been ready to join him yet. As the men backed away, she stood at the grave, wanting to speak but with nothing to say, wanting to pray but with nothing to ask for. "Let this pass," she said finally, although she wasn't sure what "this" was—this sorrow, this disaster, this life, this deep silence between them all. Whatever it was, let it pass.

Mother did not appear to want to say anything further, so Charlotte left the tea tray and walked downstairs again.

Her father was waiting for her at the bottom of the stairs, home earlier than usual. "Walk with me, would you?" he said.

"Of course."

They stepped onto the porch, where the heat of the day still lingered although the sun hung low in the sky. The air was muggy and still. Three men desultorily whitewashed one of the barracks across the parade ground, while a troop suffered through rifle drills under the gaze of their sergeant.

Her father anticipated her thoughts. "Better to have them drill in the sun and become accustomed to it than to have them surprised on patrol one day and be unready."

"I know. It's just hard to imagine that occasion around here."

"These men will be off to Riley soon enough, or perhaps Utah. Then they'll have occasion."

They took the path around the perimeter of the fort—not as picturesque as the nightly path her father had walked at West Point, but with its own vistas: the Missouri River winding below them to the north and east, and to the south the dusty boomtown of Leavenworth. They paused on a hummock overlooking the river, an Indian burial mound, or so her father said.

"So you're determined," he said.

"Yes."

"Your mother will miss you."

"And you?"

"You know better than to tease me," he said, his voice low. "Of course I shall."

They watched as cookfires were lit along the riverbank, new emigrants, probably, or boatmen stopping for the night. She would miss him too. In the months since Caroline's death, they had strived daily to relieve her mother's melancholy, and failing that, to make life bearable for each other. Sometimes they felt as much friends as father and daughter.

"You know I disapprove. Not of him, but of this scheme. He said he would send for you when the place was ready."

"Yes, I know. And you know my place is with my husband, in fair or foul."

Her father shrugged. "Young people. No sense of time and the appropriate unfolding of things. And you were supposed to be the sensible one."

"Things never unfold. One must unfold them."

Brave talk, borrowed from James, she knew, but she was tired of being the sensible one, the cautious one, the one who kept everyone else together at the cost of her own desires. When the celebrated lecturer, author, and social thinker James Turner came to town, she had demanded that her father take her down the hill, more for diversion than interest in the man's ideas. She'd heard of his philosophical romance, *Travels to Daybreak*, and sent off for a copy. It was a good story: A young man, rich and spoiled, embarks from America on a pleasure trip to the South Seas; is shipwrecked on a tiny, mysterious island; discovers the inhabitants, who welcome him into their society; and befriends the young son of a prominent family. The people of the island call it Daybreak, after their daily practice of greeting the morning sun from the island's eastern cliffs. His new friend teaches him about the laws and principles of Daybreak, which include pure democracy, universal suffrage, and the common ownership of property. The young man falls in love with his friend's beautiful sister, renounces his inheritance, and chooses to spend the rest of his life among the happy, simple inhabitants of the island nation.

Yes, it was a good story, but at first she couldn't understand the furor it had caused. People back East had started "Daybreak Societies" and gathered monthly to discuss its principles. It was debated in the literary reviews and monthlies, and the Greeley paper even speculated about forming a model community some-where within American borders. But then she went to the lecture and heard James Turner speak. Then she understood the excitement.

There was no lecture hall in Leavenworth as yet, so Turner had lined up three wagons at the bottom of a sloping meadow to make a platform, and once the crowd had assembled, he leaped upon them with an energetic spring. "Hello, fellow slaves!" he cried.

The audacity of his greeting stunned the audience. "Ain't no slaves here but that fella," a man shouted, pointing toward a black man collecting admission at the entrance.

"Oh, yes, there are," Turner replied, striking a defiant pose. "There's you, and your friend there, and myself, and—he mimed searching the crowd—well, I see nothing but slaves."

A tall, broad man, with intense blue eyes and a flop of sandy brown hair that he brushed back from his face occasionally, Turner moved with the lightness of a cat on his makeshift platform, a sheaf of notes in one hand, popping with energy like a cedar log in a fireplace. He leaped from wagon to wagon with a zest that stopped just short of recklessness, drawing in the people at the edges of the crowd.

Charlotte could not take her eyes off him. Once he gained the audience's attention, he began to work his way through his points. The tyranny of property, the false assumptions of superiority by the rich, the distortions of human nature brought about by want and greed. Occasionally someone would heckle or call out a question; Turner would stop, grin, tell a joke, draw the man in, make a point, move on. The lecture became a rolling conversational game, Turner in charge, but just barely. He seemed to relish the challenge of staying one step ahead of his listeners, entertaining and provoking at the same time. When he turned to his remedies—common ownership of land and resources, sharing the fruits of common labor, first in small communities, then growing ever larger—people stirred, grumbled, and finally listened.

Two hours later, as the people dispersed, Charlotte climbed the hill to the fort in the gathering twilight, oblivious to the chatter of the crowd. *Is this how it feels to fall in love?* she wondered. If so, it was a feeling she was glad to keep—breathless, excited, longing for the next chance to see him. His stance, poised and confident. His smile, engaging and bright, drawing everyone in. His voice, ringing over the murmur of the listeners. And his ideas! Oh, my. That was the best part of all. A truly original thinker, out here on the edge of civilization. Who could imagine it?

Her father invited Turner to the fort that evening to dine with the senior officers and their families. The two men debated in a friendly way, and she could see the pleased surprise on Turner's face when she joined in, articulating her own views. Turner had a habit of gazing intently at the person he was talking to, even when the talk was not especially important, a habit which both unsettled and flattered her. But Charlotte liked that intensity and returned his gaze with equal power. His eyes had thin, pale lashes, and when she spoke, he looked directly into her eyes, not at her birthmark. Before long she was smiling broadly, laughing, her self-consciousness gone.

It was nearly midnight when the conversation broke up, but she was out of her room by seven the next morning, for a walk to town, yes, but also in hopes of seeing him. She took care to stroll by the Leavenworth House. And there he was, in a chair by the front window, a notebook in his lap as if to write, but nothing on the page. He escorted her on her walk, and by the time they returned they had made a plan to ride out to the Delaware village in the afternoon. Her father accompanied them in the coach, where the debate continued from the previous night. Could humanity really be reformed? In one generation? Two? A hundred?

The Delawares were courteous but indifferent to their discussion. They already had their answers.

At the lecture the next evening, the Indian village was mentioned, their attitude toward private property, and Charlotte was pleased to hear her views repeated. Again they dined together, and by the end of the visit Turner had been invited to return.

Then he was off to more towns on the frontier. Charlotte waited for his letters; he was scheduled to return by way of St. Joseph, and she had already prevailed on her father to ride up with her. His letters grew more personal during the weeks of his absence, and by the time he returned to Leavenworth she was ready for what followed. Proposal, acceptance, her father's cautions and demurrals, her mother's wan inquiries, a day's tense pause, the family stepping in and out of rooms in the house with a short question and reply, then retreating for solitary thought and, finally, surrender, for, as they all knew, no one could deny Charlotte her wishes for long. Soon there was a marriage in the parlor of the family home, and she had gone from spinster to bride in three months' time.

Her father interrupted her reminiscence. "Thinking about your young man, I suppose."

"Yes."

He sighed. "Well, I was a young nonesuch once. Bless you both."

They stood in silence, their shadows projected onto the trees at the base of the bluff. Then another shadow appeared beside theirs, growing fast as a soldier came running up the slope from the fort. He saluted, breathless.

"Beg your pardon, sir."

"What is it?"

"News from town. They're fixing to hang a man in front of the hotel."

Carr strode down toward the fort with Charlotte and the soldier trailing behind. "Get my horse and gear," he called. "And tell McGrath to assemble his troop. We shouldn't need more than one." He paused mid-stride to smile at

Charlotte. "No need to drill in the hot sun, eh, daughter?"

Chapter 4

Charlotte could not resist the impulse to follow her father, so she walked behind at a distance to stay out of his sight and avoid a chiding. She would not be denied her one opportunity to see him in military action. The troopers urged their horses into a gallop when they reached level ground, disappearing from sight, but Charlotte knew where they were headed.

She hurried into town, if one could call Leavenworth a town—more a cluster of houses and shops in a continual state of construction. By the time she reached the Leavenworth House, the sun was down and shadows had gathered.

Her father sat at the point of a wedge of troopers, his reins loose in his one hand and the other hand resting on the pommel of his sword. There was a wagon drawn up in front of the hotel, a man kneeling in the back with his hands tied behind him, coated with tar and feathers. Surrounding the wagon was a crowd of forty men. One of them stood before her father, a torch in his hand.

"This ain't a military matter," the man said. "Everybody knows you ain't supposed to interfere in civil affairs."

"If this is a civil concern, then I'll see your marshal's commission and have your name, sir."

"Puddin Tane," the man said. "We caught this man out in the country with a pack of stolen goods."

"I said I'll see your marshal's commission," Captain Carr said. "And failing that—"

He drew his sword from its scabbard and rested it on his shoulder. There was a stir from the crowd, and at the sign, the troops spread into a line across the street.

"Failing that, I'll have my men clear the square."

Into the charged silence came the sound, from somewhere in the crowd, of a breech block being snapped into place. Her father lifted his nose slightly, as if smelling the air, but gave no other indication that he had heard, keeping his eyes on the leader of the mob. It was almost a nod, but not quite; but Charlotte sensed from that small move that mayhem would erupt at the firing of the first shot.

The leader of the mob raised his hands for calm. "Now, we ain't here for trouble with you boys."

"Glad to hear it." Her father nudged his horse forward, pushing between the man and his wagon. "Come up the hill tomorrow and file a report on these stolen goods, and I'll return your horse and wagon." In a swift movement he scabbarded his sword, took the reins of the wagon horse, and wheeled. The man in the wagon toppled over with a thud. "Sorry about that, young fellow," he said, not looking back.

The troop spun and joined him, and in a moment they had vanished. The crowd began to mutter and curse; Charlotte retreated up the hill. There was enough light to see by, but even in the dark she could have followed the sweaty tang of a horse troop and the faint odor of tar.

She had thought to circle the outside of the fort's square of buildings and come to the family's quarters unseen from behind. But when she reached her house her father was already there, sitting on the back steps with the young man from the wagon.

"There you are," he said. "I need your help cleaning up this gentleman."

Charlotte wanted to tell her father that she had seen it all, that she had been awed by his transformation from the mild, distant man at the dinner table to the commanding presence she had seen in the street, but she knew he would be peeved. Besides, there was a task.

"Hello," she said. "I'm Charlotte Turner."

The man stood, extending a tarry paw. "Adam Cabot, ma'am. Please don't shake it. I'll soil you."

Charlotte laughed and took his hand. "I admire your consideration, but I'm not one for hesitance. In a military home one grows acquainted with messes of all sorts."

She looked him over. The tar had been slapped on over his clothes and had not been hot, thank goodness, so there were no burns on his skin. Some scrubbing with lamp oil and soap would put him back into form. She drew a pan of water from the kitchen pump, fetched rags and brushes, and brought up a chair.

"No permanent harm done," she murmured, working a glob out of Cabot's hair.

Cabot didn't answer. He was a compact, tightly built man, clean shaven, with a narrow nose, thin lips, and dark brown eyes. Handsome but for the sticky black coating, Charlotte thought.

"That's all right," she said. "I wouldn't be conversational either, if such a thing had happened to me." She picked a few feathers out of his hair.

"I'm sorry," he said. "I just can't talk. I can't think of anything to say. Strange, and all the way into town I was trying to come up with my great final words, my Nathan Hale speech."

"Did you?"

"No," he said glumly. "Words fail me when I need them the most."

Charlotte realized in the fading light that Cabot's eyes had filled with tears. She felt his hesitation, his embarrassment, but he continued nevertheless.

"Kansas has been full of killing for three years," he said. "But until you've had the rope around your neck—"

He broke off and turned away. Charlotte's heart went out to him, but she too could think of nothing to say. She worked more tar out of Cabot's hair, but it was clear the task was hopeless. "We'll have to shave this, I'm afraid. But it will grow out again."

Her father had been watching them from the other side of the steps, stroking his beard, and at the pause in conversation he cleared his throat.

"Your life is forfeit if you stay in Leavenworth, Mr. Cabot," he said. "I suppose you know that."

Cabot started to speak but then checked himself. "I do," he said after a minute.

"So I have request for you. My daughter leaves for St. Louis on the morning packet boat. She goes to join her husband and a band of settlers who are forming a community in the south of Missouri. It would comfort me to know she had an escort to St. Louis. I do not care for her traveling alone."

Cabot's voice was hoarse. "You saved my life, Captain. I will gladly do this and more."

"Lives are lost and saved every day, Mr. Cabot. Most of the time it happens out of the common sight. When you came to Kansas, you threw your life into the bargain. You could have lost it two years ago, or you could have lost it tonight, but it had already been thrown down. The great moment came when you made your choice, not when my men plucked you out of the crowd. Saving a life when you have a cavalry troop at your back is easier than casting it down for a cause."

"You do me honor, sir."

"Have you read the Stoics, young man?"

"Some."

"I keep Aurelius by my bed to remind me that we are all on the way to death, every day, and what matters is not when or how it arrives, but what you have done on your way to meet it. 'To the thrown stone, there is no more honor in rising than shame in falling.' Keep that in mind, my friend. The streets of Leavenworth this night were not the time nor place for you to die."

Charlotte spoke up. "I never knew you to be so fatalistic, Father."

Carr sniffed. "Growing old, I suppose. Or perhaps it's the times. All seems a slide toward destruction, with nothing to distinguish us but the gracefulness of our fall." He stood up and stretched.

"It's still a young world," she said.

"I'll have to take your word for that. But you'll take my instruction, and have Mr. Cabot as your escort tomorrow?"

"Yes," she said with a smile. "I will take your instruction."

He patted her arm. "Words I rarely hear these days, and they warm my heart. Mr. Cabot, I shall send some men to fetch your things. It would not be wise for you to return to town."

Cabot awoke the next morning sore from his head to his knees. The kicks and cuffs from his captors merged with the bruises he had gotten from bouncing in the back of the wagon like a load of rocks. But at least he was alive, and ready to—to what? He didn't know. He had collapsed into sleep without thinking of today, or of the rest of his life. The captain was right about Kansas. He was marked now. Perhaps he should return to Boston. Or he could strike out in a new direction. Perhaps the captain was right about the greater parts as well. He had already thrown his life onto the table and only had to decide what number to pick.

They took a wagon to the landing with an escort of soldiers and Captain Carr, and now it was Charlotte's turn to be inward and silent.

"You're on your own after you round the bend, young man. Good luck to you," the captain said, shaking his hand. Cabot turned to unload his belongings, to give Charlotte a private moment for her farewell. A slave from the packet slouched down the gangplank to help, but Cabot waved him away. He was not about to accept the fruits of the poisoned tree now.

Father and daughter embraced as two soldiers carried Charlotte's trunk to the steamboat, a crowded vessel about twenty feet wide that inspired less confidence than its coat of bright red paint might have merited.

"Distance cannot diminish your parents' love for you," the captain told her. "Nor mine for you."

Carr turned away. "Write," he said. "Visit when you can. All good will to your husband." He mounted his horse abruptly and rode off at a fast trot.

Cabot had booked deck passage, so he arranged their trunks on the shady side of the boat, as far forward as he could manage. The porters waved Charlotte toward the ladies' cabin, but she ignored them. "We came out on a boat like this," she told Cabot. "The ladies' cabin was the dullest place imaginable, but of course we all had to stay together. I'd rather not spend my day fanning myself and talking about the heat."

Cabot kept his hat low, self-conscious. With his shaved head, he felt he looked like a convict. "Is this craft safe?" he asked a passing deckhand.

"Only lost one passenger so far, and that was a lunatic," the man said. "Couple of passages ago. Jumped off the stern down by Marthasville."

"That's not what I meant," Cabot muttered. Charlotte chuckled at his discomfort and settled onto her trunk.

"We must entertain each other," she said. "I shall tell you my story, and you shall tell me yours, and in the meantimes—" she reached into her traveling satchel— "you may read my husband's book."

Cabot turned the volume over in his hands. He had heard of *Travels to Daybreak* and the stir it had created. He flipped to the first page: *It was a fine morning in June when I set out from New York harbor on my travels to Daybreak, although of course at the time I did not realize that Daybreak was to be my destination.*

"Interesting," he said.

For the next several hours they read aloud to each other, talked, and walked the deck, though Cabot was careful not to let their trunks out of his sight for long. With the current behind them, they flew downstream at ten miles an hour or better. Parkville, Randolph, Liberty Landing came and went, cargo and passengers loading and unloading at each stop; by the early afternoon they had reached

Lexington.

The book intrigued him with its innocent idealists and their beehive-like society; a beehive without a queen, he supposed, everyone laboring for the common good. He couldn't tell whether its author seriously proposed such a community or was merely indulging in fantasies. As the steamboat continued south and east, away from the frontier and into the settled country, bottomlands thick with hemp, corn, and tobacco, the chasm between the Daybreak of Mr. Turner's fiction and the America of the present day seemed unbridgeable. Slaves in the fields, slaves handling cargo, slaves just standing by, awaiting instructions from their owners. The locals barely acknowledged their existence—they were little more than the trees or cattle, just moving parts to the landscape who happened to have human faces and who could walk, speak, and think. He looked up from the page and took Charlotte's hand.

"I'm glad they tried to hang me," he said. "I'm glad they failed, but now I know things I would never have known otherwise."

"Such as?"

Cabot choked back the emotion that suddenly rose up, surprising him. His chest felt tight, and he struggled to keep his face still. He waited until the wave passed before trying to speak. "I know what it is like to have one's very life subject to the whim of others. Few white men experience this sensation." He looked out over the rail at the thick band of trees lining the bank. "It is our great evil, this thing. This abomination."

Charlotte tapped the book in his hand. "My husband would say that it is the system of property itself that is the evil. Once we accept the notion of human ownership of God's creations, then it is a simple step to the human ownership of other humans."

"And do you believe this?"

She frowned a little. "I don't dabble in social theories. I stick to things I truly know and have studied."

"Mrs. Turner, you do more than dabble in a social theory. You commit your life to it."

"I commit my life to my husband. I devote myself to tangible things, not abstractions."

Cabot would have liked to debate further, but didn't want to be impolite by placing her in disagreement with her husband. "I should like to ask him about this matter someday."

"Why not now?" she asked. "Once we assemble in St. Louis, we will charter wagons to bring supplies to the colony. Join us for a while. You can be present for the founding of the great experiment."

They were interrupted by a whistle blast as the gangplank was thrown off and the boat lurched once again into the current. Cabot hated that sensation of motion in all directions, outward, downcurrent, rotating, all at once. He took hold of the rail.

She smiled at him, a little indulgently. "You don't like to travel by boat?"

"Only when I can't tell where we're going. I don't like drifting."

"A good motto for life, I should think. Now if you'll excuse me, I need to tend to some ladies' matters."

He tipped his hat at the remark as she strolled away.

They tied up at Boonville as evening fell, the pilot far too fearful of snags in the low water to attempt night travel. Charlotte's ticket had included a share of a bed in one of the rooms, while Cabot pushed their trunks apart and laid blankets between them to give himself a private space on the deck. As he settled himself onto the planks, he thought about her offer. Why not go to Daybreak? He couldn't return to Kansas, and he'd just as soon not go back to Massachusetts yet. Perhaps this man Turner had an idea worth pursuing. Any direction was better than none.

Chapter 5

B y the time Turner and the keelboat reached George Webb's farm, the hills had closed in on them and the river was running clearer. There were bluffs a hundred feet high or more on the outside of the bends, limestone on top of granite, crested with a fringe of cedars and blackjack oaks. Then all at once the valley would open out into rich-looking bottomland dotted with cabins and an occasional village, islands of cultivation in a sea of forest.

He thought of how he had met Webb in the first place. It had been in St. Louis, after a lecture in April. It had been a good lecture, one of his best, in the ballroom of the National Hotel. Remarkable how the slave-state Missourians took to his message of the rights of man and the evils of capital. Apparently they could appreciate in the abstract what they could not embrace in the particular. He had been exhausted but excited. Lecturing animated him, and it usually took an hour before the nervous energy subsided enough to let him sleep. He climbed the steps to the third floor, where he could look out the window and watch the omnibus load passengers for the Madison Street Ferry on its last run of the night.

Turner regretted leaving Charlotte so soon after they had married, but a lecturer's job was to lecture. With the success of *Travels to Daybreak*, more bookings came in every day; there would be time later for quiet evenings by the fire. From the window, he could see beyond the smokestacks of packet boats and steamships to Illinois in the distance across the river; or at least fires and movement on Bloody Island, which was sort-of Illinois. Cockfights, perhaps, or a boxing match; the island wasn't the scene of many duels these days. But seeing even a dubious piece of Illinois made him think of his father and the old home, if you could call three rooms above a newspaper office a home.

He had taken Charlotte's tintype out of his pocket, opened the case, and tipped it so the lamplight would not reflect. For a moment he gazed at her features, dimly suggested by the silver and gray of the picture: her intelligent, bright blue eyes, and her light brown hair, "floating like a vapor," as he loved to sing to her, making her blush. He started to hum the tune, but caught himself and looked around.

A white-haired man stood a few feet away. He stepped closer when Turner left his reverie. "Sir," he said, extending his hand. "George Webb." His face was flushed with excitement but his voice was calm. He was stocky and solid, and he gripped hard with a calloused hand.

They stepped from the hallway into a quiet alcove. George Webb was dressed in a worn black suit that had once been very fine. He did not look like a man who often dressed in suits.

"I have read your book many times," he said. He waved off Turner's thanks. "I have a proposal for you."

There was a settee in the alcove, and they took it. "I am growing old and seek to make a difference in the world," Webb said. "Since reading your book, I think I see my chance."

He had been pondering this decision, he said, for many weeks. He had a thousand acres of fine river bottom land in southern Missouri that he was ready to grant to a Daybreak Society for a real life, honest-to-God Daybreak. Ozark river bottom land, oak and hickory trees on the hillsides, sycamores and cottonwoods along the river, and a half mile or more of good flat ground between the river and the mountain, ideal for cultivation and settlement. Better land existed somewhere in the world, he was sure, but, by crack, he had never seen it. It could grow corn, wheat, tobacco, maybe cotton although he had never tried it, hemp, fruit trees, nut trees, anything a man might want to seed it with. But Webb was growing old, with only one son, who was nothing much of a farmer, and bit by bit the land had overgrown itself. Now it was down to a few acres of cultivated ground, and the rest sprangled briers and sprouts. It would be the perfect location for the great experiment Mr. Turner had spoken of, the true-life Daybreak so often mentioned in meetings of their Society and surely at meetings of other Daybreak Societies around the nation, and he was ready to grant the land.

But only on condition that Mr. Turner here lead the group himself. He would trust no one else.

And Turner, the man who sought to rise above his farm-country upbringing, the man who preferred to lecture before the crowds, to move on rather than plant roots in some isolated plot of dirt, and who was a newlywed to boot, had impulsively said yes.

In the late afternoon they came to a cluster of houses at the base of an impossibly steep mountain, and for the first time they could see a wagon road running alongside the river. A man was fishing from the bank.

"We're looking for George Webb's place," Pettibone called out. "This it?"

The man gawked at their heavily laden keelboat. "Well, ain't this a sight," he said. "Stay here, I want to show this to my brother."

"We don't travel fast," Pettibone said. "So this ain't Webb's?"

"No, this is French Mills. Webb's three or four miles upstream on the left. Who the hell are you people?"

"Simple travelers," Turner said.

"Like hell."

Pettibone and Charley poled on. The river followed the base of the mountain, a long stretch of slow, deep water enveloped in shade. After a few minutes, they could see the man from French Mills following them up the wagon road, along with three or four others, clumsily trying to conceal themselves behind the brush.

"Nothing to worry about," Pettibone said. "We're a curiosity, is all."

After an hour, the men dropped away. "Must be suppertime," Turner said.

"Whiskey time, more likely."

Ahead they could see the opening to a valley as the mountain curved off to the west and the river stayed straight. The land was level and open, but overgrown with saplings and briers. Through the brush they could see a whitewashed frame house sitting by the road.

"Don't see no landing," Pettibone said. "Maybe there's one farther up."

A mile upriver, at the head of the valley, the road came down to a shallow crossing. Pettibone steered the keelboat to the bank. "This is where I get paid," he said.

"All right," said Turner. "I'll find our man Webb and see about bringing a wagon for my goods."

He jumped ashore and started toward the house they had passed. The road was grassy in the center, not much of a thoroughfare. He paused in his walk and looked out across the valley.

So this was to be the scene of his great experiment. Just as Webb had promised, it was half a mile to where the slope of the mountain bent upward, all tillable land. They would set themselves back from the river and the road a sensible distance, for protection from floods, of course, but also to create a proper vista—the water, the road, the fields, the town, the mountain. Travelers to Daybreak would see the human in harmony with the natural, same as in the book.

Turner was elated but surprised. Who could have imagined that so many people would embrace his ideas? The last word he had gotten, fifty people were meeting in St. Louis to form a train for Daybreak—a few families, but mostly single men or husbands scouting ahead. Men across the country were uprooting themselves and their families, throwing off the burdens of their current lives, and heading here. Not in pursuit of wealth like the California or Oregon emigrants, but in fulfillment of an ideal.

The mountain was tall and thickly wooded. It cast its shadow onto the valley early, good in the summer when the shade would cool them in the evening. They would set their houses close together for ease in visiting, and at the upper end of the valley they would build a great common building, a refectory in the evenings, a schoolhouse during the day, and a place of worship on Sundays. Then a double row of houses, leading to a stable, a barn and a granary, downwind from the houses, all of them large and grand since they would be serving the whole community. In time they would create their own manufactures—clothing, ironwork, who knows what else.

He inhaled deeply, the smell of warm wet air filling his nostrils. Perhaps this was his calling after all, to be the founder of a city based on new principles. This was America, where thinking too big was less likely to bring a man down than not thinking big enough. The thick late-summer foliage of sassafras, wild rose, and briar vines obscured the immediate view, but he could sense the valley would be rich ground for planting.

There was a halloo from down the valley—George Webb heading his way with a horse and wagon. Turner trotted to meet him, and soon they were shaking hands warmly in the road.

"You found us," Webb said. His barrel-chested body trembled with excitement, and he took in the entire valley with a wave of his arm. "Here it is, the beginning of the new world."

Turner laughed despite himself. "I'm supposed to be the man with the grand rhetoric, George."

Webb clapped his shoulder. "When I was a young man this was a garden, and

I mean that in plain fact," he said. "From the house to here, it was beans, squash, potatoes, turnips. A winter's worth and more. Now look at it."

"It's still a garden," Turner said. "It's just hidden."

They met Pettibone and Charley at the keelboat. Within a couple of hours they had ferried the goods a wagonload at a time to Webb's barn, which like the rest of the farm was slowly reverting to the state of nature. They hoisted the food-stuffs into the rafters using squares of canvas gathered at the corners, and by the end of the labor they were all drenched in sweat.

"I hope you men will spend the night before you head downstream," Webb said to Pettibone and his son. "My son shot a possum to fry up."

"I'd be grateful," Pettibone said. "A home-cooked meal is a rare thing out here."

"No claims for the home cooking," Webb said. "It's just my son and me."

They walked to Webb's house, which was no mere cabin but a large, well-framed dwelling set back a dozen yards from the road, with a full front porch and plank siding that had once been whitewashed, now chalky and faded. The relative cheerfulness of the exterior was not matched by the inside, which was dark, smoky, and cluttered, clothes and tools scattered on the floor and a loose pile of cordwood next to the stove. There was a skinned possum in a pan on the table, cut into portions.

Webb opened the woodbox of the stove and blew the coals to life. He tossed in a few small sticks and blew some more.

"Company tonight," he said.

Turner had not noticed the man sitting in a chair near the fireplace. He was whittling something, blowing the shavings off his pale fingers from time to time. He did not look up for a minute.

He was as skinny as a coyote, and as he bent over his carving a broad-brimmed felt hat covered his features. When he looked up Turner saw the pale face of a man in his late twenties, framed by thin strands of yellow hair, colorless lips, and expressionless blue eyes. He took in the group with a quick glance and returned to his whittling. "Hope you ain't hungry," he said. "That possum won't divide far."

Webb stepped forward. "Gents, this is my son, Harper. We just call him Harp. This is Mr. Turner, and Mr. Pettibone and his boy."

"Yeah," said Harp, not looking up.

Webb spoke again to ease the awkwardness. "We'll throw some potatoes in with that possum. That'll stretch it." Harp didn't answer, and Turner and Webb walked out onto the front porch.

They stood in the gathering dusk, listening to the repetitive drone of katydids in the humid air. "I'm afraid my son's not too sociable," Webb said. "It's just been the two of us for a while."

"No need to apologize," Turner said. "It can't be easy to see family land handed to strangers."

Webb snorted. "As if he had made anything of it. Two thousand acres here. I'm parceling out a thousand for our project—everything north of here—" he swept his left hand across the valley. "All the way to the ford and a little beyond. He'll keep the house and a thousand acres south, down the valley and across the river. Harp's got no complaint. What's he done with the land so far? Twenty acres of corn to feed his whiskey-making, and the rest gone to cedar sprouts and broom sage."

He clapped Turner on the shoulder. "But enough of my teeth on edge. I have questions for you about the colony."

Inside, Harp and Pettibone had settled in the fireplace corner with a jug, and a grumbling Charley was slicing potatoes into the fry pan. "Don't look so glum, boy," Webb said. "Some of those are yours."

Pettibone waved the jug at them from the hearthstone. "This is a fine product," he said. "I may take a load downriver for resale if I can get Mr. Harp here to settle on a price. Damn fine product."

"It's none of my doing," Webb said stiffly. "Your dealings with Harp are your own matter."

Across the room from the fireplace was a window, with a chair and a writing desk beneath it, and books and papers strewn around—the elder Webb's corner of the room, Turner guessed. A copy of *Travels to Daybreak*, heavily marked in the margins, lay on the desk.

Harp's whittling project was on a table by the fireplace. Turner stopped and picked it up. It was a black walnut, carved into links of chain using the interstices of the walnut as the openings of the links. "Stars in heaven, this is quite a work," Turner said. "A walnut is as hard as a rock."

Harp looked up at him with the same blank expression. "Patience and a sharp knife. All a man needs."

Turner would have replied, but Webb motioned him toward the desk, where he was eagerly flipping pages in the book.

"Here's my question," he said eagerly. "The citizens of Daybreak greet the sunrise every morning with a chant, as you describe it. I wonder if this chant might be made into a song? Have we any musicians among our advance party?"

"I don't know," Turner murmured, running his finger across the passage. "It's been weeks since I received any correspondence." He hated to admit that he had no idea if the chant could be set to music, that the chant had just popped into his fancy one afternoon as a good way to open a chapter, the happy islanders all gathered to greet the morning.

He traced the words of the anthem:

Where there is inequality, let us bring balance.
Where there is suspicion, let us bring trust.
Where there is exclusion, let us bring openness.
Where there is division, let us bring harmony.
Where there is darkness, let us bring Daybreak.

September 1857

Chapter 6

"*Homo homini lupus.*"

"I beg your pardon?" Adam Cabot tilted his head.

"Man is a wolf to man," Charlotte said. "My father used to say it at every opportunity."

They rode in silence for a minute, bouncing gently on the spring seats of the wagon. The road, by now just parallel tracks through the forest, was smooth for a little while, a blessing after the miles of jolts. From the steamboat landing at Sainte Genevieve there was a plank road as far as Farmington, but for the last thirty miles the wagon roads had gotten steadily narrower and rougher.

Their subject, as always, was the trouble in Kansas, the trouble in the capital, the trouble in the nation.

"After he came back from Mexico, that is," she continued. She glanced at the young man sitting beside her. "Once he was home and started teaching again, he would get the strangest expression. He would look toward you but through you, as if there was someone behind you he was addressing. And that's when he would say it."

Cabot's face, usually so open, became careful and composed. "He'll get no argument from me," he finally said. "But wartime is a different matter. Perhaps the horrors of war blind a man to the higher possibilities of mankind."

Charlotte gazed out at the thick screen of blackjack oaks and hickories they were passing through. She had to admit the scenery was beautiful. The hills were not as high as the Adirondacks of her childhood, but the landscape was equally rugged, and in the warm light of September, Charlotte found to her surprise that she was enjoying the trip. She and Cabot had met the first group of settlers in St. Louis, fifty-four of them, and they had embarked en masse for the trip south. It felt good to be in the countryside. Cabot, innately idealistic, had taken to the plan for the great experiment despite his own recent reverses, although they could never seem to keep the conversation from drifting back to Kansas. At Sainte Genevieve they chartered wagons for the trip inland, and Adam's good humor and educated language made everyone look to him for leadership. His black hair had just begun to grow out again, and sometimes he rubbed his head with a serious expression before bursting into fits of laughter at the ridiculousness of his appearance. The Eastern cut of his clothes marked him as a butt of everyone's jokes, but he didn't seem to mind.

She could use all the idealism he had to spare. The parting from her father still made her sad. She had not handled the departure well—first the rush into marriage, then her decision to join her husband in Daybreak before she had been sent for. She could see in her father's eyes that he had doubted her common sense.

The wagon road came to a clearing. Set back from the road was a cluster of stick-and-earth huts, strange-looking affairs, five feet tall, with thin strings of smoke rising from the centers of their roofs. Charlotte could see women and children moving among the huts, dark-haired, dark-skinned, and ragged. Two of the children walked toward the passing wagons and held out their arms mutely, palms upraised, fingers loosely curled.

Cabot turned to the wagon driver behind them, a local man they had hired. "What's this?"

"That's the Creek Nation," the wagoner said. "Missouri branch. Army left them here to die during the Removal, and they never got around to it."

The wagoner cast a glance over the group, all of whom had now stopped to watch the wagons pass. "Seems like there's more of them since last time I came through here."

The children kept their arms extended as they drove by.

"Do you think—" Charlotte asked.

"I'll check," said Cabot. He handed her the reins and jumped down from the wagon, swinging himself onto the one behind as it neared. He conferred head to head with the wagoner for a moment, then just as nimbly hopped down and trotted back.

"He says no," Cabot said, lifting himself onto the seat. "They'll follow us all the way to the colony. He says the men are probably out somewhere finding food."

"Those children don't look fed to me."

"We'll go a mile or two, then I'll ride back," he said. "They'll never try to keep up with a man on horseback."

"There's a half ham in the back of this wagon. Take it."

The road descended sharply from the ridgetop, the forest changing from oak to cedar, and as they dropped into the river valley the trail grew worse, nothing more than a cleared cascade of rocks. They inched over shelves of rock one wheel at a time. A broken wheel now would cost them half a day. Charlotte checked over her shoulder at their precious load—Cabot's cast-iron Washington press and twelve trays of type. They had immobilized it in the wagon bed as best they could with sacks of flour and sugar, but Charlotte still dreaded the idea of the wagon tipping in some creek bed, thousands of tiny letters spilling into oblivion.

After the wedding, she and Turner had spent a week at Arrow Rock, truly alone for the first time. Turner worked on plans for his triumphant return lecture tour to the cities of the West—Buffalo, Cleveland, Pittsburgh, Cincinnati, Louisville, St. Louis. Charlotte had thrown herself into the role of correspondent and organizer. And in the nights she was surprised by the ardor with which she embraced the joys of marriage. The first night was awkward and strange, but the second night came easier, and by the third night she was reaching for him even before he reached for her. She knew that this new life was what she had spurned all those cadets for; by day to support and disburden her man, her original thinker, and by night to join with him, to delight in his strength and vigor. But then he had returned to the lecture circuit, and then came the offer of land for a settlement.

Of course it had all happened too fast, she knew that. But after her years of suspension, she had been poised and ready to move. The speed didn't frighten her.

But these last acts—Turner taking on the colony, just accepting the land without seeing it, without pausing to consider, without consulting her, and she in turn making the abrupt decision to join him, although he had said he would need a few months to build cabins and clear ground—these moves had been fast in a different way. They felt whimsical, ill-considered.

"Mrs. Turner?" Still strange to hear the new name. Adam Cabot brought her up short. She jumped in her seat and looked around. They were about halfway down the long rocky slope and had reached a glade. The trail edged along a bluff, giving a view of the river bottom below. She gazed out. The river shone in the late afternoon light like a ribbon of mercury; on the other side was a thick grove of cottonwoods and sycamores, with a valley beyond it, broad and long, open meadows and crop fields, and at the far end two houses, one white, one brown.

The houses were tiny against a high, thickly forested hill behind them, and the forest sent fingers of trees down its slopes into the bottomland, reclaiming the ground that human hands had cleared.

"The driver behind us says that's the colony site," Cabot said. "We descend here, and then there's a ford. Our land is just beyond."

"And—?" Charlotte looked behind her, thinking of the children on the ridge. The line of wagons snaked back as far as she could see.

"I'll get us across the ford, then ride back," Cabot said. "I've got the ham."

"Thank you." She paused. "Adam—?"

"Yes?"

"He doesn't know I'm coming."

Cabot gave her a questioning look, and she could see surprise mingled with curiosity in his features. But ever the gentleman, he didn't press her further. "Then he will be doubly pleased by our arrival." He urged the mules forward. In a short time they had reached the ford, the wagons crossing one at a time to avoid interfering with each other.

Charlotte looked upriver as they crossed. So this was the St. Francis he had written her about. It seemed a good river, medium-sized, a bit of a current, more clear than muddy. The crossing had a solid bottom and was not too deep; the mules' bellies got wet but that was all. The trees were thick and as tall as church steeples. Behind the trees she could see more hills, higher than the one they had just come down.

The mules struggled up the bank then settled into an easy walk as the track wound through the cottonwoods and sycamores on the other side. Cabot handed her the reins, hopped down and took the ham, borrowed a horse from a later wagon, and was gone.

As he trotted his horse through the forest with the ham resting on his saddle, Cabot pondered this latest bit of news. Why had Charlotte not told her husband of her coming? She was not the type of woman to travel three hundred miles for the childish pleasure of a moment's surprise. Perhaps pure devotion? She knew he did not want her out here, but couldn't bear his refusal. That would be in character with the Charlotte he'd gotten to know over the past weeks—firm to the point of hardheadedness, yet with a core of loving-kindness just below that solid surface.

Not his business, he supposed, but worrisome nevertheless. There were no private matters for this man Turner any more—he had more than fifty people to lead in this venture, with perhaps hundreds more to come. He didn't think it proper to speculate about what passed between Charlotte and her husband, but he couldn't help the thoughts that ranged through his mind. Could it be that she suspected something irregular in the man's removal to this far country? Nonsense, he told himself, with a reminder to avoid evil speculation in the future. But then nothing was regular about their embarkation on this journey.

The lessons of history led him to doubt the ideas in *Travels to Daybreak*, but he was curious to meet James Turner. Charlotte's descriptions of him made him seem a combination of Solon and Socrates, but Cabot marked that down to the rosy views of a woman in love. Not that he had any practical experience in such matters, he thought with a pang. Shy since childhood, he had never shone at the play parties and dances, and although he had had a few flirtations and walks along the Charles, he had never loved nor felt himself to be loved in that glowing way. He had yet to meet his ideal woman—someone idealistic yet practical, someone who would be a partner and confidante, not merely a dependent. A Titania for his Oberon, a match of both head and heart.

All right, so he was envious of this man he had yet to meet, who had managed to find a bright and witty—and handsome—woman to marry. So he wanted to meet him for that reason if nothing else, to learn his secret. No crime in that.

He reached the Indian village and climbed down from his horse. At first no one could be seen, but then a boy emerged from one of the huts. He looked suspiciously at Cabot for a moment before approaching.

"Here," Cabot said. He swung the ham from its resting place on his saddle.

The boy ran inside without a word.

For several awkward minutes, Cabot waited in the clearing, the ham resting on his saddle horn. Finally the boy came out again with a bundle wrapped in cloth, and they exchanged items. Cabot unfolded the bundle. Inside were corncakes of some sort, boiled rather than baked, with an odd blue sheen. Cabot broke off a piece.

"Good!" he said. They were cold and gritty.

The boy held the ham over his head. "Thank you," he muttered as he turned toward the houses.

"Thank you," Cabot replied. He waved in the direction of the huts, sure that he was being watched. He mounted his horse, reflecting on the odd ways in which the demands of dignity revealed themselves, and rode away.

Charlotte was glad for the time alone. She wondered how Turner would take her unexpected arrival. The driver in front of her was whistling "Clementine" again. He had been whistling it for what seemed like weeks. Didn't he know any other tunes? Perhaps she should teach him.

And then the wagon path opened up into a broad clearing and on the far side of the clearing she could see him. He was still far away but she recognized him instantly, although he had grown a beard in their months apart. He and another man, an elderly-looking gentleman, were paired on a crosscut saw, felling a tree. He had laid his hat and coat aside, and the sunlight caught the tousles of his light brown hair. In an instant all worries fell away.

The wagon road ran along the river's edge, through the heavy shade of the high trees, with dogwoods and pawpaws in the understory. Through the foliage she could see the river to her left, the barest of ripples on its surface. To her right the forest thinned out. There were about ten acres where trees had been girdled and were standing dead, waiting to be cut. Then cleared ground, some of it planted, some open and grassy. At the far end of the valley, the white house was set halfway up the slope, with weathered clapboard siding; and about a hundred yards closer to her, a cabin, newly built, the logs rough-hewn and not fully chinked; and in front of the cabin, Turner and the older man, who now had seen the wagons approaching and straightened from their sawing. Turner took his coat from a nearby bush, put it on, and waved his hat.

By now most of the wagons had entered the clearing. Charlotte looked behind her; there were thirty of them, one right after the other, laden with goods and people. As they caught sight of Turner, the people in the front wagons sent up a cheer, which spread down the line; even those just emerging from the forest knew that they had arrived. Charlotte joined in. Turner, still waving his hat, climbed a stump for a better view; Charlotte stood up in her wagon, reins in her hand, and waved back.

She could see his surprise when he recognized her. He paused in mid-wave and nearly lost his balance. But he recovered quickly and soon was striding to greet them.

Turner took the reins from her, tied the mules to a tree, and helped her down from the wagon. Charlotte could feel that he was thinner now; his grip was strong, and his skin had grown dark. Their eyes met as he gave her a brief embrace.

"My dear!" he said. "My dear." Then he gestured to the arriving wagons. "I must—"

"Of course," Charlotte said. He dashed to greet the others and to tie up their mules.

They gathered in front of the cabin for a brief prayer of thanksgiving; Charlotte counted only five other women and a scattering of children. They gave three cheers to the older man, who turned out to be Mr. Webb, the donor of the land. Webb was a solid, red-faced man with a large round nose, deeply cleft down the middle. Charlotte guessed him to be sixty or more. He was redolent with sweat from working the crosscut saw, and strings of white hair trailed out from under his hat, but he carried himself with a dignified air, like some Cincinnatus of the hills, and Charlotte could see why Turner had trusted him so soon and so completely. Then it was time to work—to unload the wagons, set up tents, divide the labors. "Women and children can sleep in this cabin tonight," Turner said.

A man in the crowd pointed to the white house at the end of the valley. "What about that place?"

A glance passed between Turner and Webb. "That house is not part of our colony," Turner replied. "It's the original homestead and belongs to Mr. Webb and his son, Harp."

All eyes turned to the house for a moment, as if Harp might step out of the door to be acknowledged. But Harp either remained inside or was elsewhere.

"We have much to do before nightfall," Turner said. "Let us begin."

He jumped down from the stump and led the way to the wagons, organizing the men into groups to set up a shelter and picket lines for the mules and horses, laying out piles of goods onto squares of canvas, and carrying other items inside the cabin.

Cabot trotted up on his horse. Charlotte could see him eyeing the situation cautiously, unsure of where he fit in, and she walked over to him as he dismounted.

"Here," she said, taking his arm. "Come this way." She led him to Turner. "This is the man I wrote you about," she told her husband. "Adam Cabot."

The men shook hands. "You did indeed," Turner said. "The man who cheated death. Mr. Cabot, you are welcome here, even though you are not among our adherents. Perhaps you will convert to our principles one day."

"Perhaps," Cabot said, "and even if not, I am glad to work with you now. It heartens me to see men working toward a worthy goal."

"Men and women, you mean," said Charlotte.

Cabot blushed. "You are right." He spoke to Turner again. "Your wife is an education in herself, sir. She has nearly converted me to your cause through conversation alone."

Turner smiled, the broad, embracing grin that Charlotte remembered and loved, which began as an ordinary smile then wrapped his face, warming the air for a yard around. "An education in herself!" he repeated. "An entire university, more like. I can see some grand conversation around the fireplace for the three of us."

Cabot smiled in return. "I—" He made a hesitant gesture. "Beyond my personal belongings, I brought nothing with me for your settlement, except—" They walked to Charlotte's wagon. "Except this, and I don't know what good it will do you."

He flipped the canvas cover to reveal the printing press, swaddled among the sacks and bundles.

"Stars in heaven!" Turner cried. "If I could count the hours I spent yanking on the handle of one of these. And typecases too. You know how to set type?"

"Not well," Cabot said. "I tried to teach myself but it was slow going."

Turner rubbed his chin, musing. "I learned as a boy. Tedious labor, and that's the mildest thing I'll say about it. But now I am grateful I learned, and I'm grateful to you for bringing this press. What do you think, my dear?" he said to Charlotte. "*The Daybreak Star*? Or perhaps *The Defender*?"

Charlotte waved her hand at him. "Tend to your work and name the newspaper later." She left to join the other women, who had gathered around a growing pile of foodstuffs being unloaded in front of the door. She felt momentarily out of sorts as the work swirled around her, but she shook it off and tried to make herself useful.

"These men will want to eat as soon as they finish their work," she said to the women. "Let's see what we can do." They went inside to set up a kitchen.

The interior was not as rough as the exterior had suggested. There were two rooms and a cast-iron stove, and someone had even smoothed down the walls a bit. Charotte looked out the back door and saw George Webb walking by.

"Mr. Webb," she called out. "Where do you get your water?"

Webb gestured toward the hill behind them. "Good spring at the base of the bluff," he said. "Path'll lead you right to it. Then there's a mud spring over yonder, closer. Plenty of water, but it's sulfur. And of course the river is closer yet."

Two young girls were standing near. "What's your name?" Charlotte said to the older one.

"Lucy," she replied. "This is Mary."

"Lucy, I want you and Mary to find whatever pails you can, take them up that path to the spring, and fill them with water. We will need plenty of water today."

The girls trotted off. "Mama, that lady says 'pails,'" Lucy said with a giggle.

Before long they were frying salt pork in skillets on the stove and saving the grease to cook hoe cakes. Lucy and Mary's mother, a muscular, laughing woman from Maryland named Frances Wickman, proved to be the better cook, and Charlotte stepped back to give her room.

She found a broom and began to push dirt toward the front door. The task would have to be repeated later in the evening, but there was no point in standing around like a dressmaker's dummy. Then she heard footsteps behind her and felt Turner's hands on her shoulders. She leaned back into his chest.

"My hands are greasy," she said.

"That's all right."

His arms encircled her and she felt his beard against her face. This would take some getting used to; she had preferred him clean shaven. The other women noticed his arrival but kept their heads to their work, discreet.

"You're safely here," he said.

"And so are you."

"I'm sorry the cabin is not as far along as I had hoped. Everything takes twice as long as I thought."

"It's fine."

"Did you see your picture? It's on the wall behind the door back here."

He led her to the back room, pulling the door shut, and sure enough there was her tintype in a frame, hung from a nail in the wall. And now they were alone. With the door closed, he pulled her to him and kissed her.

"Thank you for your letters," she said after a while.

"They were the best part of my day. All day, I would compose my next letter in my mind. I couldn't wait until evening to get back here and write."

"They came in great bunches sometimes."

He smiled. "That's how they were sent sometimes. People don't come along this road every day."

"Any more encounters with that bandit? You could have been killed, you know." She shivered for a moment at the thought of him dead on some riverbank, never to be found.

"No. I know. To this day I don't know why we weren't. Because I wrote the letter for him, perhaps. Or perhaps he already had all he could carry." He squeezed her hands. "How are your mother and father?"

"Well enough. My father thinks I've gone mad."

"For once, I may agree with him. I would have sent for you when things were more ready out here."

"This is your great experiment," she told him. "This is where I should be. My father will forward any letters."

"But the hardship—"

"Living without you was a hardship. Living here will merely be a struggle."

That evening, the men gathered in the yard of the cabin, many with their copies of *Travels to Daybreak* for reference.

"Let us plan," Turner said. He drew a map in the dirt of the yard. "Here is the river, and here the road along it. There is no room for houses on the river side of the road, so—" He marked an arc in the dirt. "I propose we set our houses in a row, something like this, and smooth out a new road between them. It will return to the main road right here, where we stand."

He gazed north across the fields into the forest. "Every family will have a house of its own. Single men will share, four to a cabin. That's eleven cabins. As the community grows, we will add houses along the length of the road first and then build side streets."

The group followed his gaze. To the west, the hill that hemmed in the valley rose like a dark shoulder, its shadow creeping longer with each minute. The sycamores by the river glittered silver in the fading light, and in the dimness they could almost see the houses, the streets, the city, rising from the switchgrass and stumps. They could feel the power of Turner's dream, and as the evening light dimmed it became their own dream, a collective dream, the dream of a city in the wilderness.

"Once everyone is housed," Turner went on, "we will build a large meeting house, a Temple of Community, for school on the weekdays and church on Sunday. And every week from this day on out, we will meet as a community to plan our course. What day of the week is it?"

"Thursday," someone answered. "September the twenty-first."

"Very well," said Turner. "Every Thursday will be our meeting night. And every September twenty-first will be a community holiday, the anniversary of our founding."

They divided into crews, with two-thirds of the men assigned to building cabins and one-third to clearing ground. None of the men were farmers; they were clerks, students, factory workers, shopkeeper's sons. George Webb agreed to tutor the farming group in the ways of clearing, plowing, and planting.

Inside the house, Charlotte and the other women took turns scrubbing dishes in a wooden tub. They moved quietly so as to hear the conversation outside.

"Too late to plant anything," murmured Mrs. Wickman. "We'll have to live on our stores this winter."

"What should we be doing first?" Charlotte said.

Mrs. Wickman gave her a sideways glance, and the other women drew near to hear her whispered reply.

"The way I see it," she said, "There's better than fifty men out there, and only five of us women. Those single men won't know a blessed thing about home life. More wives will be coming soon, but for now it'll be all we can do to keep them fed."

"You have two girls," said another woman. "I have one. We'll set up a kettle by the river, and they can take over the washing."

"Agreed."

Charlotte spoke up. "Fetching the water will be a burden. We should get one of the men to build us a race from the spring. It's all downhill."

"Good," said Mrs. Wickman. "One of the pork barrels will be empty by morning. We can place it at the corner of the house here for rainwater, and add more barrels as they empty."

"Which one is yours?" Charlotte whispered to her as they watched the men debate.

Mrs. Wickman pointed to a lank, bespectacled man with a flat-brimmed hat. "That's him," she said. "John Wesley Wickman. Clerk on the docks most of his life, but oh, he does love to read, read, read, and think, think, think. Don't know why he ever married me!" She chuckled softly.

With the dishes finished, they filed out the back door and came around front to listen to the rest of the talk. The debate had moved to the question of membership.

"One more thing," Turner said. "Conditions for entry. You are the pioneers here. You've already earned your place. But later on, not everyone will come with the same high purpose."

"Loafers and parasites," someone said.

"Let's just say, enthusiasts without skills or resources," replied Turner. "Despite our ideals, we must also act in the best interests of the colony. Therefore I propose that additional colonists not be admitted unless they come with at least two hundred dollars in money or goods."

"Hear, hear," called a voice.

"Admittance will be by community vote, and is provisional for six months. At six months, another vote."

"And no Irish," said a man in the front of the crowd.

The comment brought an angry buzz. Turner let it run a while before all faces eventually turned to him.

"Each of us comes from stock that was once new to this country," he said. "We cannot turn a man away for that. We must decide one case at a time."

"Besides," said another man, "when was the last time you saw an Irishman with two hundred dollars to his name?"

The group's laughter was interrupted by a rifle shot that cracked through the twilight. Men flinched and looked in all directions, checking for injury. There was movement from the white house down the valley.

Unnoticed by all, Harp Webb had come onto the porch, and from his porch had shot a mourning dove. It fluttered to the ground from the branches of a large white oak tree that stood beside the road a hundred yards from where the group had gathered. Harp laid his rifle on the railing and walked down the hill to fetch it.

"Some country this is. Shooting rifles off your front porch," said a man quietly.

Charlotte watched as Harp retrieved the bird, paying them no mind. He was a thin man with a full beard; bright yellow hair strung out in long trails from beneath his hat. He walked with deliberation, and at first she thought he was going to ignore them entirely; but as he turned toward his house, he gave the group a careless wave. Charlotte took a peek at George Webb, but other than some additional reddening of his potato nose, his face gave no clue to what he was thinking.

The incident spoiled the mood of the group for a time. Everyone gathered their things and made plans for the night in quiet murmurs. But once the wives and children settled on the floor of the cabin's front room, the incident with Harp was behind them and the room filled with talk and laughter. As night came on, Charlotte retreated to the back room. She started to unpack her trunk, but fatigue caught up with her; she took a nightdress off the top of the stack of clothing and got into bed. She hadn't realized how tired she was. The mattress was just a straw tick sitting on a rope frame, but after the long trip it felt like feathers.

Soon Turner came in and quietly closed the door behind him. He undressed in the dark, taking his nightshirt from a hook on the door, and climbed into bed.

For a little while they just held each other.

"You surprised me," he said at last. "But I'm glad to see you."

"I should hope so!" She pulled him to her and kissed him. She could feel his smile beneath her lips.

He was lean, much leaner than when he had left. Her hands caressed his sides, counting every rib.

"You'll fatten me up," he said, reading her mind.

"I'll do my best."

"Can you believe it? We're starting the community." His voice was excited. "I would never have imagined it. But here I am. Can you believe it?"

Charlotte let him talk. For now, she was just happy to stroke his chest and hear his voice again. She had been able to hear his voice in the letters he wrote, but only with effort. Now she could just close her eyes and hear him, the happy, clear voice she knew, carrying on about work crews and incorporating the town and starting the newspaper as soon as possible, about spreading the gospel of cooperation. She let the sound flow over her.

In time, the words slowed. Her caresses moved lower, finding the tail of his nightshirt, then moved underneath. He stirred and turned toward her.

Later on, he murmured in the dark, "Why did you come? You know I said I'd send for you."

"I couldn't wait. I just felt I had to be here."

"It's going to be hard. This is hard country."

"I'm not afraid. I want to be here." She could hear his breathing even out. His voice had grown soft and drowsy. Then all was quiet.

"I want our child to know its father," she said to his sleeping form.

November 1857

Chapter 7

Turner awoke to the soft noises of Charlotte, awake already, in the other room fixing breakfast. He rubbed his face, clean-shaven again. His hand felt like a stranger's, hard and calloused. Progress at a cost—he was turning into one of those muscle-bound farmers he had disdained as a youth. Typesetting was difficult nowadays. His fingertips no longer could feel the kerf at the bottom of a type stem. Out back, in the shed they had built for the printing press, he struggled with a simple paragraph, setting *p*'s as *d*'s and *b*'s as *q*'s.

Still, he'd gotten out the first issue of *The Daybreak Eagle*. And the colony was taking shape. The cabin building was going well—a cabin could go up in a hurry with twenty men working on it. They had not brought glass for windows, so for now they were hanging sheets of oiled cloth in the openings. Perhaps next year they would have enough money in the treasury to equip each house with a window; none should enjoy the privilege until everyone could. All the families had cabins now, and most of the single men. They would have everyone out of tents in another couple of weeks.

New settlers kept arriving. A man named Hess Shepherson, who had left a new bride waiting in Indiana while he checked out the Daybreak experiment, rode in on horseback in October. A few days later, one of the wagoners the group had hired in Sainte Genevieve, Ben Prentice, returned with his wife and two children. "Ben just kept carrying on about how happy you people all were, talking about share and share alike," Mrs. Prentice said, her expression dubious. "So I said all right, let's go and see. We was just renting the old place anyway." She smiled a little shyly. "I can't say no to him most of the time, I might as well admit." Prentice didn't seem like a good risk, joining up on a whim, but he was good with horses and, to everyone's surprise, had the entrance deposit in hand.

As Mrs. Wickman predicted, their late arrival in the valley meant no planting till spring; they would have to live on stores and on food bought from town. A disappointment, but not a surprise. They could spend the time in preparation, because before they could plow or plant, they had to pull stumps.

They sent Cabot to Jefferson City to obtain their town charter, and a week later he returned with news of the larger world. Panic had gripped the Northeast; banks were failing, prices were dropping. The copies of *The Intelligencer* and *Missouri Republican* that he brought back were passed around, studied, discussed. All agreed this was no time to be a chip on the surging waters of the economy.

One settler, a big man by the name of Buford, turned out to be the comedian of the group as well as a quick study in agriculture, unlike Wickman, who had hoed up half a row of corn shoots before someone noticed and stopped him. Cabot was useless with tools but good at planning. Turner and Cabot had walked off the ground for the Temple of Community, and now a crew was gathering limestone slabs from the bluffs along the river for its construction. The Temple would be larger than they now needed, but as Turner reminded everyone, they weren't building it for the Daybreak of today, but for the Daybreak of ten years from now, or a hundred.

The smell of biscuits and molasses brought him out from the covers. He slipped up behind Charlotte and put his arms around her waist.

"There's the slug-a-bed," she said, turning and tapping his nose with her fingertip. "I thought I might have to send in the dogs."

"Not all of us can see in the dark."

"Oh, I can see in the dark. And I can live on spiderwebs and hoarfrost. And I can read minds too. More shingles today?"

"Till noon. Then I need to spend some time on the next *Eagle*."

Turner had drawn shingle duty this week. Splitting them wasn't so hard, once Webb had showed him how to find the grain in a piece of wood and split along it, how to swing the mallet easily to conserve strength, how to position the froe so that the shingle wasn't too thick or too thin. By the end of the morning he would have a respectable pile. The work was repetitive enough that he could compose his articles in his mind, and then in the afternoon retire to the shed and set them into type, sometimes not even bothering to write them in longhand first if he had the paragraphs clear enough in his thoughts.

56

Charlotte paused behind him and wrapped her arm over his shoulder. "I'm glad you're keeping up with *The Eagle*," she said. "Not all the important work is done outside."

"*The Eagle* is like to be what keeps us through the winter," he said. "We'll not be self-supporting this year."

They were interrupted by a soft knock at the door. It was the youngest Cameron boy. "Papa says come out and look," he said. "Something's coming."

Turner fetched his hat and coat and stepped out the door. Up the road he could see a long line of wagons, twenty or more, led by a man on horseback.

By now just about everyone had heard the creaking of the wagons and the snorting of the horses. The group did not take the turn into the colony but stayed on the main road. The lead rider spurred into a trot for a moment and reached him ahead of the rest. Turner stepped into the road.

"Good morning," Turner said, extending his hand. "Will you stop for breakfast?"

The man was a thick, leathery-looking sort in a buff coat. He had a chaw in his mouth the size of a walnut, and he paused to spit over the other side of his horse's neck before reaching down to shake Turner's hand.

"You the leader of this bunch?" he said, indicating the colony with a toss of his head.

"Yes. James Turner."

"Heard about you. Name's Harley Willingham. I'm county sheriff. You know anything about this bunch?" He tossed his head behind him.

"No."

"Buncha Irish, out of St. Louis." He flashed a sudden smile of stubby yellow teeth. "I'm helping 'em find the county line."

The lead wagon had caught up to them now, and everyone halted. The Daybreak villagers gathered around. George Webb walked up from his house and shook hands with Willingham.

"Well?" said the wagon's driver impatiently. "What place is this?"

He was a tall man in priest's robes and a wide-brimmed black hat, and he alternated his glare between Willingham and Turner.

"Good morning," Turner repeated. "Will you—"

"They et already," Willingham said.

They shook hands, and Turner introduced himself.

"The Fourierist or whatnot. I've seen your pamphlets," he said in an unimpressed tone. The priest swept his gaze over the buildings and the colonists. "I'm Father John Hogan. Good progress. They tell me you just got here this summer."

"That's right."

He raised his voice. "Any Catholics here who would like to make a confession? I can hear it before we move on."

No one answered. Willingham rubbed his nose. "They's a Catholic church up in Fredericktown. I reckon anybody wants to go, goes up there."

"Germans and Bohunks," Hogan said. "Probably wouldn't let an Irish in."

"You're from St. Louis?" Turner asked.

"That's right. It's a fine old city for the old-timers, I suppose, but a stinking hell for the working man." He gestured to the line of wagons behind him. "Camps along the tracks, that's all they get."

"I hear there's a new panic."

"Right again. Worse back East, bad enough here. Started with the banks, now it's the factories. Beggary and starvation." Hogan reached into a pocket of his robes and pulled out a packet of papers. "We've purchased land," he said. "Know where this is?"

Turner took the packet and looked it over. George Webb stepped forward to see it as well.

"Ripley County," Webb said. "You've got a couple of more days to travel."

"That's what this man said," replied Hogan.

"Don't know why you took them this way," Webb said to the sheriff. "They've got three rivers to cross. Should have took them down to Greenville to cross the St. Francis there, catch the road to Williamsville and cross the Black there, then over to Doniphan to cross the Current."

"I thought maybe they was some of your bunch," said Willingham.

"Anyway," said Webb, handing back the packet, "too far to retrace now. This track'll take you through to Logan's Creek, but it's a rough trace. You'll be good to get across the Black by nightfall."

"We're used to rough," said Hogan. He returned his attention to Turner. "This river is the St. Francis, eh? You plan to live like St. Francis?"

"I'll take the harmony and peaceableness, but skip the talking to the birds."

Hogan snorted derisively. "As if a bunch of heathen would know anything about it. You made any spiritual provision for this lot?"

"They can take care of that on their own, I should hope," said Turner.

"I read that pamphlet of yours. You think this is 'True Christianity?'"

"We're finding our way, Mr. Hogan. I hope you find yours."

The sheriff interrupted them. "Well, like the man said, you've got a ways to go. Better pull foot."

"Good luck to you," Turner said. Hogan tipped his hat and gave his reins a twitch, and the wagons started up again. Willingham stayed on his horse and watched them pass.

"Been meaning to come out here and pay you a call," he said as they went by. "I heard you all were building a new town."

"Getting there," Turner said.

"You all Mormons or something?"

"I'm not, but I don't inquire as to the religious persuasions of my companions."

"More's the pity. Mormons got run out of Missouri once already. No niggers or such, I take it."

"No."

Willingham looked out over the fields. "This is good ground for corn, but you'll have to put a watch out for the coons." He heaved an exaggerated sigh. "You got your regular coons, and then you got them copper-colored coons up on the ridge. Both of 'em sneaky as hell." He seemed to be working his way around to something. "Nice place, nice place. So—"

Everyone waited. Finally he spoke again.

"I'd ask you about your politics. Election next year, by then you all will be eligible to vote."

"I don't—"

"—inquire about the politics of your companions, eh, Mr. Turner? Well, may I inquire about your own politics, then."

"I have generally voted Democratic."

"Northern Democrat or Southern?"

"Last time I voted, there was no such thing."

Willingham stopped surveying the distance and fixed his attention on Turner.

"Let me spell it out for you," he said. "Missouri is a slave state. Always has been, always will be. They can do what they want out in Kansas, vote this way and that, agitate every direction. But this ain't Kansas."

"You have slaves, Mr. Willingham?"

He snorted. "Hell, no. You think I could afford to feed and clothe a bunch of niggers just to polish my boots and fix my supper? But that ain't the point." He straightened up in the saddle. The last wagon of the Irish train had disappeared around the Webbs' house. "The story is, if your bunch of people has come here to upset everybody and agitate for something nobody wants, then you are like to find yourselves the object of a lot of ill feeling. And I am the law and I live a half day's ride away."

"We're not here to agitate or upset anyone, Mr. Willingham. We are here to live our own lives and no one else's."

"All right, then." He stirred his horse. "That bunch there, they looked like trouble to me. So I am wanting to make sure they don't stop short of the county line. You ain't one of them free love type outfits, are you?"

"No."

"Well then. Appreciate your vote next year."

A sudden rush of anger swept over Turner. He reached up to take the horse's reins, but seeing the suspicious expression on the sheriff's face, patted its nose instead. "Before you go."

"Before I go."

"Let me spell it out for you now. We are here of our own choosing and breaking no laws. We let alone and ask to be let alone. Our ideas about property and competition may differ from yours, but we plan to practice them in peace. In any event—"

Willingham urged his horse forward and waved over his shoulder. "All right, don't overheat yourself. Hell, you all are lucky to be up here. Go down where them Irish are headed, there's lots of pukes who'll burn down your barn just for talking funny. Up here—" he flashed his yellow grin again— "we got 'em down to a precious handful. George, your boy at home?" he called behind him.

"Don't know. He was when I got up this morning," Webb said. "Any trouble?"

"No trouble, just want to visit with him a minute." He broke into a trot down the road.

Cabot's job for the day was cutting sprouts. He had been at it for about an hour after the Irish group passed through, his hands cramped and sore from the labor, when another wagon came into the valley. A stout, middle-aged man in a white collarless shirt was driving it, gripping the reins with an air of concentration as if he were receiving coded messages through his fingers. He wore tiny wire-rimmed spectacles. Beside him on the wagon seat sat a young woman, nineteen or twenty, with dark brown hair tucked under a man's broad-brimmed hat. Her hands were folded primly in her lap.

He walked to the road to meet them.

"Your group is about an hour ahead of you. You'll probably catch up to them at the next river crossing," he said. "Just keep following this road."

The two put their heads together and spoke in murmurs. The girl looked back at Cabot.

"We are not a group," she said, with a distinct French accent. "We are seeking the Daybreak."

From the seat between them she produced a copy of *The Eagle*.

"We are in St. Louis," she said. "My father, he is great in his enthusiasm for this community."

They bent their heads together again, and then she spoke again. "We are seeking to live in here."

A few people had stopped their work to see the newcomers. Cabot extended his hand to the father.

"This is Daybreak," he said. "Welcome."

The man shook his hand and burst into a series of excited statements, all in French. It was too fast for Cabot to understand with his schoolboy knowledge of the language, but he continued to shake his hand while the young woman tried to translate.

"He is very happy," she said. "He is ready to be a farmer."

"*Fermier*," he said, making a muscle with his arm.

"*Bonjour, mademoiselle*," he said, embarrassed at how slowly he was speaking and how bad his pronunciation must be. "*Je m'appelle Cabot. Et lui, c'est Monsieur Turner, notre directeur-géneral.*" He pointed toward Turner, who had left his pile of shingles and was walking to join them.

"*Bonjour, Monsieur Cabot. Ce sont mon père, Émile Mercadier. Et je m'appelle Marie.*"

"Invite them in," Turner called out. Cabot detached himself from the man's handshake. He looked dubiously at the pudgy man, who was still smiling broadly. "Farmer, eh?"

"*Fermier*," said Mercadier, making his muscle again. "*Communiste.*"

Over leftover biscuits and spring water in the Turners' cabin, the Mercadiers told their story, the father rushing ahead in French, the daughter editing and simplifying in English. He had been forced to flee France in 1848 for his radical opinions; the family had first stopped at New Harmony, then found the Icarian group at Nauvoo and lived there until 1854. That was where Madame Mercadier had died of cholera. When the Icarians broke up, they relocated with some of the group to St. Louis, but that settlement was not doing well.

"It is communist, but it is not a community," Marie said. "The young men, they leave one by one."

As it turned out, Mercadier was no farmer, but a shoemaker, with a complete set of tools in his wagon, along with a fine-looking fiddle in a hardshell case.

"Nothing against the farming life, but Mr. Mercadier here might well be of more use to this community as a shoemaker," Cabot said. "Not just for our own needs, but this winter we will need to bring in cash or trade."

"First things first," Turner replied. "The community has to vote them in. Until then they can stay in our front room."

Cabot went back to work, feeling unaccountably irritated at Turner's peremptory dismissal of his suggestion. True, the community would have to vote. But why so quick to remind him of that? He was only making an observation, and an obvious one at that. He liked Turner—who wouldn't?—But his air of command, his attitude of knowing best, had the faint smell of arrogance about it. Cabot sensed he had been put in his place, whatever that place was.

After lunch Turner went to the shed to set type for the next edition of *The Eagle*. Cabot was right, of course. The colony was not self-sufficient yet; for the winter they would need hard money or at least goods for trade. *The Eagle* would help—he had two hundred subscribers, more or less, at two dollars a year, and another hundred or so who had subscribed but not yet paid. Food should not be a serious problem; the hogs and biddies they had brought with them had multiplied prodigiously. Mrs. Wickman had showed Charlotte how to store eggs in lime water, and by now every home had buckets and canisters of eggs put away. But they would need cash money for yard goods, more and better tools for the men, seasonings, and at Christmastime a few treats for the children—

Turner stopped in mid-word. He laid his job stick down carefully on the table, tilting it over a sliver of wood so that the type didn't spill, and wiped the ink from his hands. He stepped out of the shed, closing the door carefully, and walked the forty feet to the cabin in a slow, meditative pace.

Charlotte found herself drawn to this odd pair, the bespectacled shoemaker and his talkative daughter, and it was a pleasure to bring out her French, which she hadn't spoken in—what? Nine or ten years? Fortunately, Cabot's was just as bad, so she didn't feel alone in her mangling. Marie Mercadier's English was far better than their French, but Charlotte could tell that she appreciated the effort they were making and indulged their slow articulation. Charlotte thought of Miss de Vries, who ran the girls' school in Highland Falls that she had attended, and her insistent cries of *Repetez! Repetez!* How she would flail her arms, and in moments of frustration would squeeze their cheeks together in an effort to get them to form the vowels. She could always manage better than Caroline—

Caroline. Every time her thoughts turned to Caroline, her mind stopped and she shivered from a sudden interior chill. Poor Caroline. Poor, lost Caroline.

Turner appeared at the door with a peculiar expression on his face, an expression as if he had just discovered something, which, she sensed, he had. She stopped her conversation and walked to meet him. They stepped outside and went over to the big sugar maple in front of the cabin, where he had made her a split-log bench, and sat down.

"How far along?" Turner said.

Charlotte looked at him quizzically, then gauging his expression better, smiled. "Four months, coming on five."

He placed his hand on her belly, not soft as it had been before, but hard and muscular, firmer than even a muscle should be. "Does everyone know but me?"

"Of course not, silly. The women know. Women always see things like this. But the men? Heavens."

The baby moved under his palm. Charlotte was still not used to the feeling, this body inside a body, this living thing inside her, moving around according to its own whims and desires.

"Are you well?"

"As far as I can tell."

"Are you afraid?"

She nodded.

They held hands, listening to cicadas chir in the trees. When he spoke again, his voice was gentle. "You could go back East. You could have your mother go with you, to New York or Philadelphia."

"Women die back East same as they die here."

"But there are doctors."

"James." She was almost stern. "We live here. This is where we are. Do I look like I was born to be an Eastern belle in a velvet dress and leg-of-mutton sleeves?"

That made him smile.

"Besides," she went on. "If the worst should happen—" Her look was earnest and intent. "You could bear it better than my mother and father. If I should be with my mother and fail to deliver…." She said no more, but simply shuddered.

It was almost time for supper. They embraced and were back at the cabin, when they spotted someone running down the road toward them. It was Gus Roberts, one of the young single men who was still living in a tent at the far end of the settlement.

"Luke Wornall's bad sick," he told them when he reached the cabin. "You better come see."

As they trotted back up the path between the cabins, Roberts told him the story. He and Luke, one of his mates in the tent, had been clearing ground in the morning when Luke said he felt unaccountably tired and thirsty. At noon they had found him lying on his pallet in the tent, feverish, complaining of a stomach-ache, but he had told them to leave him a jug of water and he would join them when he felt better.

Mrs. Wickman had found him. The Wickmans' cabin was next to the men's tent, and the men were using the woods toward the river for their necessities. Wornall had apparently been trying to make it there when he collapsed. When they arrived, Turner and Roberts first, with Charlotte and the Mercadiers close behind, Mrs. Wickman was kneeling over him, patting down his face with a wet cloth. Some of the other men came in from the fields.

"Bring a blanket out here," she told them. "We'll put him on it and carry him back to the tent."

Wornall was conscious, but barely. "I'm sorry," he moaned. His face was ashen, and his breeches were wet and stinking.

"There, now," said Mrs. Wickman. They slid him onto the blanket and dragged it toward the tent. "Gently," she said. "You men better take your things out of here. I'll need several buckets of water to clean him up with. Just leave a chamber pot. Here you go, son, let's loosen up your gallowses and get you comfortable."

Roberts and the other men stared as Mrs. Wickman undid the man's suspenders and pulled off his boots. She glanced up at them.

"Well?" she said. "Ain't you never seen a sick man before?" This spurred them into action, and they quickly carried everything out. "And don't let the children down here."

When she pulled down Wornall's breeches, a flood of watery, fishy-smelling diarrhea, flecked with white, came with them.

"I'm sorry," Wornall said again, his voice little more than a whisper.

"Don't worry, son, we'll get you cleaned up. You ain't the first man's ever shit hisself," Mrs. Wickman said. She threw the breeches out the back tent flap as Charlotte and Marie arrived with buckets of water. "Open up these flaps as much as you can, get a little air in here."

Charlotte put down her bucket and turned away. "I can't—" She covered her face with her hand.

Just then Wornall doubled over in agony. Mrs. Wickman managed to get the chamber pot underneath him. He moaned and then fell back onto the mattress, his eyelids fluttering.

"Just relax, son, everything will be fine," Mrs. Wickman said. She stood up and joined the others at the tent opening.

"You might set some men to gathering brush," she said to Turner. "When this is finished we will need to burn this tent and everything in it."

Mercadier said something to Marie, who nodded, stepped forward and joined them.

"This is what killed my mother, Mr. Turner," she said. "This is the cholera."

November 1857 / March 1858

Chapter 8

W ornall died later that night, his mumbled apology the last thing anyone heard from him. In the morning they burned the tent and all his clothes, saving only Wornall's diary from the flames. The other men's clothes and bedding went too.

That first day Charlotte walked the fields alone while the bonfire blazed, sending a column of smelly gray smoke down the river valley. Her father's dinner table lectures on earthworks, landforms, and drainage came in handy in an unexpected way. North from the village was the wide river bottom, fields and areas someday to be cleared for fields—too valuable to be used as a cemetery. But on the other side of the fields, several short hollows were tucked into the mountainside, facing east toward the morning sun, sloping but not too steep. She chose one that had a good stand of trees and could be seen from the settlement, not too long a walk but far enough away to feel quiet and alone. She picked Wornall's spot and returned home to let the others know.

By then Gus Roberts and Jesse Buford, two of the other men in the tent, were ill. Charlotte had to ignore her horror of the disease from then on. The luxury of drawing back in fear was no longer available; everyone simply had to do what was necessary, grit their teeth and point themselves forward. The other women tried to get her to stay away because of her condition, but of course there wasn't time for that.

A hurried search revealed that no one except George Webb had any calomel, or at least Webb was the only one to admit to having any.

"Just as well," Turner told her. "Saves us having to decide who would get it and who wouldn't."

They set aside one of the cabins for a hospital and took turns caring for the sick men. Roberts was the worse off. Although he was a strapping young man, his size and strength gave him no advantage. They tried to cool him and to keep up with his maddening thirst, but after two days he died.

Buford was alone in the cabin for only a day, when they brought in Lucy Wickman. From that time forward, Mrs. Wickman was there day and night, leaving only to fix meals and to spend time with her other daughter, Mary. Three days later, Mary joined her sister in the sick ward, and then more and more.

Almost everyone who fell ill was from the lower side of the settlement, closer to the river, which caused some bad feeling. Talk flew around the village that it had been built too low, where the river fogs could enter the nearest houses and poison them with its bad air. But Cabot pointed out that the fogs from the river covered all parts of the settlement equally. And besides, there hadn't been any fogs when the disease struck. Suspicion also fell upon the Mercadiers until someone remembered that Wornall had taken sick in the morning and the Frenchman and his daughter hadn't arrived until afternoon, and then onto the Irish who had passed through earlier, but soon enough everyone stopped searching for causes or people to blame, and just tended to the sick and dying.

With the fall had come the sickness and then the rain, weeks and weeks of rain, everyone confined indoors for long stretches. The river had risen alarmingly—it covered the main road and crested only a few feet from their front door. It was frightening that a river so placid and harmless-looking could become that relentless, carrying logs and posts and debris downstream in its swift grip. The Hudson Charlotte had grown up on was much larger, of course, but it seemed tranquil compared to the St. Francis. There was something almost animal in the speed of this river's swelling. One of the sycamores on the bank gave way in the night, falling into the stream with a sodden crash that woke Charlotte in the dark.

The sickness persisted into the winter. Buford lingered for more than a week. Although he had been the colony's clown, with a stream of witticisms for every situation, he spent his last days possessed by an intense fear of hell, alternately praying and confessing his sins to anyone within earshot. Lucy Wickman died quickly but Mary hung on. Hess Shepherson, whose wife had just arrived at the colony the week before, fell ill on a Saturday and was dead by Monday.

About half of the sick ones recovered and were sent back to their cabins, though many had to stay in bed for weeks afterward. Glendale Wilson, the fourth young man who had shared the tent with Wornall, Roberts, and Buford, never showed so much as a mild fever. He walked around the colony like a lonesome ghost, everyone's eyes upon him and everyone avoiding his gaze.

In the end, the last one ill was Mary Wickman. Charlotte spent time with her in the mornings, helping Mrs. Wickman with her cleanup and breakfast. When Mary was conscious, Charlotte read to her; but more often she just mopped her face and kept her warm as she murmured, semiconscious, in the soft light of December, her body under the blankets as frail as a bird's, a strange contrast to the sturdy little form Charlotte had seen lugging pails of water for her mother.

For two months the weekly meetings had been suspended because of the epidemic. The whole colony seemed to be sleepwalking. Those who were well came out in the mornings, found something to do, and worked at it as long as they felt like it. Christmas came and went with no celebration, only quiet greetings within a family or across a distance. But with the waning of the disease in early January, Turner called a meeting again, walking from house to house with the news.

And at the meeting, Wickman was the first to speak. "I'd like permission from the community to bring my daughter home," he said, his voice hoarse and nearly inaudible. "I know that's not how you're supposed to do it—supposed to wait till the last person either gets well or . . . you know . . . but I don't think anybody else is getting sick. It's been days, and I—I just want her home."

No one spoke. All eyes were cast down. "Hearing no objection," Turner said after a minute, "the request is approved. We shall burn the cabin on the next favorable day." Wickman walked out of the meeting into the dim evening light. Charlotte followed.

He strode directly to the hospital cabin, where Mrs. Wickman sat nodding, reading her Bible beside Mary's cot.

"Run home and get her bed ready, Frances," he said. "Time to go." He glanced over his shoulder at Charlotte. "Can you gather up her things?"

"Of course."

And so Mary Wickman went home in her father's arms, shivering in her blankets, and was tucked into her own bed. But her body had grown rigid and her breath came in soft rasping gasps, and a few minutes later she was dead.

Only then did Mrs. Wickman break down and cry. She had been strong all through Lucy's decline and death, brushing away a few tears but keeping a smile for Mary. Now, though, she lay in the bed with her daughter, sobbing, with her body held over the girl as if to keep her warm, and her rough hand smoothing out the sweat-tangled mat of hair on the back of her head.

Charlotte quietly laid on the table Mary's few belongings—a rag doll, another blanket, a few extra clothes—and let herself out the door, as Wickman awkwardly stroked his wife's heaving back.

The next day was dry and windless. The men gathered in the morning with barrels of water drawn from the river to quench the sparks and lit a fire in the center of the cabin floor. Within fifteen minutes, the building was ablaze, flames licking out the front and back doors, the intense heat driving them all back except for Cabot and Glendale Wilson, who had been stationed on the roof of the house next door with buckets to protect its roof. Another fifteen minutes and the center beam collapsed, bringing the walls down with it and sending up a shower of ash and sparks that sent them all running to stamp out the tiny conflagrations in the weeds.

And then it was full winter and she was due. Looking back on it, there was much Charlotte couldn't remember of that time, and just as well. Her pains had been going on for a few days, but on a cold January afternoon she knew her time had come. A granny woman in French Mills had a reputation for being good with childbirth, so Turner was sent to fetch her—more to get him out of the house than anything else, she suspected. As afternoon moved into night, the pain got worse, and so did her fear, which doubled the pain. But the women of the colony gathered in the house, spoke to her calmly, and got her through her fear. Then it was just determination, or desperation, or a combination of the two. She was going to give birth or die, so she gave birth. By the time the old woman from French Mills arrived, it was mostly over. Thank God it had gone as well as it had. With the river so high, she could never have made it to Fredericktown for medical help, even if there had been any available.

So now Charlotte and Turner had a son, and the town had a graveyard. The limestone slabs collected to build the Temple of Community were put to use as grave markers, squared off and chiseled with the names of the dead. The newest one had been dug a couple of weeks ago, its mound of red earth a bright gash in the fallen leaves on the hillside—the Cameron boy, kicked in the head by a mule. John Wesley Wickman, the clumsy one, the man who seemed inept at every task he was assigned, built a sturdy bench for his wife beside the graves of their daughters. It was Osage orange, impervious to the elements, and he had smoothed it to a polish and set it firmly into the rocky slope. Mrs. Wickman went up every morning for an hour. She would leave wildflowers, sprigs of bittersweet, bright buttons, and tiny handwritten notes, which she removed on the next visit and replaced with new things. And on a bright, oddly warm March afternoon,

Charlotte found herself there as well, wrapped in her gray wool overcoat, sitting on Mrs. Wickman's bench.

Charlotte knew she should get back to the colony. There was a great deal of work to be done. But she just needed to get away. Surely not every minute had to be spent in toil and duty. It was probably more cabin fever than anything else, she told herself, but whatever it was, her need for time alone to think overpowered everything else at the moment.

She had pulled her arms in from the sleeves of her overcoat, sitting on the bench, so that the heavy woolen coat sat like a tent around her. She felt a stir inside the coat and looked down through the collar opening. Young Newton, named after her father, was squirming in her arms. She thought he might want to nurse, but after a moment he turned over, puckered his lips as if pondering some deep thought, then relaxed again, still asleep.

Charlotte sat for a while longer, until it really was time to get down the hill. She stood, and as she did, a flutter of color caught her notice out of the corner of her eye. She turned to see.

It was a patch of Harp Webb's hair that had come out from under his hat. He was sitting at the base of a tree about forty feet up the hill from her, his heavy canvas coat draped all the way to the ground, his rifle propped between his knees. Charlotte walked over to him.

"Mr. Webb," she said. "I didn't see you there."

"Ma'am." He touched his hat and got to his feet. "Feels good to stand up. I been holding that pose for three, four hours."

"Why?"

He pointed across the hollow. "I seen some turkey sign on that slope a few days ago, thought I might put one in my bag. Then when you came along I figured the turkey wouldn't show, so I decided to watch you instead."

"All this time?"

He shrugged. "Didn't have nothing else planned for today."

The idea of Webb sitting up the hill from her, watching her all this time, made Charlotte shudder. "You should announce your presence. Don't you have anything better to do with yourself?"

"You people are the ones with all the ambition. Me, I just sit and hunt the birds."

They came to the edge of the hollow and looked down at the colony.

"Not that turkey hunting ain't work of its own sort," he said. "The trick to hunting is, you got to be willing and able to outwait your animal. He pointed to a groundhog hole at the base of a tree. "Now that critter, he will outwait a man. You got to catch him by surprise. But the other animals, you wait downwind long enough, and they will forget you. Then you got 'em."

The path down to the village was little more than a trail, with weeds and sassafras sprouts growing in the wagon tracks.

"You're feeling philosophical today, Mr. Webb."

"Rally me all you want, ma'am. I do think a few thoughts from time to time. Even an ignorant border ruffian is entitled to a thought now and then."

"I'm sure that's true." She forced a smile.

"Are you now." He studied her face. "You might be surprised. Take for example, did you ever wonder why your property lines run at an angle up the river valley instead of straight north and south?"

Charlotte was flustered. "No, I never really did."

"'Cause it's an old Spanish land grant, that's why. The Spanish, they surveyed this valley first, and they just laid it out how they pleased. All that township and range stuff came later. My daddy bought this acreage from a man who had got it from the Spanish, way back when, who got it I guess from the Indians." He paused. "You should read the deed sometime, it talks all about so many arpents this way and so many arpents that way. Bet you've never seen the corner markers."

"No."

He pointed. "Blaze on a black oak tree that way, rock piles that way and that way, big X painted on the bluff over yonder."

"You know this land pretty well."

"You're damn right I do, beg your pardon. It would have been mine to inherit, till you people came along. And that ain't the half of it. When my daddy parceled off this claim for you all, he split me off the part with the house and downriver. I go all the way up that mountain, down the other side about half way, then right angle across the river to about where you can see that outcrop. Then back across the river to the house."

Harp continued to talk as they walked toward the settlement. "'Course, I ain't built no town on it, no houses or barns or corncribs or what all. I ain't got big ideas like my daddy and you all. But it's mine all the same."

"Your father is quite a man."

"Oh yeah, one of the great men of the county, they say. Always reading his books, always talking about serving the greater good. He read your husband's book over and over. Taught me to read, too, but I don't care for it. I take my lessons at the feet of Mother Nature."

"And what did Mother Nature teach you?"

Webb gave her an appraising look. "Most people only see what they want to see in nature. It ain't easy to read the real lessons."

She waited for him to continue.

"Eat. Struggle. Mate. Die," he said. "Put off dying for as long as you can. Take pleasure where you can, for pleasures are always cut short. Defend your ground."

"And you had no mother of your own?"

Webb shrugged, but his beard hid any expression. "Run off. She was from back East. The rustic life didn't agree with her, I guess."

"What about the other lessons of nature? Beauty and cooperation?"

They were halfway down the slope by now. Harp stopped and turned back toward the edge of the forest. "Oh yeah, some of the creatures cooperate. The lower creatures, the bees and the ants. And the wolves. I believe I'll part from you here," he said. "My father, he had two terms as judge, you know. Great believer in the common good, king of the ants. Didn't none of it rub off on me. Me, I just sit under trees. I watch and wait."

From their vantage point on the hillside, they could see the entire valley, two miles from end to end. The colonists' work of tree-cutting and stump removal was pushing the fields northward, into the bottomland forest, but there was still a great deal of ground to be cleared. The huddle of houses that made up Daybreak looked insignificant from up here, and the cleared fields little more than a small gap in the forest that surrounded them, forest that began just across the road and extended eastward into the distance, hill upon hill receding, the winter gray-brown of the near woods growing bluer and paler as the hills backed away to the horizon, and forest behind her, the cemetery barely hacked out and constantly encroached upon by sprouts at every edge, forest that blanketed the hillslope and stretched westward behind her, how far God only knew.

And at the south end of the valley was the original house, the Webbs' house, fronting the main road, and behind it their barn and outbuildings. Tucked against the hillside was Harp's odd collection of shacks and sheds, where he seemed to spend most of his days.

"That's quite a nest of buildings," Charlotte said.

"You should come and see sometime," Harp said, a note of pride in his voice. "Took me two years to get 'em the way I wanted." He pointed with his rifle. "That one highest up is the springhouse. This near building, that's my stillhouse, and the long one behind it is my saltpeter works. You ever seen saltpeter made?"

"No."

"Oh, it's the champion. Every so often I dig out a bunch of dirt from the cave and put it in some tubs. Then I just let the water drip through it, again and again, until I've got a good batch of liquid to boil off. Sometimes I'll have two fires going, whiskey in the one house, saltpeter in the other. Tending a fire all day ain't a half bad job." Webb's eyes darted to her overcoat, where Newton still slept in her arms. "Boy doing all right?"

"Yes, thank you."

"He takes to crying too much, you tell me and I'll fix him up a little whiskey teat. I seen it done many a time. Everybody else wants their jug filled, I charge 'em cash money, but for you, nothing."

"Thank you. I'll let you know."

He turned and started to walk toward his still, following the curve of the hill-side. Then he stopped and looked down at the colony again, his eyes sharp. Marie Mercadier was carrying an armload of stovewood into her house.

"There's a pretty young thing," he said. "Bet every man in the settlement has his eye on her."

He said nothing more and walked away. Charlotte watched him go, then walked slowly the rest of the way down the hill, Newton resting in his warm cocoon, her shadow long before her in the slanting light, shivering from what she told herself was the evening's chill.

When she reached the house, she let herself in through the back door and tucked Newton into his cradle. Turner, Cabot, and George Webb were out front, seated around the table, talking about their weekly meeting while Turner scribbled tiny notes on a folded piece of paper.

"I tell you this, my friends," Turner was telling the men. "It was easier to make decisions during the weeks when we shut down the meetings from the cholera. Just decide and go, not spend four hours arguing and then vote what you knew needed to happen in the first place." They laughed.

"How many shirts and pants will we have for Grindstaff this week, Mrs. Turner?" Cabot said over his shoulder.

"A dozen of each, I would guess. I haven't been around to collect them yet."

Every week Grindstaff, who owned the general store in town, sent them bolts of cloth and a list of requests, and every week the women in the community cut and sewed until the orders were filled. The trip around the houses to collect the finished items had become one of Charlotte's weekly tasks. Some of the money went toward their account at the store, while the rest went into the treasury.

"I'm grateful for every one of them, ma'am," said Webb. "They certainly make my finance report more cheerful."

"We all do our part," said Charlotte.

"We're on the good with Grindstaff. He'll advance us seeds for the coming year," Webb said. "But if we really want to move ahead, we need a McCormick reaper. Do the work of ten men."

"Can we afford one?" Turner asked.

"If everyone stays. But if some people pull out and take their money with them..."

"Have you heard anything?"

Cabot spoke. "Cantwell's unhappy. Says if he had wanted to work like an animal, he would have stayed back East in the factory."

"How much did he bring?"

Webb checked his books. "Three hundred and twenty dollars."

"The thing is," Cabot said, "He can influence others. He's a talker, that Cantwell."

"We've got a whole town full of talkers," said Webb. "No shortage of big ideas."

Charlotte stepped to the table and stood beside Turner. "We're ready to start planting. Once there are green things coming up in rows all down the valley, our outlook will improve. You won't hear as much complaining." The men nodded. "Besides," she added, "I thought the idea was to get off the whole treadmill of getting and spending. Debt and interest. Wages and competition."

"Easier said than done," replied Webb. "There are still taxes to pay and goods to buy. But we'll make a fist of it yet."

"If we get into a corner, I can always make another lecture tour," said Turner. "We brought in high money from those, didn't we?" He put his arm around Charlotte's waist. Charlotte didn't reply. "And there's *The Eagle*. I'll have another issue out by the first of February, I'll wager. Which reminds me, this one will finish up my ink and paper. When I ride into town tomorrow, I'll ask Grindstaff to order some more from St. Louis."

A glance passed between Cabot and Webb. "Mind your expenses," Webb said. "*The Eagle* is barely a paying proposition. More subscribers would be a help—especially the kind that pay in something besides wildcat money."

"Oh, it'll fly," Turner said. "There is only one direction on my map, and that is straight ahead. McCormick reaper, you say?"

Newton was awake now and crying from the bedroom. Charlotte left the men and went to tend him; she needed to get out on her rounds anyway. She took him to the washtub to clean him up, put a fresh diaper on him from the stack beside the door, and rinsed off her hands in the wash water before tossing it out. Motherhood had left her feeling dirty most of the time—sneezed upon, snotted upon, dribbling and dribbled upon. She soon had him tucked back under her coat as she walked up the lane among the houses.

The colony was now up to nine married women, the Shepherson widow, and the Mercadier girl. Mrs. Wickman had sewed two pair of pants and two shirts; everyone else had done one of each, except Mrs. Cantwell, who had only managed a pair of pants. "Lucky to get that," she said, her face pinched and half-angry. "Not enough that I have to do all our own housework, and then he makes me rub his feet for an hour every night."

"They hurt," called Cantwell from his bed. "I think there's something wrong with them."

"Well, thank you for this," Charlotte said, folding the pants over her arm. She didn't feel like listening to the Cantwells' woes. She was still thinking of Turner's offhand remark. Another lecture tour? And leave her home with the baby? Not that he did all that much to help with young Newton besides fly him around the room when he came in at evening time, but the idea of herself alone in Daybreak and him off, riding from city to city, getting banquets and hotel stays, seemed too unfair to tolerate.

By the time she got home, the front room had been cleared for the weekly meeting. Another reason to hurry and finish the Temple of Community—to get these packed sessions out of her house on Thursday nights. She paused outside the open door for a moment. There was barely room for all the men to stand; Turner stood on an overturned box. A few men even were pushed into the bedroom doorway.

A voice came from the shadow of the maple tree in the front yard. It was Adam Cabot's. "Quite a throng, isn't it?"

"Yes," she said. She walked over to him. "More than a two-room cabin can easily hold."

"That's what happens with big ideas," he said. "They grow quicker than our ability to contain them."

"Do you think that is happening here?"

Cabot sighed deeply and watched the milling group in the lamplight. "I am in no place to judge," he said. "Becoming the prisoner of great ideas is something of my specialty."

"And have you embraced our great idea? You've thrown yourself into our work with the zeal of an enthusiast."

He turned to face her, with a disconcerting force in his gaze. "There is no monument, no symphony, that speaks more to human possibility than a group of men and women gathered to elevate the race. A sacred task is in the undertaking here."

His intensity took her aback for a moment. "You sound like my husband."

Cabot bowed slightly toward her. "No finer compliment, Mrs. Turner."

She took his arm as they walked to the house. "Call me Charlotte, please. We are friends, and I hope we shall be friends forever. And I noticed that you didn't answer my question."

Charlotte left him at the door and went around to come in through the back. She dragged her slat-back rocker out of the front to give the settlers more room and settled in it with Newton.

When the time came for the domestic manufacture report, she stood up and delivered it over the heads of the men crowded in the doorway. How many shirts and pants were made this week; how the stores of flour, salt, and meal were holding up; what kinds of supplies needed to be brought back from town. Mrs. Cameron had requested some yards of black cloth to make a mourning dress. The last time Charlotte had brought such a request, for Mrs. Wickman back in November, someone had questioned the expense, and a fistfight nearly broke out. This time the group meekly voted its approval.

Then two hours went by in debate over the tasks for the coming week. Whether it was too early to plant. Whether it was wise to buy a McCormick reaper. How much of the valley should be planted in wheat and how much in corn. Where they should mill it, and how much they could expect for their excess. The talk went on and on, everyone chiming in, until at the end they voted to buy the reaper. The fields were still too wet for planting, so Turner announced they would be spending the week in repairs and inside work. A few men would fell trees, and others saw planks; they had voted last week that it was time to cover the log walls of their homes with clapboards. Charlotte dozed off and was only awakened by the sound of the men putting the furniture back in place and shouting good-nights in the chill air.

An hour later, just before bedtime, there was a quiet knock at the front door. The first knock was so quiet that Charlotte thought she had imagined it; the second a little louder.

On the stepstone was a small, slender man in a long overcoat, his face long and narrow, an attempt at a beard shadowing his face. When Charlotte opened the door, he removed his hat and placed it over his heart, inclining his head a bit too dramatically.

"Ma'am," he said. "I wish to speak with Mr. Turner."

By now Turner was behind her. "As I live and breathe," he said. "Mr. Hildebrand."

"The same."

"I heard no horses," Charlotte said, looking over his shoulder into the darkness. Seeing nothing, she returned her attention to the man. His voice was soft and lilting, and he seemed to have a balance about him, like an acrobat or rope walker; but somehow he also seemed curiously rooted, as though nothing could move him off the doorstone if he didn't want to.

"I avoid the roads, ma'am. There are those who would quarrel with me if they knew I was about, and I always avoid a quarrel."

Turner stepped in front of her. "I forget my manners. Charlotte, this is Mr. Sam Hildebrand. Mr. Hildebrand, my wife."

Hildebrand bowed again.

"I have heard of you," Charlotte said.

Hildebrand's glance flicked upon her and then went elsewhere. "Mr. Turner, may I have a word."

"Certainly." Turner stepped aside and held the door open.

"Outside, if you don't mind."

Turner and Charlotte exchanged a moment's worried look, but the request seemed polite enough. He took his coat off the door hook. "Certainly." They stepped outside and stood beneath the maple tree in front of the house.

Charlotte pushed the door to, but not all the way, and from inside she watched the two men converse. Hildebrand bent his head near Turner's ear; the two kept their gazes away from each other. The night was clear, with a quarter moon just rising in the trees across the river.

They spoke for several minutes. At one time she saw a gesture pass between them—Hildebrand offering something, James accepting? She couldn't quite tell.

Then whatever it was, was over, and he came back inside. Hildebrand melted into the dark.

"So?" she said.

"He and two of his brothers wanted to sleep in our barn. They're heading to Arkansas." He held out his hand and dropped two small gold coins, tinkling onto the table. "And they gave us two dollars for the privilege."

Blowing out the lamps, they eyed each other with mutual curiosity and doubt. They undressed and climbed into bed.

"Won't they freeze out there?"

Turner chuckled. "I doubt it. Three horses and four men, all in a nice bed of hay—"

He stopped, but too late.

"Wait. Four men? And only three horses? That doesn't make sense."

He wiped his hand across his face, a gesture he always made when embarrassed. "I didn't want to tell you. They've captured an escaped slave, and they're taking him back to Arkansas for the reward."

"What a disgusting business. I can see why you didn't want to tell me."

"I know. But it's cash on the barrelhead. The colony needs money."

"Perhaps we should get into the slave-catching business ourselves, then. They probably just stole a man to take down South somewhere."

"Let's not quarrel over this."

"James. I know we need the money. But some dollars are not worth earning."

"He said they'd be gone before first light. They know that plenty of people here are in the anti-slavery camp, and don't want any arguments."

"I've a mind to go out there and start one myself." But she knew she wouldn't. The deed was done; these men were going to sleep in the barn whether she liked it or not.

It was late in the night when Newton woke her, crying, wanting to nurse. She had hoped to get him to sleep through the night by now, but it was still an uncertain matter. Charlotte felt her way through the pitch-dark front room to the rocking chair and fed him there.

The whole day sat uneasy on her mind. Harp Webb in the cemetery. James thinking about a tour. And now this business with Hildebrand. Ever since Newton was born, she had felt a deep sense of dread come over her from time to time, a feeling that the world was bearing down on her too heavily. That feeling hovered over her all the time, and days like this only redoubled it. Dealing with slave-catchers! And dangerous ones at that. It was not so much that James had done it as that he had done it without talking to anyone and seemed so indifferent to the moral slope of the matter.

Perhaps she was just too touchy about the whole issue. Growing up in New York, she'd never had to think about slavery. Slaveholders were distant people, easily dismissed as greedy plantation types. Even here there weren't many slaves, a few house servants here and there, people you could imagine almost as family servants, not owned property. But to assist these people, to give them shelter? Of course, what could you do? When someone came along it would be uncharitable to deny them a place to sleep at night.

While she was thinking, Newton finished nursing and fell asleep. She tucked him into his cradle and piled the blankets over him. A warm night for March was still March.

She wasn't ready to go back to sleep yet. Turner was snoring peacefully under the covers. Charlotte put on her wool coat and a pair of slippers and stepped out the back door.

The sky was a rich carpet of stars, with the quarter moon now about to drop behind the hill. She marked the familiar constellations—Orion, the Seven Sisters, the two dippers, reclining Cassiopeia in her giant W—that stretched out over the valley. The night was still, and a faint smell of wood smoke hung in the air.

A rustle of horses stopped her breathing and made her shrink into the doorway. The sound came from the barn. At least Hildebrand was being true to his word and getting out before daylight. Before anyone awoke, they would be through French Mills and into the deep woods, down the diminishing wagon track toward Arkansas, the ill-traveled road that few travelers used or even knew about.

She heard the creak of saddles, the clinking of bits. Then the sound of three horses walking slowly down the lane toward the main road, hoofbeats quiet and unhurried, no words spoken. They were nothing more than apparitions, silent ghosts passing the house. If she hadn't known about them, she would have doubted their existence.

As the riders passed the cabin, one last sliver of moonlight caught them before they faded into the trees. Charlotte watched them enter and then leave the faint shaft of light—one man riding, then a second and a third, and behind the third a man walking, his hands folded in front of himself at his waist as if in prayer, although as he passed into the light Charlotte could see that his hands were tied, with the rope attached to the saddle horn of the third rider.

The man looked back over his shoulder at the moon. Then he slipped into darkness, and all that Charlotte was left with was a glimpse of a round cheek, a shining eye, and a black face.

April 1858

Chapter 9

The longer Cabot stayed in Daybreak, the more he felt like a true inhabitant and less like a refugee. His fellow citizens were simple people, mostly, with little to brag about in their lives, and this venture was the greatest deed they had ever undertaken. When Cabot arrived in the community, it was of less consequence to him, a young, single, educated man who would someday come into a bit of an inheritance, than it was to the family men, for whom Daybreak was an ultimate gamble. He grew to admire them, chasing their ideals into this river valley. The simplicity of their aims, and their single-mindedness in pursuing them, refreshed his faith after the disaster of Kansas. Perhaps Turner had been right all along, and the way to change the world was to change a tiny piece of it, to let the rest of the world watch and emulate. He often thought about Charlotte's question to him from earlier in the spring: Had he embraced their idea? Not entirely. But it was good to be out here in the bosom of nature, to see God face to face, as Mr. Emerson put it. And with a fine woman like Charlotte Turner to converse with in the afternoons, what better place was there to be?

With the coming of spring they had begun holding their meetings in the shell of the Temple of Community, seated on boxes or folded blankets. The walls were about three feet high now that Prentice and Wilson were working full time on them. They made a good pair. Prentice, the teamster from Ste. Genevieve, always good-humored but not particularly bright, lightened the dour mood of Wilson, who had still not gotten over being the only cholera survivor among the four men of his tent. The two men, self-appointed stonemasons, had begun the window openings and spent the day walking from place to place, stone in hand, looking for the right fit. The larger space meant that the women could now attend.

Turner always took on something of the lecture platform when he led the meetings. Cabot had to admit that performance was his gift. With good material and time, he could always move an audience toward himself, talk them through an idea or banter his way past an objector.

It was the first really warm evening of spring, a sign of warmer weather to come. Cabot strolled from his cabin toward the Temple site, enjoying the cool sun. Turner was waiting for him by a tree, a couple of dozen yards from the wall.

"May I have a word?" Turner said.

They walked a short distance down the road.

"This man Cantwell," Turner began.

Cabot nodded. Nothing further needed to be said. Cantwell, the great malfeasant, the complainer and slow worker who was never in harmony with the others, always raising objections, never producing his share. He claimed to be ill most of the time but looked suspiciously healthy.

"I hear he's planning to resign the community tonight," Turner said.

"Fine by me."

"Here's the thing. He'll want to take back his entire contribution to the community, rather than just his share of what we currently hold, and people may want to give him that, out of sympathy or just to be rid of him. But with all the purchases of seed, building materials, and the like, our accounts are pretty low. We can't have him get his entire amount back. Will you back me on this?"

Cabot paused. It would be a hardship on Cantwell and his wife to leave the community with little, but harder yet on the rest if they didn't. An ugly business, but the world was populated with ugly business these days.

"All right," he said.

"Just watch for a chance to make a difference," Turner said.

The prospect of a troublesome scene with Cantwell made Cabot tense, though everyone else seemed relaxed. The citizens lounged on the grass, discussing the coming week in easy tones, none of the usual arguments breaking out.

Not that the news was all good. The planting was going well, but some of last fall's winter wheat had been washed out in the flooding. Grindstaff had cut down on his clothing orders. People seemed to prefer the ready-mades from the factories back East. Donations from outside had leveled off, despite Turner's exhortations in every issue of *The Eagle*, and subscriptions themselves were down. The only growing source of income was Mercadier's shoemaking. They had rented him a room in town, where he stayed from Monday through Wednesday, and every week he brought back hard cash and plenty of trade.

"I am proud," Mercadier said, standing to address the group. Charlotte gave him English lessons in the evenings, and he liked to try out new phrases. "It cheers me to serve the communa-tay."

A young man sitting near Turner muttered under his breath. "You'd think with the old one gone half the week, a fellow could make some progress with the girl."

"You?" said his companion. "Good luck and best wishes. She's a hard-nosed case, she is. Now me—" Cabot quieted them with a cough.

Cantwell stood up. "I have something to say. Me and the missus have decided to go back East. We are resigning from the colony."

"Very well," Turner said. "According to our charter, any member leaving Daybreak is entitled to his share of the assets. Mr. Webb, what are the colony's assets today?"

Webb consulted his account book. "One thousand, six hundred twenty-eight dollars and fifty cents."

"And how many members on the rolls?"

"Twenty-two. Giving Mr. Cantwell a share of seventy-four dollars and . . . two cents."

"Wait a minute!" Cantwell cried. "I brought three hundred dollars to this colony. That ain't fair. I want my share back!"

"Your share is seventy-four-oh-two," Turner said. "When you joined the colony, you cast your lot with the common good."

"He didn't bring in hardly nothing," Cantwell said, pointing at one of the younger men.

"He also helped build your house."

Cantwell's voice was down to its familiar whine. "I want my three hundred dollars."

"Your three hundred dollars is in homes and seed and livestock, Mr. Cantwell. It's in that reaper out in the barn. You think we just put it in a hole in the ground?"

"All right then, I ain't resigning." Cantwell sat back down.

Cabot saw his moment. He stood up, his chin jut out. "Mr. Director, I wish to make a motion. I move we strike George Cantwell from the membership rolls."

"Second that motion," said the young man who had been at the end of Cantwell's pointing finger.

Cantwell jumped up, his face bright red. "Now wait a minute, I said I wasn't resigning."

"Cantwell, since you got here you have done nothing but complain," Cabot said. "You are always in a pucker about one thing or another. You hoe half a row of corn in the time it takes another man to hoe two. We are well to be rid of you, and if I had my way, you'd get the two cents but not the seventy-four dollars, because that is about what you are worth."

Cantwell took a step toward Cabot, but Cabot stood his ground. He had figured Cantwell for a hollow barrel. But even so, a tremble went through him as he braced himself for violence, taken or given.

"This ain't fair," Cantwell repeated. "I ain't well. When I get my health back, I'll show you who can work."

"Motion and second on the floor," Cabot said, his voice hard.

"I'll go to law on this, I swear it. You people will rue the day."

Turner spoke again. "Mr. Cabot is correct; there's a motion on the floor. Anyone else wish to speak to the motion?" No one did. "Show of hands then, all in favor? Anyone opposed? Motion carries."

The group stirred as Cantwell made his way through them, leaving through what would someday be the back door.

"Mr. Cantwell, you are no longer a member of Daybreak. Mr. Webb will draw you your share, and you can have until Monday to pack and leave."

"I swear to God you will regret this," Cantwell said, his voice fading into the distance.

Cabot watched the faces of the crowd as Cantwell stomped off. He read their minds in their changing expressions: first the painful pleasure of a lanced boil— *Cantwell is gone!*—then giddiness at the ease with which it happened—*so fast! Just like that!*—then a moment's remorse—*He wasn't such a bad fellow after all. His wife deserves better*—ending with uncertainty—*If Cantwell can get thrown out with such ease, what about me? Sent off with seventy-four dollars to my name.* And in that sequence of expressions he saw the group move from a band of equals to a group of workers with a boss, looking up at Turner with worker eyes, waiting to be told what to do. It was not what he had imagined a workers' paradise would look like. The crowd drifted away in twos and threes, the married ones joining their wives to talk as they walked home.

Turner appeared at his side. "That went well."

"I suppose," Cabot said. "Hate to see a man humiliated and sent off like that."

"Brought it on himself. He didn't want to work, so he deserves what follows."

"You're none too sympathetic."

"I'm thinking of the common good," Turner said. "Whatever advances the common good has my full sympathies, but whatever holds it back—" He paused. "Whatever holds it back is my enemy, and should be yours, too."

"I thought you might bring up that idea of another lecture tour. See what the community thinks."

"Time didn't seem right." Turner shrugged.

He awoke late that night with Cantwell's threats and curses in his mind. It was sometime toward morning; birds were singing in the darkness. So it was the common good they were protecting. But Cabot could not get over the feeling that he had done wrong. He knew what it felt like to be driven out of a place, and now here he was doing the same to Cantwell. He couldn't sleep any longer, so he got up and dressed, then sat in his doorway to await the day. Purgation and violence seemed to go together wherever he went. Could he ever find a home that didn't need cleansing of its undesirables—or where he was not the undesirable to be cleansed? Perhaps he should just return to Boston and resume some sort of normal life, find a job, earn some money, pursue his cause the ordinary way, through meetings and pamphleteering and contributions. Maybe even meet someone like Charlotte and get married.

But he knew he would not. He was here for the duration, for better or for worse.

On Sundays they held brief community meetings instead of church. There were readings from *Travels to Daybreak* and occasional performances, and Turner usually gave a short lecture. Turner woke that Sunday thinking about lecturing on their expulsion of Cantwell. It had been ugly but necessary. The ideal of the community might be equality, democracy in the pure form, but the reality was that not everyone was ready for that condition. Cantwell was not ready for it. He was like a sapling that had been bent down by a falling tree but regrown with a new trunk. Take the fallen log off the sapling, and it still won't grow straight. It was already bent. What the community had to do was give room for the saplings, let those grow straight that could, and chop out the rest. But he wasn't sure whether everyone was prepared to hear it yet. He could tell from Cabot's reaction that there were plenty of people who thought Daybreak could cure anyone of their old-world habits. Idealism was fine, but there were the boundaries of human nature to be considered.

He took Charlotte's hand after breakfast. "Let's walk," he said. "See what wildflowers are in bloom."

Charlotte, surprised, cast a querying glance at Newton. "All right, if Marie will watch him for an hour," she said.

They strolled down the Daybreak road in the warm April air. The dirt street was damp but not muddy; the Mercadiers' house was at the far end of the road, close to the Temple of Community. The rows of cabins were still rough-looking and windowless, their doors open front and back for ventilation. The planks for their siding were seasoning in the barn.

"We need to order some windows as soon as we can afford them," Turner murmured.

"Amen," Charlotte replied.

Marie met them at the door. She was dark-complexioned, with deep brown eyes that tended to squint much of the time; Turner wondered if she might be a little near-sighted. They were making the handoff of Newton when Turner felt a movement at his side and realized that Harp Webb had appeared out of nowhere.

"Stars in heaven, you move quiet!" Turner exclaimed. Harp touched the brim of his hat to the women.

"I was down by the river," he said, nodding with his head in that direction. He held up what looked at first to be a polished stick, but on second look Turner realized it was an unstrung fiddle bow. He held it out to Marie. "I've had this in the barn don't know how long. Heard your daddy was a fiddle player, thought he might want it."

Marie took its other end. "It's a nice bow," she said, flexing it slightly.

"I would have strung it, but I didn't know how," said Harp.

Marie laughed. "No special secret," she said. "When you brush down a horse, you just collect a few hairs from its tail. Three, four horses, and you have plenty for a start. Papa, he keeps a few handy all the time." She hefted the bow in her hand. "So, how much you want for this? I will ask Papa."

Webb looked surprised. "I ain't selling it!" he said. "It's a present. Been sitting in the corner I don't know how long, and I thought—"

She handed it back. "A gift is a debt."

"Well, I'm damned!" cried Webb. "I try to do something nice, and this is my thanks?"

Turner laid his hand on Webb's arm. "Please, it's just a misunderstanding," he said. "I'm sure—"

"Ain't no misunderstanding," Webb said angrily. "I understand just fine. She don't want the bow 'cause it's from me. I ain't my fine, educated daddy, but I ain't stupid." He walked away, his face contorted with anger. As he rounded the corner of the Mercadiers' cabin, they could hear the bow snap, and then snap again.

Turner felt embarrassed. "I'm sure Harp just meant—" he began.

"Oh, I know what Harp just meant," Marie said briskly. "My mama, she died when I was thirteen. And three weeks later, old Dupuy showed up with a bottle of wine for Papa, wanting me to sit on his lap while they talked. When I take a man, he will need to be someone who can talk to me directly, not come with presents for Papa. I am not to be traded for like a calf or a sheep." She swept Newton into her arms. "Now take your walk. I am fine. I have dealt with men like him before."

They strolled north to where the Daybreak road joined the main road, by the river ford. There they continued north into the woods along the bank, thick with mayapples in the rich bottomland.

"So no more Cantwell," she said at last.

"No."

"I can't say that I'll miss him."

"But?"

"But what?"

"I think I heard a 'but' at the end of that sentence."

"Perhaps there was. It was a hard way to be dismissed, in public, in front of his wife and everyone."

The trees were not fully leafed out yet. The serviceberries and redbuds had bloomed and gone, and now the dogwoods were full. Dappled sunlight fell on their faces in thin slants of brightness that made the whole forest floor seem alive with energy.

"That's what Adam said," Turner said after a while. "I think I am just now learning how to lead this community."

He was still turning the ideas over in his mind. Charlotte said nothing as they walked.

"I'm thinking about lecturing on Cantwell today. Why it was necessary to get rid of him. Daybreak is not a magic place where malcontents will suddenly become productive. People need to understand this."

She took his hand as they walked.

"We expelled him two days ago," she said. "Day before yesterday, we watched him load up and leave, and the last thing we heard was a curse from his lips. Lecture on the beauties of spring, or on the Dred Scott case. Don't rub this wound."

"All right. But this business with Cantwell has made me a better leader. I know when something needs to be done, I have to bear down and do it, not worry about what everyone else thinks. The community needs someone to do this for them, and I am that someone."

Their walk had taken them up the river to where the head of the mountain closed in. The valley grew narrower and cooler, and the carpet of mayapples thickened.

"Look at this," Turner said, walking a little way up the hillside. A cairn of rocks about three feet tall was piled at a seemingly random spot on the slope, among fallen logs and moss. "Wonder what this is."

"It's the corner of our property," Charlotte said. They sat on a log.

Turner eyed her with surprise. "You are an unending novelty."

Charlotte rested against him. As he spoke, she had relaxed, and now they sat quiet for a moment.

"I need you too," she said.

"You have me."

"I know. You can go on your lecture tour if you must. We will manage here. Don't forget, it wasn't you alone who conducted the removal of Mr. Cantwell. Adam played his part to perfection as well."

Turner chuckled. "Yes. Among you and Adam and George, I'd say we're safe."

Charlotte's look grew worried, and she drew back from him. She looked him directly in the face.

"There is something I need from you. And I need to be very serious, please."

He caught her mood and remained silent, looking back at her.

"Marie Mercadier," she said.

He nodded.

"When her father is off in town, I want her in with us. She can work with me, or help you with *The Eagle*, or whatnot, and you can walk her home at night. But I don't want her alone."

"What, you think she will scandalize the community with one of the single boys? Believe me, they've all tried to get a word from her, and she won't give them a drop. We won't find her out in the hayloft with anyone. Or is it Harp you're worried about? She seemed pretty sure of herself back there."

She shook her head. "I don't think Harp is that easy to dismiss. Call it a nameless fear if you wish. But I just don't think she should be alone."

Turner saw no need to worry. He had admired the spirited way she had set Harp down; a girl with that kind of ginger should have no trouble managing someone like him. He had seen men like Harp in lecture halls all over the country—would-be roughs who would deride from the back of the room, throw an egg if they thought they could get away with it, but shrivel when confronted by a man with any conviction. But he didn't want to spoil the moment. "All right. The two of us will have no trouble keeping her busy. To tell the truth, I could use some help with the typesetting."

"There you are, then." She rested back against him, her head on his shoulder. He kissed her. Her lips were warm and open, and he felt himself stir. They had not made love since Newton was born; he had been afraid of hurting her, waiting for a sign. He kissed her again.

"Speaking of trips to the hayloft," he said.

She smiled. "I knew you had a secret motive for this walk."

"I didn't, I swear."

"You forget I can read minds. I know what you're thinking before you've even thought it. And don't swear, it's unbecoming for a leader. Just declare."

And then her hand was inside his coat, finding its way to his skin, cold at first but he didn't mind. He took off his coat and laid it on the mossy slope. He tried to guide her down to his outspread coat, but instead she took him by the arms and pressed him onto the ground.

"I'm not going home with leaves all over my back," she said. "I get enough scrutiny as it is."

And she was atop him, her skirts spread out over his body. She found the buttons of his breeches and opened them, slipped them down, just enough. Desire swept over Turner irresistibly. He felt fabric—cotton, linen, something— but she reached beneath her garments, something was adjusted, pushed aside, and then there she was. She lowered herself down to him and held there. Lying on his back, Turner looked to the side and realized they were atop a raised, circular hump of earth. An old burial mound, maybe? But his thought only lasted an instant before he was lost in sensation.

Afterward, they walked back to the settlement slowly, saying very little, enjoying the quiet of the spring day.

"So—" she said.

"Yes?"

"Sixteen hundred dollars? That's all we have?"

"Less than that, once we subtract Cantwell's share."

"Surely George knows enough not to keep it all in one bank."

Turner laughed. "George Webb is a creature of the old ways, bless him. He has never trusted a bank in his life."

"Good for him."

"Seriously. When someone brings in some banknotes, he takes them to town, trades them for hard money at whatever discount he can get, and brings it back. And what he does with it after that no one knows, but he accounts for every penny, every week."

"No one knows?"

"Not even me. He says he has a strongbox, or maybe more than one, and he is confident they are safe and secure."

Charlotte shook her head. "I hope he knows what he is doing."

"He's made it this far."

They could see the colony through the trees now. Charlotte stopped and kissed him again, before they got into sight of everyone.

"If you have to go on another tour, you have to go. But you know I'll miss you."

"Thank you."

"Where would you go?"

"I'm thinking of a quick round to the north. Now that the railroad's made it to Pilot Knob, I could board a train there, do St. Louis, Independence, St. Joseph. Then back to Quincy, Galesburg, maybe Burlington or Davenport, on into the northern cities, maybe even Wisconsin. Then home again. One lecture per town, one day to set up, one day to leave. The take would be smaller, but there would be less time and expense for travel."

"That doesn't leave you time to get handbills printed."

"I'll print them here and send them ahead. I can do it in the late summer, before the harvest. They'll need me here for the harvest."

"You know...." They stopped again.

"Yes?"

Her look was friendly yet challenging, full in his face. "If you really want this community to strike a blow for the equality of mankind, you'd let women vote."

He stopped the jest that was about to pop from his lips. He knew she wasn't joking.

They gazed at each other, not speaking. Of course she was right. And yet, the idea of proposing this to the colony, the ridicule, the dissension—he could not let himself suggest an idea that would be voted down. The cost to his leadership would be too great.

"You know—" he began.

"Yes. I know." She didn't let her gaze drop. "And you know."

"Yes, I do."

The sun was full overhead now, and with that the air was quickly warming. As they walked up the lane, they could hear children playing between the houses and down by the river.

Turner felt a surge of warmth as they reached the village. He knew that some of his good feeling was just the happiness of a man after refreshment, but he liked to think there was more to it than that. He felt almost fatherly as he watched the children running and smelled the sweet, smoky tang of ham frying in someone's house. The community—his community—was going to flourish. He could just feel it. All they had to do was find a way to become self-supporting.

When they reached Mercadier's house, it was empty. Marie must have taken Newton out to play, he supposed. So they walked further into the settlement. Mrs. Wickman sat in her doorstep, still dressed in her mourning black. No one could muster the courage to tell her to move on, change back into her ordinary dress, start her ordinary life again. They stopped to talk.

"You're a couple of sprites, out in the woodland," Mrs. Wickman said. Her body in its heavy black dress was thick and solid in the spring light.

"The flowers are in bloom," Turner said. "You should come see."

"Oh, I've seen 'em," she said. "Took my walk up the valley." She inclined her head toward the cemetery. "Don't know their names though. I'm a city girl; only thing we ever saw growing was dandelions."

"Your husband seems to know them all."

"He's a studying man, that man. Him and his books, reads till the lamp is out every night." She gave them an appraising look. "You two are the booky types too, I'd say."

"I guess you're right about that," Charlotte said.

"No harm in it, I suppose." Her face went back to the habitual expression, distracted and lost, that she had worn ever since the girls died.

"Well. Good day to you." Turner tipped his hat and they walked on.

"Oh yes," Mrs. Wickman said. "Someone's at your house."

A big black gelding was tied up outside, its saddle off and propped against the house. Turner did not recognize it.

Inside, Marie was distractedly playing with Newton, but her face was uncomfortable and worried. At the table sat Emile, stiff, with a look of even greater discomfort.

And in the chair, still wearing his military overcoat, his hands jammed into his pockets, looking most miserable of all, was Charlotte's father. He stood up and spoke as soon as they entered.

"I've come to tell you that your mother has died."

April/ July 1858

Chapter 10

Charlotte threw herself into her father's arms, tears filling her eyes. She had always prided herself on her ability to keep things together, to keep herself under control, but this news had just come from out of the sky and knocked her down.

She wiped her cheeks and pulled back from her father a little. He looked older than he should. Had it really been less than a year since she had last seen him? His face was tired, and his overcoat seemed a size too big. His hair, which even in its best times was an uncombed mass of black and gray, seemed longer and more unkempt than ever.

"You came all this way," she said.

"Didn't want to send a letter. Besides, the Army seems to need my services less and less these days. Might as well get on a train and see the sights. See my little namesake." He smiled.

Turner was still standing by the door. Now he stepped forward and shook hands with Carr. "You've met the Mercadiers, I take it," he said.

"Yes. They were kind enough to let me sit inside till you came home."

The Mercadiers took this as their cue and excused themselves, and for a while the three were silent, watching Newton burrow into his mother's arms.

"What happened?" Charlotte said quietly.

Carr shrugged. "She just faded and faded. Only ate milk and toast. One day I came home and she said she had seen Caroline." This last sentence cost him a moment's composure; his face contorted and he rubbed his eyes. Then he went on. "Just her mind going, I'm sure. But she was so happy to have seen her that

I thought perhaps Caroline really had appeared to her. Ghost or apparition or something. After that, she talked to Caroline almost every day, upstairs, in your bedroom or in the hallway."

She laid her hand on his sleeve. "Did you ever see Caroline?"

His eyes filled with tears again. "I wish I had! Then I would know something of this world. Instead of—"

"Here," she said, rising. "Get your coat off. When did you last eat?"

"Oh, don't worry about me, I'm an old soldier." But he readily obeyed, and in no time they were tucking into pork chops and some of the remaining potatoes from last year's crop, pulled from the cellar box, a little sprouty but still good at the center. It was good to be up and moving around—activity brought relief, although Charlotte felt dulled by the blow; she looked at her hands and they seemed like the hands of someone else.

"You say the Army didn't mind you going?" Turner asked him.

"Mind? They were delighted. Too many officers. We cost too much. So I'm on indefinite furlough."

By the end of the meal they had settled matters. The cholera had left plenty of empty beds in the community; Carr would bunk with some of the younger men and stay as long as he wanted, not as an applicant for membership, but as a working guest. Turner seemed happy to have him, and Charlotte had not realized how much she had missed her father until she had him near again.

In the morning Turner took her father out to walk the grounds. Charlotte felt warm with pride as she stood in the doorway and watched her two men stroll up the lane, greeting and being greeted, Turner gesturing with relaxed confidence and Carr pausing, listening, nodding. When they reached the Temple of Community, they circled it several times, Carr testing the walls here and there and sighting down them to check for plumb. She knew Turner was deliberately distracting him from his grief and was grateful. But her own grief was just beginning to make itself felt. Yesterday's shock had given way to simple pain, not a complicated feeling, just a plain sadness that gnawed at her under her breastbone and would not go away.

As she watched them, she heard a sound behind her and turned around to see Adam Cabot walking up the road from the south. He tipped his hat to her, then looked at her with an odd expression.

"Charlotte, are you well?"

She passed her hand over her hair. In a moment the whole story was out, her father's arrival, the dreadful news, his plans to stay on. And her tears returned.

He took both of her hands in his. "I'm so very sorry. Please accept my condolences."

"I hardly know what to say. Thank you."

Cabot smiled. "No, I'm the one who's supposed to not know what to say. You're the one who's supposed to be gracious and wise." This brought a smile from her at last. "Yes, just like that."

"I assure you, I'm feeling neither gracious nor wise."

"Your father didn't come all the way out here just to tell you this news. Surely you see that."

She had, in fact, not thought about that until this moment. "I suppose you're right. He knew I would need to have him near."

He squeezed her hands. "Try again, dear. Granted, you need him. But he needs even more to have you close by. That's why he's here."

After he said it, it made sense. Her father had not been alone for nearly three decades. She looked up the lane at them; they had finished their examination of the Temple and were heading toward the fields. They looked back and waved.

Cabot released her hands with an embarrassed expression. "I should get up there," he said.

"Nonsense," Charlotte said. "Come in for breakfast. I hear Newton stirring."

"Thank you. But I've eaten."

"You have? And out for a walk already too? I hardly knew you for such a morning bird." In a teasing voice, she added, "I might think you have a sweetheart down in French Mills you're going to see. What say you, Mr. Cabot? Is there a motive for your morning stroll?"

Cabot blushed crimson and turned his head away. "No such thing."

She thought about teasing him further, but his blush was so deep she held back.

"The fact is," Cabot said after a moment, "I am undertaking a new regime for my self-improvement. The Hindus believe in a morning river bath as a religious exercise."

The statement sounded so absurd, and Cabot looked so simultaneously sheepish and defensive, that she burst out in a laugh despite herself. "I'm sorry," she said. "I just never imagined you in a turban."

"That's the Sikhs," he said peevishly. "The Hindus are—oh, never mind." He glanced up the lane. "Please—"

"Of course. I never tattle on my friends."

She watched him walk back to his cabin. An interesting man, full of surprises, she thought. She remembered the first time they had met, when he was covered with tar but still extended his hand politely—such a curious mixture of thoughtfulness and resolution. What went on in his mind? She was never entirely sure. And here he was, practicing Eastern religion out in the woods! An interesting man indeed. A good match for Marie Mercadier. Of all the men in the colony, why did he have to be the shy one? She had never seen him so much as try to talk to Marie in the evenings or visit their house on Sundays. She wondered what it was Adam really wanted.

But by now young Newton was fully awake, and it was time to stop wondering about Adam Cabot and move on to the rest of the day.

Cabot had been reading the Bhagavad-Gita for several weeks, but he still couldn't manage the emptiness of thought that was supposed to come to him over time. Instead of emptying out, his mind kept filling up with new concerns. He had re-read Mr. Emerson again as well, trying to gain an original relation with the universe by immersion in nature. He sat on a rock beside the river, and he climbed to the top of the ridge that shadowed their settlement on the west to await the first rays of dawn, but when he went to nature the only thing revealed to him was more nature. Not that the intricacies of leaves and the ripples of water weren't interesting, but he had been hoping for something transcendent, some sign that there was harmony to be found beneath all this murder and mess. In their isolated valley, news didn't arrive daily; it came every week or two, in gobbets of strife and dischord from Kansas, the South, everywhere.

Today he had sat on his rock at the river while thoughts rushed noisily in and out of his head like passengers through a train station, each of them intent, directed, but interfering with the others, jostling and shoving, giving him the sensation of aimless disorder. He should rejoin the fight in Kansas. He should return to Boston and enlist with Mr. Garrison again. He should stay in Daybreak and make a go of this way of life, build an example for the rest of the country. He should call it quits, find a wife, and start living like everyone else.

That was his problem—he wanted it all, to be contemplative and to be involved, to live in the eternal and be in the now. Or, he supposed, he didn't know what he wanted at all.

From where he sat he could see upriver and down, a good vantage point, and downriver through the trees he could see the shapes of two men coming up the road on foot, their forms obscured by the thick screen of vegetation. He fought back the panic that had gripped him in unfamiliar situations ever since Kansas and forced himself to remember that not every stranger in the woods was a threat. But as they drew closer he realized it was Turner and Captain Carr, back from hunting, rifles under their arms and a bloody bag held between them. He rose from his cross-legged squat and pushed through the underbrush to the road.

"Looks as though you two have had some luck," he said as Carr lowered the bag with a grunt.

"Luck doesn't enter into it," Carr said. "This man's a fine shot. We'll have a good bit of hasenpfeffer to throw in the pot tonight."

"Mr. Turner, you are a frequent surprise."

Turner grinned and blushed, but was clearly pleased by the praise. "I picked up a few talents as a boy."

"Do you shoot, Mr. Cabot?" asked Carr.

"Our family went on hunts occasionally, but I'm afraid I was the conscientious objector."

"Pity, it's a useful skill. Not in the law office, but certainly out here. Most of what I learned from the military manual applies, except I doubt if I'll need to take a defensive posture against a rabbit."

Cabot didn't reply. The men's rifles were military carbines, not the muzzleloaders that were common around here. He'd seen enough of those weapons to last him.

Carr anticipated his thoughts. "It's a useful skill, but not everyone has to possess it. The world needs its conscientious objectors as well."

"Does it?" Cabot said.

"Oh, yes," said Carr. "We saw in Kansas what happens when violence becomes a habit. You know that more than most. I don't know what we're coming to."

His gloomy words gave them all pause. There seemed nothing else to say. Carr lifted his corner of the sack. "Well, let's get these skinned," he said, and the two men continued up the road, leaving a bloody spot in the dust.

Cabot watched them leave and found himself wishing he could be more like James Turner. Author, speaker, town founder, crack shot. Judging by the man's size, probably a champion wrestler as well. Was there nothing the man couldn't do? On top of it all, he was married to Charlotte who, although Cabot was loath to admit it, increasingly occupied his thoughts. He didn't want to think about Charlotte and he didn't want to be envious of Turner, but there it was.

What he needed, Cabot thought, was something to occupy his mind with the same passion. The Kansas fight had done that for him; but here in the Missouri woods he felt himself to be marking time. And marking time was courting trouble.

Charlotte looked at the bag of dead rabbits on her back step and turned away abruptly. The newspapers were full of stories about violence and killing, threats of war, the uncertain future. The men talked endlessly about national honor and states' rights. And who was she? She was the woman, like all women, left to raise the children and cook the meals while all this high talk carried on.

She drew some water from the rain barrel and rinsed off the bodies. Good enough, they could be fried or thrown into a stew. But something disgusted her about the bloody little corpses, so eerily human with their heads and skin removed. She left them in the pan of water and stepped outside.

Charlotte had left Newton with the Wickmans to give herself a few hours of peace on a Sunday afternoon, but now she felt an overwhelming need to have him back. He could have wandered off and fallen into the river.

She wiped her hands on her apron as she walked. Did it have to be so difficult to keep anything clean? Dirt streets, dirty people, dirt everywhere.

She knew she was walking fast but hoped it didn't look like she was running. It felt like running, though, and she tried to put a smile on her face as she passed cabins, people, children, homes. She couldn't pay attention to them. She just needed to see Newton. She shouldn't have trusted Mrs. Wickman.

Charlotte made it to the Wickman house and walked in without knocking. John Wesley Wickman was sitting with a book in a rocking chair by the open door, a tiny pair of reading glasses on his nose. He looked up and smiled as Charlotte entered; she brushed back her hair and tried to say something but could not.

Mrs. Wickman was at the table by the stove, chopping potatoes. She wore an apron over a short sleeved dress, and her broad upper arms bulged out from the sleeves, pale as the potatoes themselves.

"Hello, dear," she said.

"Where's Newton?"

Mrs. Wickman tilted her head to one side and looked at her feet. "Down here," she said.

Charlotte looked under the table, and there he was, in his dress and diaper, pulling himself up onto Mrs. Wickman's skirts.

"He's become quite the crawler," Mrs. Wickman said. "Another couple of months and you'll be chasing him all over town."

Charlotte got down on her hands and knees and pulled him out, holding him to her face. She inhaled his scent.

"I'm sorry for barging in, I just—" She couldn't think of what else to say and sat down in their armchair. She buried her face in his tiny belly. Newton gurgled with pleasure and took handfuls of her hair.

Neither of the Wickmans spoke. Charlotte bent over and rested Newton on her thighs, still with her face pressed against his white cotton dress. He squirmed, his knees bumping against her chin.

She was not going to cry, she knew that. But what was she going to do? She couldn't sit like that forever. She wanted to shout, run, stay, laugh, weep, curse. She held her face close and breathed.

After a few minutes she pulled her face away and looked at Newton. His eyes roamed over her face, and his lips formed a smile. She smiled back.

"I just got afraid," she said.

A look passed between Mr. Wickman and his wife.

"I know the feeling," he said.

In the weeks and months that followed, Charlotte's moments of nameless fear returned occasionally, unexpectedly, with the same debilitating effects. Mrs. Wickman stopped by one morning to tell her quietly that such spells were not uncommon among new mothers. "Just hold on, they'll pass," she said.

Her advice was no help during those moments, though, and Charlotte found the best thing to do was lie down if she could, and if not, to get Newton close and hold him there, an act with which Newton sometimes cooperated and sometimes did not.

Her father continued working with the masons, and in a great piece of luck, a German carpenter named Schnack drifted into the community from Cincinnati just as they were planning the roof for the Temple. Carr let him take over and moved on to the excavation for their barn, a real barn with a stone foundation, not the log structure they had thrown up last year.

The week after the roof of the Temple was finished, there was a hard argument at the community meeting over whether to put windows in it. There was enough money to buy windows for the Temple, but not enough to put windows in all the houses yet. The men voted to finish the Temple, even though the women complained that the oilcloth and crude shutters over the window openings of the houses left them open to insects in the summer and drafts in the winter. "We'll get to the houses as soon as we can," Turner said in an effort to quiet the grumbling. "The Temple serves us all."

"So does being able to sew without getting frostbite," Mrs. Wickman said.

Turner kept his promise and brought Marie Mercadier in to help him with *The Eagle* on the days when her father was in town. She proved adept at the job, learning the typecase quickly, and had a sharp eye for proof. Now and then Charlotte took work out to the shed in the warm afternoons to keep them company, Newton at their feet while they worked and talked.

Shepherson's widow, who had only been in Daybreak a few days before her husband died of the cholera, decided to stay, having nowhere else to go, and was soon being addressed respectfully by several of the single men at lunch and after the weekly meetings. And as spring warmed toward summer, Charlotte's moments of panic abated, as Mrs. Wickman had promised.

Then it was time to plan Turner's lecture tour. Charlotte had always been the scheduler; she sent off for a train timetable and plotted the route. He could go east and west without much problem, but north-south lines were few. Eventually she worked it out so that he could make twelve cities in twenty days, assuming the trains were all running, which of course could not be assumed; so they built in another five days of travel time and began writing to reserve churches and lecture halls. Charlotte feared the loneliness that she knew would haunt her while he was gone, but they could see no way around it. The colony needed money. Turner seemed excited by the prospect of making another circuit, exercising his talents, and his excitement only added a spoonful of resentment to her dread.

One Sunday in late July, Charlotte went out while Turner polished his lecture. She took the rifle with her; if James was going to be off chasing dollars for the colony, she might as well practice bringing home squirrels. She walked behind the barn to the edge of the woods and remembered Harp Webb's words about sitting in wait. Perhaps the art of hunting was not in pursuit, but in patience. She put a cartridge in the chamber and sat on the remains of a chest of drawers that had not survived the trip to the colony and was being dismantled for kindling, board by board. The sunlight felt good on her back. She took a deep breath and set in to wait.

As she sat she could feel the familiar anxieties return, her husband's approaching departure, death all around, the clouds of hateful talk from hateful men that swirled through the newspapers. A cold knot of dread formed in her chest. She tried to push it down, keep it from rising up to her throat, where it would tighten and freeze. A movement in the field a dozen yards away caught her eye.

It was a rabbit that had twitched its ear, a tiny motion, but enough to be noticed. Charlotte had no idea how long it had been sitting there, frozen, hidden, fearful.

It was sitting in profile to her, one big eye visible on the side of its head, its ears taut and high. She was probably too far away for it to see her clearly now—she had heard they had bad eyesight—but she knew it was listening, straining to hear whether the unknown threat had gone away. Its coat was the color of the dead underlayer of grass in the pasture, and if it had not made its tiny movement she would never have seen it.

She swung the barrel of the rifle toward it and took a bead, first fixing the back sight and then raising the front as her father had taught her. She paused for a moment at the sight of the rabbit's huge, frightened eye at the end of her view. The thought flitted through her mind that sometimes she was just like the rabbit, paralyzed with a nameless dread of a threat too vague even to be pictured.

Then she squeezed the trigger, and the rabbit's head disappeared.

August 1858

Chapter 11

Turner stood beneath the pulpit of the Congregational Church in Quincy, Illinois, shaking hands and answering questions. It had been a good night for the tour. The church had been nearly full, at twenty-five cents a head, and he had sold several subscriptions to *The Eagle* on top of that. Things had picked up since he crossed the river. The Missouri crowds had been lackluster—he was too close to home to be interesting, he supposed—but Alton, Springfield, Jacksonville, all had excellent turnouts, and tonight was the best yet. From here he would hit Galesburg, Peoria, and farther north.

An older man in a black frock coat stepped up to take his hand. "Most interesting, young man. I am Hiram Foltz of this city."

"Pleased to meet you, sir. Thank you for coming."

"May I ask—"

"Certainly."

"Your settlement. It is founded on principles of equality and sharing, all things in common. But yet—I do not seek to offend—but yet you live among those for whom human beings themselves are nothing more than property."

It was a common enough question. "That is true. We hope to be an example for those around us, a demonstration that life can be lived on other principles."

"In other words, if I walk among murderers and thieves, my moral obligation is simply to avoid being a murderer and thief myself so that they may profit by my example."

Turner blushed. "Well said, sir."

Foltz frowned. "I don't concern myself with rhetorical points. Will you walk with me a short way? I wish to talk further."

It was a warm night and just dusk, so Turner agreed. They stepped outside the church. The air was heavy with a number of different smells, all of them unpleasant. Foltz's frown wrinkled a bit more.

"A breeze would be good, or a rain," he said. "But I believe neither is in store."

They walked toward the Mississippi, a few blocks to the west. Most of the merchants had laid plank sidewalks in front of their buildings, but occasionally they had to drop down to street level. Foltz had a crooked leg and used a cane; he noticed Turner's glance.

"Fifteen years ago, I was part of the Missionary Institute at the east end of town," he said. "We were all Lane Seminary boys, radicals to a man. We would get a buggy and a fast horse, cross at the ferry here after dark, and ride into Missouri. See if we could find a slave or two, load them up, return here by daylight. If you could get them as far as Peoria or Springfield, you were safe. The trail would be cold, and the Missourians didn't like going that far into free soil. One night, someone spotted me crossing the river, and by the time I got to Palmyra there was a crowd waiting," he continued. "That's where this limp comes from."

They had reached the front street and stood on the boardwalk, looking at the packed brown dirt that sloped to the river. A couple of steamers were tied up at docks, and a half dozen skiffs were scattered along the bank.

"Fugitive Slave Law put an end to all those adventures," Foltz said. "Now I'm a mere businessman." He pointed down the street with his cane. "That's my cigar factory just past the slaughterhouse. Horrible smell but the money is good."

"So after fifteen years of your effort—"

"Yes. Things are no better. Actually worse. Every day of my life, men send their slaves over here with loads of tobacco or bills to collect, and there's not a damned thing I can do about it."

They walked upriver a block and then turned back toward the center of the city. A couple of whores standing in the entrance of a building stepped out of the shadows toward them. One was tall and fair-haired, a bit like Charlotte in her shape, although her face was unpleasantly painted. Covering a scar, perhaps? Turner couldn't tell in the dim light. The other was short and dark, plump, with a round face. The women retreated under Foltz's glare.

"What hotel are you in?" Foltz said.

They were at the town square, where light from taverns and hotel parlors cast slanting patterns of shadows across the streets and into the common. Turner pointed across the square at a three-story brick building. "Miller's."

"Nice enough," Foltz said. "I'd offer you my guest room, but unfortunately I have a new son-in-law in residence at the moment."

Two farmers had brought their cattle to the slaughterhouse and were trying to bed down their herds at opposite corners of the square. One cow was sleeping in front of the door to the city hall, and the men had to step into the street to go around it.

"If you make use of the services of one of those ladies, make sure you go to your room, not theirs," Foltz said. "Most of them will have a panel thief in the next room. And whatever you do, don't fall asleep until after they've gone. More than one man has stepped out here in the morning with nothing but his socks."

"I'm a married man, sir," Turner said.

"These cribbers would starve if not for married men," Foltz said with an appraising glance. "But my apologies for the thought."

"No offense taken."

"Will you walk two blocks more with me? There is something at my house I want to show you."

They left the square and walked up the main street. Soon they were in a quieter, darker district, and stopped in front of a tall white house.

"We'll step into the dining room," Foltz said. "The family will be asleep upstairs."

He let them into the house, and they walked quietly through the parlor into the dining room. Two heavy pocket doors separated the rooms; Foltz pulled them closed before lighting a lamp.

"No point in waking the household," he said.

On the dining room table, a railroad map of Missouri, Illinois, and Iowa was spread out, its corners held down by books. "I was intrigued the minute I read your handbill," Foltz told Turner. "And your lecture this evening only confirmed my interest. For I perceive, sir, that you are an idealist."

"That depends on what you mean by 'idealist,'" Turner said. "I do not live in the world of ideals. Daybreak is very much real."

"Of course, of course. All the more intriguing. You have not merely speculated. You have felled trees, built homes, cleared ground. But you've done it in pursuit of your ideal."

"That's true."

Foltz gestured to the map. "Could you show me, please, where this colony of yours is located? I have a notion, but am not sure."

Turner studied it. The map was out of date; it had the rail line snaking down from St. Louis only as far as De Soto. He traced with his finger the route from there to Pilot Knob. The road from Arcadia to Fredericktown was marked, and the one from St. Louis south through Fredericktown, Greenville, and into Arkansas. The course of the St. Francis River didn't seem quite right, but no matter. He slid his finger to a spot an inch southwest of Fredericktown.

"There," he said. "As close as I can tell."

Foltz drew close and peered at the spot. "And from here to the Mississippi? What sort of terrain and people?"

"A couple of fine river bottoms, very well peopled. In between, it's rough, rough country, a few hill farmers but not much else."

"And how would you travel from there to the river?"

Turner leaned back in his chair. He had guessed something like this was coming. "The easiest path is right up to St. Louis. Everyone knows that. Mr. Foltz, I need to tell you right now that I am not going to allow our settlement to be used as a stop on the Underground Railroad. We depend on the good will of our neighbors. If it became known that we were harboring runaways, we would not long continue in existence."

"I have no intention of asking you for such. As I told you, the fugitive slave law has cramped our activities considerably. I would not ask you to risk fines and imprisonment."

They sat and considered each other. Finally Foltz spoke again.

"May I ask why are you undertaking this lecture tour? Surely your colony needs your leadership."

"I hold it as no shame to tell you that we are not yet self-supporting. We must have money to survive. Perhaps another year will make us independent of the outer world, but we are not today."

"So this tour is for cash."

"Yes."

"What would you say if I told you that this stop on your tour could yield you two hundred and fifty dollars over and above what you were anticipating? And that is in gold coin."

Turner waited.

"This situation will not last forever," Foltz said after a moment. "How it will end I do not know. Compromise, separation, war, who knows. What I do know is that when it all breaks loose, there will be thousands, perhaps millions of colored people trying to escape. We in the National Anti-Slavery Society will be ready to assist."

"And—?"

"And I would like to send you a young man from Philadelphia to board at your settlement for a few months. He will be a traveling botanist, making sketches and collecting specimens in your part of the country. He will entice no runaways and transport no fugitives. He will simply be making observations, gathering information. He is single and comes from an impeccable background."

"Impeccable for a city of the East, perhaps. But I don't need to remind you that these hill settlements have their own standards."

"Everything involves risk, Mr. Turner. You led a group of people out there with no idea of what would happen yourself. Surely others might accomplish something as well."

Foltz took a bottle from a side cabinet. "At any rate, let us drink to the continued success of your travels." He poured two glasses, diluted it a little with water from a pitcher, and handed one to Turner. They saluted each other and drank. Foltz held his glass to the lamplight. "Tennessee whiskey," he said. "Not your local corn." Then a disgusted expression came over his face. "I see them everywhere. Working the fields of corn and barley, out in the woods cutting the oak for the barrels, the maple for the charcoal." He drained his glass. "Even as I plot their freedom, I drink their blood. No wonder it burns going down."

An image came to Turner—the Hildebrand brothers in the darkness, their captive in tow, the tossing of a couple of coins into his hand—and a wave of shame and embarrassment came over him at having been complicit in the deed. He stood up abruptly and reached to shake Foltz's hand.

"I will be back through here in a few weeks," he said. "I will have an answer for you then."

He walked back to his hotel through the darkening streets, the whiskey warm in his belly. Of course he could not bring the question to the community. Too many people were soft on the idea of slavery in the first place, and even those who opposed it wouldn't want to antagonize the neighbors. Except for Cabot, of course, and probably Charlotte along with him. That man's passion for abolition gleamed from his face. The two of them would probably see joining the Railroad as a fine thing, not a rash act that would attract the wrath of the entire county. No, if he brought this man to the colony, he would have to do it alone and keep his purpose behind a curtain.

On the town square, the taverns were still brightly lit, but the cattle had all bedded down. He could see the two whores at the corner toward the river, hoping for some traffic from the steamboats, perhaps. He could tell they had spotted him—they edged in his direction. He considered for a moment. After his declaration to Foltz, it would be hypocritical of him even to think about calling over one of those ladies; but he definitely had an itch, and a man had needs.

Turner pointed to the short, dark one, and waited for her in the shadow of a building's corner.

"Got a dollar to give a girl?" she said with professional brightness.

"A dollar, eh?" he said. "What's a dollar buy me?"

"You have a room?" she said. Turner gestured to the hotel. "Nah, they won't let me in there. Come down to Water Street with me." She pulled at his shirt buttons.

Just then the girl glanced over his shoulder and darted away. A night marshal strode toward them. "Don't make me chase you!" he shouted. The girl stopped in her tracks. "Let's have a look."

The night marshal passed Turner and took the girl by the elbow. "This woman bothering you?" he said.

"Not at all, just making conversation," said Turner.

"I'll bet you were." The marshal turned the whore's face to the light from a tavern. "I don't recognize you," he said to her. "New in town?"

"Yes, sir," she muttered.

"Just in from your pappy's farm, too, I'll wager." The girl didn't speak, and he cuffed her lightly on the top of her head with his open hand. "Or chased out of New Orleans for spreading the pox, more likely. Here's the rule, you toothless little bitch. Stay below Third Street." He shoved her in the direction of the river.

"Now, just a minute," Turner spoke out. The marshal sized him up.

"Defending the lady's honor, now?" he said, approaching Turner with a hint of menace. "That's precious. Trust me, sir, these whores know the rules. I take it you're a traveler, so I'll explain." He gestured to the square. "Up here, we keep it clean. Down by the river, look for a red blanket over the transom, if you fancy that kind of thing." He touched Turner's chest with his nightstick. "But I'd take my smelling salts, if I were you."

As the marshal stepped away, Turner exhaled with relief. What had he been thinking? This would just be his moment to get robbed, or exposed, or written up by some humorous newspaperman. He would have to wait to get his itch scratched. He walked into the lobby of his hotel and climbed upstairs, giving no glance to the sleepy desk clerk.

With Turner gone, Charlotte met with Adam Cabot and George Webb for a few minutes every evening to talk about the colony's progress. They would carry a couple of the benches from the Temple of Community out under a maple tree and sit, go over the day, and plan for tomorrow, with Newton playing nearby. It was full summer. The men worked after dinner till dark scything hay and hoeing corn.

Now that the Temple was finished, the community had begun eating their dinner together, taking shifts to keep enough dishes on the table. It was chaotic at first until the women figured out how much food to make and how to serve it so that the last group's meal wasn't cold and sparse. But the shared meal, the laughter and teasing of the men over incidents of the day, the time for announcements and plans, made Daybreak feel more real to her, more like an established community than a mere cluster of cabins.

Webb had the precision of a lifelong farmer, and when he announced it was time to cut hay or pick beans, they obeyed his instincts. He could no longer keep up with the scythers so he drove the team instead, instructing the young men about how to stack the hay on the wagon. The new barn was all but finished; Charlotte's father had placed it on the slope of the hill behind the community, so that the wagons could drive in on one level and dump hay into the main loft and grain into the bins, and the cattle could be fed on the lower level. A simple thing, really, Carr told everyone, a design you could see all over New England. The walls of the bottom level were built of the local stone, just like the Temple. The cattle already liked to congregate in the cool interior in the afternoons, even though with plenty of grass in the pasture they were not yet being fed.

The crops looked good this year. This was their second cutting of hay; the first had been harvested in late June and already made an impressive stack in the loft. The men were turning the rows of cut hay with their forks, and if no rain came in another couple of days, would add it to the great stack in the barn.

The days were hot and the nights warm and humid; it was hard to tell which was more uncomfortable. If they left the oilcloth down over their window openings, the air inside was stifling, but if they raised it, the mosquitoes plagued them. So they lingered outside as long as possible, until darkness or fatigue pushed them in. One night a great storm of meteors lit the sky overhead as they sat on their benches; everyone stood in the street to watch the spectacle in the muggy night.

"Your old-timers would say this is a sign," George Webb said.

"And what do you say, George?" Cabot asked.

"I say we make our own signs," Webb said, his head tilted toward the sky to watch. "We read the page of Nature as best we can, but we are always reading it in our own language, try as we might to read it in hers."

"You're a man of enlightened views," Cabot said.

"Don't sound so surprised!" Webb said, laughing. "Even us simple hill folk are entitled to an idea once in a while." He quieted Cabot's protestations with a wave of his hand. "It's all right. I'm just having some fun at your expense."

"Seriously, George, how did you come to be so open to new ideas?" Charlotte said quietly. "It's not common, you know—for country people or city."

"Same as the two of you, I would reckon," Webb said. "Reading, reading, reading. Ever since I was a boy, books were my constant companion. When I come out here to try my luck, I brought half a wagonload of books with me, and every trip to St. Louis I brought back more. This place might be isolation, but I could bring the world to me."

"And yet—" Charlotte stopped, realizing that what she was about to say might seem impertinent. But Webb read her thoughts.

"Yes," he said. "And yet my only son bucks everything I do. He won't pick up a book. I build up a two thousand acre farm, he won't cultivate more than twenty. Just enough to keep his whiskey business going." The anger in his voice was impossible to miss. Charlotte and Cabot sat quiet. Charlotte had the feeling that she had triggered a spring that might better have been left untouched.

"And yes," Webb went on, "maybe my offer to place Daybreak on this land was not a pure decision. Maybe it came from frustration, or pique, or what have you, at the sight of this fine river bottom land going back to forest. When I was a young man, by God, I would not have sat on my tail end all day and watched whiskey drip out of a spigot." He stopped abruptly. "But I embarrass myself. You don't need to hear an old man's railings."

"I don't hear any railings," Cabot said. His voice was soft. "I hear the hard-earned wisdom of a fine and generous man."

"Oh, go on," Webb said. But Charlotte could tell from his tone of voice that the old man was pleased.

It was at one of these after-dinner meetings that Charlotte realized her feelings toward Adam Cabot had changed, deepened, and that she could easily become attracted to him if she allowed herself to. The idea came to her while he was talking. Something about the way he spoke started it, maybe his habit, like Turner's, of looking directly at the person he was talking to, as if there was no other person anywhere. That intensity, the look, brought back memories of their long talks during their trip together to Missouri. She remembered other things as well: the curve of his wrist as he held the reins, the three-notes-descending tone of his laugh, the way they became comfortable with each other immediately, and remained comfortable even without speaking. His earnest idealism had encouraged her during the long journey. There was something of that wonder in him yet; he spoke often of wildflowers he had seen or unfamiliar birds. Set against the hardcore practicality of survival, it was his unguarded gentleness that she thought of first.

Turner was the only man she had ever been with, of course, and her only real suitor. Those ardent cadets of past years had not been interested in her for herself, but in the idea of her, what she represented. She knew full well why she loved and had married Turner—his determination, his gift for talk, the intensity that gave him the ability to imagine and then create Daybreak. It was all still there, and she still loved it all, and of course there was Newton. But yet she wondered if she had made the right choice. Perhaps she should have waited, encouraged other men. It was a silly thought. What other men?

And why on earth think about such a thing now? She had never been a flirt. Still, she had to admit she had always been drawn to Cabot's easy conversation, his manners, his quick mind. Nothing would be wrong with enjoying a little tender feeling. She liked being near him. It felt warm and good.

She began to imagine Cabot as her suitor, her lover, her husband, pleasing fancies that filled her with a tingling warmth. He was clean-shaven, unlike most of the men, and his habit of taking a morning trip to the river gave him a curiously fresh smell. Even in the evening, when all the men were drenched in sweat from the day's work, he was different. She noticed it when they spoke and remembered it later in the evenings.

In the night she returned her thoughts to Turner and loved him all over again. The intensity with which he embraced her was unforgettable. She pushed stray thoughts from her mind and focused on him, remembered the length of his body pressed against hers, the feel of his shoulders as he moved into her. She imagined him there with her, closed her eyes and pressed herself beneath her gown.

But in the dawn Cabot walked past her house from his visit to the river, his hair slicked back and wet, and she thought of him as he must have looked a few minutes before, lowering his body into the cool water. He was a head shorter than Turner, his body compact. She was sure he must be a fine dancer. She imagined them dancing, his hand light on her waist as he guided her through a courtesy turn. She would have to organize a dance for the harvest.

Newton was asleep in his crib. She stepped out into the humid morning air. Cabot had already passed the house and was gone. She was still in her gown. Turner had had a great flat stone brought up from the river last year and placed in front of the door as a step, a stone that took four men to get off the wagon. It was cool under her bare feet.

Charlotte stepped off the stone onto the packed dirt of the yard. But she couldn't think where to walk. So she just sat down on the doorstone. A wren warbled from a dogwood tree across the road. It was going to be another miserably hot day, she could already tell. Soon the others would be waking. But for now she would sit in the stillness and listen to the sounds of the morning, listen and think about her life.

How had she gotten to this place? What was she doing here? Had she made a decision or just been swept along by events, one thing and then another?

She couldn't say. But here she was, with a child sleeping behind her and the road and the river in front of her, and a little town full of people off to her left.

She thought about the three lives she had in her care at this time, her husband, her father, and her son. All three were here, so of course she would never go anywhere until—until whenever something else happened, she supposed. And then what? She was a stick on the river, carried along by currents she could not control and could barely even feel. She knew this was her role in life, but that knowledge brought her no comfort. It would be good just once to take charge of herself, to make her own decisions.

The predawn light was quickly brightening. She went inside to start Newton's breakfast.

Chapter 12

The lectures at Galesburg and Peoria went well. Decent crowds, good halls. But in Princeton, the Converse Hall was practically empty, except for a group of Swedes who came up from Bishop Hill. Large, rough, mournful men, they sat silently through his lecture and then filed out at the end as if on command.

"What's going on here?" Turner asked the janitor, the only man remaining in the room.

"They've never been the same since their leader got killed," the man said. "They thought he was going to rise from the dead. Guess what, he didn't."

"No, I mean everybody else," said Turner. "Where is everybody?"

"Gone over to Ottawa for the candidates' debate tomorrow," the janitor said. "Bad time for you, sorry about that. But nobody don't want to talk about nothing else all week than the candidates' debate."

So Turner found himself riding a hack to Bureau Junction the next morning to catch the train for Ottawa, a slow choker that never got up enough speed to outrun its own cloud. They crept along the river until they got to La Salle, where the train stopped for no apparent reason for a half hour. By then the August day had turned scorching, the train was packed with passengers quarreling over the election, and Turner thought for a moment he would just get out and walk. Since Springfield, he had been keeping the proceeds from the lectures in a pouch strapped to his chest to ward off pickpockets. In the crush of the crowd, it galled him miserably.

But after La Salle they made better time, stampeding from the train as soon as it slowed. Everyone else seemed to know where they were going, so Turner fell in with the stream and soon found himself in the city square along with five or six thousand other people.

The candidates were seated on a wooden platform at one end of the park, mopping their faces as other speakers heated up the crowd. Judge Douglas sat upright on a straight-backed chair with the air of an experienced politician, acknowledging the heat only by wiping his face occasionally with a large hand-kerchief. The challenger, Lincoln, sat more like the farmers who used to hang around the newspaper office. He shifted from ham to ham and jiggled one leg, and dust seemed to gather on his charcoal suit even as he sat there.

Douglas spoke first and went straight to the attack. Turner had generally voted Democratic in the past, and he had to admire the senator's debating skill. He gave Lincoln enough rhetorical questions to answer that he would have to spend the rest of the afternoon on the defensive. And sure enough, Lincoln took the bait, replying and replying and replying, unable to get to his points until nearly an hour had gone by.

The crowd looked to be Republicans mainly. They cheered Lincoln at every turn, finally carrying him away on their shoulders awkwardly after the whole thing was over. Two of the men holding him up were short, so Lincoln's legs dangled halfway to the ground. But as Turner stood in the trampled square, watching the throng disperse, he didn't feel like cheering for either candidate. The whole debate had seemed to devolve into *you're-a-liar-no-I'm-not, and he-loves-niggers-no-I-don't.* The train was headed back to Princeton. He needed to get back to the hotel and pick up his things, but he stopped at the post office long enough to send a note to Hiram Foltz back in Quincy.

From there he went north to Dixon and Galena, then crossed into Wisconsin for stops in Janesville and Milwaukee. "You should go to Chicago, friend," said a man in Milwaukee. "That's where things are going on."

"I thought that place was a swamp," Turner said.

"Swamp it was," said the man. "They decided to raise the city. Brought in more dirt than you ever seen, dirt by the wagonload. They're putting jackscrews under the buildings, crank 'em up, fill in underneath. Never seen nothing like it."

Turner's return train went through Chicago, but he had not reserved a hall. Besides, it was getting close to harvest time. So he didn't try to stay, but stood on the platform and gazed east, looking at the glints of the lake that he could see between the roofs of houses and hotels. The city was just as the man said, booming and noisy, excited conversations in strange languages passing between people who rushed past him on their way to somewhere important. Sure enough, some houses and buildings, even whole blocks, had been raised up seven or eight feet. Others were up on jacks, and the streets were a crazy patch of heaved dirt and brick, ramps and sudden drop-offs, planks pitched out into the streets across gaping holes where the dirt had settled unevenly.

Between trains a man sidled up. "Where you headed, friend?"

"Quincy."

"We're bigger'n Quincy now. Quincy's the past, we're the future." He gestured out at the city, where Turner could see a two-story brick house creeping down the street, rolled on logs by a straining team.

"So it appears."

"Spending the night?"

Turner looked at the man more closely. He was small but muscular, balanced on the balls of his feet like a boxer, but with the practiced smile of a pimp.

"No, just catching the next train."

"I got a girl in a wagon down here, entertain you till your train comes."

"No thanks."

"Nice wagon, wooden sides, nobody peeks in. Pretty little gal too."

"Thanks, but—" Something about the man didn't seem right to Turner, and suddenly he stopped what he was about to say and backed away, turning abruptly and running toward the station end of the platform without another word.

"Hey!" shouted the man, but Turner didn't turn around until he reached the station door. Then, feeling momentarily foolish, he looked back to see the man running about ten yards behind him. Another man had come out of nowhere and was running alongside, a heavy cudgel in his hand. When they saw that Turner had reached the door, they leaped off the platform and disappeared down the tracks.

Turner stayed inside the station house until the Quincy train was called.

That night the train pulled off without notice on some siding somewhere, and everyone had to sleep in their seats. They reached Quincy about noon the next day; Turner walked to Hiram Foltz's cigar factory on the riverfront, dodging another herd of cattle destined for the slaughterhouse next door. The factory floor was filled with men, some black, some white, sitting at wide tables covered with stacks of tobacco leaves, more tobacco leaves in their laps. One of the men glanced up as Turner entered.

"Upstairs," he said, indicating the stairway with a nod of his head.

Foltz's office was on the third floor, where the noise and smells were less. He came out from behind his desk and shook Turner's hand. "So you've decided to help us out."

"I have my doubts," Turner said. "But I have to admire the firmness of your convictions."

"Those opposed to us are equally firm in their convictions," Foltz said. "Regardless, I am glad to have you on our side."

"I didn't say I was on your side. I just said I'd take in your man."

"Good enough."

They set off for his home, walking as quickly as Foltz's limp would allow. His wife, a lean, serious-looking woman with her hair pulled back tightly from a center part, met them at the door.

"Your fellow is out back," she said.

In a kitchen chair propped against a shade tree, a young man in his early twenties was reading a book of poems. He was wearing a derby hat and a bright yellow vest. He was slender and pale, and he absently picked a tooth with his little finger.

"May I introduce you," Foltz said. "James Turner, this is Lysander Smith."

"Ah," said Smith, standing to greet him. "The rustic utopian." Before shaking Turner's outstretched hand, he plucked a blade of grass and stuck it in his book to keep his place.

"So do you know anything about botany?" Turner said.

"God, no. Does anyone? Linnaeus, I suppose, but he's dead, thankfully. Fear not, I am a masterful faker." Smith gave him a mischievous smile.

"So how do you propose to pass as a botanist?"

"Oh, my good fellow! I have my books, and my sketchbook. And my little glass. And I shall press leaves."

Turner spun and walked inside, beckoning to Foltz. He stopped inside the door to Foltz's summer kitchen.

"Does this man realize what he is embarking on?" he said, half angry.

"He has been thoroughly instructed. He comes from a fine line, the Philadelphia Smiths."

"I don't care about his line. That man will stand out like a wart. I can't believe you would send him on this task."

Foltz pursed his lips. "Mr. Smith is a free man. He chooses what to undertake and what not to."

"He's a young fool, from what I can see."

"I'm not this boy's father. Neither are you. He wishes to offer himself to my cause, and I'm willing to take him at his word."

They stepped back outside. Smith had returned to his book.

"Let me tell you about Daybreak," Turner told him. "We are building it with our own hands, house by house, acre by acre, based on principles of equality and shared wealth. It is an experiment in living, and people are investing years of their lives into it."

"Ooh, I hit a nerve. Very well, it's not a rustic utopia. It's an experiment in living."

"I'm not going to endanger this community for your noble cause or anyone else's."

"Oh, dear fellow, it's not the noble cause that interests me. Foltz here is the noble cause man. I am seeking—" He paused dramatically. "Ad-*venn*-ture."

"Please be serious. This is not a game."

The mocking expression dropped from Smith's face. "Different people are serious in different ways, friend. What's a man like me to do if he wants to break out of the cage? I am looking for something large, something to throw myself into. And do I look like the military type? The National Anti-Slavery Society will work as well as anything else."

"And you want me to help you play out this dream."

"No, Mr. Foltz wants you to. If you don't put me up, someone else will."

Foltz cleared his throat. "As I said before, it seems to me you are both idealists. You both are looking to create something great."

Smith's amused look returned. "Mr. Turner here is the creator. I am just looking to play *dans le forêt*."

Turner turned to Foltz. "And how long would you expect this forest adventure to last?"

"I'd like to have Mr. Smith back here by June or July of next year. If this mission goes well, we have other places to send him."

"And just so we're clear—there will be no slave-stealing, no actions to bring suspicion to our community. He is just there to make observations."

"Agreed."

"You'll have to buy and care for your own horse," Turner said to Smith. "We are a working community, not a hotel."

"Mr. Smith is well provided for," Foltz said.

Turner looked at the two of them. He could hardly believe that he was about to go in league with them, the bedrock abolitionist and the young fop. But with the lecture proceeds and the subscriptions, Foltz's money would cap this trip's success. He shook their hands.

Adam Cabot's eyes snapped open and he gazed into the darkness. He could discern dim shapes in his room. An hour to dawn, maybe, or a little more.

In the dream that had awakened him, he was back in Boston, somewhere in the Irish slums across the South Bay, walking from tenement to tenement on a benevolent mission of some sort. The people greeted him as he walked from room to room; he was known to them. But the buildings had no central stairs, so when he traveled he had to climb outside the walls and ascend on stone ledges that grew narrower as he ascended. This did not frighten him and seemed quite natural, although he was aware that he was in danger.

Some people thought dreams had special meaning. To him they seemed a jumbled mess of memory and fancy, a stew of impossibilities that only made sense in the retelling. Still, that sense of being at ease on a precipice—

He should get ready for his morning meditation. He was going to the river today and soon there would be enough light to see by. Generally he liked the river better than the hilltop, although a couple of times he had very nearly stepped on a snake as he followed the path in the dimness. There was something elemental about it—rock, river, trees. Movement and stillness. The high hill behind him, an uplift of the eternal earth itself, the river in constant motion before him, and the village perched between, so insignificant and temporary by comparison. It was a good place to gain perspective.

He dressed and stepped into the dark street. No lantern light could be seen from any of the houses. That was the way he liked it, walking through the village with everyone still asleep. He headed south past the houses of the Wickmans, Captain Carr, all the villagers one by one, until he reached the junction of the street with the main road, where the Turners' house stood.

There was a figure sitting on the stepstone in front of the house. As he approached, it stood. He could tell it was Charlotte, dressed in her everyday brown shift and apron. He thought of turning around; he thought of walking past as if he didn't see. But he slowed, stopped, lifted his hat.

"I hope you don't mind," she said quietly. "I have a request for you."

Cabot was startled but smiled. "Of course."

"I'd like to see this contemplation spot of yours. Perhaps I will take up the practice myself."

An uncertain look sped across his face. "Do you think that would be proper?"

"I can manage my own sense of propriety."

"Of course." He gave a slight bow. "This way."

They continued down the road toward Webb's house. Neither of them spoke for a while. The air was warm and moist already.

"You'll be good to start your haying early this morning," she said at last.

"I don't know. George wants to wait till all the dew burns off."

They were reaching the end of their valley, where the mountain curved back toward the river from the right. Soon they would be in the narrow passage where the road to French Mills traversed a slender spit of ground between high bluffs and the river.

But before they reached that place, Cabot veered off down a tiny trail—not even a trail, just a hint of easier walking through the underbrush—that led to the river. At the end of the path was a large slab of limestone that sloped at a gentle angle into the water. Half a dozen turtles plopped into the river as they approached.

"I'm afraid the turtles have had to learn to share their rock with me," Cabot said.

He sat on the rock near the edge of the water and crossed his legs. The breezeless air closed them in.

"What do you do here?" she asked him. The quiet of the morning made them both speak softly.

"Usually I spend a few minutes in the river. Not today." He reached forward and touched the water. "When it's warm I immerse myself. If not, I just dip whatever feels right. Then I sit and contemplate for a while."

"Contemplate what?"

"The book says I should contemplate the emptiness of existence. I try, but more often I just let my mind rest on whatever it rests on. Then I push that out and let it rest on something else. Sometimes it finally gets empty, but not always."

They sat on the rock about a foot apart. Sunrise was still a few minutes away. Cabot's heart raced, although he tried to keep his manner calm. Surely she understood the impropriety of the two of them together, but there she was, inches away from him. And for what purpose? Did she mean to offer herself to him? Was there a secret she wanted to discuss? Propriety be damned. He was glad for the intoxication of her near presence.

What had she asked? Ah, yes, what he did here. "I don't come here to learn about the wild creatures, but I do. The deer come down to drink at the other side, over there." He made a small gesture. "And twice I have seen a black bear work his way through the woods across the river, sniffing and digging like a hog."

He kept talking, despite Charlotte's eyes, which were distractingly blue. His words sounded like nonsense to him. "The way I see it, this rock must have fallen off the bluff many years ago. It goes way out into the river, then there's a deep hole right where the rock ends."

"You should fish here sometime."

He smiled. Always the practical one. "I suppose I should."

Silence came over them again, and they sat as if listening, although there was little to listen to. Cabot found himself admiring Charlotte's ability to be still, to remain quiet and do nothing. It was a skill rarer than it might seem; he had to work to attain it, and Turner surely did not have it. He thought about the journey to Daybreak that he and Charlotte had taken, and how they all had changed since then. Turner had gained an intensity and a sense of certainty that had no doubt always been there but now was less fenced in by social constraints. Charlotte had changed, too. Motherhood and the cholera battle had made her tough, but not in a harsh way, just tough in the sense that she knew more about the struggles of the world and was capable of looking them in the face. Perhaps his ideas about the benevolent influence of Nature were true, but not in the way he had imagined. Perhaps Nature showed you her teeth, and you gained wisdom from learning the severity of her bite, discovering your ability to withstand it.

"You look deep in thought," she said. "Would you care to enlighten me?"

Cabot looked her full in the face. "I was thinking about how we have changed since we first met."

"How have I changed?"

"You are stronger, more sure of yourself."

She laughed. "If you only knew."

"And have I changed?"

Charlotte lifted her hand from her lap and placed it on the rock between them, where Cabot could easily place his hand on it, should he desire to. He thought she would like for him to. But the thought of what might happen if he did frightened him. Could he be that kind of man? Could she be that kind of woman? In the yellow light of morning he observed how brown the back of her hand had become. She noticed his glance and read his thoughts.

"Yes, brown and spotted," she said. "Nothing to do about it, I suppose. The price of a working life outdoors. Mother used to scold Caroline and me if we ventured outside without our hats and long sleeves. Caroline was always better at obeying that command."

Her hand still rested between them.

"But we all lose our pale complexions and grow brown over time," she said. "Yes, I think you have changed."

He laid his hand on hers and felt its warmth. Then he curled his fingertips around her hand, knuckles scraping stone. Her fingers curled, too, and gave his hand a slight squeeze.

As if pulled by a single string, they stood up, hands still clasped. She was on the upper slope of the rock, her back toward the bank. He paused for a heartbeat, then leaned forward and kissed her.

The earth seemed to lurch under his feet. Trees swayed and the sound of wind filled his ears. But all he could feel was Charlotte's lips beneath his. He held the kiss, held it longer, then released her hand, released the kiss, and turned away, embarrassed, his heart hammering.

He looked back. Charlotte was gazing at the river, where a muskrat swam by leaving a silent V in the water behind it.

"I should go see about Newton," she murmured.

"Yes."

She brushed off her dress. "Thank you for sharing your spot."

Was this to be it? A single moment, a mere glimpse of what could have been? Better not to have kissed at all, then. He seized her shoulders and pulled her toward him. She tilted her face to him, eyes closed, and he kissed her again, more passionately this time. And she pulled him closer, arms around him, one hand on the back of his head, and kissed back. For a moment everything fell away, everything stopped. But then she broke off, her hand lightly brushing his cheek as she turned away and walked up the path. He didn't try to stop her.

"This spot can be your spot too, you know. Come out and meditate anytime you like."

She gave him a skeptical look and a smile, and they both knew that meditation was far from their minds.

August/November 1858

Chapter 13

Morning found Turner and Smith catching the early packet boat for St. Louis. Smith still wore his preposterous derby hat perched high on his head, but had changed into a black and white checkered vest.

"If you're looking to blend in, you might want to drop the Eastern manner," Turner told him as the boat dropped its planks and pulled out into the current.

"I am who I am," Smith said, but his tone was nervous.

"And who is that, exactly?"

"About what you'd expect. Rich family, lazy childhood, trips to Europe, bored to death. Family's rid of me now. Had to leave Philadelphia. Caused a little scandal."

They sat on a bench by the railing. The early birds had all rushed to the west side of the boat to get in the shade, but Turner took a spot away from the crowd. "The river twists and turns so much, you'll be in the sun anywhere you sit," he told Smith. Foltz had kept his promise, and with another two hundred and fifty dollars in gold coins in his possession, Turner could no longer keep the money strapped to his chest. He had it in his valise, swaddled in cloth so no passerby could hear any tell-tale clinking, and sat with one foot on either side of it.

"So has your upbringing taught you anything useful in life?" he asked Smith.

"Oh, indeed. I learned how to comport myself with an air of authority, and that if I wanted something I should just take it and not ask. And enough Latin grammar to avoid embarrassing myself."

With the current behind them, they made St. Louis by nightfall. Turner slept on the deck with his valise for a pillow, his belt tied through its handles and then wrapped around his biceps. Smith went ashore; in the morning he returned watery-eyed and smelling of whiskey.

"I like this town," he said with a wan smile.

They caught the Pilot Knob train, and by the time they had reached Jefferson Barracks, Smith was asleep, his head bouncing against the window pillar beside their seats, a small string of drool hanging from the corner of his mouth. He woke up after they had passed Potosi and gazed out at the blur of blackjack oaks and red cedars as they sped by. There had been rumors of new mineral strikes in the area, copper, iron, maybe even silver, and they could see men with picks and shovels digging into hillsides seemingly at random.

"This is it?" he said.

"It gets wilder as we go."

"Lovely."

By the time they reached the Pilot Knob depot, a lonely shack set up close to the iron mines, Smith seemed mired in gloom. "Now what?" he said as they dragged their cases away from the landing.

Turner looked at the sky. It was already well past noon. "We get a room. It's a hard day's travel to the colony, with two fords along the way. Not something to try at night."

They found a room at the hotel across from the courthouse in Ironton. Turner was exhausted from the trip and fell into bed as soon as it was dark, dropping his shoes at the end of the bed and using his valise as a pillow again. For a few moments he thought about how he would explain the presence of Smith. Charlotte would probably smell him out within a minute. He might have to tell her the truth despite his doubts. Surely she would see that stepping publicly into the slavery question at this moment would be poison to their place in the community—the sheriff had made it clear how even a whiff of abolition sentiment would be met. But anyone else? Was there anyone else in Daybreak he could trust with the truth?

Smith stayed up and sat in a chair, looking meditatively out the window. Turner fell asleep with him still there but at some point in the night felt him clamber into bed. When he woke, though, Smith was already gone. Turner instantly reached for his valise—found it undisturbed—and blinked in the morning sunlight. Then a piercing whistle brought him to the window. Smith was out in the street atop a wagon loaded with supplies, holding the reins on a hearty-looking team.

"All right, then," Smith said. "Let's go to Paradise."

Charlotte avoided Cabot for the next several days, not because she didn't want to see him, but because she did. She knew that if they met, she would kiss him again, and she wasn't ready for that or for what could happen after. She wasn't sure if she ever would be. All she knew was that she wanted to be transported back to that moment by the river when time stopped and the world seemed full of possibilities again.

In the evenings they still met, she and Cabot and Webb, and she smiled to herself at Cabot's obvious nerves. She thought she might feel awkward around him as well, but instead she felt powerful, the possessor of a secret. It was a good feeling, though she recognized its corrosive force. As soon as the meetings were over they walked away in opposite directions, neither trusting themselves to speak. Lying in bed at night, with Newton in the crib beside her, she imagined Cabot climbing in with her, his tender hands and his clean smell. But at the same time, she missed Turner and wished he would hurry home from his tour. She didn't know how those feelings could coexist, but they did. Two men, two powerful emotions. Two loves? She didn't want to let the word enter her mind.

Turner's letters said the tour was going well, with hard money to get them through the winter and, strangely enough, a paying guest to bring back to Daybreak.

"We ain't a hotel," George Webb sniffed when she read them the letter. "Don't know what he's thinking there."

"The Oneidans do it," Charlotte said. "The curious come out to gawk, and they charge them for the privilege."

"We ain't the Oneidans, thank God," Webb retorted. But Turner's letter had been posted from Quincy, and he was headed home. So there was no time to debate or ask for more information.

The hay was dry, so all the men turned out to put it up, with Webb supervising the stacking in the barn. There was an art to it, he insisted; the men dutifully tossed their forkfuls in the places and direction he showed them. Shortly before lunchtime, the young German carpenter, Schnack, was brought in from the fields close to the river. Unskilled with the pitchfork, he had reached down with his hands to load some hay onto the wagon and picked up a copperhead along with it.

Charlotte was still in the Temple cleaning up from lunch when they brought him in. Two men were holding him up. He seemed capable of walking, but occasionally his legs wobbled and he sank to his knees. He was groaning and mumbling, mostly in German. Sweat poured from his face and dripped off his chin. His right hand was bright red and swollen, with two clean puncture marks between the last two fingers.

Everyone looked at Charlotte.

"Put him on a table," she said. She turned to the little Prentice girl who had been helping her clean up. "Missy, go fetch a bucket of cold water from the springhouse. And then go find Mrs. Wickman."

She turned to the two men who had brought him in. "Take his boots off, for heaven's sake. We have to eat off these tables." To the clean-shaven one, she said, "I'll need your razor."

"Oh, Gott," moaned Schnack. "That is my good hand.'

"I'm not going to cut off your hand, Thomas," Charlotte said, and that calmed him. She wiped the sweat from Schnack's brow with the cleaning rag in her hand. His teeth chattered as she lifted his hand from the table to inspect it. Newton, unknowing, played at her feet.

The puncture wounds were small and bright red. One was in the fleshy web between his fingers and the other was in the knuckle joint of the little finger. The hand reminded Charlotte of a cow's pink udder.

The girl returned with a bucket of water, breathless with importance. Charlotte lowered the man's hand into the bucket. The cold water felt good as she held Schnack's swollen hand down. Hayseeds and grime floated to the top. As she rubbed off the dirt, she could see a bright red streak running up Schnack's forearm.

The clean-shaven man arrived with his razor, and as Charlotte wiped it on her apron she signaled with her eyes for the two men to hold Schnack's arm. She laid it on the table beside him, waited for a moment for the men to get their places, and then split the skin in a fine line across the puffy swelling of his hand, opening the vein.

Schnack howled in misery. "Oh, Gott! Cut it off, just cut it off!"

Charlotte rose from her work and looked him in the eye. He looked like a cow about to be slaughtered. "Don't be such a baby. Didn't you ever hit your hand with a hammer?"

"Oh yes, ma'am. This one, I run clean through with a sixteen-penny nail one time." He raised his other hand.

"Then settle down." Schnack clamped his lips with an embarrassed expression.

She bent down, put her lips to the wound, and began to suck. Her mouth filled with blood, which she spat onto the floor. She sucked again. Was there venom? She couldn't taste anything. It tasted just like blood, just like the taste when she bumped her lip against a tooth. She spat, sucked, spat, sucked, spat again, pressing her thumb against the back of Schack's wrist where a vein protruded over the bone.

George Webb arrived from the barn and examined Schnack's arm, which was now swollen to the elbow. "How big was the snake?" he asked.

"Two foot, three foot maybe," Schnack said. "Three foot probably." Webb gave the other men a look. They shrugged.

"Kill it?"

"Hell, no. I just drop my hay and run," he said. "I never seen no snakes in the city."

"One of you boys ought to go tell the others," Webb said. "We have a huffy copperhead out there someplace. On second thought, both of you might as well go. He's in good hands here."

"Mr. Webb, am I going to make a die of it?"

"I should think not. Well, I need to get back to work." Webb turned and left.

"We'll have you back pounding nails within a week," one of the young men said.

"Yeah, we'll fix a hammer to your stump," said the other one.

Schnack cried out in frustration and pain, and Charlotte glared at the men. "Before you go back to the fields, help me get this man to his bed," she said. They lifted him from the table, still weak-kneed, and steadied him as he walked to his house. Charlotte brought Schnack's boots and placed them at the end of his bed. She dragged a straight-backed chair over to the bed then laid his hand on it. "Keep it lower than your heart," she said. She wrapped the wound in a towel, loosely, so that more blood could drain out. "Do you want some water?"

"Yes, please."

"I'll bring you some. Thanks, boys, that's all I need for now."

She decided to walk to the springhouse for another bucket of the cold spring water instead of fetching it from the nearest pump; somehow the spring water was more refreshing. She stopped by the Temple, where the Prentice girl was entertaining Newton, and poured out the first bucket onto the floor, sweeping the water and blood out the door.

Mrs. Wickman had finally been located and appeared at the door. "How's the boy?"

Charlotte shrugged. "I did the best I could. You should look in on him."

"Land, I have never treated a snakebite. Wouldn't know what to do."

"Neither did I. Just went by guess."

Mrs. Wickman swept up Newton and nuzzled him. "What a big-uns we are getting to be!" She surveyed the wet floor. "Looks like everything's under control here."

Charlotte's mouth and lips felt strange. She couldn't tell if it was venom or just her imagination, but she wanted to rinse out her mouth at the spring. "I'm going to fetch some water for Mr. Schnack," she said. "Want to walk with me?"

"No, I need to get to my sewing," she said. "I'll stop by his house on my way back. I'll take the youngun so you don't have to carry him to the spring with you."

They parted, and Charlotte hurried to the spring with her bucket. She knew her need was probably imaginary but felt urgent anyway. But she stopped short when she came near and found Harp Webb in the springhouse, kneeling at the spring, filling jugs.

He heard her, though, and turned quickly. "Hey," he said. "Hope you don't mind."

"Water should be free to all, Mr. Webb," she said. "Don't you think?"

He didn't answer. "I would use the spring up closer to my house, but it's got that sulfur taste. Don't mind it myself, but you got to keep the customers in view."

Charlotte watched him immerse a jug in the split wooden barrel they used to catch the water.

"Ever wonder why that is?" Harp went on. "Two springs, not fifty yards apart, and one of them is all sulfury and the other has nothing but sweet clear water?"

"No, I have to say that I haven't."

"I thought I told you about learning your land. Thing is, my spring comes out higher up the mountain. Runs out of different rocks and such." He kicked at the rocks in the wall of the springhouse. "This here's limestone of some sort. Your water gets all sweetened up by it. Mine is just a surface spring, dries up in the summer."

"Once again, I am put to shame by your knowledge. I mean that sincerely," Charlotte said.

"You never know when a piece of information might come in handy." Harp finished filling his jug and then stepped away from the spring. "You go ahead, I have a bunch more to do."

Charlotte dipped her gourd into the spring, rinsed and spit, then filled the bucket. She started to hurry away, impelled by the nervousness that Harp always evoked in her, but stopped at the door.

"Mr. Webb, do you sell your whiskey in smaller amounts?" she said.

"Sure. By the thimbleful if you want it that way. Dime a quart, two bits a gallon. Anything less than that, five cents maybe."

"I'd say just enough for a couple of glassfuls. One of our men was bitten by a copperhead this afternoon, and I am thinking this might help him."

Harp nodded. "Who got bit?"

"Mr. Schnack, the young German."

"The barn-building fellow."

"Yes."

"Too bad. Never been bit myself, but I've seen 'em bit, and it's no fun for sure."

"Well, thank you."

"I'll bring it by this evening."

"No, just take it directly to his house. I'll ask your father to pay you out of the community funds."

Harp's face was expressionless, but Charlotte knew he recognized that she didn't want him coming by her house—especially with Turner gone. She turned to leave. Harp cleared his throat.

"Them Indians from across the river is into your sweet corn," he said.

"Really? How do you know?"

He gave her a sideways look from under his hair. "Like I said, you can learn a lot if you watch and wait."

Charlotte wondered with a shiver whether he had seen her out walking with Adam Cabot. Given his love of showing off knowledge, he surely would have said something, or made a hint. Still, it was an uncomfortable thought.

The next morning Charlotte was in the cornfield before daylight to test Harp's claim. In the predawn dimness she could barely see. She tried to move quietly down the rows, but their broad leaves rustled against her arms.

When she got to the spot nearest the ford, she crouched down. The absurdity of her being out there struck her. What was she trying to prove? Did she think she could scare them away? Or even want to? Harp Webb probably laughed himself to sleep last night knowing she would be unable to resist the need to prove something to him, even though she couldn't say what she had to prove.

Crouched in the rows of corn, she listened for unusual sounds, watched for strange sights. She steadied herself with her hands pressed to the ground on each side. Perhaps she was becoming a farm woman after all; the ground felt good under her fingers. She felt a small, sharp rock underneath her right hand and picked it up. It was not a rock at all, but an arrowhead. The men were always bringing in arrowheads or bits of pottery from their plowing or hoeing, but this was the first one she had ever found. Surely this valley had once been home to a town or village.

She looked at it closely. It was small and delicately crafted, the kind of point that might be used to hunt small game or birds, she imagined. For a moment she indulged herself in the picture of a village on this very spot. It was a perfect spot—the river close at hand, good springs, rich soil. There would have been canoes pulled onto the bank, huts and cooking fires, an industrious craftsman sitting in the shade, shaping a piece of flint, this very piece of flint, years ago. She would show this to Adam today—he would enjoy thinking about the earlier civilization that had once existed on this spot, now vanished, plowed under like so much compost.

Then a young boy came up from behind and practically ran over her back, rushing down the row with an armful of corn.

He hadn't seen her in his haste and knocked them both off balance. Charlotte stood up in surprise and they faced each other.

He was no more than twelve and thin as a cornstalk himself. He wore a pair of baggy trousers but was shirtless and barefoot. With one hand he clutched half a dozen ears of corn to his chest; the other was outstretched as if to ward off a blow.

So Harp was right. Charlotte felt irritated at the boy, at them all. They could have just asked. But she also felt sorry for him, so thin. She wanted to show him she meant him no harm.

She held the arrowhead out to him, gesturing for him to take it. He took it from her, cautiously, as if suspicious of a trick. For an instant he examined it in the dawnlight. Then with a look of disgust he threw it in the dirt at her feet and dashed off toward the river, breaking down several cornstalks as he crashed across the field but not dropping any ears of corn.

Charlotte picked up the arrowhead and put it in her apron pocket. She walked back to her house in the quiet foggy morning and sat on the doorstone. A half hour later, Adam Cabot walked by on his way to his contemplation rock.

He stopped and faced her in wordless invitation. Charlotte's heart pounded as she fingered the arrowhead in her pocket. She could walk to him, show him what she had found, a conversation would start. She would walk with him to the river. There they would talk, they would touch. They would kiss. All she had to do was stand up and walk, walk with him down to the river, and her life would take a powerful turn. Something would happen. Something great, something terrible. Something both great and terrible. She felt herself poised on the edge of a bluff, peering over into the vastness beneath her feet. She took a deep breath.

She was not ready to take that step. She stayed where she was and waved at Cabot. He waved back, hesitantly, and walked on.

She told herself that it was the thought of Harp Webb's prying eyes that had held her back, or concern for the sleeping Newton, but she knew it was her own lack of nerve. Perhaps someday she would gain that nerve, but not today.

Late in the day, Turner arrived home in a rented wagon from Arcadia, a slender young man beside him wearing a bowler and a loud vest. "We'll put him up in Adam's cabin," he said cheerfully. "Two educated young men from the East, they'll have plenty to talk about."

His story about encountering Lysander Smith in Quincy and accepting his request to use Daybreak as a home base for botanical studies didn't ring true to Charlotte, and in the evening he told her the full story.

"You aren't going to ask the community?"

"How can I? Word would get around, and Daybreak itself would come under suspicion." He paced the floor of the front room. "And please, I must ask your complete confidence as well."

Charlotte considered. True, everyone in the area—and even some of the members of Daybreak—thought of abolitionists as dangerous fanatics. Acknowledging one in their midst, even one who promised not to do any agitating, would cause tension.

"He could just stay at a hotel somewhere," she said.

Turner held her shoulders. "One more year and we can sustain ourselves," he said. "I truly believe that. The money this man brings will carry us through the winter and into that next year."

"At least, let's tell Adam. He will be thrilled to have a fellow believer."

Turner snorted. "Him least of all. The man's a true idealist. He's already been tarred and feathered once, and with this man Smith as a confederate, who knows what he'd get himself into."

Another few minutes and he had won her over. He always did. Charlotte guessed that surely Adam would suss out the true nature of Smith's stay.

That night Turner was even more ardent than usual. At first, Charlotte did not quite feel the same level of response, but soon enough, his passion swept her away and she remembered how much she had missed him. She lay awake after they had finished, grateful for his return. Perhaps now her sense that life was out of order would go away.

It did not. Lysander Smith annoyed her at every turn. He left tips at the dining tables, which no one knew what to do with, eventually deciding to turn them over to George Webb to avoid dissension. He stayed in bed until well past breakfast, reading, and then wandered around the community getting into everyone's business. For a while he decided that he would adopt the Grahamite diet, inspiring Cabot to join him. Within a few days he had abandoned it as boring, while Cabot stubbornly carried on with it, chewing steadily on his heavy bread and piling on ever more vegetables in his effort to purify his body and soul. Smith's supposed botanical trips rarely lasted more than three days and tended to end with his returning hung over with tales of the nightlife of Memphis that only agitated the young men; Charlotte couldn't imagine that he was fooling anyone outside with his story, but saw no sign that he had revealed his secret to Adam.

Schnack's hand turned blue near to the point of blackness, and his arm swelled up to the size of his calf; but the swelling stayed below his elbow and after five days returned to something like normal. He could not bend his hand properly but could manage a saw with his thumb and two forefingers, and soon he was back at work. And for whatever reason, the corn stopped disappearing.

For about a week in the fall, Smith amused himself by guessing everyone's weight and proved alarmingly good at it.

"A hundred forty, forty-two at the most," he said to Charlotte one evening, walking past as she sat in her doorway snapping beans. He clapped his hands in glee at her startled glare.

"Mr. Smith, you do not amuse me."

"That's all right. I'm only seeking to amuse myself."

Charlotte didn't answer.

"You're a woman of the East," he went on. "We have a lot in common, you know. We should ally against these rubes, bring a little life to this place."

"You forget I'm married to one of these rubes, Mr. Smith."

"Now how could I forget that? Doesn't mean you and I couldn't enhance our cultural life, *sub rosa* of course."

"You disappoint me."

"Only because you don't know me well yet, Mrs. Turner. I grow less and less disappointing with acquaintance."

"I have no idea what you're talking about."

"You don't?" He grinned at her. "Just as well. I have no idea what I'm talking about half the time myself."

Charlotte stood up and brushed the bean stems from her apron. "I cannot tolerate this pertness, Mr. Smith. Please go away."

He tipped his hat and left, whistling a snatch from *Traviata* she vaguely recognized. Charlotte went inside with her bowl of beans, upset with Smith, upset with Turner for having brought Smith here, and upset with herself for having let Smith get on her nerves. She couldn't stand the man's cheek. How could he have been so forward? Was it something about her? Had a brief encounter with Adam Cabot put "loose woman" on her forehead for all to see?

She pushed these ideas away and went back to work.

Smith's claim to culture wasn't entirely a lie. A few days later, the sounds of a violin emerged from his house after dinner. He was playing that same aria he had hummed earlier. Listening to it as she passed by, Charlotte remembered: it was the lament the heroine—what was her name?—sings in the middle, giving up her true love at the pleadings of his father. Violetta, that was it. She stopped and rested her palm against the wall of a house. She and her father had gone to see that opera, the two of them, back in New York, when she was just a girl. She remembered this moment, how she had wanted to cry out, *Don't do it! He is your one true love!* from her seat. She could see the tragic turn the story would take, how he would misunderstand, even though she thought she was doing a good thing for a good reason, giving up her happiness to save his family name. Or perhaps the tragic turn came earlier, before the story even starts, when she went astray in the first place, with all the suffering and sadness growing out of that decision.

Now she believed the tragedy came from simply being born of woman, few days and full of trouble. Here she was just twenty-four herself, and she had already suffered all the loss she thought she could stand, a sister lost, a mother lost, the pain of childbirth. The most melancholy part of it was that her troubles were no more than the ordinary, no more than others had to bear, much less than some. So this was the price of being alive. But why did it have to hurt so much? Why did the simple facts of living and dying cause so much pain? For a moment she wondered if people grew inured to the struggles of life as they aged, but then she thought of the Wickmans and reconsidered.

After the opera, they had stayed in the city, and the next morning her father had allowed her to visit Mr. Waters' store and buy a collection of tunes from it. At home her mother had bid her to play the tune at the piano and sing it as best she could. She had complied, in the parlor twilight, though her talents were hardly up to the task, and her mother had cried at the beautiful sadness.

All of a sudden the loss seemed fresh again, almost too much to bear. And here she was out in the woods, where no one else would know the song, know where it came from, know what it meant. She looked up the dirt street to her father's house. Was he hearing this music? And was he remembering it? Was this the place she was destined to live from now on?

This was no time to cry. This was nothing to cry about. She was not going to cry.

Lysander Smith kept his eccentricities to the outside world. Inside the cabin, he was peaceable, even restrained. Cabot learned his true mission at Daybreak in less than a day.

"And what brought you to this wretched locality?" Smith asked. "You don't look like the *De Re Rustica* sort to me."

"Driven from Kansas but didn't want to go back East," Cabot said. "Or at least not yet."

"Not want to go East? What, you're a flagellant? Or perhaps you're a miniature Wordsworth. All this nature just annoys me."

"But surely you understand the power of a higher call."

Smith sniffed. "Hm. I'll admit, the notion of fighting slavery has its draw. But like you, I am a refugee as well. I raised a cloud of dust in Philadelphia and had to be out of reach for a while."

"Didn't kill anyone, I hope."

"Do I look like the killing type?" Smith asked with a laugh. "If I do, then you're the one who needs spectacles, not that pretty little French girl who is always squinting her way around."

"Does she? I hadn't noticed."

"Not your type, eh. Not mine, either. I could have guessed you would prefer a brood mare to a filly. Kansas, you say?"

"Yes, Leavenworth. I met Mrs. Turner there, and she persuaded me to join the group."

"The lady but not the man?"

"Yes." Cabot was increasingly uncomfortable with the direction of the conversation.

"Well, then. *Trés convenable.*" Smith laughed. "Don't worry, your secret is safe with me. Besides, she's not my type either."

"I don't know what you mean about a secret. And what would you say is your type?"

"Come with me to Memphis sometime, and I'll see if I can find you a specimen."

Cabot left him to his reading and stepped outside. Surely there was work out here that needed doing. There was always work. He walked toward the barn, thinking about Smith, of all people the least likely to be engaged in the cause of abolition. By all signs Smith was a talker and not a doer. But here he was, advancing the cause in some small way, while Cabot stood to the side. Who was the true abolitionist and who was not?

And even Smith, a complete stranger, could see that he … that he….

That he was in love with Charlotte Turner.

He had never voiced the words to himself, even silently, but when he did so he could not deny their truth. And what was he to do about this fact? An honorable man would leave the colony immediately, manufacture some family concern, a father in failing health, a mother in need of assistance. But he knew he had no intention of doing any such thing.

Evidently he was not an honorable man.

He had kissed her, and she had kissed him back—twice—and all the careful slip-stepping since then could not erase that. He would do it again, if ever given the chance. And he would go further, he would steal her away from his friend, he would make her his. He was certain of it.

"You're looking deep this morning."

Turner's voice made him leap. "Lord, you startled me."

"Sorry. Planning your next campaign?"

"Something like it." He paused in his walk. "Listen, I know why Smith is really here."

Turner eyed him without speaking.

"He told me almost as soon as we shook hands."

"I should have known he couldn't keep a confidence. What exactly did he tell you he is here to do?"

"Scout routes for the Anti-Slavery Society, identify likely spots for a future escape effort."

"But not to conduct slaves northward himself?"

"No."

"Good enough. That was his promise."

They resumed walking to the barn. "But why not?" Cabot said. "Why not use this colony as a station? We're isolated, we could travel at night, Mississippi and Louisiana through Arkansas to here, from here a day's travel to Illinois, a week's more to Canada."

Turner seized his shoulder. "Don't speak a word of this again. If anyone needn't be told of the danger of abolition work, it should be you. We have a great work a-building here, and I'll not have you or anyone else endanger it with schemes such as that. Even a hint of Kansas over here would have men with torches after us in a week. You heard what Harley Willingham said." He sighed and watched a hawk circle the ridgetop. "The real problem is how to keep this Smith from opening his mouth again. Thank God he spoke to you, and you can be trusted. But if he blabs his business in some whiskey den in town, we'll all be lucky to get out of the county alive."

Turner's gaze dropped from the circling hawk to Adam's face. "I said you can be trusted. You can, can't you?"

"Of course," Cabot answered. Every word they spoke now seemed fraught with extra meaning, and Cabot felt as though all his phrases began and ended with "I love your wife."

"Then act like it. See if you can put this Smith on a leash and keep him on it." He spun away toward the Temple of Community, leaving Cabot on the path, flushed, angry, guilty, and with nowhere in particular to go.

Lysander Smith wrote regularly to Hiram Foltz but assured Turner that he wasn't revealing anything incriminating in his letters. "I'm not quite that great a fool, to trust the discretion of a backwoods postmaster," he said. But when a mention of Daybreak appeared in the *New York Weekly Tribune*, Turner knew the source.

"Do you like it?" Smith cried, gleeful, when Turner showed him the copy of the newspaper, which Mercadier had received in the mail from a friend in St. Louis. "I knew my little tendril would find a crevice."

Word has reached us of yet another experiment in social reform being carried out deep in the forests of Missouri. "Daybreak," its founders call it, and daybreak it surely represents to the souls who inhabit it. The community is founded on principles of common ownership and complete democracy, and we understand it has no particular religious bias.

We fervently hope that the principles of equality and justice represented by this community will serve as a beacon to its neighbors, residing as they do in a state where these qualities are denied to many of its inhabitants.

Turner had to admit that he liked the recognition. But the glancing reference to slavery wouldn't be helpful with the local folks. Sure enough, a month later came a piece from the *New York Herald*, clipped out by someone and sent anonymously in the mail.

Our friends at the <u>Tribune</u> report that more <u>sprouts</u> of one sort and another are appearing in the Western states. We remind our friend that <u>sprouts</u> only grow to maturity in their home soil. Many the sprout that flourished at <u>daybreak</u> has withered by sunset.

But there was little time to think about newspaper arguments. The wheat needed to be harvested and stored. The new reaper lived up to its claim. It clattered through the fields in a quarter of the time it would have taken the men, or less; everyone followed behind, tying up shocks of wheat and propping them together to dry.

Charlotte had seemed a little peculiar to him ever since he had returned. Turner didn't inquire into it, thinking it might be one of those women's moods people whispered about. Perhaps she needed to get out of the colony for a day. So when it came time for the trip into town, he arranged with Marie to watch

Newton for the day and surprised Charlotte with the idea of accompanying him the night before.

They were up before dawn, their breath hanging in the air, the wagon loaded with clothing for Grindstaff's general store. Charlotte had their list in hand. With the harvest coming in, this was a light week. Once they had all the wheat onto the threshing floor and then into the granary, they would need to haul it to the mill, wagonload after wagonload, but for now there was food in the storehouses, and this trip was more a luxury than anything.

As he double-checked the harness on the farm wagon, Turner noticed Adam Cabot, on foot, disappearing around the bend in the road past Webb's house.

"Now what do you suppose he is up to?" he said to Charlotte.

She cleared her throat. "I believe he has some morning religious practice."

"He would," Turner said, adjusting the hames.

They forded the river in the cold morning and were past the Indian camp before sunup. No smoke rose from the huts and no signs of life could be seen, but the place still had the sense of being inhabited. Charlotte sat close to Turner on the wagon's spring seat, her body warm against his side. He shifted the reins to his left hand so they could clasp hands under the lap blanket.

Grindstaff stepped out onto the platform in front of his store as they approached. "Well, if it ain't the outlanders," he said, "or *auslanders* as them goddam Germans say from up north of town, excuse the swearing ma'am, bad habit I know, but habits once entrenched are harder to remove than a chigger. How the hell you all doing down there on the river? Excuse me, ma'am."

"Well and good," Turner said, stepping down from the wagon and shaking hands before helping Charlotte down.

"Listen, I got to tell you something," said Grindstaff. "I'll pay you for this order of clothes, but I can't order no more this week. It may be a while before I order any more too."

Something about the way Grindstaff looked—his leathery face and chaw of tobacco—reminded Turner of Willingham, the sheriff, and he was immediately suspicious.

"Can't or won't?" he said. "Maybe you just don't like the way we live?" Charlotte laid a quieting hand on his arm.

"Hell, I don't give a goddam how you live, excuse me ma'am," Grindstaff said. He spit into the street and led them in the store. "You seem like good people. Hell, at least you can speak English, unlike them goddam Germans, in here all the time muttering and shit. 'You take fifty cent? We give you fifty cent,' buncha cheap bastards. And the Polacks or whatever the hell they are, don't know what they eat, but damn it makes their breath stink." He paused. "Excuse me ma'am."

Grindstaff waved a hand at his shelves. "No sir, here's my problem. People ain't buying." The pants and shirts from last week lay on the shelf in neatly folded stacks. "I sold one shirt and one pair of pants from last time. People are going for these goddam factory-mades, they're a little cheaper but not that much, and yours are a damn sight better made, I tell 'em hand-stitched last longer, but they don't seem to care. Things are looking up, people got a little money in their pockets, all of a sudden they don't want homemade stuff, they want things with a label from some goddam place back East."

"Then why do you stock those factory-made shirts in the first place?" Turner asked.

Grindstaff looked at him as if he were a madman. "I'm a businessman, friend. I put stock on my shelves and hope to sell the damn stuff. Stock that sells, I put more of it on."

Turner blushed. "Of course. Foolish thing for me to say."

"Don't let you hunt or fish on their land, either, the Dutchy sons of bitches. Time was, you didn't have to ask, you just went hunting. Nowadays, half the time they won't even let you if you ask. Sons of bitches. Excuse me, ma'am."

They made their purchases, left the new clothes, and hurried out. Turner was embarrassed at their lack of success. All those women, cutting, sewing—for what? It would be hard news to break. And the lack of exchange items meant that Grindstaff's ticket would be rising faster than ever—he would soon be wanting hard cash for his goods.

"Let's not hurry back," Charlotte said. "We have the day."

They rode south down the Greenville road at a leisurely pace. Charlotte had packed a lunch, so they stopped along Twelvemile Creek and let the horse drink while they spread their food out on the wagon gate. The day had warmed enough to let them take off their coats.

"I guess it's time for a new plan," Turner said.

"And what is this new plan going to be?"

"I wish I knew."

They chewed their ham in silence.

"I have an idea for the next issue of *The Eagle*," Charlotte said. "Should have mentioned it to you earlier."

Turner waited.

"It's been ten years since the Seneca Falls Declaration. I'd be interested to read your musings on what kind of progress we've seen since then."

Turner groaned. "I thought we agreed not to confuse the issues in people's minds yet. Economic equality and equality of the sexes are separate matters."

"We didn't agree. You said 'no' and I acquiesced."

He knew she was right, but that didn't make it any easier. "I can't endorse the thing, I hope you know that. We would lose too much support."

"I didn't ask for that. I just said it would be interesting to read your thoughts."

"But if I don't endorse it...."

"If you don't endorse it I'll be intrigued to see your logic."

There was no way out. Might as well surrender. "All right then, I'll take that as a commission. Now let's see if we can find a track that will take us back home."

Sure enough, there was a wagon trail that cut toward the west less than a mile later. It ran along a creek bed for a while and then turned abruptly up a hill. It grew rougher and rockier, and for a while Turner thought he would have to admit defeat and turn around, but then they passed a lone cabin with a couple of kids scuffling in a bare space under the trees, what passed for a yard. A thin man with a peppery beard came out on the porch and watched them silently.

"This road go through?" Turner called out.

"Yeh."

"Well, where does it come out at?"

"Any place you want, if you take it far enough, I reckon."

Turner held back a retort. Comedians. "Where does it come out close by, then?"

The man looked down the wagon track as if he were following it in his mind. Finally he spoke. "Take it straight, you get down to the river ford at Trace Creek. But there's a cutoff a mile or two before that, takes you back to Cedar Bottom and up that way."

"Okay, thanks." Turner chucked the reins. Even the horse seemed impatient to move on. The man watched them out of sight, but the children never stopped rolling in the dirt.

The wagon trail was just as the man said. It followed the ridgelines, and when he took the right fork it came out near the Indian camp, empty as before. Turner had never noticed the trail before—it was just a couple of indentations emerging from the trees—and supposed it had probably been an Indian trail once. The sun was starting to get low in the sky when they reached the rocky outcrop that overlooked Daybreak.

Turner stopped the wagon and tied the reins to a little oak. He wanted to look at the colony for a while. They sat on a ledge at the edge of the bluff.

They couldn't see the river crossing from where they sat—it was hidden in the woods below them—but they could see the main road all the way to the end of the valley, the Daybreak road branching off to the right, the rows of houses along both sides. There were thirty houses now, a village to be proud of, from the Temple at the north end down to Turner's house at the south, where the Daybreak road rejoined the main one. The broad fields between Daybreak and the mountain were dotted with stacks of wheat, and closer to them, the corn shimmered deep green in the low slant of evening sunlight. People were walking to and fro, tiny, seemingly aimless in their movements although Turner knew that each one would have insisted on the significance of their movements. But from high above, they seemed in random motion, like ants on a hill.

The bottomland forest, which had filled half the valley when he had arrived, was being pushed back toward them; the fringe of dead trees that had been girdled for this winter's cutting was visible, and beyond it the belt of stumps yet to be pulled. Another few years and they would have the entire grove cut down, maybe forty more acres for crops. At the base of the mountain beyond, where the pasture gave way to forest, he could see some of the community's hogs rooting; George had begun tolling them closer and closer to the barn with melon rinds and ears of corn, in anticipation of butchering day later this fall.

"We're going to have to manufacture something," Turner said, mostly to himself.

"What?"

He pointed at the community. "How many people you think that river bottom can sustain? Just from the food grown on it."

Charlotte nodded. "I see what you mean. Even if we clear the whole valley, we can't support more than twenty or thirty."

They looked down at the people.

"What about the reaper?" Charlotte asked.

"We harvest faster, but we don't harvest more."

Again she nodded. "So we need another source of income. *The Eagle?*"

"Good if it holds up. But not enough."

"Donations?"

"Would you like to live on the goodwill of others?"

They lapsed into silence again.

"So what shall we do?" she asked.

"If I only knew," Turner said.

They started the wagon down the rocky slope to the ford. Turner did not know what else to say.

"Have you asked Adam? Maybe he will have an idea," Charlotte said at one point. Her voice sounded strained.

"After the harvest is over. I'm not eager to let anyone know my thoughts on this just yet."

"Very well." She seemed to be deciding whether to say something. Finally she said, "This man Smith...."

"Yes?"

"I'm afraid he's going to cause more problems for us than he's worth. He pesters Marie with suggestive remarks. He even made such remarks to me once."

Turner chuckled. "I guess you set him straight."

"Of course," Charlotte replied. "But Marie is younger, and besides, no woman should have to put up with this nonsense in the first place."

She was right, naturally. Turner had observed Smith's behavior but had written it off as the posturing of a silly young man determined to shock the world. Smith would have to be spoken to—not that it would do any good.

The weeks went on, the harvest was complete, and first frost came early. Turner thought that a ropemaking venture might work. They could plant part of the bottom field in hemp and set up a ropewalk between the main road and the river, where the ground was flat. All it would take was patience and labor. He spoke about his idea with Cabot and Newton Carr privately first, and they walked up and down the road, measuring the distance they could set up a good straight ropewalk. Two hundred yards easily. Cabot had another idea: if they set it up close to the riverbank, they could dig out a little raceway and run the rope-jack with water power. Carr, ever the engineer, pointed out that they didn't need to make a raceway for a paddle wheel; the small amount of power they would need to turn a ropejack could be gained simply by setting a piling directly in the river and mounting a wheel on it, with the other end of its shaft mounted on the bank. He immediately began sketching what he would need.

He sold the plan to the community at their next meeting.

"Hemp's a nigger crop," Grindstaff said when Turner approached him about seed. "Grows like hell in the river bottoms, so I'm told. But yeah, if you want to make rope, I'll sell it for you. And probably get you a good price, too."

Turner had begun planning his commentary on the Seneca Falls Declaration as soon as Charlotte had suggested it, and as cold weather took over he spent his afternoons in the print shed, composing. All summer they had kept the door to the shed wide open, trying to draw a breeze, but now it was closed, and they lit a fire in the stove to keep their hands warm and the ink soft.

His plan was to have Marie set the original declaration down the left column. By the time she finished that, he would have his comments ready for her to set in the column alongside.

He would use the simile of a flower to explain his point. Just as a flower does not spring up and bloom in a day, neither do conditions of equality in the world. First the root would have to be firmly set, the root of right relations in the economic sphere, from man to man. And as we could see by observing the world around us, not only was that root not set yet, it was still the barest of seeds, with communities like Daybreak the first tentative sprout. Once firm and healthy, the plant would produce its finest blossom—the right relations between man and woman.

He liked it. He could imagine this column forming the basis for his next lecture tour—maybe next year? Who knows. Emerson toured every winter. He had half a mind to ride up to St. Louis and hear him again, pick up a few tricks, maybe even meet the old master himself.

Turner was toying with the idea of making an allusion to the slavery question, perhaps the right relation between the races was, what, the seed? And the abolitionists were trying to rush the plant's growth. Then he realized that the whole metaphor was the same one that had been used in the *Herald's* snide little remark. It must have gotten lodged in his mind, and he had used it without thinking. That recognition irritated him, and he was about to scrap the whole column and start over, when he noticed that Marie had stopped typesetting.

At first he thought she was merely proofing her work without a proof sheet, as any good typesetter could do, reading the column backward and from right to left. Her back was to him. But then he saw her wipe a tear from her eye with one knuckle and then wipe the knuckle on her printer's apron. Her slender shoulders hunched forward. Turner walked to the layout table.

"Marie," he said. "What's wrong?"

She glanced up, embarrassed, and wiped her eye again. "Nothing's wrong," she said. "It's just—" she gestured at the Seneca Falls Declaration, now fully set and filling a whole column of type. "I've never read this before. It's so—so— glorious."

"Really? Never read it?"

"Never even heard of it," she replied. "It was written, what, years ago?"

"Ten," Turner said. "Eleven now, I suppose."

"And signed by all these women—and men too. A hundred of them, it says here."

"Yes."

She ran her finger over the type. "I am a lucky woman," she said. She gestured to the sheets of paper on the table beside her. "These great sentiments. My father and mother, all their lives they dream of a better world. My mother never sees more than a glimpse. But my father, he never lets this dream go away. For a time, he thought maybe someday we will live it out in France, but now it's all empire, empire, the new Napoleon. We will never go back to France—" She stopped, and added quietly, "And we never want to, either. We are here today, working for this dream. We were meant to be in this place." She smiled.

Marie's eyes were set in their usual squint, but the expression did not make her unattractive; it gave her a half-smile and an expectant look, as though she was perpetually anticipating some surprising treat. Her dark hair was braided and pulled back to keep it out of her work, and she had it tied in an ornate knot. Turner could see why all the young men wanted her.

"You are a great man, you know," she went on. "You have great ideas, strong ideas, and you do not just write them down. You make them happen. All around us, we see your ideas coming to life."

Turner smiled back at her. "Marie, I need to ask you something."

"Yes?"

"This man Smith. Is he bothering you? I hear tales that he is behaving in all too familiar a way."

She laughed. "Mr. Turner, surely you know I can manage a foolish man like Smith. I have managed all the Daybreak boys, and even Harp Webb has only been around one more time. Smith is the least of my troubles."

"All right. But please know that if you ever need assistance—if—if this Smith becomes a problem—" He didn't quite know what else to say. "Marie, you should marry," he finally added. "You are young and attractive. You keep all the young men here in a constant state of excitement hoping to attract your favor. You could have any man in the colony."

She half-turned away, looking at the floor. "I will not marry," she said. "I am like you, I have strong ideas. And one of those ideas is that I will not marry just to be convenient. I will only marry a man I love and admire."

Marie turned toward Turner and looked him in the eyes, her arms at her sides. "Surely you understand these convictions."

"Of course."

"And the man I would marry—" She paused but continued to look directly at him. "He cannot marry me." The room was quiet. Turner understood and a rush of desire flooded through him. He knew it was insane, but took a step toward her. She did not step back.

December 1858/February 1859

Chapter 14

George Webb squeezed Cabot's arm as they walked to the evening meeting. "Hog-killing tomorrow. I know this isn't your calling, so just watch me and follow along. Your job is to scrape hides and to stay out of the way of the boys who are gutting. Things can get very slippery. Good way to lose a finger."

Before dawn, they hung block-and-tackles from one of the big oak trees near the barn and placed the wash pots beneath them. "Not boiling, just scalding," Webb warned the crew of ten- and twelve-year-olds whose job it was to tend the fires.

Everyone stayed out of sight of the barn until the strongest young man of the colony, Schnack the carpenter, gave the sign that he had tolled the hogs into the pen with slops and latched the gate behind them. Then everyone came forward to inspect.

"Twelve, not counting the babies," Webb said, standing with one foot on the gate to peer over the hogs, which were milling restlessly, spooked by the throng of people. "We'll let those two young ones go—there and there—so that makes ten. Good show. We won't have to kill again till January, if that."

He nodded to Schnack, who was hefting a nine-pound hammer. "Take one at a time so you don't get too far ahead of us. I'd get that old sow first, her and the big boar. They'll be the most trouble. And mind the tushes. Don't get in there with them until you've got those two killed."

Schnack swung himself up and sat on the gate as the hogs milled by, looking for a way out. The old sow and the boar were easy to spot; they were half a foot taller than the other hogs and weighed a good three hundred pounds each. He sat, hefting the hammer, while the boar passed by a few times; then when it passed again, swung the hammer over his head and brought it down hard directly on the hog's skull. It dropped with a groan and lay twitching in the dirt.

"Well done!" Turner cried.

"Like pounding spikes," Schnack said. The men moved in and dragged it out of the pen, then fastened the ropes around its hind feet and hoisted it up, sticking its throat just above the breastbone to drain the blood while its heart still beat. Then it was time to scald and scrape, working as fast as they could while the other hogs circled in the pen.

The old sow was warier. She stayed at the far end of the stall, alternately watching Schnack and chasing the other pigs away from the best slops. Finally Webb grew impatient and had two of the men climb into the stall, using a half-finished wagon bed as a shield against the sow's tusks. They pinned her in one corner of the stall, where Schnack stunned her with two swings.

"That was the king and queen of that herd," Cabot said as they hoisted and stuck the sow.

"They'll have new royalty by spring," said Webb.

Cabot couldn't help feeling that Turner's eyes were on him all the time, although he knew it was probably his imagination. Scraping the hide was simple work but hard; he followed Webb's instructions and stayed clear of the men who were gutting and splitting. Charlotte, moving among the men, was always at the periphery of his awareness. He could hear her quiet voice and her ready laugh. He kept his head down and scraped. "Not too hard," said Webb over his shoulder. "You don't want to slip and cut through the skin, not that these brutes have a soft hide."

The rest of the killing went easily after the two old ones had been finished off. With the pigs unable to see behind themselves, Schnack could easily work his way around the pen. By morning's end his hammer was covered in blood, and he was drenched in sweat and dirt. Schnack wanted to catch the blood for *blutwurst*, so the women held pans beneath the hogs' pierced necks before they were hoisted into the tree, one by one.

"Now what?" Charlotte called to Schnack. She held a steaming bowl of blood at arm's length. Her breath frosted in the air.

"Put it in a crock somewhere to let it cool," Schnack said. "Somewhere safe. Don't let no dogs get after it. I'll mix it up tomorrow."

"All right," she said. Cabot tried to be nonchalant as he watched her walk toward the print shed. Made sense. It had a secure door latch and was unheated for the day. He lowered his head, thinking, and felt in his pocket. On one of his walks he had snipped some sprigs of bittersweet, and wanted to give them to her. The bright orange berries were so cheerful against the gray of the winter forest.

Charlotte placed the bowl of blood against the wall of the print shed, steam rising from it in the chilly air. She saw the proof page of Turner's column lying in a shaft of light on the composition table, and although she knew she should get back to the work outside, she couldn't resist.

It was good. She could hear Turner in it, musing, talking to himself, working himself around to a position. It wasn't where she wanted him to be, of course, but he was making a turn. That was always his way—he never admitted to being wrong, just reasoned and reasoned until he found himself in a new position, which somehow wasn't supposed to be a contradiction of the old.

She smiled at his phrasing and recognized that he was trying out a new lecture. What did this mean? He was already thinking ahead to next year, knowing that the colony would need more cash. Or was this just a fallback plan in case the ropemaking didn't work out? Or was it simply that he was tired of living in Daybreak and needed the excitement of a lecture tour to keep himself interested? If that was true, she would insist on going along.

The latch on the door clicked open. Charlotte turned. There stood Adam Cabot, wearing the expression of lip-quivering resolution that a man gets when he is about to launch into something regrettable.

He closed the door and walked toward her, his gaze intense. He stopped about a foot away. They stood in silence. Then he pulled some bittersweet vines, twisted into a tight wreath, from his coat pocket and handed them to her.

"These are for you," he said. "I thought of you when I saw them—so beautiful, so much life in the cold."

Charlotte's face felt hot. Then Cabot stepped forward again, took her by the shoulders, and kissed her.

She reached up and kissed him back, willingly, hard, and for an endless moment she felt the same sensations as she had the previous time, by the river. She was bodiless, expanding, growing lighter and lighter, like a cloud on a summer day. She stumbled backward a little, and mindful of the bowl behind her, drew away to catch her balance. Cabot caught her and pulled her toward him.

"I must know," he said. "Is this attachment real?"

"Of course it is real," Charlotte said. "What do you take me for?" Her weightless feeling vanished; she walked to the other side of the composing table. She tried to choose her words. "It is just as real as this table. No less so. But the words on this page are also real, and this colony, and the people in it. One reality does not obliterate the others."

His face contorted with unhappiness. "So this hardscrabble life in the woods—this is to be your fate?"

"Apparently it is. At least for now."

"You were meant for higher things, Charlotte. What happened to making the world a better place?"

"You imply that we are not."

Cabot frowned. "That's not what I meant. But with so much going on in the country, it is hard to just cultivate your garden. This man Lincoln—"

"Didn't impress James much."

"But at least Lincoln is in the arena, and I am not."

Charlotte turned toward the door. "There is work to do. We can discuss our various futures another time." She paused at the threshold, noticing her appearance for the first time, bespattered with blood and hair, bits of skin and fat. These clothes would take a great deal of washing before they became clean again. "Please wait a few minutes before leaving. It will not do for us to be seen leaving this building together."

"I love you, Charlotte."

Her hand was on the latch. She closed her eyes and held her breath. She imagined him behind her, his hands on her shoulders, turning her toward him, pulling her to him, insistent … was that what she wanted? Did she want him to stop her from leaving, to turn her around, to kiss her again, to insist she face the truth about her feelings? What would happen then? She waited, expectant, hungering to feel the heat from his body against hers. But he stayed where he was, and she opened the latch. "I know you do."

She left the shed and strode toward the barn, disappointed in herself. Disappointed in life. Of course she loved him. Why couldn't she say it back, and at least give the man a little comfort? She told herself that it was to avoid giving him false hope, but inwardly she knew she was afraid to speak the words, afraid of the feelings they might unleash, the chain of events that could occur, the great unraveling of lives and fortunes. As if a chain of events wasn't already in motion. As if she had the power to redirect it by her simple acts of word and will.

She made five more trips to the shed, lining crocks of blood against the far wall. Adam had disappeared. Back at the oak tree, the men scraped hides, split heads, and cut off feet for pickling. The youngsters scooped out the brains and separated the internal organs into tubs.

George Webb stopped her. "Seen our man Cabot?"

Charlotte scanned the group. Nowhere. "Perhaps—"

Webb raised his hand. "It's all right. He's a city boy, with a delicate stomach. All this bloodletting takes some getting used to."

Frances Wickman brought out a coffeepot as the fifth hog went into the scalding pot. As she walked among the men, handing out cups of coffee, Charlotte noticed something different about her shape, or perhaps it was her posture. There was a baby on the way, she felt sure. Another reason to be careful about Adam: only a fool would think to keep secrets in a community with this many watchful eyes.

The men gratefully stopped to rest. After he had finished the killing, young Schnack had attacked the scraping with enthusiasm, eager to show off his strength, but even he was puffing for breath.

"That's a tough-hided old bunch," he said to no one in particular. He pulled a couple of cold biscuits out of his coat pocket.

Charlotte followed Mrs. Wickman back to the Temple after the coffee had been drunk. She helped her rinse the cups and waited until everyone else was out of earshot.

"Frances," she said, "Are you—?"

Mrs. Wickman blushed, smiling. "Can you tell already? I think I'm only two months along."

"Just had a feeling, that's all." She embraced her. "And was this—"

"Anticipated?" She shrugged. "Not exactly. I didn't exactly try to avoid it either. We didn't really talk about it, just . . . you know."

"Of course. I'm delighted."

Charlotte's thoughts must have been easy to read, for Mrs. Wickman quietly said, "I know it'll never replace Mary or Lucy. Wouldn't want that. Not so sure about the Mister, though." She looked mournful. "I think he just misses children being around, you know."

Charlotte left her with another hug and a promise not to tell. There was no time to stand and talk.

By the end of the day all were exhausted, but the hogs were cut up and ready for salting the next day. The children had taken the bladders, tied off the ends, and were playing kickball with them. They raced around the fields with their new toys, returning to the lard kettle now and then to snatch hot cracklings. Schnack had sidled up to Charlotte and asked her to set aside some onions for his wurst recipe.

"I'll work it up tomorrow," he said. "Just like mama used to make. You see."

Charlotte thought about telling him that her mama had never in her life made sausage out of anything, much less blood, but held her remark. She left Schnack sorting through the tub for the best lungs.

Cabot had left the shed and walked to his cabin, thinking to wait a few minutes, circle the village, and return from the other side. Lysander Smith was sitting in his doorway, a copy of *Travels to Daybreak* in his hand, keeping his place with a finger.

"In the book, you don't work nearly as hard," he said. "You should call it Backbreak, not Daybreak."

Cabot didn't feel like talking but stopped anyway, his mind churning. So she didn't say she loved him. All right. He understood why she couldn't. But surely no one could kiss like that without love. Or perhaps one could, and he was a fool.

"That's why it's a book. You could have helped, you know."

"I know."

"But you're a paying guest, of course."

"It's not that. I'm just—ah—intimidated, shall we say. Killing, chopping, all that."

"Perhaps you should have stayed in Philadelphia, Mr. Smith."

"Perhaps so. But back to my original observation."

"Yes?"

"What's so ideal about this place? It looks like just another work farm to me. I don't see the point."

Cabot felt his color rise. "Mr. Smith, you do not see what we see. You see only the surface of things. Where you see toil, I see community. People building a small place in the world where status is not determined by wealth, where all are equal." He felt surprised at himself for defending Daybreak so vehemently.

He had come to the place as an outsider himself, and here he was, talking like one of the true believers at the Thursday night meetings. Perhaps he had become one of those true believers at last.

"A pretty dream. I'll take the world as it is, thank you."

"Really. You prefer the world as it is, eh?"

"I didn't say that. The world is a horrid place, and we both know it. I just said I'd take it, rather than trying to live in an imaginary alternative. You can have your pretty dream." He paused and looked toward the hog-killing scene. "And next year you're going to make rope. The fun never ends."

Cabot was about to make another comment but paused. "You're right. We need to do something just for enjoyment. Any ideas?"

"None that you would approve of." Smith smirked.

"You know what I mean. The cultural life."

"What, don't you think Mr. Turner's Sunday lectures are fun?"

"How about a dance? I've heard you play, and old Mercadier knows quite a few airs and reels. A Christmas dance would be a fine thing."

Smith waved the book at him. "For God's sake, listen to you! I thought you were more intelligent than to fall in with this troop of monkeys. Look at them, working like slaves, and for what? The common good, the community? Don't make me laugh. You're all intoxicated by the great ideas of the great man, and what has it gotten you?"

"A community of fellow strivers."

"An island of dreamers in a sea of strife."

Cabot turned away, stung by the dose of truth in his words. Smith rose and put his hand on his shoulder. "All right, you'll have your dance. If there's any way to get my hand up that girl's skirts, it would be to make music with her old dad."

"Mr. Smith, you shock me."

"Oh, don't act so righteous." Smith leaned close. "There is always a woman, isn't there?"

Cabot did not answer.

The Christmas dance took place a month later. Smith and Mercadier had managed to work up some dance tunes, everyone emerged with their best clothes, and the tables and benches in the Temple were pushed to the walls.

Marie, for once, lowered her shield against the young men and danced every dance, her cheeks flushed and a smile on her sober face. She even danced once with Turner, who showed himself to be good on his feet.

Though the idea had been his, Cabot felt detached from the festive mood. Charlotte had given him no chance to speak with her alone since the encounter in the print shop. Every day he felt nothing but longing and ache for the woman he could not have, or could have if she would only allow it. He could not force gaiety into his gloomy manner, but tried to conceal it as best he could by keeping himself across the room from Charlotte and Turner, hugging the wall as the dancers swirled and stomped.

He felt a shoulder rub against his. It was George Webb.

"You're the picture of fun," Webb said.

"Sorry. Somehow the mood isn't there tonight."

"You should dance."

"As should you."

Webb snorted. "You never seen me dance. I'd frighten the children." The music shifted from a heavy jig to an air, and the two watched the dancers shift position. "Besides, there's an overage of men. Let's stroll out."

Stars filled the clear winter sky, but the air was not yet the jaw-numbing cold of January. The men pulled their coats around themselves and stood on the steps of the Temple, gazing down the moonlit valley toward the river.

"Two months ago, cornfields," Webb said. "A year ago, pasture scrub. Five years ago, forest."

"And next year?"

"Hell if I know. Hemp, so they say."

"So *we* say."

"So *he* says. Just hope it ain't back to pasture scrub by then. Let's walk down and look at this ropeworks."

They followed the rows of stubble down the slope to the main road. Across the road was the level ground where men had been clearing brush in a long, narrow line between the road and the river; the ropewalk had to be straight, and it had to be covered, so the hemp wouldn't twist wrong or get wet. Cabot could see where the posts for the framing were to be set.

"Hell of an operation," said Webb. He pulled a flask of whiskey from an inside pocket of his coat and handed it to Cabot.

"I didn't know you drank," Cabot said.

"It ain't my son's product. I wouldn't give him the satisfaction." They gazed up and down the cleared path. "How did we get into the rope business, anyway?"

"We took a vote."

"I suppose so. Still. We always take votes but they always come out the same. Mr. Turner gets a bright idea, and we all hop to say yes. Lecture tour, newspaper, this Smith fellow, and now a hemp farm. Weren't supposed to be this way. Supposed to be a democracy, everybody with a say, everybody makes the decisions."

The liquor warmed Cabot's throat. He handed the flask back. "Truly spoken," he said. "Without equality in the decision-making, our equality of ownership means nothing."

"Truly spoken," Webb repeated, taking a drink and returning the flask.

The lights from the Temple shone across the empty fields, and from where the men stood they could hear faint music from inside. They stood in silence for a while.

"There will be snow in a day or two," Webb said. Cabot didn't answer for a while.

"So what do we do about this?" he finally said.

They turned and strolled toward the Temple, sensing that their presence would be missed before long. A breeze from the north lifted Cabot's hair and stung his cheeks a little. "Mr. Turner is a good man, and the idea is sound," Webb said, choosing his words. "But forming the idea is different from carrying it out."

Cabot knew they were pausing at the threshold of a cabal, reluctant to cross over. "I'm tired of playing the junior lead in this drama," he murmured, surprised that he had said the words aloud.

"Rightly so," Webb said. "You're a sharp man. But I ain't asking you to betray your friend."

"What are you asking, then?"

"I'm saying you and me, when we get together before the meeting, we are half the group. If we keep ourselves together, we can block any foolish ideas, rein him in. Maybe over time the man gets the point that he ain't the emperor."

"And with three votes, we can enact our own ideas."

Webb stopped at the foot of the Temple steps, startled. "You don't think she'd vote against her own husband?"

Cabot hesitated. "On the right issue, perhaps."

As if on cue, the Temple door opened. Charlotte stood in the beam of light.

"There you are. Don't tell me you two are out here nipping at the jug," she said.

"We just stepped out for a moment," Cabot said apologetically. "We'll be right back."

"And what draws you out here at this hour?" She walked down the steps to join them.

"Just wanted to inspect the ropeworks, see how it's going," Webb said. They both wore embarrassed looks.

"Ah, the ropeworks," Charlotte said. She gazed across the fields toward the river. "That is quite a piece of work."

"You can say that again," Webb said. They stood in silence in the moonlight. Suddenly Cabot felt emboldened.

"Actually, Mrs. Turner, we came out here to talk," he burst out. "And it concerns your husband."

He could feel Webb's eyes on him as if he had just blurted out a state secret. "I don't think this is such a good idea," Webb said.

Cabot turned to her. "May we speak to you in confidence?"

"Go on. But if I am not comfortable with this conversation, I will ask you to stop."

Cabot nodded. The two men looked at each other again, and Cabot cleared his throat. "Mrs. Turner, we are beginning to worry."

She waited.

He composed his thoughts. "One of the founding principles of this community is democracy, as you of course know." A passage from *Travels to Daybreak* came to mind. "'Some would say that the wise should rule. But who are the wise, and how do we know them? By their exercise of judgment. And how do the wise become wise? By the same exercise of judgment. And the wisdom of many is greater than the wisdom of one.'"

"You have a prodigious memory," Charlotte said with a smile.

"Go on, go on," Webb said, now impatient.

"In any event. We are concerned that Mr. Turner is forgetting this principle. We began noticing small things. How duties are assigned. Whether others' opinions are recognized. Then we received Mr. Smith without warning or consultation. And now this rope manufacture, which, yes, we voted on, but with less than complete understanding."

"But why meet like conspirators?" Charlotte said. "Why this moonlight trip to the woods?"

"Fact is, ma'am," Webb said, "we're not sure how your husband will take it if we were to talk to him directly. He's been acting touchy."

"Then treat him like your leader." Charlotte's face glistened with sweat from the dancing; she shivered in the chill night air.

"One thing, Mrs. Turner," Adam said.

It felt formal and strange to call her "Mrs. Turner." Even with his own feelings set aside, their friendship was such that they could use first names. But he knew George Webb would hear the change, and wonder.

"Yes?" she said, her voice steady.

"Could you talk to him? Nothing too serious, just let him know that there are people who are concerned about our democratic principles?"

She nodded, but with a grimace. They walked up the steps to the door of the Temple, the men on each side of her. Light streamed out the windows, and the strains of fiddle music could be heard over the shuffling and clumping of feet and the random din of voices. The music stopped. There was a burst of applause.

They stepped through the doors. Turner was leaning against the wall by the two musicians, watching the dancers. Charlotte walked straight across the floor to him and took him by the arm.

"Dance with me, James," she said. She turned to Mercadier and Smith. "Play to wake snakes."

And then it was the dead of winter, time for indoor work, repairs and mending, the cattle in the barn most of the time, even the hogs staying close. The ground froze too hard to dig post holes, so work on the ropewalk stopped.

In late January the river froze over. Children scooted out on the ice, greasing the soles of their shoes so they could slide better. When he was sure that the ice would hold, Charlotte's father organized a work crew. "Perfect chance to set up that water wheel," he said. Tied together in case the ice broke, they chopped a hole in the ice eight feet from the bank. Carr peered down through the water. "Perfect, perfect," he muttered.

Some of the crew took a wagon up on the ridge and chopped down cedar trees, stripping off the limbs and leaving only the trunk. "Cypress would be better, but you work with what you've got," Carr said. Then they drove the tree trunks deep into the riverbed, brutal work in the cold and wet; the men came in shivering at lunchtime with their pants encased in ice. After ten tree trunks were driven into the river bottom, Carr had the men bind them together with heavy rope. "Now for the rocks," he said. "Biggest we can load."

For the next several days, crews took wagons into the hills, prying rocks out of the frozen ground or chiseling them from outcrops. Standing on opposite banks, the men used ropes to pull the rocks onto the ice and into the ever-growing hole. After a couple of weeks, Carr ventured out on the newly formed ice and gave the piling a violent shake in all directions. He declared it firm.

"We'll mount a keeper for the axle on top, and have ourselves a fine little wheel," he said. "Not much power but enough for this job."

One evening Charlotte found the moment to speak to Turner about Cabot and Webb's concerns, bringing the subject up without warning after dinner to see his response. "Do you think Daybreak has become less democratic lately?"

"Sure," Turner said. "Good thing, too. We'd never get anything done."

His casual reply surprised her. "Doesn't that worry you?"

"Why should it worry me? We'll get more democratic once we're self-sufficient. It's all part of the plan."

"But what if others don't see the plan? What if they want more say now, not later?"

Turner puffed a sigh. "Everybody wants perfection. Why can't they be happy with improvement?" He looked at her suspiciously. "Why? Have you been hearing something?"

"Just odd comments, that sort of thing. You know how people talk, especially the women." She felt uncomfortable concealing the names of Cabot and Webb.

"I hope you stood up for me. I need you to stand up for me on this."

"It's not an issue of standing up or not, sweetheart. It was just talk, the general mood of people. So I wanted to ask what you thought."

"Here's what I think. I think things around this community improved quite a bit when we got rid of Cantwell. So if we have some new complainers, maybe it's time to clean things up again."

"James! If I had known you were going to make such a fuss I never would have brought it up."

"Oh, I'll make a fuss all right. The last thing this community needs is another bunch of malcontents stirring up discord."

Charlotte let the conversation go. She hardly knew what she could tell the men. But she felt obligated to pass along something, so one morning after breakfast she found Cabot on the street and took him by the arm.

"Where does your work lead you today, Mr. Cabot?"

"Nowhere in particular. I thought I might go out to the barn and see if I can be of use. Wickman is supposed to be mending harness. I don't know any more about that than he does, but we can be ignorant together."

"You should let Mr. Mercadier help you when he gets back from his days in town."

Cabot smiled and blushed. "Emile helps in a supervisory capacity. He inspects everything we do and tells us to re-do about half of it."

No one was nearby, so Charlotte leaned close and said, "Stop by the house today if you can. I'd like to talk to you about that subject we talked about at Christmastime."

She could feel him grow tense at her nearness and saw the quick look of adoration in his eyes and the agony when she didn't return it. Feel for him as she might, Charlotte would not encourage him—that could only lead to things she was unprepared to deal with. Cabot nodded stiffly and went on his way.

In the early afternoon, Cabot knocked at the door. Charlotte let him in quickly, embarrassed to feel like a sneak.

"I spoke to my husband," she said quickly. "He is suspicious of those who would question the method instead of focusing on the outcome. You and George should bide your time, keep your eyes on increasing our prosperity, and not raise questions of the democratic process until later on. George was right. He is very touchy on this subject."

"But democracy is part of the outcome, not just a process," Cabot said. "If all that mattered was making money, we could have just formed a joint-stock company and been done with it."

"I'm only giving you my advice," Charlotte said. "I can't tell you what to do. But I don't see anything good coming from questioning his leadership at this moment."

"I'm not questioning his leadership. I was explaining this to Lysander a couple of days ago. Debate and examination are an essential—"

"You were discussing this with Lysander Smith?" Charlotte interrupted. "An outsider, and an odd one at that? Adam, I thought you would have better judgment."

Cabot's expression grew defensive, almost pouty. "I've gotten to know Lysander better than most, sharing a house. He's not so bad. You should give him more credit."

"Oh, for heaven's sake." She stared at him in amazement. "A couple of privileged characters from the first families of the East, that's all I see you two having in common. Even if you do like him, he's not one of us. He's a visitor. You shouldn't trust him with our private debates."

"I'm sorry. But I find him very astute."

"Astute. Right. Well. Good luck then." Charlotte opened the door, and Cabot stepped out. They kept their posture friendly, although their faces were set.

Cabot bowed and adjusted his hat. "I owe you my thanks for speaking with your husband," he said. "I do appreciate that, even though I can't agree with your opinions."

"I know." She clasped his hand. "Adam, please think before speaking. With James, with Mr. Smith, with anyone."

His face softened. "Of course, Charlotte. This community is my home. I am not about to speak foolishly and put it in danger."

She feared he already had, by talking to a man like Smith, but chose not to repeat that fear. And as if drawn by the mention of his name, Smith appeared in the street, walking past the house on his way south.

"Holding hands in the street," he teased. "My, this is a modern town."

They dropped their hands, and Cabot was about to speak, but Smith waved his hand. "Oh, that just makes you look guiltier. Cabot, I'm going to visit Brother Harp for a while. Care to join me?"

"I have work," Cabot said briskly, stepping down from the doorstone.

"Work, work, work," Smith said. "You should learn the habits of these rustics. They don't work until they have to. And sometimes not even then. Webb the Younger and I shall spend the afternoon philosophizing by the fire."

"I can imagine," Charlotte said.

"Oh yes, we'll have our dram," Smith said to her. "I respect that you are a temperance community, so I have Harp keep my stock at his house. It's forty-rod rot, but I fear he has a corner on the local market." He tipped his hat. "Off to work with you then."

Cabot drew his coat around him and headed toward the barn. Charlotte stayed in the open doorway as he left. Smith smiled his mischievous smile at her. "Just teasing, you know."

"So you say. A tone of constant irony gets wearying after a while, Mr. Smith."

"Poor Adam is too honorable for his own good. He would be better off if he unbent just a little, don't you think? Let himself down from that hook of duty he hangs himself upon?"

"But then he wouldn't be Adam."

His mocking smile broadened. "So you do love him, then."

"Mr. Smith, don't make fun of good people."

"But it's so much more enjoyable than making fun of the bad ones. The bad ones don't even notice. I'll sit there and mock Harp Webb all afternoon, and he won't even feel a sting."

"You might be surprised at what Harp Webb notices." A breeze rattled the branches of the trees, and Charlotte looked out into the February sky. "Another few weeks, and you can begin your botanical work again."

A cloud passed over Smith's face. "God, don't remind me. I don't know why I ever let that idiot Foltz persuade me to this project."

Charlotte smiled despite herself, happy to know that at least something made Smith uncomfortable. He certainly spent most of his time inflicting discomfort on everyone else.

"Seriously," Smith went on. "Why should I concern myself with the comings and goings of people out in this benighted landscape? They can all go to hell, black, white, the whole lot of forest apes. You and Cabot are the only people I can talk sense with. There's a reason people live out here on the frontier. The rest of society can't stand them. It shits them out, and they land out here in the woods and rocks."

"This is hardly the frontier, Mr. Smith," Charlotte said dryly. "If you want the frontier, you'll have to go west a few hundred more miles."

"It's frontier enough for me. Well. Time to go find Webb the Younger and drink. Then perhaps I'll see if I can get Marie Mercadier to speak to me in French. That always lifts my gloom. Quite the little printer's devil, that one."

Smith wandered off down the road, and Charlotte turned inside. Standing in the open door had chilled the house, so she fetched an armload of wood from the woodbox in back. The chill would wake Newton from his nap soon; she could hear him stirring in his bed. No point in fetching him yet. She could get in a bit of mending before he woke and perhaps chop some onions for tonight's soup.

March/May 1859

Chapter 15

The seeds for the ropemaking operation arrived in March in heavy sacks with a rank smell that repelled even the mice in the barn. "They say the Indians used to grind up this stuff for flour," George Webb said, rolling some seeds between his fingers. "Course, they say that about everything. You'd think the Indians were roaming through the woods eating the bark off trees, like beavers."

When Thursday came, the day to ride into town to fetch Emile Mercadier from his shoe shop, Marie made a show of begging to go along with Turner. "I have a new jacket for him," she said, showing a solid-looking garment of heavy brown cloth. "He will be so happy."

The morning sun was warm on their backs as they forded the river in silence. They worked the wagon up to the ridgetop, still in silence. "It is going to be one of those lucky false spring days, when everyone thinks that spring has really come," Turner said when they finally reached the top.

"Why lucky?" said Marie.

"Gives you hope. You know that spring is on the way."

"Perhaps," she said. "But I don't like the false part."

They did not speak again for a while, although the air between them was heavy with intention. And when Turner passed the Indian camp and turned the wagon down the little-used wagon track, Marie did not ask what he was doing. He took them a hundred yards into the forest and then stopped beside a plum grove. He got down and tied the horse to a tree, and when he turned around, Marie had gotten into the back of the wagon and spread out a blanket. She was lying on the blanket with her dress pulled up to her neck. Turner leaned over the side of the wagon and kissed her.

"Take everything off," he said. "I want to see your whole body."

She looked dubious but did as he asked. Turner climbed into the wagon and kneeled above her. Her nude body was pale and slender, small breasts with dimpled nipples, a fuzz of brown hair on her arms and legs.

"I'm cold," she said, so he lowered himself down and covered her with his body. "That's better," she said. He unbuttoned his trousers.

Marie did not appear to enjoy herself, at least not the way Charlotte did. She made a noise at one moment, and Turner pulled back, afraid of hurting her; but her expression was serene.

"Why are you doing this?" he said afterward.

"Because I love you. Charlotte was right. You are a silly fellow who doesn't often understand the mind of a woman."

He propped up on one elbow and pulled his coat over her body. "She said that, did she?"

"Not quite. She tries to tell me about men. She thinks I am a child who needs her advice. And when she talks about men, I think she is usually talking about you."

"So I'm the model? Or the cautionary example?"

"Maybe both." She returned his frank gaze. Under the coat, Turner could feel her hand between his legs, caressing him. "And why are you doing this?"

Turner didn't know what to say. "Because you love me. Because you let me."

Marie looked into his face and then up at the sky. "That wasn't what I was hoping for. But it will do."

"What were you hoping for?"

She waved her hand between their faces. "Never mind. It doesn't matter. A hymn to my beauty, maybe."

Turner wanted to say more to her, to comfort her with his affection. But he had no desire to be dishonest with her. He knew his motives were impure, so why be coy about it? She was young, she was fresh, she was good-looking, and they shared grand ideas together.

They did not linger. Emile would be expecting the wagon before long. But Turner was glad to have time with Marie when he did not have to look over his shoulder or listen for someone approaching. He unhitched the horse and pulled it around, and they headed toward town. Marie smoothed out her dress and sat quietly beside him in the wagon; she held his hand while they rode through the woods but released it whenever they neared a farmhouse. They talked of the next issue of *The Eagle*, of the hemp field and rope factory, of the other citizens of Daybreak.

Mercadier was surprised to see his daughter, but she was ready for him. "I finished your new coat!" she cried, hopping down from the wagon and flourishing it. Turner hurried to pick up their mail and goods. He did not meet Mercadier's eye during the ride back and thought he felt Mercadier's gaze on him a few times, but eventually decided it was his own guilty conscience at work.

Lysander Smith started his ostensible botanical expeditions as soon as the weather got warm, disappearing for longer and longer periods of time. He had been gone for two weeks in May when Turner was awakened from a sound sleep by Charlotte shaking his shoulder.

"There's a man at the door," she said. She had lit a lantern and held it up for him to find his pants. Turner wiped his face and tried to shake off the heaviness of sleep.

"Who is it?"

"I didn't open the door. He didn't say."

They tiptoed out of the bedroom, leaving Newton asleep in the trundle. Standing in the yard was Sam Hildebrand. He held his horse's reins in one hand and grasped his belt buckle with the other.

"Sorry to trouble you," he said. His narrow face was deeply shadowed in the light of the lantern. "You know a man named Smith? Says he lives here."

"Yes," Turner said. "He's been boarding here since fall."

"That's what he said." Hildebrand swung into his saddle. "You need to get yourself a mount and come with me. This Smith fella is in trouble and he asked for you. I'll wait for you down past Harp's house." He pointed south with his head.

"But can't—" Turner looked around at the night.

"Lives are at stake," Hildebrand said and rode off.

Turner threw on some boots and a shirt and went to the barn to saddle a horse. In the black of the barn's interior, he lit a lantern. The horses, sleeping in their stalls, stirred at his movements. He picked a big gray gelding and saddled it up.

Hildebrand was waiting at the narrow place where the road ran between bluffs and the river. As soon as Turner came into view, he reined his horse south again.

"What's this all about?" Turner called to him.

Hildebrand turned in his saddle as Turner rode closer. "Let's gab about this when we get farther on," he said. "Right now I want to make time."

He took off at a fast trot, breaking into a canter when the splashes of moonlight let them see the road better. Turner's gray was a strong horse, but Hildebrand's was clearly more accustomed to long, fast rides, and Turner struggled to keep up.

They followed the road for five or six miles, then Hildebrand suddenly veered off to the east into the woods.

After the first crash through the underbrush along the road, Turner found himself in open forest that was easier to ride through than he had imagined. The shade of the trees made it harder to see, though, so they had to pick their way more slowly. Turner tried to stay far enough behind Hildebrand to avoid getting whipped by limbs, but close enough to follow his path.

They reached the river. Hildebrand rode directly in, looking neither to right nor left. Turner would never have attempted a river crossing by night, but followed Hildebrand's track precisely, and sure enough, there was a trail of packed dirt that led up the bank on the other side. They climbed up a steep slope a couple of hundred feet or more before the path leveled off, following a ridge.

He lost track of how long they rode like this, working through the mottled darkness of the forest. It felt past midnight, but all Turner knew was that the night seemed to be getting darker.

They kept following the ridgeline. It seemed to Turner that they were heading generally east, but he could not tell for sure. The stars were only intermittently visible through the canopy of leaves, and he had to concentrate on keeping up.

Eventually the unseen path Hildebrand was following opened up into a trail, not quite wide enough for a wagon, but a clear trail nevertheless. Hildebrand slowed his horse to a walk and then came to a stop and looked around. He sniffed the air.

"Here's where we go down," he said.

They dropped off the ridge into a long hollow that ended, to Turner's surprise, on another road. Before Hildebrand rode out onto the road, he stopped again and listened.

"Here's the thing," he said. "Your friend Smith may already be dead, and if he is, you need to deal with that like a man and not act a fool. One killing is plenty." He urged his horse out into the road. "These men up here are going to want to ask you about him, and you'd be wise not to get caught in a lie." He reached into his saddlebag and pulled out a revolver. He checked its chambers and then put it in his belt.

They rode past the shoulder of the ridge they had just come down. To Turner's surprise, Hildebrand began to sing. As they rounded the ridge, Turner could see a bonfire in the next hollow, a hundred feet from the road. They rode into the hollow, Hildebrand still singing, and as they got closer a man stepped out of the shadows with a shotgun lowered at their chests. He wore a flour sack over his head with two rough holes cut out for his eyes.

"It's me," Hildebrand said. "That's him." The man looked at Turner without speaking but stepped out of their path.

They rode into the firelight and dismounted. Near the fire were two other men with flour sacks over their heads. One was enormously tall and fat and wore a shirt with the sleeves torn off, revealing huge fleshy arms. The other was a much smaller man who still had on his coat, despite the heat of the bonfire, and because of the coat Turner did not notice for a moment that he was missing his left arm. Behind the fire, Turner could see three horses tethered to the trees.

The one-armed man spoke to Hildebrand. "This the man?" Hildebrand nodded. The man walked up to Turner and stood uncomfortably close, his face about the level of Turner's breastbone.

"Welcome to the party," he said. "Your friend's been here for a while." He turned and walked back toward the light.

A few feet away from the fire, Lysander Smith was lying on his side on the ground, his hands tied behind his back. He struggled to lift his head as the men walked toward him. One of his eyes was bruised shut, and dried blood covered his face. Turner recognized his yellow vest, but the rest of his body was the universal color of dirt. His hair was thick with caked blood. One ear appeared to be sitting wrong on his head.

"You know this man?" said the small man. His empty coat sleeve was folded up and pinned.

"Yes," Turner said. "His name is Smith." His throat was suddenly dry and his voice didn't come out for a moment.

"That's what he said too." The man walked over to Smith and poked him with his toe. "I guess your name is Smith after all. Seemed a little too convenient for me."

Turner made a move toward Smith, but everyone reacted toward him, and he stopped. "May I?" he said to the small man, showing his handkerchief.

"Suit yourself," the man said. Turner knelt beside Smith and wiped his face. Smith's jaw was slack, and saliva trailed out of the corner of his mouth.

"You fellers have been busy," Hildebrand said.

"We rowed this boy up Salt River for a while," the one-armed man said. "Ain't that right, pal?"

"Yeah," the big man said. His voice was high-pitched and tinny. "We rowed him."

Turner put his hand under Smith's head and used some of Smith's saliva to clean out around his eyes. The look in Smith's one open eye was terrified. Turner wanted to stand up, get righteous, exercise some rhetoric, but he remembered Hildebrand's warning and held himself in check. He straightened up.

"Gentlemen," he said quietly. "What seems to be the problem?"

"What seems to be the problem," the man said, "is that your friend here is a nigger-stealer and a sodomite. Set him up, how about, pal."

The fire popped and crackled high into the black sky, and Turner's face felt hot. The big man propped Smith against a small maple tree.

"I don't know what you mean," Turner croaked.

The one-armed man glanced off into the dark at the edge of the fire. Turner followed his glance. Another man lay on the ground, bound and bloody. A black man.

"Wouldn't have caught him if it hadn't been for some of our local niggers," the man said. "Came to their owner, said there was a runaway hiding out in the woods, came to them for food, wanted to get away from a crazy white man who was wanting to hold his dick. Ain't that right, Cuffy?" He walked over and poked the runaway with his boot. The man groaned and stirred a little. He kicked him harder. "I said ain't that right?"

"Yes'r," the man said.

The small man walked back to Turner. "So are you a nigger-stealer too?"

The eye-holes of the flour sack were dark and empty. Turner looked into them anyway. "I am not," he said.

"The shit you aren't," said the man.

Turner could see no point in repeating his denial. He stood and faced the man silently.

The third man, still holding his shotgun, edged out of the firelight. "I can't breathe under this thing," he said. "I'm going to step over here and take it off for a minute. Catch my breath."

"Fuck you are," the one-armed man said, turning toward him. "Anything happens here, happens with all of us. Ain't nobody going to say, 'Oh I didn't see nothing. I wasn't there. I was off feeding the horses.' You stay right here." He turned back and spoke to Turner. "So tell me about this man Smith."

Turner tried to hold his voice steady. "He's been a paying guest at our settlement since September. He's a botanist."

"What the fuck's a botanist?"

"A man of science, he studies plants. He's looking at plants."

The big man spoke up. "That's what he said. That's what he said too."

"Oh, shut your ass and let me think," said the little man. "Of course they'd have a story cooked up."

All this time, Sam Hildebrand had been squatting at the edge of the group, twirling a leaf between his thumb and forefinger. The one-armed man turned to him.

"What do you think, Sam? Think this man's telling the truth?"

Hildebrand continued to twirl the leaf. "This ain't my concern," he said. "You asked me to fetch this feller, and I did it. Everything else is your ball of yarn."

This just seemed to make the one-armed man angrier. He stomped back to Smith. "Plant man, eh?" He shook the young tree that Smith was propped up against. "What kind of tree is this, Mister Plant Man?"

Smith arched his head back stiffly a couple of inches. "I … I can't—" He faltered. "I can't see. I can't tell." The effort of speaking opened up a crack in his lip, which began to bleed again.

"He's got little drawings in his book," the big man said.

"Yeah, and he had a nigger down on the creek bank too." The small man went over to one of the horses and brought back a looped rope. "It's a maple tree, you piece of shit. How do you fancy the idea of getting hung from a maple tree? Will that suit you?" He put the loop over Smith's head and tightened it, then tossed the other end of the rope over the nearest branch.

Turner started for the small man. The big one got between them, grabbing Turner by the shoulders and flinging him backward like a child. Turner hit the ground, gathered himself, paused in a crouch, tried to think of his next move. He had a knife in his pocket. But….

His thoughts were interrupted by the click of a revolver's hammer locking into place. All eyes went to Sam Hildebrand, who had stood up and was facing them, his revolver pointed at the ground.

"Calm down, boys," Hildebrand said. "You want to scrap, go someplace where you can charge admission for it."

The silence that followed was finally broken by the small man. "Sam's right, boys. We're here on business." He squared off toward Turner again. "Paying guest, huh?"

"That's right."

"Who paid you?"

"He did."

"Oh yeah?" The man thought for a moment. "Where's he from?"

"Philadelphia."

"And you know anything about this nigger-stealing?"

Turner did not move his gaze from the hollow eye-holes. "No. I do not."

They faced each other in silence. Finally the one-armed man turned to Hildebrand. "What do you think, Sam? Think this bastard's telling the truth?"

"I told you I ain't in this business. I fetched him, you got him."

"Well, ain't that convenient, Mister, Mister—" The man's voice sputtered and came to a halt as his attention once again settled on Hildebrand's revolver. "So you can't vouch for him?"

"I don't vouch for him nor accuse him either," Hildebrand said.

"You think he's a truthful man?"

"I got no reason to think he ain't."

The man faced Turner again. "Will you swear? Swear on the Bible that you and your people ain't got nothing to do with this man?"

"Like I said, he's our guest, and he's made himself welcome." Turner swallowed, trying to keep his throat moist. "He's never said a word about stealing slaves. And yes, I will swear."

Hildebrand interrupted again. "An oath made under threat ain't valid. Everybody knows that. You just got to take this man at his word or not."

The little man seemed to take this as a vote of confidence. "Well, since Sam here vouches for you—" He paused. "—says you're an honest man, that's good enough for me. Good enough for you boys?" The other two men muttered unintelligibly. "Just so you know, we ain't letting no Underground Railroad start up around here. You bear that in mind."

Lysander Smith's voice croaked up. "I didn't mean—"

The small man walked over to him. "Well, the Philadelphia lawyer wants to make a speech. Speak up, Nancy."

Smith looked up at him and tried to smile. "I didn't mean anyone—I didn't mean any harm."

The man punched him square in the face. "Fuck you, Nancy. This may be how you do things back in Philadelphia, but they ain't how we do things out here. We'll take this nigger back south, because he's worth money plus a reward. But you—" He picked up the end of the rope from the ground. "You are a worthless Nancy-ass piece of unnatural Eastern shit." He walked to one of the horses and whipped the rope around its saddle horn several times. "And we're going to hoist you up."

The man took the horse's reins and led it forward a few feet. The rope lost its slack almost immediately, pulling Smith to his feet. The loop around his neck tightened. His cheeks bulged, and he flailed from side to side, trying to find air.

"Please!" Turner cried. "This man's worth something. He comes from a wealthy family. I'm sure they'd pay—"

"God's shit!" said the one-armed man. "What do you think we are, kidnappers?"

Turner turned to the two other flour sacks. "Please! You can't kill this man." The men shuffled their feet.

The one-armed man spoke up loudly. "We are deputized to do whatever it takes to find and return runaways. And I say this is what it takes."

He gave the horse's reins another jerk, pulling it forward a couple of feet. The little maple tree swayed downward under the extra weight of Lysander Smith being lifted off the ground. His feet dangled in the air, kicking wildly.

"If he tries to help his friend, shoot him," the one-armed man said to the man with the shotgun.

"You heard him, mister," the man said to Turner in a weak voice. He waved the shotgun in Turner's direction.

Turner thought about testing the man's resolve, but the big man stepped toward him too and picked up an axe handle from the ground. The end was matted with blood and hair. "If he don't stop you, I will," he said.

Smith thrashed wildly, and a trickle of blood ran from his nose. The young maple tree from which he was dangling bent further; it was too small to support a man's weight. Smith's feet touched the ground. Straining against the rope that bound his hands, he balanced on his toes.

"Shit," the one-armed man said. "Hold his feet up, pal."

The big man looked nervously at the struggling man. "I ain't holding nobody's feet."

166

The tree drooped lower. "Goddamit, one of you bastards hold up his feet!" He pulled the horse another few feet, and Smith lifted off the ground again. The tree swayed under the struggle, and for a moment Turner thought the limb might break. Smith's face was purple in the firelight. His toes scraped the ground. He tried to bounce up and down to give himself some slack in the rope.

"You should have tied his feet," said the man with the shotgun.

"Just take the fucker's fucking feet and hold them off the ground!" said the one-armed man. "This won't take more than another couple of minutes."

"That's bad luck," said the big man.

"Bad luck! I'll make you think bad luck, you waste of shit."

"Oh you will, will you? I'd like to see that!" Smith was still thrashing and it seemed to Turner that he might be getting one of his hands loose.

Sam Hildebrand stood up abruptly. "Jesus Christ Almighty," he said. He walked up to Smith, put his pistol to the base of his skull, and pulled the trigger.

The roar of the pistol shot seemed to have made them all deaf and mute. All Turner could hear was its echoes in his ears. Everyone stood silent. Smith's body twitched and trembled a few times and then hung still.

Hildebrand put his revolver in his belt and walked to his horse. "You can let him down now, you ninny," he said. The little man backed up the horse, letting Smith's body sink to the ground.

Hildebrand mounted up. "You boys better get the hell out of here. That shot might wake somebody. Don't forget your nigger." He looked at Turner. "He's all yours now."

He rode off into the dark, leaving the men in their flour-sack masks silent. Then in a frenzy of activity, they gathered themselves and disappeared, tossing the runaway slave over the neck of one of their horses. Turner could hear them cursing and arguing as they rode away.

Turner untied Smith's hands and carried his limp body away from the fire. At the base of a tree, he found Smith's coat and pocketbooks. His horse shied away when he tried to lift the man's body over its neck, but after a couple of attempts he managed to heave it up. He led the horse to the road and climbed into the saddle.

The road was unrecognizable to him in the dark, and even if it had been daylight he wouldn't have known it anyway. It seemed to run east and west, but he had no idea where from or to. He went back the way he came, and when he saw the knocked-down brush where he and Hildebrand had come through, turned the horse into the woods again.

He gave his horse a loose rein, and it worked its way up the slope until soon they were back on the ridgetop. Turner let the horse find its way, urging it forward whenever it wanted to stop, and after a while he began to think it knew its way home.

Turner's mind was numb. He sensed danger lurking behind him, as if the murderers might change their minds and pursue him as well, but he didn't hasten home. Logic told him that they had been just as shocked and scattered by the sudden end to Smith's life as he had, but logic was not what made him plod through the dimness. It was the overwhelming sense of failure, the recognition that he had led the colony into a dangerous place with no clear way out. He felt a deep foreboding that the limp body bouncing across the horse's neck was simply the first of many, and that he should have known their adventure would come to this. What had he been thinking, taking dozens of bookworms into the woods? They would be lucky if the place didn't kill them all.

Daylight seeped into the air imperceptibly until at one moment Turner noticed that he could make out the bark on the trees. And sure enough, by full dawn his horse had led him to the river crossing.

Turner stopped to let the horse drink and took Smith's body down. He dipped his handkerchief in the river to bathe his face. The body was still warm, though cooling fast, and the caked blood came off with a little wiping. The handkerchief wasn't much good on his hair, though, and Turner ended up dipping the back of Smith's head into the river to wash out the blood. It trailed downstream, a pink tendril that disappeared into the common flow within a few yards. Blood lost in the water, a life lost in the night. Everything vanishing downstream. He smoothed out the hair as best he could, but it still looked like a stringy knot.

An hour later he was at Daybreak. He had tied Smith's coat around his head to try to make less of a spectacle, but with the man's arms and legs dangling halfway to the ground on each side, it was still a gruesome load to bring home.

As he passed the Webbs' house, Harp came out onto his porch. "Told him not to drink that shit from downriver," he said. Turner looked up at him silently and kept riding.

A dozen or more people had gathered around Turner's door, alerted no doubt by Charlotte, and watched as he arrived. George Webb and a couple of others helped him take Smith from the horse and carry him inside.

"Did he drown?" someone said. "His head's all wet."

But when they laid him on the table, face up, and everyone could see the burnt-looking bruise across Smith's neck and the wound in the back of his head, no one asked any questions for a moment. Charlotte picked up Newton and took him into the back. Adam Cabot drew in a sharp breath and left the room.

Smith's hair had fallen across his face. Webb lifted it with his thumb and examined the marks of the beating. "How many were there?" he said.

Turner didn't feel like talking quite yet. "Three," he said.

"Hildebrand?"

"Sam wasn't one of the three. Three plus Sam is what I meant."

More people arrived as the news spread. Turner knew he should go out and say something to them, but was too tired. He didn't know what he would say anyway. Go home before it's too late, perhaps. He went into the back room and lay on the bed, where Charlotte was curled up with Newton playing count-the-toes. He kicked off his boots and rolled over on his side, embracing her. Newton squirmed between them with delight.

"You're home," she said. "It's all right."

"No, it's not."

She said nothing, simply placed her arm over his head and drew him to her.

There was a quiet knock at the bedroom door.

"Adam Cabot's saddled up a horse," a voice said.

Turner rolled onto his back and didn't move any further. Let him go if he wanted to play hero. He wouldn't even know which way to ride. Who knows, maybe Cabot knew Smith's little secrets himself. At this moment he didn't care.

"I'll go see," Charlotte said.

He heard her voice outside the window, hailing Cabot as he rode down from the barn. "Adam, where are you going?" she called.

"Fredericktown," Cabot said.

"What on earth for?"

There was a pause and a rustling. "To fetch the sheriff. Charlotte, we are not outside the boundaries of civilization here."

"Of course. Godspeed." The sound of a horse riding off.

Turner closed his eyes. The sheriff. Good luck. All he wanted to do was let the night's events vanish for a while. He kept his eyes closed as he heard Charlotte come into the room and take Newton away, leaving through the back door and shutting it behind herself quietly. The image of Smith's dangling body and kicking feet lingered in his mind. Then blackness swept over him, and he was asleep.

May / August 1859

Chapter 16

Cabot reached Fredericktown shortly after noon and found Sheriff Willingham at his home taking a nap. He waited on the porch until Willingham came to the door, scratching himself. "There's been a murder out at Daybreak," he said.

Willingham walked to his stable and saddled a horse without a word. "Do you want to hear what happened?" Cabot said.

"Not yet," Willingham said over his shoulder. "There's water for your horse yonder, and the missus will give you coffee if you want it."

Cabot let his horse water, but skipped the coffee as Willingham led his mount outside to a stump from which he climbed into the saddle.

"You're not taking a weapon?" Cabot asked as he rode up beside him.

"Is somebody out there going to try to shoot me?"

"Of course not."

"All right then. If I have to chase a man, I can always borry a gun, or come back here to load up gear. No point in weighing myself down."

They arrived in the colony late that afternoon, with Cabot riding ahead pushing the pace, and went straight to the Turners' house. Willingham spit out his chaw before he came through the door. Turner was sitting in a chair in the corner, and a group of women had gathered, awaiting permission to wash Smith's body. "Ladies, y'all need to clear out while I talk to this man," Willingham said to the women. He pulled some chairs away from the table into the center of the room and leaned over the body of Lysander Smith.

"They done quite a job on him," he said.

"The big one had an axe handle," Turner said, his voice flat.

"That'll do the trick," Willingham said.

Turner repeated the story of the night before. No one interrupted. When he reached the part about the black man and the killers' accusation of sexual misadventure, Cabot could feel the air in the room grow tense. He walked to the table and looked over Willingham's shoulder into the face of the dead man, its bruises changing from red to a purplish gray. So many secrets had been concealed behind that face. Could one man ever truly know another? Or were the feelings of another always dark? He considered himself and the secrets he concealed, and supposed it was just as well that the path into the labyrinth of a man's heart was so hard to find.

"So there was four of them," Willingham said at the end. "Hildebrand and the three fellas with sacks."

"You know this Hildebrand?" Webb asked.

"Oh yeah," Willingham said. "Ain't nobody in the law who don't."

"I knew his daddy," Webb said. "And I remember him a little. His daddy was a little rough around the edges."

"He didn't seem like part of the group," Turner said. "But Hildebrand was the one who ended up killing him." His voice was weary. He swayed to his feet. "If you'll excuse me, I'm going to bed."

Turner stumbled into the back room, shutting the door behind him. The men stood in silence around the corpse.

"Seems to me like old Sammy kinda done this boy a favor," Willingham said after a while.

"Are you going to bring him in?" Webb said. "To question if nothing else. Obviously he knows at least one of these people."

Willingham cleared his throat. "Let me spell it out for you," he said. "Number one, this fella ain't easy to find. He stays out of town, and I ain't going to waste a lot of time chasing after him in the country. Number two, your man here crossed the river, rode south a ways, and picked up another road. That might have put him out of my jurisdiction, so I'll write the sheriff down in Wayne and see if he knows anything."

"How many one-armed men are there around here, for God's sake?" Webb said. "Harley, a man's been killed here!"

Willingham's voice was calm, but an irritated edge crept in. "Number three. This fella was, we all agree, in the act of stealing a nigger from somewhere down south, and to hear what these flour sack fellas said, was also performing some kinda unnatural act on him. How much chance that a jury would convict some-body of killing him? Lots of folks would just say tough luck, so long. I'll pursue this, but don't get your hopes up."

Cabot turned away. Smith had been such a small man; it was easy to imag-ine a horse lifting him off the ground, harder to imagine his weight breaking down a tree.

"George, can you gather up six men?" Willingham said. "I need a coroner's jury to pronounce cause of death."

Charlotte had stepped outside with the other women while the sheriff conducted his examination, quietly gathering rags and drawing pails of water. When the men came out, she exchanged a look with Willingham, who nodded, tight-lipped. They stepped inside in silence. Charlotte walked over to Smith and laid her hand on his chest.

Of course he was an idler and a pest. No one could dispute that. His yellow vest was stained and filthy; she tried to smooth out some of its wrinkles, but they were too deep. She wrung out a rag and wiped his face.

"We could move him to his cabin and do it there," Frances Wickman said quietly, moving up beside her. "Messy job."

"No, this is all right," Charlotte said. "This table and floor will need scrubbed anyway."

Mrs. Wickman removed his shoes and carried them out the back while oth-ers started in on the body, covering his man parts with a sheet for modesty's sake while washing away the dirt and blood. Charlotte, at the head of the table, did the best she could with Smith's face and hair, although the great hole behind his ear could not be fully hidden no matter how she combed.

Sheriff Willingham startled her by silently appearing at her side, catlike, and plopping a friendly hand on her shoulder. "I'm sorry to have disturbed your home like this, ma'am," he said. "This man, friend of yours?"

"Of sorts. More guest than friend. But yes, he was a sympathetic young man at times, though difficult at others."

The sheriff nodded solemnly. "Ain't we all. You didn't have any idea he was acting contrary to the laws, did you?"

Color rose in Charlotte's cheeks. "Mr. Willingham! It is not my place to tell you how to do your job, but we all heard quite clearly who shot Mr. Smith. It is he who you should be investigating, not Lysander Smith."

"All right, all right, I heard that already," said Willingham, backing away. "Just trying to get the full story. Coroner's jury has finished up, so I'm releasing the body to you. He have any family around?"

"Philadelphia is all I know about. We'll bury him here."

"If you want to have a likeness made, there's a man in town's set up a shop."

Charlotte contemplated Smith's ravaged face. "No. I imagine they have better images of him already."

Turner slept through the rest of the afternoon, dinnertime, and into the late evening. At some point in the night Charlotte felt him leave the bed. She followed him; he was sitting in the doorway, staring out into the night. She squeezed into the doorframe with him, her arm over his shoulder.

"Right before my eyes," he said.

She could think of nothing to say to him in return.

They buried Smith in the Daybreak cemetery, a few yards up the hill from the Cameron boy. Harp Webb showed up dressed in a clean white cotton shirt and some new work pants, Daybreak made, bought from Grindstaff's store. He even took off his hat, revealing a bald spot on top of his head surrounded by the bright ruff of his yellow hair. Turner gave Smith a graveside eulogy, somewhat lackluster and disjointed, but Charlotte supposed it was the best he could muster under the circumstances. He didn't mention the slave-stealing, although of course everyone had heard the story by then.

Charlotte spoke to Harp afterward as the group dispersed. "You surprised me. Thanks for coming."

Harp fixed his hat over his head and squinted into the distance. "Little skunk was a good cash customer. I'm going to miss him. Liked to sit and talk too. Don't know who I'll have around to talk to now. That boy could tell more crazy stuff in one night than most people could in a lifetime." He smiled, his teeth nearly the same color as his hair. "I ain't been up here in a while. Remember that time I run into you up here?"

Charlotte was in no mood to get friendly with him. Something of that feeling must have shown on her face, for an ugly look suddenly came over him and he turned to walk away. But then he walked back to her. "You want to know some things, Mrs. High-and-Mighty?"

"I'm sure you're about to tell me, whether I want to know them or not."

"Oh, I can tell you things. No doubt about that. Don't think they'd matter to you. Seeing as how you know everything already."

Harp always seemed to find her weak spots. Charlotte folded her arms and waited for him to speak.

"Ever wonder what people think about this place? People out and around?"

"No, I can't say I ever have."

"More's the pity. You should stop and think about that some time. You've got neighbors, you know. You want to be citizens of the world, but you're living here and now."

"All right," Charlotte said. "Tell me about my neighbors." She met his gaze, trying not to look hostile.

"Your neighbors don't think you'll make it another year," Harp said. "We talk about you all and your big ideas. Everybody pitching in for the common good. Lots of big talk, very pretty ideas. Hell, you all haven't been through a bad year yet. See how much everybody pulls together when it don't rain for a couple of months, or when we get a hard winter and there ain't enough food to go around. Most people I know, they grew up here or came here young. They ain't just playing farmer. They know it's devil take the hindmost in this world, and if you want something you better not count on anybody but yourself. We are born alone, and we scratch and scrap alone." Charlotte's face burned and she started to make an angry retort, but stopped herself. It would only give him satisfaction.

"A lot of people think I ought to have took you to law," he went on. "'Cause of my daddy splitting up his land and all, giving you people half. But if I wait a couple of years, you folks will give up and move on, go play something else. I could say more if I wanted, but I don't care to."

"I don't care to hear it anyway."

"Fine with me. I got whiskey to sell."

"I'll tell you something, though. This settlement is a good place, with people trying to make the world better. The devil can't get the hindmost if there aren't any hindmost."

"Pretty words. You can say all you want, but the world is what it is. Bunch of fools, your man running around the country giving speeches and that Cabot taking a bath every day and this one—" He gestured back toward the graveyard. "This one drawing his pretty pictures of plants and trying to steal slaves and God knows what else. It's not mine to speak ill of the dead, but if you want to know what the neighbors are thinking, most of your neighbors think he got what he deserved."

"Do you think that?"

"I got no opinion. I don't have nothing to do with slaves, buy, sell, nor catch. Too much risk for the reward, if you ask me. I'm just saying."

"It's all about advantage, isn't it? Taking the advantage, holding the advantage."

"Yes, ma'am, it is. I didn't make this world, I'm just living in it. You folks can have all the meetings you want and vote to do this and do that, but in the end, you're living in the same world I am. And if you haven't took advantage, you'll find out that somebody has took advantage of you."

By this point they were the only two people left at the cemetery. Turner had strolled part of the way down the hillside and was waiting for her. Harp touched his hat and walked away through the fields toward his house.

"Everything all right?" Turner said when she joined him.

Charlotte's lips were set. "I hate that man."

They walked the rest of the way home in silence. There was to be a meal in the Temple of Community, as after every burial, but Charlotte didn't want to go there just yet. Apparently Turner didn't either. He sat down at the table, his eyes focused on nothing.

They had spoken very little since yesterday. Charlotte figured she wouldn't rush him into conversation. What was there to say about it anyway? In an inside pocket of Smith's coat they had found a little sketchbook, with drawings of plants in about half the pages. She leafed through it as they sat; the pictures were careful, spidery pen-and-ink sketches, well done, but with odd labels: "large leaves," "near Piggott," "tree."

"I don't think he would have fooled anybody," she said.

Turner shrugged. "I should never have let him come," he said after a moment. "I knew he was a lost man the first time I saw him."

"This man Foltz should be ashamed of himself," Charlotte said. "Sending a boy out here to play spy. Plotting imaginary escape routes for imaginary slaves. He's the one who shouldn't have let him come, not you."

Turner shrugged again. "Maybe so."

Something about his apathetic tone irritated her. He was probably right, he shouldn't have brought Smith here, but that didn't make any difference now. No point in moping. If he wasn't going to be angry, she wasn't going to be angry for him.

Charlotte picked Newton up abruptly. "Well, let's head to the Temple," she said.

"You go on," Turner said. "I'll be along directly."

Charlotte left without answering further and started walking toward the Temple. She hated feeling this judgmental, but it was hard to resist. Turner and his big plan had gotten Smith killed, and now he was feeling guilty about it. Well, it was a little late for second thoughts.

Newton was struggling on her hip as she walked, probably wanted to nurse again. He could just wait. Cabot and Webb would no doubt want to talk to her soon and carry on some more about her husband's inadequacies, and they could wait too. Who had made her the dumping ground for everyone's opinions? Even Smith had unburdened himself on her.

Newton started to cry and reached for her breast. "Need, need, need," she said, smacking his hand away. That only made him cry louder. She sat on the ground in the shade of a tree and held him on her knees at arm's length. His face was pinched in unhappiness, but he stopped crying for a moment as they regarded each other. He sniffled.

"No," she said, "I'm not angry at you. I'm not angry at him either. I'm angry at the whole human race." She opened her blouse and let him nurse.

Late spring turned into summer, and the whole colony stayed somber after Smith's killing. As the news spread that he had been caught stealing a slave, a further pall came over them; no one went so far as to say he deserved his hanging, but there were always sideways looks whenever his name came up. Turner wrote to Hiram Foltz, sending Smith's belongings back, and was surprised when Foltz wrote back asking for a refund on the unused part of Smith's room and board. "I guess that's how he got to be a wealthy man," Turner said. "If he wants his money back, he can come and get it." Cabot, bundling up Smith's things, brought out a packet of papers that Smith had entrusted to him—a series of detailed maps of the Bootheel, northeast Arkansas, and even Tennessee and northern Mississippi, with roads, plantations, river crossings, and landmarks all noted—and sent it to Foltz. "He never wrote anything down until he got back here," Cabot said. "I told you he wasn't as foolish as everyone thought." Neither Charlotte nor Turner could work up the nerve to ask him how much he knew about the other secret parts of Smith's life, afraid of what they might find out.

Frances Wickman grew larger, and larger still, and even larger, and by June it was clear that she was carrying twins. She stayed in her chair most of the summer, fanning herself, uncomfortable, her feet planted flat as if she were on an unsteady boat. Charlotte visited her in the evenings. "This twin business is not a good thing," Mrs. Wickman said gloomily. "One baby is hard enough, but two? I'm too old for this nonsense." She pulled Charlotte's hand to her belly. Charlotte could feel the live things inside, bumping aimlessly. "If something happens to me during all this . . . " She raised her hand to quiet Charlotte's protestations. "I'm in no mood for silly assurances, missy. If something happens to me, I want you to raise these babies, at least until the Mister finds a new wife, if ever."

"Of course I will."

"Speaking of babies—" Mrs. Wickman eyed her cautiously. "I'm surprised young Newton hasn't had himself a little brother or sister yet."

Charlotte blushed. "It just hasn't happened, I guess. And since Mr. Smith was killed, Turner has, I don't know . . . ."

"Not been attentive? Honey, that's easy to see. You're not the only thing he's neglecting, either. The meetings lately have been a disgrace, people all talking at once, nobody making plans."

"You're right. I know you're right."

"It's not my place to say more. But your Mister should wake up."

The hemp field grew in dense profusion, so thick that even a child couldn't walk through it; as the weather grew hot and dry, the hemp only seemed to thrive. The same was not true for the corn. Its leaves twisted and frayed at the tips, and the ears seemed alarmingly small. No afternoon thunderstorms came to relieve the dry days. The ground grew hard, and sumacs and sassafras turned color early, their bright red-orange spattering against the dull green backdrop of the forest's edge. The mechanical reaper couldn't handle the thick stalks of the hemp, so they had to cut and shock it by hand, miserable work in the merciless sun.

Turner seemed to be sleepwalking through the days. He made no plans to lecture and even gave up his Sunday afternoon talks in the Temple. As the months passed, it became clear that Sheriff Willingham was going to do nothing about the killing, either from fear of Hildebrand or simple lack of interest. Only Cabot and Emile Mercadier refused to let go of the injustice. Cabot wrote to Governor Stewart, and after more than a month he received a strange, rambling reply that promised everything in general and nothing in particular. "We need to get a new man to run for sheriff," Cabot said at the weekly meeting.

"We've got a bloc of twenty votes we could swing his way. George, anyone you would suggest?"

"I retired from politics quite a while ago," Webb replied, uneasy. "Besides, I don't believe Daybreak should get involved with politics. We should be above politics."

"I used to believe that too," Cabot said. "But by God, where else do you go when the law won't operate? I've half a mind to run myself."

"Watch your language, sir," said another of the men. "There are ladies present." Cabot blushed and sat down.

Mrs. Wickman's day came on an August afternoon. The granny woman from French Mills was fetched, bearing a bag of herbs and remedies. She boiled water on the stove and brewed a tincture.

"What is it?" Charlotte asked.

"Evening primrose," the woman said. "And this and that. Brings the labor on stronger and quicker."

Frances was already sweating with the pain. "Remember what you promised," she said, gripping Charlotte's hand. The lowermost of the babies seemed to be turned wrong; the granny woman probed and pushed, looking for a way to deliver the baby. It was nearly midnight when the first one, a girl, emerged, with the next one soon after. "Both girls," said the midwife.

"Mister was hoping for at least one boy," Frances whispered.

"He don't have no say in the matter," the granny woman said. "That's up to the Lord."

"Sarah," Mrs. Wickman croaked through dry lips. "Sarah and Penelope. Tell the Mister that's their names."

Charlotte stayed until sunrise. Mrs. Wickman was weak and drenched in sweat. She had lost a good deal of blood, and she fell asleep as soon as they got her cleaned up and laid onto her pillows. Mr. Wickman had gone to Cabot's spare bed—Lysander Smith's former bed—to sleep.

She returned home to find young Newton in bed with his father, curled up against his side in a tight knot of knees and elbows. Turner was awake and smiled at her as she entered, but did not move, letting Newton sleep a little longer. Charlotte changed into her nightdress and curled up with them.

"Well?" Turner whispered.

"They all made it through," she whispered back. "We'll see in the morning. Frances seems in good shape, considering what she's endured. Both the babies are alive. One is stronger than the other."

"Boys or girls?"

"Both girls. Sarah and Penelope."

Turner chuckled quietly. "Penelope. Now there's a name."

"She seemed quite certain."

"Penelope it is, then."

They lay in the growing light. "New life," Charlotte murmured after a while.

He raised up on one elbow. "Is that supposed to mean something?"

Charlotte was too tired to hide her feelings. "Everything means something, don't you think?"

"What does it mean, then?" His voice was rising, and she put her finger to his lips. She leaned close to his ear.

"People are born and people die," she said. "You can't always control or predict that. Out there, people are waiting for you to direct them. It's time for you to stop thinking about the things you can't change and start thinking about the things you can."

Her finger was still pressed against his lips.

"Daybreak is the child of your brain," she went on. "It's time for you to decide whether you want it to keep going, because right now it's sliding out from under you."

She rose up from the bed and walked outside. Still in her nightdress and barefoot, she walked down the road past Webb's house. She reached the path to Adam's meditation rock and walked through the brush, stepping carefully among the weeds.

No one was there. Had she been hoping to find Adam? She was too tired to face the question. Instead, she stepped onto the rock and stood at the water's edge, listening to the grinding of the cicadas and the songs of the morning birds.

The rock was slippery underwater and she gripped it with her toes. First ankle deep, then knee deep. The current pulled gently at her. It was not especially swift in this spot, but there was a slight tug. And when the water reached her thighs, it felt stronger, more insistent. But she could maintain her balance.

Her cotton nightdress was heavy with water. She felt farther out with her toes. The rock seemed to slope endlessly into the river.

When the water reached her breasts, she stood motionless. Little eddies swirled out from her. She held out her arms, straight from her sides, parallel with the surface of the river.

One more step and her head was under, and now the current was almost too strong. She leaned against it, fighting to regain her balance.

Underwater there was no sound but the rush of the river in her ears, or perhaps it was the sound of her own body, the blood rushing through her veins, the beat of her heart, the simple sounds of being alive that were usually drowned out by the echoing rattle of the world. She couldn't hold her breath for long, so she stepped back, her hair dripping. Then she took a deep breath and stepped in again, holding herself under for as long as she could before backing up again.

Charlotte wiped her eyes and remained in the water with only her head and neck showing. She watched the trees across the river as the sun began to peek through them.

After a few minutes she began to feel slightly ridiculous and backed out of the river the same way she went in. But it was all right. She was soaked and dripping but felt better somehow. She sat on the rock and let the early morning sun warm her. When the nightdress had dried out a little, she walked up the dusty road back to the house.

September 1859

Chapter 17

In late September they spread the shocks of hemp on the ground. George Webb showed them how to lay the stalks in even rows so the dew and frost would soften the outer shell and make the inner fibers pull away. After Charlotte's scolding, Turner tried to act more like the leader of the colony again, but the murder of Smith had sapped him of the urge. Colony politics and projects bored him. He found himself daydreaming of Marie Mercadier's soft young body and scheming ways to get her away from the village so he could experience its pleasures, schemes which rarely succeeded. There was always work, the never-ending work of crops, livestock, and simple upkeep of the colony, and in the rare occasions without work, there was someone else around. But they managed, now and then, to escape, and in those moments nothing else mattered. Turner told himself his sensual pursuits were for relief from the pressures of leadership, but in his heart knew this was a mere excuse. He was adrift but he liked the sensation of drifting.

And Newton Carr put his water wheel into place. At the moment there was nothing for the wheel to run, so they let the shaft rotate freely in its keeper; when the time came for it to turn the ropejack, they would engage the gears. Carr and Turner stood on the bank admiring the wheel as it rotated slowly in the river, each paddle dipping into the water ever so slightly.

"Not enough current here to run much of a machine," Carr said. He sounded disappointed. "Still, I'd like to think of a use for it for during the months when we're not making rope."

Turner watched the wheel turn lazily in the river. The paddles were about a

Steve Wiegenstein

foot square. He had imagined them bigger, but Carr had said they needed to be lightweight or else the whole thing wouldn't turn. Even so….

"Maybe we could use it to lift water out of the river," Turner said. "Put some little buckets on each paddle with a trough up at the top, something to tip the water into the trough, then run it out toward the fields."

"Never work," said a voice from the road behind them. "Ain't got enough elevation. Best you could do is dump water up here by the ditch, and you'd still have to carry it the rest of the way."

They turned to see who was offering the advice. Standing in the road was a young man, fifteen or so, small and wiry, his clothes ragged, wearing a battered hat that looked two sizes too large, but with such a rakish air that it seemed almost stylish. He grinned, a broad smile that verged on a smirk, and touched his brim.

Something about his features seemed familiar to Turner. He squinted up through the underbrush.

"You know me, Mr. Turner?" the young man said. Then it came to him.

"Charley Pettibone!" Turner said. "You've grown up."

They clambered up the bank to the road, where Turner introduced Charley to his father-in-law. Carr surveyed the water wheel from the vantage point of the road. "I believe you're right, son," he said. "More of a slope here than you would think."

"Yessir, I've got a good eye for such."

"How's your father?" Turner asked.

"Dead, sir, I'm sorry to say," Charley said. He added "sir" so automatically to his words that it came out "deadsir."

"I'm sorry to hear about your father," Turner said. "He was a good man."

"Got run over by a steamboat, is what happened," Charley said. "We was tied up in the big river south of where the Arkansas comes in, going to cross over the next day to pick up a load at Rosedale. Steamboat come along in the night, hugging the bank real close on account of the low water, being summer and all."

"Good heavens, when did all this happen?"

"Two months ago. He shoulda seen us. It was night and all, but they had lanterns, I seen 'em. We were sleeping on the boat, and I felt the bow wake push us up against the bank. I woke up fast, let me tell you. Grabbed me a tree branch and hung on. And when it passed, their wheel sucked our boat right under. I hollered at Daddy, but he was a heavier sleeper than me. And the steamboat just

182

went on by. Some feller at the rail just hollered, 'Can't stop! Can't stop!' And boom, just like that they were around the bend. I called out and called out, but I never got no answer. Found me a fork in the tree branch to sit on till morning and by then there wasn't nothing to see."

"You should have reported this," Carr said.

"Wellsir, that ain't so easy. And no steamboat captain is going to go to the sheriff or whatnot when he gets down to New Orleans and say, 'Oh by the way, I think I run over a feller back up the river a ways.'"

"So what have you been doing since then?" Turner said.

"Working my way aroundsir, just doing what I can find. All I got is right here." He lifted up a canvas sack that was hung over his shoulder by a piece of string. "I'm traveling kinda light right now."

"You have any family?"

"Nosir, not a one."

"So where are you headed?"

"Wellsir," Charley said, gazing up at the sky. "In point of fact, I was headed here."

"Were you now?" Turner said. "Do tell."

"It's like this," he said. "Morning comes, and I climb down out of my tree, fish around in the river and on the bank for what I can find, which ain't much. Can't find my daddy nowhere, thought he might have got hung up in the brush downstream maybe, but no such luck. I work my way through the swamps and finally get to a plantation, and the lady there gives me food and such. A few days go by, and the master rides me out to the main road in his buggy. He drops me off at the junction with a big sack of food, and he says, 'Up the road is Pine Bluff, and down the road is Natchez. Take your pick.' He drives off, and I stand there for a while. I get to thinking about everything you told us while we were on the boat, all about your town you're starting up, new way of living, so on and so forth. And I think, all right then, up the road it is. And here I am."

"But Charley," Turner said. "You have no family. How will you live? What will you do?"

Charley blushed but looked up again, as if studying the clouds. "Wellsir, I was kindly hoping that you might take me in," he said at last.

The words "Of course, dear boy!" were about to burst from Turner's lips. But he held back. Perhaps it was time to take people's advice and think before acting. Instead, he said, "That will take a vote of the community. In the meantime, let's get you some food."

At his house, he introduced the boy to Charlotte and listened as he retold his story. "And where have you been sleeping?" she asked him as she hurriedly stirred up a new pan of hoe cakes.

"Barns, mostly, ma'am. Corn cribs. Couple of times people have let me sleep in their house."

"Well, we shall have no more of that," she said. "You can stay here as long as you like." She looked over at Turner. "Right?"

"Certainly."

"We'll make you a pallet here on the floor. Or perhaps you can sleep at Adam's house." She frowned. "No, that might not be a good idea. Adam has been feeling rather put-upon lately. We shouldn't be volunteering him for things. You'll stay here."

"Yesm," said Charley, stuffing down hoe cakes as soon as they came off the skillet.

"And then at meeting this week, we shall present Charley's case to the community, don't you think?"

"My thoughts exactly," Turner said. Or perhaps not entirely exactly— he had assumed that they would board him with Cabot. All right, so Cabot was feeling skittery these days. Who wasn't? And all that "Adam" this and "Adam" that didn't feel quite seemly to him. It was over-familiar. A moment of jealous speculation passed through his mind, but he quickly discarded it as a silly notion. Charlotte and Adam were the souls of probity.

Of course, so was he.

Charlotte brought Charley Pettibone to meet Cabot before the community meeting, cleaned up and in a borrowed pair of Turner's trousers. When Charley stepped inside and took off his wretched hat, he revealed a wad of curly brown hair that appeared never to have known a comb.

"Your bed's over there," Cabot said, gesturing to a cot at one side of the room. "Hope you have better luck than the last man who slept in it."

"What happened to him?"

"Beaten, hung, shot by some of your fine local citizens."

Charlotte interrupted. She sensed skepticism, even irritation, in Cabot at this flat-faced Southern boy, attitudes that he was trying to hide. Jealousy of the attention she was paying to him, she supposed, with a shiver of satisfaction that she could still incite jealousy in a man, even one she had so firmly set aside. "Charley doesn't need to hear all that right now."

"It's all right, ma'am," Charley said. "It's a hard world, I know that."

"A hard world indeed," Cabot said. "Well, we'd better get going. Can't keep the people waiting."

Charley excused himself, leaving the two of them standing in the front room of the house, in a silence that suddenly became awkward.

"You're not leaving," Cabot said.

"No," she said. "Not yet."

Cabot glanced nervously at the windows, but Charlotte already knew that the oilcloth that covered them only let in light, not sight. "Come over here," she said.

He crossed the room, and Charlotte took him by the shoulders. "I haven't had the chance to tell you that I'm sorry for the loss of Mr. Smith. I know you and he were friends."

Cabot wrapped his arms around her, and for a long time they simply stood there, not moving, barely even breathing. Charlotte could feel his shoulders slump. He inhaled deeply. And then he was crying, his chest heaving, gasping in great gulps.

"He was a good man," he choked out between sobs. "I know he troubled us all with his sharp tongue and his odd ways, but God knows he didn't deserve to die for it in a strange place, with none to comfort him. I know how he felt, alone among his enemies, a rope around his neck. There's no greater fear. No greater sense of the cruelty of the world."

He turned away from her, wiping the tears from his face. "I'm sorry," he said. "I shouldn't keep you. They'll miss us at the meeting."

"No, they won't. Not for a while. And I don't care."

They embraced again, and this time there was something different in it. Charlotte knew the feelings between them had not gone away, would never go away.

She lifted her face to his.

His kisses were hungry and mad, wild kisses that covered her lips and neck even as he smeared her face with his tears. In seconds they had gone from sympathy to passion, their bodies binding tighter until she could feel every inch of his flesh pressed against her from shoulder to knee.

Even with no lamp lit in the fading autumn twilight, the room seemed too bright. She closed her eyes. That was better. She unbuttoned his shirt and pressed her palm against his chest, feeling it rise and fall beneath her hand.

With no sense of conscious motion she found herself sitting on the edge of Lysander Smith's cot, Cabot kneeling on the floor between her legs, and her hands embracing his bare sides beneath his shirt. Their kisses deepened and turned slower and more forceful. And then there it was—his hand, both his hands—under her dress, caressing the back of her knees and then moving up, caressing the underside of her thighs, touching her in places where only one man had touched her before.

She needed to be closer. She needed to have nothing between them. Her fingers touched along the ridges of his spine.

As she leaned into him, the cot tipped over with a crash and Charlotte fell forward, knocking Cabot onto his back on the floor. Her eyes popped open as she tumbled onto him, and the ridiculousness of their posture—Cabot flat on the floor, Charlotte above him with her legs straddling his torso, like a wrestler about to make a pin—made her laugh. She leaned down and kissed him again. Their eyes locked.

"This is madness," he said.

"Yes," she said softly.

Charlotte climbed off him then, turning her back as he buttoned his shirt and smoothed his hair. Cabot righted the bed with an embarrassed air and gestured toward the Temple, where they knew the community had begun to gather.

"I need to—" he said.

"Yes," she repeated. He stepped quickly through the door, leaving her to straighten out her wrinkled dress in the growing darkness.

At the weekly meeting, Charley told his story again.

"So where are you from, actually?" Wickman asked.

"Wellsir, that's a good question," Charley said. "Great state of Arkansas is the best I can do. My daddy and I moved around a lot. He had a strong fondness for Fort Smith, but me, I only went there once."

"And how old are you?"

Charley ran his hand across the top of his head. "Dang. Let me see. I think I was five in '49, so that would make me fifteen?"

"Where's your family?"

"Ain't got none I know of. My mama died with the birth fever, not with me but with what would have been my little sister, but she died too. Ain't got no grandma nor grandpa I know of, nor uncles and aunts neither."

Cabot spoke. "No offense, but we're not running an orphanage here. We want settled families. People who are going to build a life. Our standard has always been that new members have to bring two hundred dollars with them, but since you're not a legal adult I'm not sure how that applies." There was a murmur in the crowd at his words. "Harsh but true," said a voice from the back.

George Webb stood up. "I tell you what. You seem a likely young man. You can board with me. I could use the help. When you get to be a man, you can decide for yourself if you want to join the Daybreak community, and if you're not working out, I'll tell you to pack up and go. Fair enough?"

"Fair enough," Charley said softly.

Webb turned to the group. "Is that acceptable to everyone?"

There was a general nodding of heads.

"All right, then, that's settled," Webb said, and sat down.

Charley turned out to be a good worker, an endless talker, and an incorrigible flirt. He took a quick eye to Marie, and now it was Turner's turn to be irritated. "You're just a boy," he told him. "You shouldn't be chasing after girls older than you."

"Wellsir, there ain't any younger ones around here," Charley replied. They were loading hemp stalks into a wagon to take them to the ropewalk. "She's the youngest you got. And she's pretty, too."

"There are bound to be girls on the farms around here. Just look around."

"Oh, I'll find 'em all right. I got a way about me."

"Whatever you say, Charley."

Splitting the hemp stalks proved to be the hardest part of the ropemaking. Even after lying on the ground for six weeks, they were still tough; the fibers had to be pulled away from the stalks carefully or else they would lose their value. Before long, everyone's fingertips were raw and bleeding around the nails. Carr had the idea of having the children walk over the stalks to break them, which helped, but it was still tedious work. Finally, there were enough fibers laid out along the ropewalk to start the jack. The shaft was pulled into place, the gears were engaged, and slowly the ropejack began to turn. Round and round it went, twisting the hemp and pulling the strands together, and all along the walk they could see the fiber gradually twisting into a rope.

"How will we know how to stop it?" Turner asked Webb.

"Just by feel. Eventually it will feel like it's supposed to. For now, we just need to keep stripping out more stalks."

Charley's romantic zeal made it even harder for Turner to find time alone with Marie. They went weeks without a moment together, as Charley always found an excuse to visit them in the print shed when they were composing *The Eagle*.

"You ought to teach me how to read," he told Marie. "I'd like to read what you all are writing."

"I'm not writing anything," she answered. "Mr. Turner does all the writing. I just set it into type."

Charley sniffed. "A dollar says you'd write better than him. He's smart and all, but I bet you're just as smart. What do you think, Mr. Turner?"

"I know never to bet against you, Charley."

Turner knew it was unwise to keep up his affair with Marie. Secrets were hard to hold in Daybreak, maybe impossible. But he didn't want to stop. The pleasure was part of it. He could get the same pleasure from Charlotte anytime, but the thrill of the forbidden added to his pleasure with Marie, and her young body was firm and supple, a delight to handle. There was also the pleasure of knowing that this young beauty, coveted by everyone in the community from Charley on up, was his, all his. And in those snatched moments when he took her into his arms, he could feel in her admiration the lost sense of purpose that had led him to Daybreak in the first place. The pall of Lysander Smith's death lifted, and for a little while he felt his old spirit-stirring energy break through the lethargy that had overtaken him.

Out in the fields, with only labor to occupy his mind, he wondered about Charlotte and Adam Cabot. Lately, they had seemed stiff and strangely careful with each other, avoiding direct interactions. He had never seen them do or say anything compromising, but there was just a sense of something. He didn't like it.

After lunch one day, he saw Harp Webb clatter up the road with a wagon full of whiskey jugs and bags of saltpeter, off to visit his customers. He walked out in the yard to the edge of the road.

"Going to town?" he called.

Harp looked down at him suspiciously. "Wagon's headed that way, ain't it?"

"Just making conversation. How's your new boarder working out?"

Harp grunted. "That little pissant ain't my concern. My daddy's the one who hired him. I have my own affairs to tend to."

"You like him all right?"

"Oh, he ain't bad. Gets on your nerves with the yessir and nosir all the time, but what the hell."

"Good worker."

"That I wouldn't know," Harp sniffed. "He comes over here to do all his working."

"Don't I know it. That boy's underfoot all the time, following me around like a pup."

"Maybe it ain't you he's following around," Harp said, winking. "All he wants to talk about of an evening is women. Daddy don't like it, thinks it's unchristian, but I talk to him anyway. I'll tell you something," he said, leaning down. "He says he's had a woman, but I don't think he ever has. I've got half a mind to take him up to the Indian camp and get him some for real."

"You mean—"

"Sure, they put out. You just stand in the clearing and jingle the silver in your pockets, and see how long it takes."

"I didn't know."

"That don't surprise me. The list of things you people don't know seems to have no end, as far as I can tell."

Turner let the remark pass.

The rope brought a good price, and the poor corn crop made Turner wish they had planted more hemp. On the evening of their next weekly meeting, he walked home with George Webb and Cabot. They stopped at Turner's house to rest and talk with Charlotte, and he brought up the subject of next year's planting.

"We'll have to rotate the fields," George Webb said. "That corn has worn out the lower field, and we need to let it go to pasture next year. We can put the corn where the wheat is now, and move the wheat to the hemp field. So the hemp will go where the pasture is."

It seemed sensible enough. Then Cabot surprised them all.

"I am planning to ask for a leave of absence from the community for six months, starting early next year," he said. Turner saw him glance toward Charlotte, whose face was expressionless. To their stunned silence, he added, "I intend to run for the legislature, and I will need the time to travel around the county."

"Oh, for God's sake!" Webb exploded. "Of all the crazy ideas. Republican ticket too, I'll wager."

"Yes, Republican. I don't think it's so crazy," Cabot said. "I think I have a lot to offer."

"I didn't say that," Webb said, standing up. "But you couldn't get elected in this county, whether you took six months or two years."

"Maybe you're underestimating the people of your county."

"Maybe you just don't know them as well as I do. Tell me this. Who's our state representative now?"

"Mr. Anthony."

"What does he do? Where does he live?"

Cabot was silent.

"Who was representative before him?" Webb continued. "How about that?" To Cabot's continued silence, he answered, "John Polk, that's who. And Josiah Anthony has a big farm up by St. Michael's. If you want to get into politics you have to know these kinds of things. You can't just have ideas. Otherwise you'll find yourself going up to your opponent's brother-in-law and asking for his vote, and wind up getting a punch in the eye for your troubles. And do you know how many votes Mr. Frémont got in this county last election? None. Zero."

Cabot crossed his arms. "Is that all anyone thinks about? Who's related, who lives where? It seems to me that there are important things happening in this country, all around us, that people ought to be thinking about."

"Oh, they ought to," Webb replied. His face was red and puffy. "But they aren't. And they don't vote on them either. They vote on whether they know you, or if their preacher knows you, or if they've done business with you. And as soon as they elect you, they start looking for reasons to complain about you. Trust me, Adam, politics is no place for the idealist."

"Sounds to me like you've lost your ideals," Cabot said, a little petulantly.

"Oh you may think what you like," Webb said. "When I first ran for office, back in thirty-six, I was a young man too. I figured I was smarter than every-body else and could help direct the county the way it needed to go. But a couple of terms on the County Court taught me that people only want politicians to get them what they want and the hell with everybody else. If you want to make the world better, the place to do it is right here, not out there."

The two men regarded each other. "Think about it," Webb said. "Whether you take a leave is not what's important. Just don't waste your time on something you'll come to despise." He sat down.

"Adam, do you really think you need six months?" Charlotte said.

"Well, four months anyway," Cabot said. He turned to Webb. "Do you have any idea who else might be running?"

"Not a glimmer," Webb said. "I got out of that long ago. You can expect there'll be half a dozen, though. There's always plenty of people want to run for office."

Turner held his tongue. Adam was a good man to talk to, intelligent and informed, and worked as hard as anyone. But if he had affections toward Charlotte, it wouldn't hurt to have him out roaming the county for a while.

"Well, this is for the whole community to decide," Turner said after a moment. "Besides, election time is months away. Let's keep this among ourselves and discuss it again when the time gets closer."

They stood to leave. In the doorway, George Webb turned to speak.

"I—" he said, then stopped. "I—" A look of surprise passed over his face. "It's—" Then his look of surprise turned to one of fear, turning to bewilderment, turning to panic. They all gazed at him in wonder at the bizarre expressions that were passing over him.

Cabot took a step toward him. "George?" he said. Webb's expression was now one of utter terror.

"It's under—" he said. Those words were all he got out before he collapsed in the doorway. Cabot was the first to reach him.

"Good Lord!" he cried. "Sit him up."

They propped Webb against the doorframe, but it was no use. His eyes were glassy and unfocused. Turner knelt before him, calling his name, but could not tell if he heard or understood. A moment later his head fell to his chest. George Webb was dead.

Chapter 18

Harp Webb had his father's funeral at the Methodist church in town, although Turner had offered the Temple of Community. "It's up to him,"
he told Charlotte. "I never heard George express any wishes." Charlotte hadn't
either, although she also knew that George had neither set foot in nor mentioned the Methodist church since she had known him. But they dug his grave
in the Daybreak cemetery, just up the hill from Lysander Smith's.

Everyone turned out on a chilly Saturday morning for the service, except
Charley Pettibone, who had disappeared into the woods before dawn with a
squirrel gun, speaking to no one. The church was packed. Charlotte felt more
like an outsider than ever when she saw the line of elderly men and women
trooping up to shake Harp's hand at the front of the church. On her shoulders
she could feel the weight of the gazes and whispers of the old settlers as they
pointed toward the Daybreak group. She didn't know any of them. The sheriff
was there, as were other dignified-looking souls in heavy black suits, people
from Webb's political days. A murmur went around the church when the circuit
judge came in, a somber, silver-haired man who placed his wide-brimmed hat
over his heart and held it there throughout the service.

The Methodist preacher had much to say, but the words washed over her
as she sat in the ranks of mourners from Daybreak, three full rows at the back
of the church. She was lost in her own thoughts. Lord knows she would miss
George, not just the man who had given the community its start, the man who
knew so much more about farming than any of the rest of them, but a man
whose simple, firm beliefs in their ideals reassured her that the community did

indeed have a purpose. They would have to make their own way now, and she could only hope that some among them would have the wisdom, or at least the common sense, to take his place.

She studied the hard-faced men and women in the rows ahead, old settlers who sat impassively through the service, their expressions solemn but unmoved. Pinched faces, thin noses, set jaws, people for whom hardship was the normal way of life and sudden death no surprise. Would she become one of these oak-hard Ozarkers? She looked down at her calloused hands and ragged finger-nails. Apparently she was well on her way.

Her husband, sitting beside her, wore the bland expression he always brought out for public occasions. He was looking more and more like a country politician himself these days, not the restless lecturer she had fallen in love with. Perhaps that lynching had done its work, brought him into line, knocked down any thought of changing the world outside of Daybreak. True, the idea had always been to perfect the community and let it serve as a beacon to the world, but lately it just seemed as though simple survival was all they were after. What good was it to be idealists if all it brought them was struggle? She looked again at his face. What was he thinking, really? She could no longer tell where his thoughts were, and that was troubling.

The hairs on the back of her neck prickled, and she glanced behind her. Adam Cabot was one pew back, his cow eyes fixed on her. She turned away quickly. Now there was someone whose thoughts were all too easy to discern. He should behave with more discretion.

Then the funeral was over, and they stood as the casket was carried past. Now for the long wagon ride to Daybreak. She took Turner's arm.

On the steps of the church, Turner signaled to Cabot with a flick of his hand. "Let's go last," he said. "We need to talk."

Charlotte thought briefly that he had noticed Cabot's gaze as well, but when they were on their way home, the two of them in the wagon and Cabot on a horse alongside, he said simply, "We are going to have to elect a new treasurer."

She looked at the line of wagons ahead, most of the village. Who could do the job? Her father, of course, but he was not a member and showed no interest in becoming one. Emile Mercadier was committed to the cause, but getting on in years, and hardly a practical man. Marie was sharp enough. Would the colony accept someone that young? Not to mention a second female. And then there was—

"John Wesley Wickman," Cabot said.

"That's who I was thinking, too," said Turner. He wiped his face with his palm, a nervous gesture she had noticed more often lately. "And something else we need to talk about. We need to find what George did with the treasury."

Cabot reined to a stop. "You don't know?"

"He never told me. Never told anyone, as far as I know."

"You're joking."

"No. He didn't believe in banks, we all know that. Whenever we needed money, he would show up the next day with the exact amount, always in gold and coin. And the books were always square, down to the penny."

"But where are those pennies?" Charlotte said.

"I wish I knew. He's got to have a strongbox someplace close."

They rode in silence for a mile, digesting the news. Charlotte fought back panic. What had been hidden could be found. Surely George had left instructions.

"We'll have to talk to Harp," Cabot said.

Turner nodded. "I know. But I wish we didn't."

"He could try to keep it for himself."

"I don't think so," Charlotte interjected. "He's a strange one, but he has his own sense of right and wrong. Just up and stealing something is not his way."

"You should go," Turner said. "He likes to talk to you."

"Don't remind me," she said. "But I need at least one of you to go along."

"You'd better do it," Cabot said to Turner. "I can't stand the man. I'll just get his back up."

The two of them walked over to Webb's house after lunch the next day, when they felt sure that Harp would be up. He seemed to keep completely irregular hours; some days he would be out before dawn, and other days he seemed to lie in bed till the late afternoon.

He was awake and waiting. "You're here about your strongbox. Well, didn't take you long, I'll give you that."

"You know about that, then."

"I know he kept one. Not sure where he kept it. His room is over there." Harp gestured to a bedroom at the end of the house. "Help yourself."

Charlotte hated the feeling of walking around in the dead man's room, only days after she had seen him die. All the little things—the bedsheets, the razor and mug, the stack of worn books by his bedside, the reading glasses—seemed shabby and inadequate to the man she knew. The room seemed as impersonal as the cell of a monk, but at the same time she could feel George's presence in everything.

"Well?" Harp called.

Turner looked under the bed, between the mattresses. Nothing. He checked the wardrobe for a false bottom. He worked his way around the walls, looking for flaps in the wallpaper or hollow spots behind furniture.

"Not yet," he called back.

They looked for loose floorboards, flaps in the chairs, hidden shelves in the ceiling. Finally they emerged, unsuccessful, into the front room.

"No luck, huh?" Harp said. "Don't surprise me. The old man was a crafty sort. Didn't give you a hint or nothing?"

Neither of them answered. They were looking around the room. "I'd be surprised if he hid it anywhere else in the house," Harp said. "Too much chance for any old somebody to find it."

Turner took the poker from the mantel and stirred the fireplace ashes. "Here," he said. "There's a loose stone."

Charlotte and Harp watched as Turner pushed the coals to the back with the fireplace shovel. Sure enough, the stone directly beneath the andirons wiggled in its bed; there was no mortar around it. Turner pried it up with the poker.

Under the stone was a heavy metal plate.

"Son of a bitch," Harp said. "I've spit tobacco on that rock many a time."

Turner flipped up the plate with the poker, revealing a deep square hole, its sides trimmed, and a bound metal box at the bottom.

"I take it that's not yours?" he said to Harp.

"Hell, no," Harp said. "I keep my money up in my cave."

"If you don't mind, I'd like to have our third director present when we open it," Turner said. "So we all agree on what we see."

"Suit yourself," said Harp.

Turner stepped onto the front porch and waved to Cabot, who was sitting on the Turners' doorstep holding the account book. He walked over.

The box had a clasp but no lock. Turner balanced it on the porch railing, made sure all four of them could see, and opened it.

There were three cloth bags in the box, each with a number of gold pieces. Turner counted them out.

"Two hundred dollars," he said at the end. Cabot did not even bother to open the account book. They all knew there should be at least three thousand.

"That ain't much," Harp said. "You people been working for three years and that's all you got?"

"Let me think," said Turner. "I need to think about this."

"In case you want to ask," Harp said, "I'm fine to tell you that money ain't mine. It's yours."

"Thanks," Charlotte said.

"I ain't no thief."

"I know that."

"While I got the three of you here, there are some things I want to tell you," Harp said. "First, let me ask you this. You know the difference between a warranty deed and a quitclaim deed?"

"No," Charlotte replied. Turner and Cabot looked at them curiously.

"Well, you might ought to find out," Harp said. "'Cause what you got over there is a quitclaim deed, and now that the old man is dead you might find out other people got claims. Just 'cause the old man signed off his interest in the property don't mean you own it clear."

"Is this true?" Turner asked.

"You ever seen your deed?"

"No."

"Then go on up to the courthouse and take a look. And another thing. I own this house now, and that little fartknocker that's been living here needs to go. You people want to take him in, fine. But from me, it's time for him to root hog."

"But surely your—" Charlotte began.

"Oh now, ma'am, you're going to tell me what my father would have wanted? Here's the thing. My daddy don't live here any more. This is my house now, and I'll run it how I want. "

Charlotte shivered. "I didn't mean to suggest—"

"Here's the thing," Harp said again. "The old man was your friend, he liked people with big ideas, he brought you all here and cheered you on. But that dreamy shit is not for me, and you all just need to stay out of my way."

Turner tucked the strongbox under his arm and stepped down from the porch. Charlotte and Cabot followed. But then Cabot turned, stepped up one step, and extended his hand.

"No hard feelings," he said.

"Right," Harp said dubiously, shaking Cabot's hand.

"I hope you wouldn't mind if we came back for a second look sometime."

"Suit yourself."

They waited until they were home before asking Cabot what he was up to.

"Simple deduction," he said. "Think about it. George Webb was a smart man and an honest man. Agreed?"

"Of course," Charlotte said.

"He didn't trust banks, because he'd seen them fail too many times. But he knew that keeping your money at home would attract robbers. And robbers could force him to show them where he hid the money."

"Right."

"So the money in the fireplace is for the thieves. The rest of the money is hidden somewhere else."

Charlotte saw the sense in what he was saying.

"He didn't tell Harp about the hiding places because perhaps he didn't have the same level of confidence in Harp's honesty that you do, Charlotte. And he didn't tell us because, well, I don't know."

"So you think—" Turner began.

"I think there's another box somewhere nearby with the rest of our treasury. It has to be close enough to get to, but not where it could be accidentally or easily found. Like I said, George Webb was a smart man."

Turner nodded. "A little too smart for his own good, or ours at least. But at least we know what we have to do."

"This news isn't going to go over well with the community," Cabot said.

"Let's not tell them," Turner replied.

Cabot grimaced. "I have to say this. George and I had grown quite concerned about the way decisions are being made. Too much keeping in the dark, too many things done without votes or discussion. And I have to say, I agreed with him."

Turner cast a look toward Charlotte. "Is this what you were trying to tell me about this spring? This is your talk-among-the-women?" She looked away. "Well, you can complain all you like about secrecy, but perhaps you should stop having private conversations with my wife."

"I'm sorry," Cabot stammered. "We meant no—"

"And don't tell me you meant no harm. Those are words I don't care to hear. Meaning harm and doing it are separate things."

Cabot turned to leave. "I'm sorry," he said.

Turner took his arm. "Please," he said. "Give me a day or two to find this other box, and then if I haven't found it, we'll lay it out for the community. I just don't want to create a panic."

"Very well," Cabot said, embarrassed. "And please understand, George and I didn't want to involve Charlotte in our discussions. She just stumbled on us one day."

"Yes, your secret discussions. Let's save that for another time."

When Cabot opened the door, Charley Pettibone was sitting out on the stepping stone, his bag on the ground beside him. He stood up.

"Guess I'll be on my way," he said. "I ain't had much success at sticking, I guess."

"You'll do nothing of the sort," Cabot said. "You'll share my house, if you don't think it's a bad omen to sleep in a dead man's bed."

"Don't believe in 'em," Charley said. "A man makes his own luck, good or bad. That feller didn't want to get hung, he shouldn'ta been stealing people's niggers, is my opinion." He paused and looked nervously at Cabot. "Um, I guess you must be some kind of abolitionist, then."

Cabot smiled. "I suppose I am."

"Wellsir," Charley said. "I don't see why we can't just keep politics out of it. People don't have to agree on everything."

"Charley, you're a philosopher," Turner said. "Who would have thought it?"

"Don't know nothing about that," Charley said. "But if you'll put me up, sir, I'll work off whatever rent you charge."

"That's just it, Charley," Cabot replied. "In this community, we all hold everything in common. I don't own that house. We all do. And you're going to be one of us."

Charley looked suspicious. "Do I gotta take a pledge or something?"

Charlotte stepped into the yard and embraced him. "Just work hard and look out for the others."

Turner went to the barn after dark and found a slender iron rod, which he carried back to the Webbs' house. Harp let him in without a word. For an hour he poked at the walls and floors, listening for hollow sounds, feeling for anything loose. Then he came outside with a shaded lantern and probed with the rod under tree roots and bushes. Nothing.

Naturally, someone saw him, and two days later he had to admit to the community meeting that their savings had gone missing. Immediately half the men were on their feet, calling out questions and recriminations.

"Harp Webb stole it, is what happened!" one man cried out.

"We ought to just burn his house and then sift the ashes," said another.

"So we're ruined? Is that what you're telling us? We're ruined?"

Turner tried to calm the frenzy but the angry buzz continued.

"Here's what we'll do," he said. "We'll keep looking for the money. It can't be lost forever. And in the meantime Grindstaff will keep us on his ticket at the store. We don't need the cash—"

"And what about our taxes?" someone interrupted. "Think the county collector will keep us on a ticket?"

The quarreling started again. Turner waved his arms in the air, vainly seeking quiet. Then Emile Mercadier stood up and walked to the front of the meeting. Except for Newton Carr, he was at least twenty years older than anyone else in the room. Everyone fell quiet.

"When I was in France, I was a poor man," he said. "I come to America a poor man. I come here a poor man. So what are you telling me? I'm a rich man now and I got to worry about losing my money? You all been rich men all this time?

"Mister Webb, he done his best by us. He knows the banks, they take your money and they give you their notes. You try to spend the notes somewhere, everybody look at it like you printed it yourself. So he doesn't tell anybody where he hides the money. Well, nobody ever thinks they going to die today." He shrugged. "But sometimes you die anyway. In France, we had a saying: 'Life is an onion. You cry while you peel it.'"

"What the hell is that supposed to mean?" a man shouted.

Cabot stood up. Since Webb's death he had been tiptoeing around the community, rehashing his final angry words, blaming himself, tiptoeing around Charlotte, around Turner, afraid to meet their gazes for what he might see in Turner's look and what he might not see in Charlotte's. Who was he kidding? He was a thrown stone, a man already living on borrowed time. What power need he give to the looks and words of others? "It means we have had a setback, but we don't just quit. We move ahead. Cry if you want, but peel the onion."

Mercadier's comments settled everyone down, although heads inclined together from time to time and the sound of whispers and low conversations continued. But at least there was no rush to leave, although a young man named Trimble, a recent arrival, packed up and left a week later.

On a late October afternoon, Charlotte was sweeping the yard when a wagon came up from the south, driven by a weathered man with a full beard. He stopped in front of their house, his gaze directed into the distance ahead, where the water wheel could be seen slowly rotating through the trees.

"I hear you all got a rope mill," he said, tilting his head toward the bed of the wagon. In it was a full load of hemp stalks, well retted, ten feet long or more. Two children were riding the load to hold it down. "How much you pay for a load? I got four more wagonloads at least where this come from."

Charlotte looked up at him. "We don't have any cash to pay you right now," she said, "but we'll mill it on shares. We'll give you half of whatever we get when we sell it up in town."

The man looked at her suspiciously for a moment. She could see him calculating in his mind. "All right," he said. "Fair enough."

"Where are you from?"

"Coldwater."

"Your neighbors grow any hemp?"

"Oh, some. Most everybody has a little. Farther south you get some good-sized patches."

"Drive on up the road a little. There are some men in the field who'll help you unload your wagon. And when you go back to Coldwater, tell all your neighbors about the deal you got from us. For every one who comes up here with a decent crop and tells me you sent them, I'll add fifty cents to your settlement."

The man grinned. "Name's Atwell," he said. "Just remember that when people show up and say, 'Atwell sent me.'"

She reached up and shook his hand. "Good to meet you, Mr. Atwell."

Atwell chucked his horses and drove off, the children bouncing in the back, and Charlotte waved at them as they rode away. About twenty feet down the road, the man stopped and turned around in his seat. "Hey, you remember that fellow Brown, caused so much trouble over in Kansas?"

"Yes."

"Tried to start a nigger rebellion back in Virginia. Took over the arsenal and sent out a call to arms. It's all over the telegraph." He tried to think further. "Nothing to worry about, though. They got him cornered."

Charlotte waved her hand at him but did not know what to say in return.

"Can you imagine a bunch of niggers with guns?" Atwell said. "What a world." He started the wagon forward, but stopped and turned around again after another few yards. "Bet you'd get a better price if you took it to the railhead in Pilot Knob and shipped it to St. Louis," he shouted back at her. "These local boys got some sharp teeth."

"I'll look into that!" she called back. "Thanks!"

Excitement grew in Charlotte as the wagon drove away. Of course! That was what they should have been aiming for in the first place. Not just making their own rope, but running a factory. There would be detractors, no doubt. She could hear them already, the men who would say that factory work was what they had left behind when they came to Daybreak, the ones who wanted just to live off the farm. And yes, it was hard work, harder than anything else they did. But James was right—their plot of ground couldn't support a town. Once the money started rolling in, the criticism would stop.

She should tell James. He would want to know immediately, even though he was working on *The Eagle* and did not like to be disturbed. He would want to greet Atwell, add his welcome, ratify the deal. And he would want to know this news from back East.

She hurried to the print shed with the news and opened the door. And in the moment she saw everything—everything, the composing table with no type set out on it, the jobsticks still hanging from their pegs, Marie lying on the table with her dress up around her neck, and Turner above her, his pants thrown into the corner, the sound of his grunts, his bare legs tense and muscular, moving back and forth in that all-too-familiar motion—in that moment she felt her life, her world, her entire self turn as if on a pivot, a hard turn to the left and down, down into she knew not what. Then she turned away and shut the door behind her and ran back to the house.

September 1859/November 1860

Chapter 19

T he news spread through the village by sunset. No one had seen anything, but the combination of events—Turner carrying clothes and linens out to the print shed, Charlotte's tear-streaked face as she strode to her father's cabin, Marie's sequestration in her house—made it all too clear what had happened.

Charley Pettibone brought Cabot the story when he came in from the fields. "Now ain't that the rinktum," Charley said. "No wonder I never got no purchase on that gal. King rooster was keeping all the hens to himself."

A chill settled in the pit of Cabot's stomach as he rushed to put on his coat. He would go to Charlotte, take her in his arms, offer his comfort, let her know that he would never have treated her like such a cavalier. He would take her away if she wanted. Or together they would drive out this man, this cad. He envisioned himself in confrontation, and the calm but fierce things he would say. James Turner was a big man, but even a tall tree might prove rotten when struck by a well-aimed blow. Cabot clenched his fists.

Then he stopped and slowly removed his coat and hat. He hung them back on their pegs. Who was he to go out like Galahad, defending women's honor? He was already a fool, no call to add "hypocrite" to his titles.

What had possessed Turner to behave so rashly? How could he have wanted Marie when he already had Charlotte? Love? Lust? He thought of Charlotte's hand in his as they sat by the river, the firm yet yielding press of her lips, her hands slipping around his back and pressing him to her. He remembered their frantic fumblings right there, on the bed of his own cabin. Love or lust—he could understand them both.

For two days he composed what he would say to her when the time was right. He would doff his hat and bow respectfully, tell her of his concern for her happiness; he would offer his family home in Boston as a haven in her time of distress. He would not press her, but would make clear that she had an alternative to staying in Daybreak.

And then he rounded a corner of his house the next morning and nearly bowled her over in the street as she was walking to the Temple for her day's work.

His careful words fled. They regarded each other in silence. "I'm terribly sorry," he finally stammered. "I had no idea."

Her face closed into a frown. "Neither did I, obviously."

"No. Of course not."

"I'm ... I want to be your friend."

She smiled. "You have always been my friend. I never imagined otherwise."

"Then...."

She placed the palm of her hand flat on his chest, a gesture that felt both like a friendly touch and a message to stop. "Then be my friend." She walked away before he could say more, leaving him baffled, his great speech lodged in his throat. He remembered to remove his hat, but by that time she was fifty feet away.

Turner hid himself away in the print shed, unsure how or if he could show himself again. He thought of leaving in the night, heading west somewhere, ending the embarrassment and shame by an utter disappearance with nothing left of his memory but packets of money that would appear from time to time. But he knew such a move would solve nothing. Plates of food appeared on the step sometimes. Although he liked to imagine that Charlotte was bringing them, he doubted that was the case. He ate sometimes, and sneaked to the woods to do his business at night or during mealtimes, when he thought he could avoid an accidental encounter with anyone.

From the window of the shed he could see the road, the people coming and going between their homes, the occasional horseman and wagon passing. The mill wheel turned slowly in the river. On the second day a couple of wagons appeared from the south, and on the third a half dozen, loaded with hemp. Turner recognized what was happening. Word had gotten around about their rope mill, and the farmers were bringing their crop, selling on the shares, no doubt. It was a fine thing—breathing room for the colony at a badly needed time. He guessed Charlotte was behind the idea.

It was Newton Carr who came to see him, accompanied by young Newton, who climbed onto his lap. Carr settled into a chair by the door and looked at him with calm but unflinching eyes. Turner could not meet his gaze.

"It's a good thing they outlawed the code duello," Carr said at last. "I'd have to try to shoot you, and from what I can tell you're a damn good shot."

Turner didn't know what to say.

"Emile would like to thrash you with a stick," Carr went on. "If I were you, I'd let him do it. You deserve a good thrashing."

"Yes, sir."

Carr tipped the chair back and leaned against the wall.

"In the Army we had this problem a lot. Hundreds, thousands of men, off in some lonesome place. Wives and daughters around, but always way more men than women. The rule was, go into town. Don't find your satisfaction within the regiment."

Young Newton climbed down and began to explore the printing equipment. Ordinarily the shed was off limits to him, so he examined every item with great interest. Turner kept an eye on the typecases and the ink. As long as he didn't get into those, he would be all right.

"Didn't work, of course," Carr continued. "Human nature being what it is. Hell on morale. You'd get some lieutenant, thinks one of the men is after his wife, not a good thing. David and Uriah all over again. Challenges, duels, you could forbid it but they'd wait till later. Not good, not good."

Turner listened.

"The key is, you've got the unit to think about. You can't forget the good of the unit. That's the commander's job."

Carr walked over to the press and idly examined some of the proof sheets.

"Cabot led the meeting last week, did a good job," he said. "Very creditable. The ropemaking business went over pretty well. We're writing to some merchants in St. Louis to see what they offer."

"Captain Carr," Turner said. "What should I do?"

Carr regarded him. "I expect you've run through all your choices in the past few days. You could run off, but I don't have you figured for that big a coward.

You could bluff it out, try to pretend it was all a big misunderstanding. But if I have raised my daughter right—and I think I have—she won't let you by with that. And even if she would, I won't." He leaned forward. "And then you would have to decide whether you could shoot me, because by God I would intend to shoot you. Or you could do what you already know you need to do. Apologize. Her first, then Marie, then everyone. Apologize and make amends, try to patch the harm as best you can, although harm once done cannot be undone. What else can you do?"

"I don't know if I can face everyone."

"Oh, for God's sake, man. You've made a mistake. You're a human being. Do you think you're the first human being who's made a mistake?"

"But how can they trust me?"

"They don't trust you. Doesn't mean you can't regain it. What's black turns to gray over time."

Charlotte walked through her days enveloped in a shell of silence. No one knew what to say to her, so they said nothing. And she had nothing to say in return. What was there to say? She had come upon her husband and the Mercadier girl engaged in the act of nature, and her world had spun down and crashed. And yet the world itself moved on at its own pace, children to care for, chickens to feed, cattle to milk. So she awoke in the morning and went to her duties, as if her life had not been blasted.

It was his arrogance that came back to her again and again, his doing it in the shed not thirty feet behind the house. Evidently he thought everyone in Daybreak was a fool, or that he had been given the gift of invisibility. And the girl—Charlotte resented her, the silly thing, but could not bring herself to hate her for long. Not many years had passed since she had been the impressionable young woman, carried away by Turner's grand ideas. She wondered about them, how long they had been involved like this, what he found in her that she did not provide. But she cast away those thoughts. Better not to know.

And what was she to do now? The question haunted her. Run away? To where and to do what? She knew that was Cabot's grand idea, to leap into the void and make a fresh start, although thank God he had been gentleman enough not to bring it up. She could read his thoughts in his face. The idea was tempting, if for no other reason than the escape from the present pain, but she knew it was not real. Duty called her here, duty to Newton and her father and Daybreak; it was not in her power to change that. Perhaps James would fly to a new life with his little squab. If so, Godspeed, and let them be merry. As for herself, she had a house to keep and a child to raise.

Several days later, Charlotte was in bed, half-asleep, when she heard the latch on the back door click open. Turner took off his shoes and knelt beside the bed. She didn't speak to him for a while. She could hear Newton's soft snoring from the trundle bed on the floor.

"Don't touch me," she said.

"I won't. I just want to tell you that I'm sorry."

"Oh, well. That solves everything."

"Just let me back."

She rolled over and spoke toward the wall. "You live here. You're entitled to live here. I have nowhere else to go. Don't expect anything."

He put on his nightshirt and climbed into bed, careful not to touch her.

"I'm sorry."

"So you said."

At some point in the night Newton climbed out of his trundle and fell asleep in the bed with them.

They did not speak for several days, although Charlotte could tell he wanted to. On the night of the weekly community meeting, he left the house early. Walking to the Temple of Community, Charlotte saw him standing at the Mercadiers' door, hat in hand, while Emile raged. He arrived at the Temple a little later and sat beside her.

"I'm trying to apologize," he said. "To you, too."

"I know. But maybe we're not ready to be apologized to."

The meeting was painful. Some people sat with their arms folded, averting their eyes; others glared. Some of the glares were aimed at her, and Charlotte realized that with Turner sitting beside her, people were assuming that she had taken him back. Cabot led the meeting, which came to a quick, strangled end.

Afterward they walked home in silence, keeping a distance between them, until they reached their house.

"Stars in heaven, I miss George Webb," Turner said.

Charlotte sat down on the doorstone. "Me too."

"How are we going to know when to butcher the hogs? And how deep to plow? And everything else George knew?"

Charlotte looked at him. "The same way George knew it. By asking, observing, learning. George didn't just come by all that knowledge at birth, you know. What he knew, you can learn. We all can learn."

"Thank you. You're right."

"Of course I am." Her old teasing smile appeared, but only for an instant.

"I really do love you. I hope you know that."

She turned serious. "Say that if you want. But I don't love you right now."

As winter approached, Turner discovered that he did indeed know more than he had thought. The wisdom of the many, which he had written about in *Travels to Daybreak* years ago, worked to identify the best time for bringing the hogs in. And everyone seemed to have a clear notion of how much wood needed to be cut for the cold days ahead, and where it should be cut. And it was while preparing the stall where the hogs would be driven and killed that Turner, scraping out manure with a shovel, hit a thick plank an inch under the dirt, lifted it, and beneath the plank uncovered George Webb's other strongbox, with stacks of double eagles wrapped in oiled paper, lined up in neat rows, every dollar accounted for. The next week, Turner stepped up to take his usual place at the head of the community meeting, and no one objected.

Adam Cabot did not speak again of leaving the colony to run for office. But he only talked to Turner when it was necessary, and Turner feared their friendship had come to an end. There was no Christmas dance.

Charlotte let him stay in the house, although she was careful not to touch him in bed. But over time, the daily labor of parenting eased feelings between them; they found themselves laughing together at some silliness of Newton's.

In early January, she came home from the Temple after lunch cleanup and took his hand. "We need to go to Mercadier's," she said. "The women are talking. They say Marie is planning to leave."

Emile did not want to let them in, but Charlotte insisted. When Marie came into the front room, the bulge of her abdomen made it clear what was happening.

"Marie," Charlotte said. She reached for the girl's hands, but Marie turned away. "Where do you think you will go?"

"Up into town, I guess," Marie said, her voice soft. "St. Louis if I have to."

"And what will you do?"

"What can I do? Serving girl, I hope."

Charlotte shook her head. "A serving girl with a little child? Are you dreaming? No one would take you in. The only way for you to find a place would be to leave the child in a foundling home and pretend it never existed. Even then you'd always be in danger of discovery. You could be turned out into the street at any moment."

Marie looked up defiantly. "Then it's whoring for me, I suppose. Lysander Smith always used to say that French whores are big sellers up in the city. They pay extra."

Charlotte took her hands this time and did not let go. "You are going to do nothing of the sort," she said. "You are going to stay right here and raise this child where it will have a grandfather to teach it." She looked sidelong at Turner. "And where its father will support it the way an honest man should."

Marie began to cry. "I am so sorry," she said. "I have made such a mess."

"No," Charlotte said. "You've only helped make the mess. And you know the housewife's lament, whenever there's a mess there's a call for a woman to come clean it up. A mother cannot just think about herself." She looked intently at Marie. "You're in a predicament, but it is not forever. Running off to town or St. Louis or wherever, and the life it would lead you to, is forever."

Marie wiped her face. She had not looked at Turner during the entire conversation. Charlotte led him to the door, but before it closed she turned back to Marie once more. "Come to dinner tonight," she said. "The only way through this is straight ahead."

"Forgive me," Marie said.

"Not yet," said Charlotte. "Let's see what happens."

Turner did not try to speak to Marie at dinner that night, or for the rest of the winter and into the spring. The year began with a feeling of suspension, as if everyone was waiting for something to happen, although no one knew what that something was. On their trips into town, the talk returned incessantly to national politics. Would there be union or dissolution, would the dissolution lead to war, and if it did who would be to blame: everyone had an opinion, everyone had a prediction, although the opinions and predictions shifted week to week. The hanging of John Brown seemed to give everyone a sharpened sense of the stakes. Riding into town one day, Turner actually saw a fistfight come rolling out of a tavern, like a Hogarth engraving come to life. The colony, with its rhythm of plowing, planting, and hoeing, was a relief. Its demands were set by nature, not by the latest shipment of newspapers from the cities.

In April Turner was walking to lunch from the fields when, passing the

Mercadiers, he saw movement at the curtain, and Marie opened the door a crack. She gestured him inside. Her belly was large.

"I don't think it will be long now," she said. "I'm afraid."

Turner took her hand. It was the first time they had touched since that day in October. "We will look out for you," he said.

"I know. But even so…." She was right, and he did not try to reassure her further.

"Are you well?"

"Yes. Tired. My back aches. But nothing else." She bit her lip. "We should think about a name."

The thought had not occurred to him. "What was your mother's name?"

"Josephine."

"How about Josephine for a girl, then?"

She smiled, her smile still as beautiful—and as rare—as he remembered. "And a boy?"

"For a boy, something American. A good old American name." He paused. "George?"

"Yes," she said. "George. I will tell my father. They will not ask you."

"I suppose not," he said.

Turner did not want to end the conversation. It felt good to be talking with Marie again, even though he knew they shouldn't be.

"Remember the time in the wagon?" he said. "A year ago?"

"Of course."

"I'm sorry for what I said then."

She frowned. "Don't ever be sorry for saying something honest."

"But still. It was unkind."

"I like kindness. But I prefer honesty, if I have to choose one or the other." She paused. "I know we can never be together. But I still love you, you might as well know that."

He smiled. "Isn't it strange? I didn't love you then, but I love you now. As if that did either of us any good."

She released his hand and held the door open a little. "Oh, it does us good. It does me good, anyway. Now go eat your lunch."

He stepped out into the street and walked to the Temple. At lunch Newton climbed up beside him to eat; he was at the age where he wanted to follow and imitate his father in everything. Turner put his arm around him as they spooned up their spring greens and salt pork together.

Charlotte did not want to attend the birth, but she had developed a reputation for being good at deliveries. So when the call went around the settlement early one afternoon, she went. The delivery was not complicated, quite fast really, a black-haired little girl who began to squall almost immediately. She returned home after dark. Turner was reading a book by the lamp.

"A girl," she said. "Josephine. After her mother."

"And—?"

"Both well."

He did not inquire further, and she was in no mood to talk. She put Newton to bed quickly, sat in the rocking chair by the window, and tried to read.

"She won't be able to baptize her," she said after a while.

"Surely she could find somebody," Turner said.

"Not a priest," Charlotte said. "I assume they're Catholic. I didn't ask."

"Maybe that Irishman that was through here a while back. He seemed eager for work."

She looked up. "Don't be flippant," she said. "This could be important to her."

"We've never had Newton baptized."

"It's not the same. We could have if we had wanted to."

"Yes."

The birth of the child only seemed to polarize the community further. A couple of families left amid comments about countenancing an immoral situation. Charlotte's refusal to drive Marie away met with approval from a few and incredulity from most. But everyone—including Turner—was caught by surprise at the next weekly meeting, when Adam Cabot stood up. He calmly reminded everyone that they had forgotten to hold their annual elections as provided in the Daybreak Charter, without needing to mention that the reason for the omission had been the breaking scandal, and nominated Charlotte for community president.

The outcry was even greater than when Turner had had to tell them about the missing money. Some insisted that a woman could not be elected to the office, but Cabot was ready for them with a copy of the articles of incorporation. Someone else nominated Turner, someone else moved that the elections be postponed for a week, and soon motions, objections, and simple shouts of confusion were flying.

"Gentlemen," Turner said, when quiet finally came over the crowd. "We organized ourselves on democratic principles, and we would do well to live up to them. Two nominations have been made and both are in order. Let us vote."

And Charlotte won.

So there it was. Turner walked home from the meeting alone, stunned. He sat in the dark house, thoughts tumbling in his mind. Was he just to become another citizen of Daybreak, the child of his own mind? But how could he? Nothing made sense.

Charlotte got home a half hour later, Newton asleep on her shoulder. "I didn't put him up to that, in case you are wondering," she said, lighting a lantern. "I suspected he was up to something, though."

"Charlotte," Turner said. "It was my book. This whole place is my idea." He hated the petulant sound of his voice.

"You could have spoken in your own behalf, you know."

"It wouldn't have felt right. Let democracy take its course. But God! To have you be the agent of my humiliation. I suppose this must feel like sweet revenge."

Charlotte's eyes filled with tears. "I don't want revenge!"

"Then why did you let your nomination stand? You could have refused."

"Yes," she said. "I could have refused, if I didn't mind dishonoring the principles of duty and cooperation you founded this community on. 'Where there is division, let us bring harmony.' Remember? You may have written the book, but you're not the only believer. If the citizens of Daybreak want to elect someone else president, that's their right. And you have no call to let your hurt feelings or personal ambition get in the way." She paused, and a sheepish smile came over her face. "Oh, all right. It did feel like sweet revenge. But only for a minute."

She was right, and he knew it. And he had to smile back at her admission. "You think you can do the job."

"Of course."

"And me? What am I to do?"

"I don't know. I have a vague notion it might be good for you to see things from a different place. And believe me, I won't forget that this colony was your idea." she said. "Now what's going to become of it?"

"You tell me. You're the new president. What are your big plans?"

"What's to say? Plant, harvest. Spread the word about the ropewalk. Publish *The Eagle*. Hold the community together."

"Your plans sound a lot like mine."

"And why shouldn't they?" she said. "James, your dreams are my dreams too. Surely you know that."

He did know it, but felt bruised nevertheless. How did she know what was good for him and what wasn't? He could decide that for himself. The fact remained that he had been voted out of office in his own community.

For the next several days, he couldn't help feeling angry about his ouster, but there was nothing to be done about it, and after a while he resolved to make the best of his life as an ordinary citizen of Daybreak. He took John Wesley Wickman to the side and handed him the strongbox.

"George Webb was thinking along the right lines, but maybe he was too careful for his own good," he told him. "It's not a good idea for everybody to know where we keep our money, but one or two people, anyway." That night, Wickman spread the word that he had decided it would be a good idea to put a fence around his yard. He spent the next day digging postholes. As Turner walked past on his way to the cornfields, Wickman gave him a significant look, and the next morning Turner noticed that all the posts had been set securely, with dirt packed tightly around each post. Wickman was up before breakfast interlacing the rails.

"You must have worked late on that job," Turner said to him.

Wickman paused in his railsplitting. "They're not set as deep as they look, if you know what I mean," he said. "But they'll hold."

"That's good."

"Six posts," Wickman said, pointing at them with his finger and giving Turner another look. "All six of them. Put 'em in last night, after dark."

By June, Sheriff Willingham had paid a call on the community, explaining that he was responding to a complaint that Daybreak was harboring people of loose morals. Charlotte sent him off with the smiling, but uninviting, answer that the community had already performed its own investigation and was satisfied that the demands of morality were being met. Willingham, with the election drawing near, was not interested in stirring up a troublesome case, and rode away handing out campaign ribbons.

Turner tried to get to work on the next edition of *The Eagle* but found himself unable. What could he write? Of course the change of leadership would have to be mentioned, but how to do it without raising more questions than he could answer? He puzzled for days, scribbling on loose sheets of paper, but nothing seemed to make sense without sounding mealymouthed or deceptive. He wished he had Marie with him—she had a good sense of expression, and could set the type faster besides. But Marie was still hiding away, avoiding them all for the most part, although he could hear the hungry squalls of the baby from time to time as he passed their cabin.

Finally he decided just to make a virtue out of it and embrace the vote as a victory for forward-thinking principles. He played off his column in the edition from a year ago and declared that in the rich soil of Daybreak, the cause of woman had taken a great step forward, one for which the rest of the nation was not likely prepared yet, but which signaled the way ahead. Leaders could rise from anywhere, even from the ranks of the weaker sex. He knew this raised the thorny question of suffrage but decided to ignore it. Let that rest for another day.

They hoed corn, planted wheat, waited for the hemp to complete its growth. The news from the rest of the country was not good, and the tension of waiting reached an almost unbearable point. It was Lincoln and Douglas all over again, only this time the tall man was a more experienced campaigner, and when Bell and Breckenridge entered the race the talk was that the whole issue might end up in the House of Representatives, where the Northern states had the advantage. But after the last ears of corn were binned, and the wheat reaped and milled, and the final parcels of hemp, brought loose or in bales by farmers from as far as two counties away, were finally run through the mill, the waiting came to an end.

The candidates split the vote badly. Judge Douglas won Missouri—and nowhere else. But the Republican managed a clear majority in the Electoral College, and the talk ran to secession and war.

And Harp Webb filed a quiet title suit in the courthouse, laying claim to Daybreak and the entire thousand acres.

April 1861

Chapter 20

A dam Cabot drew his knees under his chin and waited for sunrise on his meditation rock. As with all his efforts at self-improvement, he had neglected his morning ritual, but lately he had been feeling more and more of a need to get his mind clear.

The world was headed for hell. South Carolina had gone out, then six more states. Compromises were floating around Congress, but no one seemed in the mood for compromise. Most worrisome, word had just come north that militias in Arkansas had seized the federal arsenals at Little Rock and on the Mississippi. As long as the crisis was in South Carolina or Virginia, it seemed distant; but Arkansas was all too close.

He no longer felt at home in Daybreak. Not just the mess with Turner, although that was part of it, of course; they avoided each other in the fields and at the table. The knowledge that if the tables had been turned, and Charlotte had been willing to break her vows and run away with him, he would have glad-ly taken on the reprehension, only doubled his discomfort. So why did he stay? He had spent many mornings in this spot, searching his heart like a good New Englander, and always came around to the same disquieting conclusion—he stayed because he would rather be near Charlotte Turner than anywhere else on earth even if all he drew from that nearness was the anguish of unattainability. It was foolish, it was corrosive, but it was his decision and he was going to live with it.

But beyond that, the great troubles in the country made him restless. Daybreak had been his refuge when his life had been in danger, but now it felt more like a place of exile. Four years since he had fled Kansas, and what did he have to show for it? Had the common life moved him—any of them—any closer to perfection? It was hard to see it. Perhaps it was time to stop trying to perfect himself and leap back into the fray, a messy man in a messy world.

And this business with Harp Webb. Harp had hired the old settlers' lawyer in town, so they had gone to the other lawyer, a young man just down from St. Louis who could speak a little German and was getting most of his business from the recent immigrants. The three directors—Charlotte, Wickman, and himself—had visited his office in Fredericktown.

"Well," said the lawyer, whose name was Herrmann. "It's an interesting case."

"Lord help us," Wickman said.

"No, I really mean interesting. The title to this property has some clouds on it, all right, but not between George and his son. George's title was cloudy when he acquired it, and so was the man's before him, and the man before that. I've seen this sort of thing before. Your first settler comes in, grabs some ground, doesn't really ask whose it is, just acquires it by adverse possession over time. Frankly, if there are any claimants to your land, they are more likely to be French or Spanish, way back from colonial times, than Harp Webb. Maybe even Osage, although I can't imagine an Osage winning a court fight, or attempting one for that matter. So I'd say his suit has little merit."

"Yes, but—" Charlotte said.

Herrmann smiled indulgently. "Don't you fret, ma'am," he said. "We'll take care of you."

Cabot cleared his throat. "Mrs. Turner here is actually our community president."

Herrmann's smile turned confused. "Ah. Well. Then."

"On the face it has little merit," Charlotte went on. "But in court? How would it proceed?"

"Well," Herrmann said. "Let's say it didn't get thrown out in the first place. Mr. Webb would probably claim that there had been verbal promises, statements made by his father about inheriting the whole property, something like that. We would counter with the lack of written documentation of such promises, the fact that a careful man like George Webb would surely have written something down if he intended to leave your parcel to Harp. In real estate law, verbal promises are quite weightless."

"You don't suppose he has something, some scrap of paper he's been holding onto?" Wickman said.

"Well, even if he does, it wasn't recorded with the county," the lawyer said. "To be a valid document, it would have to be filed with the recorder, or at least notarized and witnessed."

They left the meeting feeling uneasy. The law might be in their favor, but if Harp Webb got in front of twelve local folks, talking about a promise from his father, anything could happen. Especially since his opponents would be a group of outlanders with strange ideas.

Charlotte stood at the washbasin scrubbing potatoes and looked out the window at the children playing in the grass of the side yard.

At least she would have one achievement in her term as president, she thought. A week after her election, the other women of the village approached her after the men had gone to the fields.

"Every day they go out in the sun and the breezes, and we are here in the stale air and dark," Frances Wickman said. "Nought for air or light but front door and back. It's time we put windows in these houses."

Charlotte agreed immediately, and after a month of lobbying, the men voted to approve her proposal to order windows from the city and pull two workers out of the fields to install them. There was grumbling about the time it would take away from the field work, but the proposal passed easily. Charlotte suspected that some of the women had used the *Lysistrata* tactic to influence their husbands' votes. Following the principle of equality, the same windows were ordered for each house, and everyone drew lots to see whose would be installed first. And no oiled paper, either. Real sash windows that could open and close.

So now she could stand at her window and watch the children. Frances had brought out a chair and was sitting in the shade of a tree, while her twins played. Sarah staggered in a circle around her, hanging on to her legs or the chair legs, walking now but still unsteady on her feet. Penelope was not walking yet; her legs came out at a bad angle from her hips, and her knees didn't bend quite right. When she pulled herself up, her feet stuck out to the side and she formed a tiny capital A. Then she would plop down, surprised. Her features were small and pretty, though, and her inability to keep up with her sister never seemed to bother her. Sarah was a determined explorer, wandering far from her mother, an intent expression pinching her face into a frown as she picked up sticks and grass, tasting each thing before moving on to the next object of interest.

And Newton, almost four now, playing with the babies because there was no one else to play with. His face was a mass of freckles, and he had a shock of thick sandy blond hair that flopped over his eyes. He moved with aimless energy, bouncing from one imaginary adventure to another, talking to himself. He had found a broken wagon spoke somewhere and used it as a walking stick, magic wand, and poking rod wherever he went. Newton's imagination and unfocused energy reminded her of his father, and she both smiled and grimaced at the thought.

She knew it was time to do something about Turner. It had been a year. She supposed the right thing to do would be to forgive him and get on with life. He had been suitably repentant, and she knew he had not strayed again. But when she saw him, he did not move her the way he had before; there was a coldness in her feelings toward him that she could not shake. Forgiving, all right, she could do that in Christian charity; but getting on, that was the stumbler.

Out the window she saw Marie Mercadier approach Mrs. Wickman, with little Josephine swaddled on her shoulder. She could feel her face harden again. How much charity was one person expected to show? Marie wouldn't have been in Daybreak if Charlotte hadn't insisted on it, but even so, seeing that girl and her daughter around was a pebble in her shoe every day. She still believed it had been the right thing to do; but "right" wasn't the same as "pleasant." Josephine made no effort to get down from her arms, although she was nearly as old as the Wickman girls, and Marie did not put her down. The two of them just stood apart and watched.

The sun dropped a little farther behind the mountain, casting a shadow over the window; and in the darkened glass she glimpsed her reflection. It was a hard face, an angry face, a face she didn't like. She looked away.

Her father was walking up the road toward the house. From his posture she knew something had happened. He stopped and tousled Newton's hair as the boy held up something and explained it to him, some new intricacy he had discovered in a walnut hull. Then he walked on.

Charlotte met him at the door.

"I've been recalled," he said. "It seems old officers aren't as useless as once imagined."

"Oh, Father." She embraced him tightly. "Where do they want you?"

"Back to West Point for now," he said, limply returning her embrace. "God knows after that." He sat down. "If fighting breaks out, and I think it will, we're in for a mess. You never know where fighting will lead you. I'm too old for this. Mexico was bad enough, but the idea of Americans shooting at Americans—" He broke off.

Charlotte watched the children. Josephine had finally gotten down and was squatting in the dirt beside Sarah, poking something with her finger.

"I take it our money's well hidden?" her father said.

"Yes."

"I mean truly well hidden?"

"Yes." She looked over at him in surprise. "Why?"

His face was drawn. "You would have to see war close up to understand. Once the law of the gun is in force, nothing is safe. You should start keeping the cattle in the woods. Have some of the young men watch them—whoever stays here, that is. I imagine most of them will want to go cover themselves with glory."

There was a knock at the door. It was young Schnack, breathless, his face and hands still dirty from plowing.

"Come to the Temple," he said. "Something's happened."

They hurried out to see everyone in the community converging on the Temple. Horses had been left in the field, still tethered to their plows. Frances and Marie picked up their children and hastened ahead of them. No one spoke, but there was a strange air of urgency.

When they got there, Turner was at the front of the meeting hall, talking in low tones with a man who soon left, got on his horse, and galloped down the road. Turner stepped onto the dais.

"The South Carolina militia has begun bombardment of Fort Sumter, in Charleston harbor," he said. "It looks like war is upon us. That's all the news at this time. We'll have a community meeting tonight to talk things over. Perhaps more news will come our way by then."

"I'll ride up to town and find out more," Schnack said, excited.

"Just finish your plowing," Carr told him. "You've got a hot horse out there. She'll need water and a cool down. News will come our way soon enough."

The crowd broke up, small groups talking intensely. Turner saw Charlotte at the edge of the crowd.

"I'm sorry," he said. "I overstepped."

"That's all right. We do need to meet."

There was no more news that evening, but everyone wanted to talk over the few scraps they had. It was hard to imagine that the fort could hold out for long. "It was meant to guard the city from attack by sea," Carr said. "I was there once. It was never meant to be defended from the land side."

Everyone was grateful at the governor's announcement that the state would remain neutral in the conflict, but Carr just sniffed. "Everybody always wants to stay neutral until the hotheads take over," he said. He was visibly glum. After the meeting was over, Charlotte took him to the side. "Most of my best cadets were Southern boys," he said. "I don't know how many of them will stick with the government."

A few days later he was packed and gone, but not before he took Charlotte out to the barn. He scratched aside some dirt in the floor of the hayloft to reveal a hole he had dug. "Old George had the right idea," he said. But Carr's hole was larger, and he only pulled away enough dirt to reveal one end of a canvas bag. "The rifles and ammunition are in there," he said. "If this spreads, guns are the first things people will look for."

"You really think this is going to get bad?"

"Who can say? But I wouldn't be surprised. *Homo homini lupus.* Protect the children."

By the time Carr had loaded his belongings on the wagon to catch the train to St. Louis, more news had come. The fort in South Carolina had indeed fallen quickly, the president had called for all states to send troops to help put down the rebellion, and the governor had refused. "We're in for it now," Carr said as he mounted the wagon. "Pray for a quick victory, one side or the other."

And then it was Charley's turn to go, a few days later. Except he was heading south.

"I can't say I know nothing about this whole deal," he said. "But I'm an Arkansas boy, and they say Arkansas has went out, so I guess I'll go down and see what's what."

"The country needs farmers a lot more than it needs soldiers, Charley," Charlotte told him.

"Well ma'am, that's the truth," he said. "I ain't been much of a farmer either, but I done what I could. And you know what they say about the ladies and a man in uniform." He grinned.

"That's only true for the live ones."

"Oh ma'am, I plan to stay alive. Little fellow like me, they may just make me the drummer boy or message carrier or something."

"You know how to play the drum?"

"Can't be no harder than poling a boat."

And then he was gone, a twenty-dollar gold piece placed in his pocket by Turner. "God bless you, Charley," he told him. "Stay safe, and come back to us when this is all over."

Harp Webb never spoke to them as he rode by; he would look straight ahead, grim-faced, without stopping. His trips to town grew more frequent and less predictable; Charlotte did not know what he was up to, but figured it could be nothing good. In early May they heard from Herrmann that Harp had asked for a jury trial. "Unusual for a civil suit, especially a real estate matter," he said. "I'd be surprised if the judge grants his request."

But Charlotte was not surprised when the judge granted the request, setting a trial date for September. That was the one good thing about it—a jury trial would take longer to put together. If they were lucky, some criminal cases might come up, and their dispute would be put off even further.

In the evenings she found herself sitting outside with Turner, two chairs parked in the shade, just as in earlier days, letting Newton play until dark and waiting for the summer evening to cool down. She noticed that whenever they were outside, Marie stayed indoors with Josephine. Small comforts.

"What's going to happen, James?" she asked. "What's going to become of us?"

"I wish I knew," he said. "There's talk that the governor has reached agreement with that general in St. Louis. But with Arkansas seceding, there's like to be an invasion, and the quickest way from St. Louis to Arkansas is right through here. On the other hand, anytime there's uncertainty, there's opportunity. Maybe the price of beef will go up, and we could get a contract with the military, switch the fields over from grain to cattle. Could be a boon."

"No," she said. "I mean us. What's going to become of us, you and me?"

"Ah," he said. He was silent for a long time. "I can only tell half that story."

"What's the half you can tell me?"

"My half," he said. "I am going to stay here unless I am called. I don't think I will be, not with all these young men rushing to the fight. They should be enough to settle things. But if I am called, I will go. And I am going to love you and Newton till the day I die."

Charlotte found herself about to respond as she always had before, scoffing, skeptical, but her heart was not in it. She had might as well admit what she had always known at some depth, that she did love him, that while her hurt had not gone away, neither had her love, not completely. She was tired and sad. Danger around them, men leaving for who knows how long. She thought about the face in the window she had seen earlier. Was that destined to be her face forever? Harder, harder, ever harder?

She took his hand. "You may have no choice in the matter," she said. "I fear that events are going to compel us much faster than we can shape them."

"And the other half of the story?" Turner said. "The half that you can tell me?"

He waited in silence while she thought. "I'll be here," she finally said.

In the gathering darkness a rider came down the road, his horse's belly wet from the ford. Turner waved at him as he passed. "Hello, friend," he said. "What news from the wider world?"

The man stopped and looked them over. He wore a broad hat that shaded his face and a leather coat despite the warmth of the day. "That depends," he said. "What side you on?"

"We are maintaining a neutral stance," Turner said. "We are friends to all."

"Hm," said the man. "See how long that lasts." He shifted in his saddle. "All right, Mr. Neutral Stance," he said. "Guess you heard the arsenal at Liberty's been taken over. The Federals keep switching generals. Governor's called for the State Guard to muster up. There's a big camp of 'em up in St. Louis, out on the west end of town." He scanned their faces for signs of reaction. "How about you, mister? Going to join?"

"I've got crops in the field and a family that needs me," Turner said. "More than the Governor."

The man did not answer. He looked down the road. "That Harp Webb's house?" he said.

"That's it."

"Thanks," he said, and rode on.

"Now who do you suppose that is?" Charlotte said after he rode out of sight. She watched him as he tied his horse to Webb's porch railing and stepped inside.

"More trouble, is my guess," Turner said.

They turned quiet again. Charlotte did not like to think that they were going to have to wonder from now on about everybody who came down the road, whether they were friends or enemies. It would be a hard way to live.

It was almost too dark to see. Time to call Newton inside. Lamps were being lit all up the road. She could see them flickering in the evening. A

Steve Wiegenstein

whip-poor-will called from the fields, and after a while was answered. If she hadn't known better, she would have thought it to be a perfectly ordinary end to a perfectly ordinary day.

May 1861

Chapter 21

Emile Mercadier came home from town later in the week with copies of the St. Louis newspapers. The men stood at the doorway of the Temple and passed them around, reading over each other's shoulders.

MASSACRE! read the headline in the *Missouri Democrat*. The dispatch said that a body of federal soldiers had raided the Missouri State Militia's camp, taken everyone prisoner, and then fired on a group of onlookers as they marched them back to the Arsenal. In tones of outrage, the newspaper described the brutish German soldiers, like modern-day Hessians, speaking their guttural gibberish as they fired volley after volley into the frightened crowd of women and children.

"Good Lord," said Prentice. "It says here that three dozen were killed."

"Here's the *Republican*," Emile said.

Its headline read FIGHT IN ST. LOUIS, and the story described how arms and cannon, stolen from Federal arsenals in the South, had been confiscated. According to the *Republican*, the troops had narrowly averted the takeover of the St. Louis arsenal, with its large cache of arms and ammunition. Missouri had been saved for the Union. An "unfortunate incident" was mentioned, in which a drunkard tried to cross the path of the troops returning to the arsenal with their prisoners, fired a pistol at the soldiers, and a confused fight ensued, with civilians getting caught in the middle.

"Well, something happened," Mercadier said.

They read the newspapers again and again, trying to make sense of the incident, but it was as if two different events were being described. The Army had captured the militia camp and taken their weapons; townspeople had been killed. Beyond that, all was fog.

But everything had changed. Blood had been shed, not at a fort no one had heard of in some distant state, but nearby, on the home soil.

"Now what?" Cabot asked.

"I wish I knew," said Turner.

What else was there to do but plant and hoe? Following Newton Carr's advice, they had built a pen on the mountain for the cattle. Two people went up in the morning to drive them down for milking and pasture, and then two others would drive them up again in the early evening. The chickens could not be hidden away, but they had begun burying crocks of eggs. Most of the community thought this hiding was a silly precaution, but Charlotte had insisted.

There had been no word from Herrmann, the lawyer, for a couple of weeks. Given the uncertain times, Cabot felt nervous about this silence; surely at least a letter would be in order, he said to Charlotte and Wickman at their next directors' meeting.

"You think Harp Webb will keep after this lawsuit, with all the other troubles in the country?" Wickman said.

Charlotte looked glum. "Harp's like a rat terrier. He's not the type to give up on anything."

"Very well, then," Cabot said. "I'm going to town tomorrow to find Herrmann. Do either of you want to come along?"

"Oh, I don't think so," Wickman said. "I'm not good in these kinds of sessions, all hard talk and bargaining. You two should do this."

Charlotte met Cabot's gaze. "All right," she said. "I'll go."

"If you need to talk to—" Cabot began, but she cut him off.

"I'm the president of this community. I don't need anyone's permission. And let's take my phaeton for a change. I'm tired of farm wagons with no springs."

As he wiped down the phaeton the next morning, Cabot nervously wondered what was in store. Going out in the fancy carriage with him would set tongues wagging. Was she ready for that? Was he? And what were her intentions? She knew how he felt. He decided to let her take the lead in the conversation. There was nothing he could say that she didn't already know.

With the tall wheels of the phaeton speeding them along the road to town, they spoke only of the war and the coming visit with the lawyer. Once there, they found the streets nearly empty. All the war talk had frightened everyone into their houses. Herrmann's office was locked. No one answered Cabot's knock. After a minute, though, there was movement at an upstairs curtain, and a few moments later Herrmann let them inside.

"I'm not going to be able to represent you in September," he said abruptly. "I'm leaving for St. Louis. It's not safe for a German speaker around here."

"Who are we supposed to get?" Cabot said.

"I don't know. There's a lawyer in Ironton, Emerson is his name. He might take your case. Try him."

Herrmann paced his living room and looked out through his windows from time to time. "The native-borns are in a fit," he said. "All the Germans around here are pulling in their heads like turtles. I tried to talk some of them into moving back to St. Louis, too, but they're stubborn. Gotta hold down those farms."

"What's happened?"

Herrmann looked at them incredulously. "You haven't heard anything, have you? Good Lord, you're just like those old Dutchies, head down and nose to the dirt." He peeked through his curtains again. "Very well, here's what I know. That business up in St. Louis has the state buzzing like a tree full of bees. I thought Missouri would stay in the Union, but now I don't know. I hear General Harney and Governor Jackson are going to meet to try to calm things down. The governor's a Douglas Democrat, so maybe there's hope. But in the meantime, he's brought back old Pap Price to command the State Guard, and they're forming regiments all over the state. Refusing Lincoln's call for troops was—well, it wasn't good."

"But you? Why are you running?"

"Those soldiers who shot into the crowd in St. Louis were from the Home Guard—Germans every one of them. That's not going over well. Sam Hildebrand's already been through here once. He killed a fellow out in the Flatwoods, some farmer who looked at him cross-eyed. There's a bunch from around here forming a Vigilance Committee, looking to pay him back for that. In other words, this is not a good time to have enemies, and I've antagonized too many people as it is."

"I hope you'll forgive me for saying this, but—"

"I sound like a coward? You don't have to tell me. If somebody had told me I'd be running like a rabbit at the first sign of trouble, I'd have laughed, or maybe spit in his eye. But your tune changes once you see a fellow you represented in a lawsuit brought to town in the back of a wagon with a hole in his forehead."

"So you're catching the train out of here."

"Actually, no. Somebody's burned the railroad bridge. I hear the Federals will be coming down to build it back, but I'm not waiting. I'm taking the road straight north." Quietly, he added, "You folks should consider it too."

Cabot laughed. "I won't speak for the others, but I've been tarred and feathered, and damn near lynched. It'll take more than a marauding local to run me off."

Cabot and Charlotte climbed into the phaeton in a state of gloom. "Stop at the stable before we leave," Charlotte said quietly. "I want to talk to the liveryman."

The stable owner greeted them with a wave, but Charlotte leaned down from her seat before he could speak. "How much will you give me for this carriage?" she said. "I'm of a mind to sell it."

The liveryman circled the phaeton, rubbing his chin. "This ain't really the place for fancy rigs," he said. "You couldn't haul a sack of potatoes in this thing."

"That's not what it's for," she said. They leaned forward so he could inspect the upholstery on the seat and back.

"Five dollars," the liveryman said.

"Oh, don't joke," Charlotte said. "Twenty, and that's half of what it cost me. It's hickory, top to bottom."

"I see that. But what it cost you is not my concern," the man said. "Ten is as high as I'll go."

"All right, but it has to be in hard coin," she said. "Send a man out to pick it up any time. We live out in the country and need it to ride home in."

The stable owner reached up and shook her hand. "Where you folks live?"

"Daybreak," Charlotte said. "Heard of it? It's down past Cedar Grove, across the river."

The man's smile disappeared. "Yeah, I've heard of it. Wish I'd have known that's where you were from."

"Why? Because you would have cut a sharper bargain?"

He shrugged. "I hear that place is some kind of abolitionist hideout."

Charlotte leaned toward him. "I'm an abolitionist, but I can't say as much for the rest of the townsfolk. And I'm right here, so you can't say I'm hiding out, now can you?"

"No, ma'am, I'd say not."

"Hard coin. Remember that."

When they reached the edge of town, Cabot said, "Do you think that was wise?"

"To hell with wisdom," Charlotte said. "What has wisdom ever got me?"

The day was bright and warm, and as they passed the farms along the way, they could see people in the fields, working as always, and it was possible to imagine that there was no war, that life was proceeding as it always had. But as they passed, men straightened from their work and watched them suspiciously until they were out of sight. Heads inclined together, and occasionally a man would walk with exaggerated casualness toward his house. There was a war on, all right.

When they reached the wooded ridgetop that ended with the Indian camp, Charlotte put her hand on his arm."Listen," she said.

Cabot reined the horse to a stop. They sat in silence, and he thought briefly that she had meant for him to hear a birdsong, or a sound from the forest. But then she spoke.

"I've not been as consistent or honest with you about my feelings as I should have been," she said, choosing her words. "And for that I am sorry." Cabot tried to demur, but she raised her hand. "Pursuing you and kissing you, then avoiding you. That must have felt like coquetry, and I hope you know I'm no coquette."

She stepped down from the phaeton and walked up to caress the horse's nose. Cabot stayed in his seat. "Would you have been a better match for me than James? Yes, I think you would. But it's a match we didn't make, and I'll not bemoan my fate. Without James, there would be no Newton, and that is something I can never call a mistake. I have to live the life I have, not the one I might have had."

"I know." He could think of nothing else to say. He knew she was right but hated to speak the words.

"I know you love me. How could I not? And if I am unable to say the words or fail to show affection in return, it's not from want of feeling, but from knowing that some feelings breed disaster. I don't have to look far to see that truth."

She climbed into the phaeton and took his hand. "I have forgiven James, and so must you. We have always been a tiny island in a hostile sea, and now those seas are stormy. We must hold together, Adam, as hard as that may be."

"Does Daybreak have a place in the world anymore? Perhaps it's time for us to leave our island and enter the sea."

Charlotte looked thoughtful. "I'm afraid I don't see you as a warrior," she said. "I want you here for your safety. And for my—" She squeezed his hand. "Well, I guess for the selfish pleasure of having you near. I would have said I want you here for your wise advice and your help in running the colony, but I am sick to death of appeals to duty and greater causes. I want you here to talk to me and keep me halfway human."

Cabot tried to keep his face from twisting into a grimace. Why couldn't she have been self-indulgent a year ago, when there was room for personal desires? Now with war afoot, his heart had grown painfully crowded with allegiances in all directions.

"You ask a great deal of me," he finally managed.

"Yes," she said, releasing his hand. "And it's not fair, and I'm sorry. But there I am."

Cabot chucked the reins and did not reply.

Turner heard the news from town with foreboding. If Herrmann's reports were right, it would soon be unsafe to ride to town for supplies, and the idea of selling their rope up north was in danger as well. Perhaps these talks between the general and the governor would work out.

With Charley gone and Webb dead, it was harder than ever to keep ahead of the work. Turner found himself in the cornfield from early to late, planting and hoeing. Even those who weren't the best farmers, like Wickman and Cabot, pitched in, returning to the fields after dinner.

It was a late June evening when Turner found himself the last man in the field, along with Cabot. Cabot had still not been friendly to him since the incident with Marie, but the quiet of the evening and the fatigue of their work seemed to ease the tension. They worked their way down adjoining rows and rested when they got to the end. They rested their hoes on the fence by the road and sat on a stump, looking back at the village.

"Let's work our way back on the next two rows and then call it a day," Turner said.

"Sounds good to me," Cabot said. But neither of them was ready to stand up yet. They stayed where they were.

Cabot spoke again after a while. "We came out here to change the world. But I think the world may be changing us instead."

Turner did not answer.

"Ever since I was a boy, I wanted to change the world," Cabot continued. "I remember when Charlotte loaned me your book to read, on the steamboat coming out. I didn't accept the reasoning, but Lord, what a force of feeling was in it! What grand sentiments—I could feel what man was really capable of. It was as though clouds had parted and I could see a mountaintop—and realized that I too could climb to that height and be the person I could see up on that mountain." He paused, seeming a little embarrassed at his rhetoric. "I guess you felt something like that when you were writing it."

"No," Turner admitted. "When I wrote the book I wanted to be celebrated. It didn't dawn on me that people could actually try to live this way, or want me to lead them. I only wanted to be famous." They could see people in the colony moving about, finishing up their chores. "Strange," he said. "It's only after having lived here that I truly feel idealistic. Before, it was all just abstraction, but now ... I see people living their ideals. And I know what's possible."

Cabot sighed. "But I don't think the world is interested. Everyone is talking union, slavery, and war. We are going to be forgotten."

"Maybe," Turner said. "'Mute inglorious Miltons,' you think? There are worse fates. We could have just been mute and inglorious." It felt good to laugh together.

"Or perhaps this other cause is the one we should have chosen. Perhaps Lysander Smith was on the right path."

"He chose his, and I chose mine. I don't want to look back." Turner stood up. "Speaking of inglorious, I guess we had better hoe our way home."

They picked up their hoes and walked to the rows of corn. As they did, a rider crossed the ford and came up the road—the same leather-coated man who had ridden by a few weeks earlier.

"You boys live here?" he said, inclining his head toward Daybreak.

"Yes," Cabot said. He rested his hands on the end of his hoe and looked the man in the eye.

"Here, spread a few of these around then," the man said. He reached into his saddlebag and pulled out a sheaf of handbills. "I want to make Greenville before I quit tonight."

"What's been happening?" Turner said.

"All hell is what's been happening," the man said. "The Federals put some abolitionist in charge. Governor and the legislature are on the run. They got chased out of Jefferson City, heading southwest is what I hear. Ain't going to be no neutral state, that's for sure."

The man rode on, and Turner and Cabot read the bills.

MUSTER CALL
All ABLE-BODIED MEN between the ages of 18 AND 45
Are Called to Muster
To Defend the State Against the YANKEE INVADER
By Order of the Legislature
May 11, 1861
Report to Your County Seat and Await Orders

"Well, you wondered 'now what' the other day," Turner said. "Looks like this is what. Everyone will want to see this. We can finish the corn tomorrow."

The men gathered at the Temple and studied the handbills.

"I'm not going," said Wickman. "I'm not able-bodied."

"Me neither," said Glendale Wilson. "I'm feeble-minded."

After the laughter had ended, Prentice said, "I don't know. It says it's an order."

"But who's going to enforce it?" Wickman said. "They want volunteers. I don't volunteer."

"We know that for sure," Prentice said back. "Like when there's weeds to be pulled."

But after the banter, the men sat quiet and passed the handbills around some more.

"I guess I'll go," Prentice said. "I'll tell you boys what I hear."

"I'm a Baltimore man, not a Missourian," Wickman said. "Don't know what they'll do in Maryland. And besides, I've got the Missus to think about. And the little ones. We've already lost the two, and I think losing me would…." His voice drifted away.

"Well, I can't go," Cabot said. "I'm a Yankee invader."

"No, you're not," Prentice said earnestly. "You're a good man, everybody knows that. This bunch that's marching across the state, they're different…."

He stopped and was silent.

"No, they ain't the Germans," Thomas Schnack said. He had said nothing till then. "What I hear, the Germans got told to stay in St. Louis. These are regular Army, with maybe some Germans. But still, I don't think I go to this muster call. I don't think I get a very friendly greeting."

One of the men poked Prentice in the ribs. "Who knows, maybe if you join the State Guard, you'll meet up with Newton Carr. Just hope he ain't pointing a cannon at you."

That thought rendered them gloomier than ever, and the group broke up and headed for their homes. As they were blowing out the lamps, Cabot took Turner by the arm.

"I want you to know," he said, and then stopped. "I want you to know that nothing improper passed between Charlotte and me on that trip to town. I want you to know that."

Turner's face was sorrowful. "I knew it in my heart," he said. "I'm the only one fool enough for that."

They shook hands wordlessly and parted.

At home, Charlotte listened to his account of the meeting, although he left out his final conversation with Cabot. "Prentice can't be thinking about joining up," she said after he was finished.

"I think so," Turner told her. "He's a Missourian born and bred, not like you or me. Or most everyone else here, for that matter. We're all transplants."

"But we're Americans."

"Yes. But loyalties out here—"

Charlotte's expression grew grave. "Perhaps I should go talk to him."

"I imagine his own wife is doing plenty of that."

They dressed for bed quietly once it was dark. Newton picked up their mood and went to bed without his usual fussing about staying up later. Sometime in the night, Charlotte reached for Turner, the first time she had done so since the day she had found him with Marie. Her embrace was tight and fierce, not the passion of pleasure, but of possession. He felt as if she were molding herself to him, clinging to him like a drowning man would cling to a branch. In return he gripped her just as close, and through the night they rocked and writhed, arms and legs entwined, their open mouths a breath apart.

The news was spotty for the next few weeks. Prentice came back from the militia meeting fired up with enthusiasm and apologetic toward the rest of them. "I have to do this," he said. "Anyway, it's only a ninety-day muster, so I should be back in time to help with the harvest and the rope work."

Emile continued to keep up his shop in town, but one week in mid-July he returned, bringing all the newspapers as usual, but shaking with fear. "Bad things, very bad things," he said. "The Federals, they take over town, and Ironton too, is what I hear. They gonna protect the iron mines and the lead mines, and the railroad. So I think, hey, this looks like good business, and I go over to introduce myself to the captain. I tell him shoes and boots, made and repaired. But then I get a mile out of town today, and a bunch of men, five of them, they ride up behind me." He shuddered. "The man says, don't do no business with them damn Yankees or we kill you. They mean it too."

Turner listened to his story while everyone else passed around the newspapers. "It's all right, Emile," he said. "We don't need you to go into town anyway. There's plenty to do around here."

"But the money!" Mercadier said. "And I think maybe I put us into danger by going over so quick and talking to the soldiers. You think?"

"We need you more than we need any money," Turner said. "And as for danger, there's plenty to go around. I doubt if you can add to it or subtract from it."

The newspapers wrote of the legislature fleeing to the southwest, Springfield or beyond, of a new convention of all Union men convening in Jefferson City, of the possibility that martial law would be declared. As he read, an idea came to Turner. He knew he should talk to Charlotte about it, but knew also that she would try to stop him. And if it failed, he wanted to be the only person to feel the consequences. But he knew he owed her something.

In the morning he saddled a horse. "I need to go into town to talk to this captain," he said. "I don't want any hard feelings over Emile not showing up at his shop any more. And I want him to understand why."

"Do you think it's safe to do that?" Charlotte said.

"Well, I don't have any enemies yet, at least not that I know of," said Turner. He paused. "And I want to see if I can get something done about this court case."

She gave him a questioning look, but he said nothing further. "Be safe," she said.

He crossed the ford and made his way to the top of the ridge. The country-side which had seemed so inertly beautiful a short time ago now seemed full of menace. He listened for threat in every sound. But the road was empty, and all the farmhouses he passed were quiet. He rode briskly, not wanting to linger. He had not armed himself. He guessed that anyone he might meet would probably be better armed and quicker to shoot.

The quiet ride into town gave him confidence, and he stopped at Grindstaff's store. Grindstaff did not come out front to greet him as usual, but stayed inside.

"I tell you right now, I probably ain't got what you need," he said as soon as Turner walked in. "I ain't got much of nothing."

"That's all right," Turner said.

"You can't count on the railroad any more, and there ain't many goddam steamboats running. People are sitting on the bluffs playing potshot with the pilot houses. Besides, these goddam Federals have about cleaned me out."

"I thought it was supposed to be dangerous to do business with them."

"Hell, I ain't got no choice. Running a store is what I do. Anyway, these boys, they don't ask, they just take. Lucky thing their money's good."

"Did Herrmann the lawyer leave town?"

"Yep, he's a gone goose. Didn't nobody see him leave, he just up and went."

"So where are these soldiers, anyway?"

"Right up the street." Grindstaff pointed toward the center of town. "They've took over the goddam courthouse, and they set up a barracks across from it, in the hotel. Pretty fancy quarters for a bunch of soldiers, you ask me."

Turner looked down toward the courthouse. He could see a small group of soldiers drilling in the street, with a handful of townspeople idly watching them. "Well, I need to go talk to them," he said. "I need to tell them that our man Mercadier isn't coming back to town anymore. Apparently some rebel boys are—"

"I know. They're warning off everybody. They come and talked to me too. I had to tell them, hell, I can't move my store, and if I close it I'll starve. I may not like these Federal bastards, but here they are and I can't do nothing about it."

"How'd they take that?"

"Not so good. But I trade with 'em too, on the sly, and take their State Guard scrip. It ain't worth shit, so I gotta charge the Federals double just to come out even. So I figure I'm square with these rebel fellas."

"Local boys?"

"Mostly. A few up from the Bootheel to organize things. I hear they're putting together a real regiment down around Jackson or somewhere."

"Well, tell them not to shoot me. I'm just going in to tell them about Emile."

He left his horse tied up at Grindstaff's and walked to the courthouse. A soldier at the door eyed him suspiciously.

"I'm here to see your commanding officer," Turner said.

"What for?"

"I represent the community of Daybreak, southwest of here. I'd like to speak to the commander."

"Wait here." The man disappeared inside. Turner stood in the sun, aware that the idlers across the street were watching him. In a minute the soldier returned.

"Five cents," he said.

"What for?"

"To see the captain."

Turner turned away. "Go to hell."

"Oh, all right," the soldier said. "A man's got to eat. In here."

What had been the county clerk's office had been turned into a head-quarters. Two men were in the room—a captain at a table, some papers in front of him, the only man he had seen in a full uniform so far, and at another table to the side, a telegraph operator gazing at a silent machine.

The captain looked up. "Well?"

Turner had been rehearsing a number of ways to do this, whether to proceed cautiously, test for a response, try to negotiate—but at that moment decided to go straight ahead.

"I am here to report a man who I think is aiding and abetting the rebels," he said.

August 1861

Chapter 22

Turner said nothing to Charlotte after his return from town, but when a patrol of soldiers—a sergeant and four nervous-looking recruits— showed up outside their door one morning a week later, she guessed he had something to do with it. They stepped into the yard to speak to them.

"Are you Harper Webb?" the sergeant said. None of the men got down from their horses.

"No," said Turner.

"You know Harper Webb?"

"Yes. He lives in that house." The five men turned their heads as if pulled by a magnet in the direction of Turner's nod.

"We have a report says he may be involved with the rebels around here. You know anything about that?"

"I wouldn't know anything about any rebel activity around here, Harp Webb or anyone else," Turner said coolly. The sergeant eyed him with suspicion.

"That's what everybody says. You know if this Webb keeps any weapons?"

"He has an old long rifle, a muzzle-loader," Turner said. "Beyond that I don't know."

"Good news, boys," the sergeant said. "He'll only have time to shoot one of us before we get to him."

"Oh, he's a quick fellow," Charlotte said. "I'll bet he could shoot two or three of you."

"Well, ain't she a saucy thing!" the sergeant exclaimed. "Ain't you never taught your wife about manners, plowboy?"

"You can keep your opinions to yourself where my wife is concerned, mister," Turner said.

"That's 'sir' to you, plowboy," the sergeant said. He snatched his quirt from its holder on his saddle and swung at Turner, but Turner leaned back a little and the blow missed. "I'd say both of you could use a lesson in manners."

"You can step down from that horse, mister, and we'll find out who gets called 'sir.'" Turner watched his face and waited to dodge another swing of the quirt. He felt unaccountably angry. Perhaps the war sentiment had infected him too.

"By God! I've half a mind to do it. This whole county is a nest of rebels as far as I'm concerned, and we're better off without the lot of you." But the sergeant stayed on his horse. "Well, enough of this. I have orders to bring in one person, not two, and if I got down off this horse I'd have to bring in two. But watch yourself, mister. I ain't got patience for smart alecks." He turned his horse. "You two ride past, you two stay behind, and I'll knock at the door," he said to his soldiers. With a last glare at Turner, he rode away.

They watched as the men positioned themselves. Harp had been watching too, for as soon as the soldiers surrounded the house he stepped onto his porch, barefoot and wearing a cotton shirt and pants.

"Are you Harper Webb?" the sergeant said. Webb just nodded. "We have orders to take you in. You are suspected of helping the rebels."

"What rebels?" Harp said. "Ain't no rebels around here."

"Very funny. You and your neighbor up there ought to join a minstrel show. Boys, search his house. You other two, search the barn."

"What are we looking for, sir?" said one of the men.

"Anything suspicious, you ignorant clods," the sergeant said. "If you don't know what it is, bring it out here and I'll look at it. And saddle up his horse while you're there."

The men scattered, and the sergeant stepped onto the porch with a piece of rope. "Hold out your hands, I gotta tie you up."

"Let me put my shoes on first."

"All right," the sergeant said. He called in the house. "Bring out a pair of shoes."

"The ones by the back door," Harp called.

"You're a calm one," the sergeant said.

"What, you want me to cry?" Harp said. "Go to hell."

The sergeant made as if to strike him, but stopped. Harp didn't flinch.

"You're in the mood to hit everybody today, ain't you?" he said. "You forgot the lady back there. Or were you planning on hitting her on your way back?"

This time the sergeant didn't restrain himself. He slapped Harp across the face with the back of his hand and braced himself to strike him again with his fist; but Harp didn't swing. "I ain't going to make your job easy for you," he said. "You want to shoot me, I ain't going to help you."

By now the two soldiers from the house had appeared on the porch. One held a pair of brogans in his hand.

"Give him his goddam shoes," the sergeant said. "Whole valley full of smart alecks. This is the United States Government you are dealing with, sonny boy, and you had better learn that right now." He turned to the soldiers. "Find anything?"

"No, sir," said one. "It's just a house."

The other two came in from the barn, one leading Harp's horse. "Anything?" the sergeant asked.

"About forty gallons of whiskey out in the barn," one said.

"Whiskey maker, are you?" the sergeant said.

"Be careful with that," Harp said to the soldier. "Some of them crocks is what I use to piss in when I don't feel like getting up."

The soldier wiped his mouth reflexively and then put his hand down again just as fast. "Got me there," he said with a grin.

"This ain't a joke," the sergeant said. "Mount up and let's go."

Harp climbed on his horse, and the sergeant gestured for him to hold out his hands. "You don't have to tie me up," Harp said. "I ain't going nowhere."

"I know you ain't. But I'm doing it anyway."

He tied Harp's hands together at the wrist and looped the rope around the saddle horn. "Say goodbye to your friends there," he said as they passed.

"Oh, they ain't my friends," Harp said. "I can guarantee you that."

Charlotte and Turner watched until the men had ridden out of sight, crossing the ford toward town. Then they went inside.

"Well," Charlotte said. She was thinking over the implications. The ease with which Turner lied to the soldiers bothered her, but not nearly so much as his not telling her in the first place about informing on Harp. "Is that what this war is about?"

"You know full well—"

"Yes. Harp was going to take our land. I know that. But I think I would have liked to have fought him in court instead."

"And would that have been more fair?"

She knew it would not have been, except that Harp would have been the one taking unfair advantage. She looked at Turner and knew she did not have to say it.

"It's just … strange. It feels strange. It feels calculated. And you've never been a calculating person. Lord knows I can't stand Harp Webb, but to see him led off like that, trussed up like a pig—"

"I know what you mean."

"I guess we might as well get used to it," she said.

Turner took his hat off its peg and got ready to go to the fields, but Charlotte took his sleeve. "James," she said. "We must not let this war change us. Promise me that you will not let this war change you."

"I can promise you that I will try," he said. "God knows what lies ahead."

"Perhaps we should go ahead and clear out of here. There have to be safer places."

He stopped at the door. "If you really believe so, you should bring that up at the next community meeting. You're the president. That's too big a question to be decided by just you and me."

Turner walked out, took his hoe from where he had left it resting against the wall of the house, and headed for the fields. As he walked away, Charlotte watched his figure diminish against the mountain, which was rich in deep summer green. Other men were walking out of their houses, joining him in the fields, and she could see them greeting each other as they met. She knew it was just her fear talking, but couldn't help longing to be back in New York, far from this turmoil. At the same time, as she watched the men begin their labors, and saw the women come out of their houses to sweep the steps, mind their children, shake their rugs, she knew that this community was no longer an experiment to her. It was her home, one that she had chosen just as surely as she had chosen Turner, and one she would never willingly leave. On the side of the distant mountain she could see the gravestones. They had buried loved ones here. They were no longer just visiting—or playing, as Harp had accused them. They were bound to this place now, war or no war.

The news from outside was sporadic and confusing. Charlotte's father wrote that he had begun training a new class at the Point, but had almost immediately been rushed south to help throw up earthworks around Washington. The Army of the Potomac had suffered a disaster, and the rebels were expected at the gates of the capital within days. There was a silence for several weeks. Then the mail brought two letters at once, although they had been written a week and a half apart. Charlotte opened them in order.

The first said that the rebs had unaccountably failed to follow up their victory at Bull Run with a march to Washington, and that their days of frantic trenching had been for nothing—a turn of events he was perfectly satisfied with, as they had not had enough time to put up more than the simplest of breastworks, and if it had come to a fight, he had little doubt but that they would have been overwhelmed. As it was, they spent their days drilling recruits and their evenings at leisure; he had already seen two plays and a concert.

Charlotte opened the second letter and read:

My darling daughter,

Since last I wrote, much has happened, and I regret that, carried like a leaf on the river of events that rushes us all to our destinations, I have failed to write you as often as my heart impels. I am well, and pray you are the same.

I am no longer in Washington, although fear of this letter's interception prevents me from stating my whereabouts with greater exactness. I am now a colonel, in charge of a regiment, that lost its previous commander to the fortunes of war; but having no superstition in that regard, I have no concern for my personal safety beyond what I feel for all of my men. The identity of my regiment must also be obscured, but I assure you, they are good, stout boys, and you would smile to recognize the names of some of my junior officers. I am told that Caroline's husband has been recalled from the West, and has acquitted himself well in several engagements.

My recall to the field of arms has given rise to thoughts of larger scope, of this world and the next, so I hope you will permit a father a few moments of reflection. Great forces are at work in the world, but I cannot comprehend them. We are down to the four of us now, you, me, and your husband and son, and it is from that foundation that all our calculations must begin. The woodchuck in its den, the swallow in its cliff crevice, sleep in their beds while storms rage around them, but for better or worse we are not animals or birds. We strive, we aspire, we seek something greater while forgetting what we have. But in these times you must think like the woodchuck. Dig so deep that the storm overhead is but a faint rattle. Decide what matters, and grip it to you. Everything else, no matter how sweet, familiar, noble, or comforting, is expendable, and you must be ready to let go of it. Please remember that.

I am, and will always remain, your devoted and loving

Father

Charlotte held the letter carefully in both hands, as if it were made of fine bone china. She did not want to fold it up and lose sight of the words. For the first time since the war began, her heart overflowed with the fragility of everything in her life, how every letter from her father could very well be his last words to her. After a while, she did fold up the letter. She tucked it into her apron pocket, but reconsidered and placed it in the crack between her new window frame and the wall, where she knew it would be safe.

The local reports were no clearer. The Union Army had been beaten badly near Springfield, its general killed, and it had retreated to St. Louis. But the rebels had not followed. They had retreated too, down into Arkansas or somewhere. And in the empty space that opened up, groups of men began appearing.

At first they rode by urgently, as if on their way to somewhere, or from somewhere. But then the groups rode more slowly, watchfully. Instead of staying on the main road, they would ride through the cutoff to Daybreak, walking their horses and peering into house windows as they passed. They rarely wore uniforms, or what uniforms they had were a nondescript half-colored garb. And in the slanting light of near-dusk over the mountaintop, no one could have told anyway whether the uniforms were blue or gray or something in between. The men in the fields warily watched them go by.

Four of them rode up and stopped one afternoon in the late summer. One of them, a man with a wide hat and a gold tooth, dismounted and came to the door. Charlotte met him on the step.

"Can we trouble you for a dipper of water?" he asked, tipping his hat.

Charlotte fetched the dipper and bucket from the barrel in back. The man was standing in the doorway, and she could tell that he was studying the contents of the house.

"We hear there's a man makes whiskey around here," he said as he walked back to the horses and passed the bucket. "This the place?"

"You passed it," she told him. "It's that house there."

"Think he might sell us a jug or two?"

"Hard to say," she said. "He's in jail up in Fredericktown."

"I've heard about that," the man said, mounting his horse. "Thirty or forty of our boys locked up there, and another bunch over in Ironton. Trumped-up charges of one sort or another."

"I wouldn't know about that," Charlotte said. "We don't get much news out here."

The man handed back the bucket and tipped his hat with a flourish, smiling broadly, his gold tooth glinting. "Well, thank you, ma'am. And God bless Jefferson Davis!"

When Charlotte didn't respond, he looked at her suspiciously. "What's the matter, ma'am, don't you support the cause?"

"I just gave you a bucket of spring water, didn't I?"

"That you did." He smiled again. "This settlement up ahead, is it friendly?"

"Friendly as any, I suppose."

"What I mean is, is it a rebel town?"

She looked at the man's face. "It's like every town. Some think one way, some think another. We try to work together and not let politics divide us."

"This ain't politics any more, ma'am. It's war now, and there's no splitting the pie." He looked out over the village. "Prosperous looking little place. Strange, don't see no cattle though."

"A bunch of men came by and took them last week," she said, surprised at how easy it was to lie. "Milk cows and all. They were dressed about like you, but they didn't say what side they were on."

"No hogs either."

"Where did you grow up, man? The hogs are in the woods this time of year."

That seemed to satisfy him. He backed his horse out of the yard. "Thanks for the water. I was just testing you with that Jeff Davis remark. Point of fact, we're scouts for Plummer's regiment. God bless Old Abraham!" He squinted at Charlotte, waiting for a response.

"God bless us all," she said, "and grant us a speedy end to this conflict."

"They told me you hill folk were a crafty lot. Let's go, boys." The men rode through the village fast, pausing at no more houses.

About sunset two more men came through behind them. One was a large man riding a big Belgian that looked more suited for plowing than road travel; the other was a little one-armed man on a nervous black gelding that he had trouble controlling. The horse was bridle-shy and kept pitching its head. Turner was in back of the house, washing up, and Charlotte was watching Newton out front.

"Did four men come by here earlier today?" the one-armed man called from his horse. "Strangers?"

"Yes," she said.

"Ha!" the little man said. He turned to the big one. "I told you those shit-birds would take this road instead of the other one." He turned back to Charlotte. "How long ago?"

"A couple of hours."

"Couple of hours!" the large man said to his companion. "We'll never catch up to 'em."

"Oh yes we will," the little man said. "They'll stop and make camp. We'll come up on 'em in three hours or so. Ma'am, they say anything else?"

"They said they were scouts for someone named Plummer, but that's it."

The large man lifted his hat and wiped his forehead with the back of his sleeve. "Who's Plummer?" he asked.

"How the hell should I know?" the one-armed man said impatiently. "It ain't one of our people, I know that much."

"I don't know," the big man said. "If they stop and camp, won't they put a man out?"

"These bastards ain't smart enough to put a man out. Besides, we'll see their fire a mile off." He jerked the reins of his horse, which bucked up and nearly threw him, and yanked it toward the north. The two men rode off at a trot.

Turner had never come out front, which seemed strange to Charlotte, since he usually took pleasure in greeting passers. But as soon as the hoofbeats of the horses died away, he emerged around the corner. His face was grave. He sat down on the doorstone, took a knife out of his pocket, and began to whittle a stick with shaking hands.

"That's them," he said in answer to her unspoken question. "That's the men who killed Lysander Smith. I never saw their faces, but I'll never forget that voice."

Chapter 23

The sound of that voice was all it had taken to bring back the entire awful scene in Turner's mind: the beaten body of Lysander Smith, the arrogant bastard who organized the lynching, the bent tree, the single shot. But instead of the numb despair that had overtaken him the first time, Turner was now overcome by something new. It was a pure, simple hatred. He wanted to kill the men who had killed Smith, kill them all, kill them any way he could. It was a new emotion in his heart, and it felt strange. But it was there, and he couldn't pretend it wasn't. He felt like a coward for having hidden behind a corner of the house while they spoke to Charlotte, and wondered what he would have done in different circumstances.

He did not have long to wonder. Sometime in the night—midnight or later—the front door banged open. Turner and Charlotte woke with a start. Turner threw on some clothes and lit a lantern. In the front room, the one-armed man was sitting on the floor just inside the door, which he had not bothered to close. He held a pistol at Turner.

"Fix me a place to sleep," he said. "And put my horse away. I need rest."

Turner lifted his lantern. The man's face was scratched and he was dirty and sweaty, but he did not appear harmed otherwise. Through the open door he could see the horse, lathered, its reins tied to the hitching rail.

"Don't worry," said the man. "I ain't being chased, not tonight anyway. Hurry up, I'm tired." He showed no sign of recognizing Turner.

Charlotte had put on a dress and stood in the bedroom door, her hair down. She looked at the man and began to spread some quilts on the floor.

"We don't have any extra pillows," she said.

"That's all right. I'll use my boots."

"Where's your friend?"

"My friend met with misfortune," the man said. "Lesson learned. Always travel with someone who makes a bigger target than you."

He waved the pistol at Turner. "What are you waiting for? Brush down my horse and cool him off."

Turner put on his boots and stepped out the door. "All right. I'll put him in our barn." He paused in the doorway. "What's your name, anyway, sir?"

"My name is Mr. None-of-Your-Business, but you can just call me Fuck-You," the man said. "Treat that horse good or there'll be trouble."

Turner stepped out, closing the door behind him, his mind racing. He untied the horse's reins from the rail. The horse was too tired to fuss; it followed Turner to the barn, where he unsaddled it, brushed it down, and gave it a pail of water. The horse appeared to have gone through some rough brush, but otherwise it was unhurt.

He returned through the back door, took off his shoes, and lay on the bed. Charlotte lay beside him; he could tell she was awake. She started to whisper something, but he put his finger over her lips. They lay there, silent, for a few minutes, until the sound of snoring could be heard from the front room. Then he let himself out the back door as quietly as he could, his shoes in his hand.

He put on his shoes in the yard and walked through the darkness to Cabot's house. He let himself in without knocking and made his way to Cabot's bedroom. He shook his shoulder gently.

"It's me," he whispered to the startled Cabot. "Be quiet."

Cabot wiped his face and tried to clear his eyes. In the dim light of his room he could see Turner pacing beside the bed, his big frame looming over him. The stars were bright and there was little moon. Turner leaned close.

"One of the men who killed Lysander Smith is sleeping on my front room floor," he said. "And I mean to kill him." He stuck out his jaw as if daring Cabot to disagree.

"Here and now?"

Turner paused. "No. This cannot be connected to Daybreak. Everyone in the county thinks we're a Yankee town as it is." He resumed pacing. "Something like this could get us burned out. No. It has to be done somewhere else, and on the quiet. Not even Charlotte can know. All right?"

"I don't like the sound of this. Is that how this war is to be fought? Killings in the dark of night?"

"This isn't war, my friend. This is a private killing. I'm sorry if it seems less honorable than a killing in broad daylight."

Cabot considered, then decided. "All right."

Turner reached out and patted his shoulder in the darkness.

"What are you thinking?" Cabot asked.

"This man is a stranger here, and he's on the run. He'll head south before daylight. We will be waiting for him down the road a ways. And no gunshots to attract attention." He thought for a moment. "All right, I've got it. Meet me at the barn. Make no noise." And then Turner was out the door, closing it softly behind him.

Cabot dressed in the dark, troubled but impelled by Turner's urgency. So it had come to this. He had endured all the battles and humiliations of Kansas, he had traveled to Daybreak, all in the hope that there was a better way for mankind than strife and subjugation. He had wanted them to be a light unto nations, a sign that the human race was capable of overcoming history through intelligence and good will, and here he was preparing to ambush a total stranger in the dark of night. And what about Charlotte, alone in the cabin with this man? Who was not to say that harm might befall her?

No time to think about that now. Turner would not wait long, and whatever else he might think, Cabot did not want him to enter this fight alone.

In the barn, a tall black horse was sleeping in a stall, and Turner was waiting with a couple of axes and a thick loop of rope. He handed one of the axes to Cabot.

They walked out the back end of the barn and went south through the fields, circling behind Harp Webb's empty house, until they reached the road. They followed it south until they reached the bluffs where the river bent back in toward the mountain. The road ran hard against the bluff along a narrow ledge of ground, with nothing between it and the river but a few cottonwood and sycamore trees and a little underbrush. Turner looked over the ground a while, then tied the rope around the base of one of the trees and laid it across the road. He gathered leaves from the roadside and covered the rope with them. Cabot watched but did not ask questions.

"In daylight this would be obvious," Turner said when he had finished, keeping his voice low. "But our man won't wait till then."

He took the trailing end of the rope and led it off behind a boulder at the base of the bluff. He motioned Cabot over.

"I'll be behind here," he said. "You get behind one of those trees. When they reach this spot, I'll snap the rope, and we'll come at him from both sides."

He disappeared into the shadow of the boulder without another word. Cabot crossed the road, looking for a pool of deep shade under one of the big trees, and picked out his spot. It was good. He could see a long way up the road, almost to Webb's house. He squatted down to wait.

In the predawn darkness he listened to the sounds of the forest. He heard mice or chipmunks rustling in the undergrowth and once, possibly, the whoosh of an owl's wings as it swooped down on something. He rested his shoulder against the trunk of the tree, hefting the axe. When his knees began to ache from squatting, he let one knee rest on the ground instead, and then shifted to the other one after a while. Something splashed into the river behind him; it sounded big, a beaver maybe, but he realized that all sounds seemed magnified in the silence. Could have been a mink or a muskrat.

He had to admit, it was a perfect spot for a bushwhacking. The horse would rear, the man would be thrown, and it would all be over in an instant. He hefted the axe. He'd gotten pretty good as a tree feller over the years, no expert to be sure, but good enough to keep pace with the rest of the men. Of course, a tree was not a moving target. Could he do it? He had no idea. What if it all went wrong? They would both be killed, then or later, no doubt about that.

It was barely daylight when they heard the sound of hoofbeats on the road. Cabot lifted himself onto the balls of his feet and waited.

The black gelding was coming along at a slow pace, its rider peering into the darkness ahead of him to see his way. When the horse reached the concealed rope, Turner yanked it up in a swift wave directly under its nose. The horse reared and let out a wild neigh, throwing the one-armed man neatly over the back of his saddle, then trotted down the road.

They ran out from their hiding places. The man had landed hard on his back in the middle of the road with a groaned curse. Turner swung his axe high over his head and brought it down, but the man was quick enough to put up his hand and duck his head. Instead of a clean hit through the neck, the blade caught him on the side of the hand and slid down his arm, peeling back the left side of his jaw.

The man reached for the pistol in his belt, but Turner stomped hard on his bloody hand, pinning it to his belly.

Cabot stood over him, hefting the axe, and in the instant he was about to swing he locked eyes with the man on the ground. The man's expression was not one of hate or fear, but rather intense concentration, as if he were trying to remember a name or add numbers in his head. The surprising ordinariness of his look stopped Cabot for a moment; he wondered if he appeared the same, focused and thoughtful. Then the moment was over as the man jerked his hand free from Turner's foot just as Turner struck him a second blow square to the side of the head. Cabot heard the *thwack* of the blade in the man's skull as a spray of blood spattered his face.

That did the trick, he thought, and relaxed his grip on his axe.

To his surprise, the man rolled over and tried to rise. But with only one arm, he could not rise up and pull his pistol at the same time. He got to his knees, his head held low to avoid a sideways blow, but his position gave Turner time to pull his arm back and then, with a full swing, bring the axe down hard on the back of the man's head. With a moan, the one-armed man fell face down in the road. Turner stepped to one side and swung one more time, cutting right through the neck bones. The man's legs quivered for an instant and then stopped.

Turner stood in the road, panting. Cabot's heartbeat drummed in his ears.

"Just like butchering a damn hog," Turner said. He looked at his bloody axe and then at the man at his feet.

Cabot said nothing. He could no longer hear the sounds of the forest, just the blood rushing in his ears. He was sweating heavily. "I'm sorry," he finally stammered. "I just couldn't...."

"That's all right," said Turner.

Cabot stepped up to the body of the one-armed man. "You're sure this is him?"

"Oh yes." Turner squatted beside the body and rolled it over. The man's eyes were open and sightless, and his jaw hung slack. Part of his cheekbone was exposed, a shiny white, where Turner's first blow had hit. "I didn't get to see his face the time before, but this is him all right. I'd like to say something to him, but I don't know what that would be."

"What's his name?" Cabot said.

Turner shrugged. "Don't know. Man Who Killed Lysander Smith."

Bile rose in Cabot's throat and tears welled up in his eyes, but he swallowed hard and blinked the tears away. There was more to be done.

"Well, let's get this man out of here." Turner looked around. "We can toss him in the river."

"No," Cabot said, his mind finally engaged. "He'll get snagged somewhere. And even if he floats downstream, somebody will spot him at French Mills. Or Jewett, or Shelton's Ford, or somewhere. We have to bury him."

"You're right," Turner said. They looked around. Obviously they couldn't take him back toward Daybreak or drag him up the bluff. Their gazes turned to Harp's land across the river.

"That'll work," said Cabot. "The ground over there is soft. Let's float him across, leave him somewhere, and then come back after supper."

They picked up the corpse and carried it to the river. It was heavy and clumsy to maneuver, and the two men struggled to get it into the water. But it floated easily; they were able to pull it across with little difficulty. By the time they reached the other side, the gray light of dawn was giving way to a filtered yellow. They dragged the body up the bank and into the flat scrubland.

"This would make a fine farm," Cabot said as they dragged the body in. "Too much work for Harp, though."

About forty feet into the woods, they decided they had gone far enough and laid the body under a big cedar tree. "Don't guess we need to mark the spot," Turner said.

They waded back across the river and scattered dirt over the bloody spot in the road. "Better rinse off that axe," Cabot said. Turner took it to the river's edge and immersed the head. By now it was almost full daylight, and they could see themselves better, wet and bespattered like a pair of hunting dogs fresh from bringing down a deer. "Am I as big a mess as you are?" Turner said.

"A bigger one, I expect."

"We're pretty bad, then. We better get cleaned up."

They left the axes behind one of the cottonwood trees and looped up the rope, then walked home in silence. What was there to say? They had just killed a man. No conversation seemed to measure up. Their pants and shoes were wet; they squeaked as they walked. Turner slipped into his house quietly; Cabot thought he had made it home without meeting anyone, but just before he reached his door, Emile Mercadier came around the corner of his house, back from an early morning trip to the woods no doubt.

"What happened to you?" Mercadier said.

"Slipped and fell in the river," Cabot said, ducking his head and turning away. Emile gave him a look but said nothing. The weight of the deed—and the need to keep it secret—was heavy on him. He wasn't sure how long he could go without telling someone. He tried to tell himself that this was war now, and war would call him to tasks he had not imagined before; but it felt a lot more like simple murder.

Inside his house, Turner changed out of his wet clothes and dropped them into the washtub out back. He could feel Charlotte's eyes on him and resented her gaze, but at the same time was grateful for her silence. The world seemed to be moving at a faster speed than he was.

They had been in the cornfields for two hours before Turner remembered the man's horse, which had run off at the first moment of the attack; and as if thought could spawn existence, he looked up from his hoeing and there it was, coming up the valley at a slow, aimless walk, the empty stirrups flapping gently as it walked. The other men in the fields caught his gaze and straightened up to watch it.

"Looks like somebody's got thrown," said Wilson, in the row of corn next to him.

Cabot was closest to the road. He stepped in front of the horse, which had lost most of its spunk since morning, and took its bridle in his hand. The horse made no effort to get away. Cabot patted its neck and led it to the fence.

"What do you think, Turner?" Wilson said. Turner said nothing. He didn't know what to think. He wanted the horse to disappear. "What do you think?" Wilson repeated, and Turner looked around. The men were all looking at him, and he realized that they were waiting for him to give them guidance.

"You're probably right," he said to Wilson. "Probably threw somebody. Let's tie it to the fence rail. The owner will be along soon."

By lunchtime, no rider had appeared. "I think we ought to unsaddle it and put it in the barn," Cabot said to the group. He led the horse to the barn.

"Maybe we ought to walk down the road a ways, see if the fellow got hurt," Schnack said.

Turner tried to think of what to say, but his mind couldn't seem to work fast enough. "Good idea," Cabot called out over his shoulder. "Turner and I'll walk down and take a look."

Turner was surprised at how quick Cabot's mind was working. "I'm sorry I got you into this," he said once they were out of earshot.

"It's all right," Cabot said. "It'll do us good to see the place in daylight anyway."

They had reached the place in the road. The dirt they had scattered had concealed most of the blood, but even a casual eye could see that something had happened there. Flies had gathered on certain spots, which though covered with dirt, still had a disturbed look.

"Not much to do about it now," Cabot said. "It'll be dry by the end of the day."

They walked on, another hundred yards or so, and then returned to the colony.

"No sign of anybody," Cabot said to the rest of the men.

"I tell you what," Schnack said. "I think some fellow's got himself bushwhacked and the horse just run off."

"Didn't hear any shots," said Wilson.

"Hell, he could have got bushwhacked ten miles down the road, or day before yesterday," said Schnack. "I sure don't recognize that horse. It's a fine one, though."

"If I was to bushwhack somebody, I'd make sure I caught their horse," Wilson said. "Plenty of money in a horse like that."

"I don't want to hear this kind of talk," Turner said. "Bushwhacking and killing." He walked away from the group and returned to his row of corn. He hoed and hoed, chopping up the weeds, focusing his entire self on the next weed, the next tuft of grass. The men could stand and palaver all day if they wanted.

He reached the end of his row and started up the next. A few feet down it, he stopped and looked up. The men, shamed by his action, had all returned to work. Turner walked through the rows to Wilson.

"Saddle that horse and run it on up the road," he said. "Take it across the river so it won't come back. If anybody comes along and sees it in our barn, they'll think we're the ones who bushwhacked its rider. And then there will be hell to pay from somebody. Rebels, Federals, somebody, you can bet on it." He looked around. All the men had gathered around him.

"He's right," said Schnack. "That there horse is bad luck for sure."

"Do it now," Turner told Wilson. "And if it turns out it's just a rider got thrown, well, his horse went thataway. He can chase it to the next county as far as I'm concerned."

They heard the bell ringing for lunch. Turner was glad. He was hungry.

August / September 1861

Chapter 24

Charlotte guessed well enough what had gone on in the early morning; and when Turner said after supper that he needed to go out for a while, she did not ask why. He returned late and wet, and in the morning she saw another set of muddy clothes in the washtub. The next morning she washed them along with everything else, just another row of clothes on just another line.

On the surface nothing seemed different. Turner worked the fields with the men, joining in the weekly discussions about what could be expected from the corn and when to cut and shock the hemp. Subscriptions to *The Eagle* had dropped off to almost nothing since the start of the war; few people seemed interested in news of the Daybreak colony anymore. But Turner worked on the next issue in the late afternoons anyway, fussing over wording and muttering at his farmer's fingers on the type.

She would not have known how to ask him, or what she would say in response to his answer; so she just let the incident remain unspoken. But unspoken it hovered between them.

Later in the week, Sheriff Willingham came down the road, riding in the center of a large Federal cavalry patrol. He tipped his hat to Charlotte as he reached their house.

"Morning, ma'am," he said. "Your husband around?"

His simple words chilled Charlotte, a deep cold that started in the pit of her stomach and radiated out until only her head and hands seemed warm. "He's out in the fields," she said. Her mouth was dry; the words came out scratchy.

"Should be coming in for lunch soon. Care to join us, Sheriff?"

"We got to push on, but thanks the same, ma'am. We could use some water, though, if you don't mind. Your spring water here is always fine, I been telling these boys." He nodded toward the horsemen.

"Of course. Climb down and rest a minute." Charlotte went behind the house and dipped the bucket in the barrel. She watched her hand as it moved through the water and was grateful to see that it did not tremble. When she returned, the horsemen had all gotten down and were sitting in the shade of the big maple tree, their horses tied to the rail.

"Actually, it ain't 'sheriff' any more," Willingham said as she handed the bucket around. "Martial law's been declared. So now I'm the provost-marshal."

"What's the difference between a sheriff and a provost-marshal?"

Willingham grinned sheepishly. "I ain't completely sure. One good thing is I don't have to run for election."

One of the military men got up from the ground and strode over to where they were talking.

"A provost-marshal serves at our pleasure," he said. "His job is to enforce the civil code and assist us in managing the civilian population. But to be quite frank with you, madam, in time of war we have one task, and that is finding the rebels and destroying them. We are here to tell you and everyone down this valley that anyone who is a rebel, who supports the rebels, who aids and abets their cause in any way, is an outlaw and subject to punishment that will be both immediate and severe."

"Mrs. Turner, this here is Sergeant Ford, who is in charge of this bunch. Sergeant Ford, this is Mrs. Turner," Willingham said. Ford touched the brim of his hat and looked at Willingham.

"We've finished our water. Find this man and let's move on."

Willingham flushed. "If you don't mind, ma'am, think we could go out in the field and find him?"

But the men in the fields had seen the cavalry troop arrive and had come to see what was going on. Turner was the first in the yard.

"Good day, sheriff," he said.

"Provost-marshal," Charlotte corrected. Turner gave her a questioning look. "I'll explain later."

Willingham shook hands with Turner. "I'll get right to it," he said. "The state's under martial law now, and we gotta root out the rebels. You all seen any suspicious characters come by here lately?"

"Yes," Turner said. "Four men rode through a while back, and then two more later on in the day. They were all heading north."

The cavalryman gave a complacent smile and waved his hand. "Oh, we know all about those boys," he said. "Couple of local horse thieves thought they'd jump one of our scouting parties. Or maybe they were rebel scouts. Doesn't matter, killed them both." He looked at the group appraisingly. "Did they stop here, spend the night?"

"The first bunch stopped for water, like you men," Charlotte said. "The last two just rode on through."

By now everyone had gathered. "I don't think Mr. Willingham here is being clear enough, so I'll tell you myself," Sergeant Ford said, raising his voice so everyone could hear. "The United States Government is in control of this region now. Anyone who is a rebel, or who assists the rebels in any way, or who conceals their operations, is subject to martial law. This means imprisonment and confiscation of property. Any man under arms who is not in uniform is considered an outlaw, and subject to summary execution. Now let's move on to the next settlement." He walked to his horse and swung himself into the saddle.

"These boys kinda dampen a man's enthusiasm for loyal citizenship," Wilson said, a little too loud.

The sergeant took a pistol from his saddle holster and leveled it at Wilson. "That's the kind of seditious talk that gets you put in jail or worse, sonny boy," he said. "I've half a mind to put a ball in your guts right now. The lot of you can consider this your warning. There won't be a second one." He put the pistol back in its holster and jerked his horse's reins.

Charlotte stepped forward. "My father is Colonel Newton Carr of the United States Army, and I will not be spoken to in such a way!" she said. "If you want loyalty, you had better deserve it."

"I don't care if your father is the Lord God Jehovah himself," Sergeant Ford said. "We're going to rid this countryside of rebels if we have to kill every man in it."

He rode away, leading the patrol down the road toward French Mills. "Be right there," Willingham called after him. Once the soldiers were a few yards away, he said to Turner, "I want to apologize for my companion's lack of manners."

"It seems to be a common problem these days," Turner said.

"Well, yes...." Willingham watched them go. "They're the catbirds right now, anyway."

"I thought you were a Southern man, Sheriff," said Turner. "You stood right here a few years ago and lectured me on Missouri being a slave state now and forever."

"That's the truth," Willingham said. "But when there's a strong wind blowing, you can either ride it or fight it. Right now those fellas have the towns, the railroads, and the mines, so they're blowing pretty hard. Maybe one of these days the rebels will take over, and they'll hang me for working with the Federals, or I'll have to run off. But for now I'm putting my chips on their color."

"But what about out here, in the country?" Turner said.

Willingham shrugged. "Out here, I don't know what to tell you. Figure things out as you go, is the best I can say." He cast a look down the road. "I tell you one thing. I would rather have just sent out letters, or rode out here by myself instead of with all these soldier boys. A crowd of Federals like that draws trouble as sure as shit draws flies, and the bigger the pile the more flies." He stopped and put his hand over his mouth. "I embarrass myself. I apologize, ma'am. Best I should look to my own manners."

"It's all right," Charlotte said. "These are difficult times."

"You can say that again. Well, I'd better catch up with these boys. If some puke with a powder horn is sitting on that bluff up ahead, I'll be harder to hit if I'm in the middle of that bunch than out by myself." He tipped his hat. "Goodbye, folks. Good luck to you."

They watched him ride away. "So that's our law, is it?" Wilson said. "Well, thank you very much."

At the community meeting that week, Wilson resigned. "I'm going up to St. Louis to enlist," he said. "It's only a three-month enlistment, and they're giving out bonuses. If I'm going to have people shooting at me, I'd just as soon know which direction they're shooting from." No one said anything, but eyes naturally turned to the Widow Shepherson. Wilson had been paying call on her for more than a year, and the quiet assumptions that a community makes had been made regarding the two of them. But her face was composed, and she remained silent. It was not clear whether this was a parting, or whether promises had been exchanged.

At the end of the month, fifteen women and children came up the road from the south. Most of the children and about half the women were barefoot, their feet bleeding, and they moved with the slow urgency of the starving. When they reached Harp Webb's house, they stopped and knocked on the door, over and over, until it was clear that no one was home; then they moved up to the colony.

Charlotte's was the first house they reached. She spread them out under the maple tree to rest and brought them leftover biscuits from breakfast, which they divided among themselves, a quarter of a biscuit to each.

"We'll cook lunch soon," she said. Newton was hiding behind her skirts, looking at the strange assembly. "Run down to Mrs. Wickman's and tell her we've got company," she told him. He ran off, looking over his shoulder every few steps.

"I remember this place," said one woman, the oldest of the group. "We passed through here a few years ago."

"You did?" Charlotte said.

"There was a whole train of us. Father Hogan was leading us into the wilderness. My name's Flanagan, Kathleen Flanagan."

"The Irish group," said Charlotte. "I remember you. What happened?"

"Some of the boys went off to enlist," she said. "Don't know what's become of them, the mail don't get through. Then bushwhackers started coming around, stole the cattle and anything else they could find. Some of them said they were procuring for one side or another. Maybe they were, I don't know. If you put up an argument, they shot you down. We've lost four men already, my husband included. The rest of the men sent us off, said it was too dangerous. They're going to try to hold things down until the war's over."

"Are your men armed?"

"Some hunting rifles, nothing special. They don't go out to the fields any more except in groups."

They were interrupted by the arrival of Mrs. Wickman, who came running with some chunks of salt pork in her apron. "We're having pork and beans today," she said. "I fished these out. This'll tide you over till lunchtime."

The group divided the chunks of meat and fell to eating, the children licking their fingers to get every taste. Charlotte had Newton bring pans of water; after they had drunk their fill, they bathed their feet. "We don't have enough extra shoes to go around, but we can help some of you," she said. "That house over there is empty. Perhaps you can stay there for a while."

The Irish women looked at each other in silent consultation. "Maybe so," Mrs. Flanagan said. Our men want us to keep heading north, but some of these babies ain't fit to travel. We can rest up for a few days."

By now more of the Daybreak women had arrived and were seeing to the children while their mothers rested. Charlotte looked up to see Marie Mercadier sitting at the base of the tree, a toddler in her lap, washing its feet with a damp cloth. She walked over to her.

"I'm not too sure about this little one," Marie said.

Charlotte looked closer at the child. His skin was pale and clammy, and he was breathing in shallow gasps. She looked around. "Who is the mother of this child?" she called.

"He ain't got one," said a girl standing nearby. "She died. I been carrying him part time."

"Are you his sister?" Marie asked.

"No ma'am," said the girl. "I just didn't have anybody to carry."

Charlotte put her hand on Marie's shoulder. "You still have your milk?"

"Yes." Their gazes met.

"It may not help," Charlotte said. "But we should try."

Marie nodded. She lowered her eyes, turned away, and opened her blouse to the hungry lips. A flash of pain pierced Charlotte, knowing the same gesture had been performed for Turner somewhere, but then she returned to the moment, remembered the advice in her father's letter, and let go.

The Irish group stayed into the fall. Emile Mercadier made shoes for all those who did not have them. To everyone's surprise, the baby, whose name was Angus, survived. Kathleen Flanagan spent much of each day sitting with Marie, tending the child. Mrs. Flanagan proved to be a sociable, talkative woman, with a hearty laugh and strong opinions. When the hemp had been fully retted, the Irish helped break the stems, pick out the fiber, and feed it into the jack. But as October drew on, Mrs. Flanagan announced that it was time to start north again.

"Our men will not know where to find us, assuming they survive," she said. "We must place ourselves where we can be found." But she asked for a private conversation with Charlotte and Marie. Although Charlotte had never spoken of her troubles involving Marie, Mrs. Flanagan somehow sensed them; she did not ask to meet in Charlotte's home. Instead, they sat on the porch of Harp Webb's house, where the group had made its quarters.

"I am bound north with my people," Mrs. Flanagan said. "They need me, and I will take them. But the child should stay behind. "His father is gone, maybe forever. His mother is dead. And there is nothing ahead for him but the foundling home, the workhouse, and God knows what else." She took Marie's hand. "Will you take him in, girl?"

"Yes," Marie said. Her voice was low.

"I understand your own little one is without a daddy."

"Well...." The moment was acutely painful, but Charlotte sat silent, waiting to hear what Marie would say. "Not in the legal sense."

"Then God in Heaven is her father, and let her not be ashamed of that," Mrs. Flanagan said. "This boy, give him your name. His family name is Flynn, and you can tell him that someday. But Mercadier is a fine name. I'll venture there's not another Angus Mercadier on the earth. In fact—" She hesitated. "In fact, your father has asked me to return here after I have fulfilled my duties, and take on the name Mercadier as well. But I need to know if you have any objections."

"Objections!" Marie cried out. "Heavens, no, I have no objections!" She jumped from her chair and embraced the woman.

"Your father plays a fine fiddle," Mrs. Flanagan said with a sly smile. "Jigs and reels and fine airs that I thought only an Irishman could master."

"Then we shall dance," Charlotte said. "I'll send the word around. Tomorrow you leave us, so tonight we dance. Let the rebels and the Federals battle as they may, and Lord knows we may all be dead by Christmastime."

"If your neighbor ever returns to his house, give him our thanks, though the house was not willingly lent," Mrs. Flanagan said. "We broke nothing and stole nothing, and we are leaving it cleaner than we found it."

Charlotte did not answer.

In the night they danced in the Temple of Community, women for once outnumbering men, the chairs and tables pushed against the wall as always. Emile's fiddle sounded thin and lonely to Charlotte; she remembered how well the annoying Mr. Smith could play, and how he matched Emile's melody or harmonized with it, his own playing wandering off into its own odd reaches before returning to the main theme. And she missed George Webb, with whom she had never gotten to dance, she suddenly recalled. So, determined not to miss another such chance, she danced every song, pulling men out of their chairs and dragging them onto the floor. There weren't enough people for a quadrille, so they stuck to simple line and pair dances, and at the moments when she partnered with Adam Cabot, Charlotte remembered that this was how she had first begun to think of him, the two of them gliding across the floor. A deep mournfulness inhabited his eyes now; it pained her to think that she had helped put it there. And, she thought, perhaps such a look was in her own. It was best not to face the mirror sometimes.

In the morning the Irish waded across the chilly river on their way north.

Mrs. Flanagan had refused the offer of wagons to take them to town.

"We are under our own power," she said. "What becomes of us will become of us. And should your wagoners be killed by bushwhackers on their way home, I could never forgive myself for having led them out into the open. Till we meet again."

Then they were gone, and Daybreak returned to its former rhythm, finishing the year's ropemaking, plowing the field to sow the winter wheat, listening in anxious silence for the sound of horsemen. Turner finished his edition of *The Eagle* and bundled the copies to take to Fredericktown. "I don't know if I'll be able to get them mailed," he said. "I may have to bring them back. But at least it's done."

A few weeks later, a little past dark, they heard slow, solitary hoofbeats passing their door, and went to the doorway to see Harp Webb riding past. Harp stopped his horse.

"Yep," he said, "They let me out. Never could put nothing on me, and the place was getting filled up with honest-to-God rebels. So it was hang me or turn me loose, and they turned me loose." He spat onto the road. "Even gave me my horse back, the damned fools." He looked toward his house. "I see it's still standing. Heard you loaned it out to some white niggers while I was gone."

"It was an emergency," Turner said. "It was a desperate circumstance."

"Yeah. Desperate circumstances all over."

"We'd do the same for any group that needed our help," Turner said. "Loyal or rebel."

"Still trying to play both sides," said Harp. "That'll come back to haunt you someday."

"I don't see it as playing both sides. I see it as helping my fellow man."

"Doesn't matter how you see it. What matters is how some officer on one side or the other sees it. That sergeant who came to get me, he wanted to hang me from a tree branch so bad it was downright comical. Lucky for me he had orders in his hand, or I wouldn't have made it to the top of the hill. He had plenty of hanging to do once he got to town, though. That old feller was the best recruiter Jefferson Davis ever had. Only about half those boys in jail were rebels when they went in. The rest of them were like me, fellers that somebody had jigged on for their own advantage. But they were all sure enough rebels when they got out, those that didn't end up doing the dance, that is." He started his horse forward again. "See you later."

Charlotte and Turner shut the door. They looked at each other in the lamplight.

"Are you afraid?" Charlotte asked him. His gaze was steady and even.

"No. Are you?"

Charlotte smiled. "No, I'm not afraid."

October 1861

Chapter 25

Turner worked his way across the field, shocking cornstalks. It was his turn to go up the mountain and bring down the cattle for milking, and he figured he would do that before returning home to wash up for supper. The October air was clear and fine; it was a day no one minded working outdoors.

The only other one left in the field was Cabot, four rows over. Turner had the feeling he was lingering to talk, and in a few minutes Cabot came over. "I have reached Charlotte's father through an acquaintance of mine in the War Department," he said. "He is well. His regiment is in Virginia attached to the Department of the Potomac, under McClellan."

"Thank you," Turner said. "I'll pass along the news."

Cabot picked up a cornstalk and absent-mindedly twisted it around a shock. "I sent word to him that I would like to serve as his aide, if he needs me. Obviously I'm no good for fighting, but an army needs clerks and correspondents too."

Turner straightened up from his work. "What about Daybreak? Don't you think Daybreak needs you?"

"Oh, I know it does, of course I do. But we're in a time of sacrifice now. I feel called back East."

Turner was sick at heart, although he didn't doubt Cabot's good intentions. But was this what the colony was to come to? One by one, men trailing off to join one side or the other, until no one was left but wives, children, widows, old men—and him?

"You should tell Charlotte," he said to Cabot. "She will make sure

Wickman refunds your share."

"Oh, I don't want my share," Cabot said. "I intend to return someday, when all of this is said and done, and we can return to our common labors."

"I bless that sentiment," Turner said. "But I fear that by the end of this war, our common feelings will be gone."

They stood in silence, contemplating the uncertainties ahead of them. And as if they needed any illustration of their fears, up the road from the south came a man walking. He was haggard and bearded, a rifle held low in one hand, wearing something resembling a uniform.

"What do you think?" Cabot said in a low voice. "Soldier, runaway, beggar, or thief? Or some combination of all?"

"Good Lord," said Turner as the man drew nearer, passing Harp Webb's house without a glance. "It's Prentice."

They trotted down the road to him, meeting him at the edge of Daybreak. "Stars in heaven, man, it's good to see you alive!" Turner said. "All your arms and legs intact, too."

"I'm welcome, then?"

"Of course you're welcome!" By now some of the children had spotted them walking into the settlement, and Turner sent one to find Mrs. Prentice.

"Thought maybe you'd all gone over to the other side," said Prentice.

"No sides among friends," Turner said. "Has it been three months already? Your enlistment up?"

Prentice gave him a scornful look. "My three months turned into six the minute I got there," he said. "Probably turn into a year next. But I ain't staying a year, that's for sure. I'll take a shoe leather discharge first."

"You look hungry," Cabot said. "Let's get you some food."

The mention of food struck a nerve with Prentice. He looked behind himself in alarm.

"I don't have much time, boys," he said. "I'm with a foraging party. The rest of 'em stopped in French Mills, but I told 'em I thought I knew of a farmhouse up the road. You've got to give me some food to take back, or else the whole party will be here in an hour. And they'll pick you clean. There's two thousand men over on the Fredericktown road, eating their way north."

"What do you need?" Turner said.

"Couple sacks of corn should so it, and a chicken or some eggs. And do you have bread? Some real bread?" Mrs. Prentice and their three children came running down the street, and Prentice tottered up to meet them. "And can you have somebody boil a pot of water?" he called out over his shoulder. "I want to boil my clothes, get rid of these graybacks."

In an hour Prentice was headed back south, a sack of provisions over his shoulder and a smile on his face. The community gathered at the junction to send him off. His wool outergarments were still damp, but he didn't mind. "At least I'm the only thing living in 'em," he said. "Throw away them underclothes," he said to his wife. "They ain't fit to keep. And pick 'em up with a stick when you do, unless you want to get acquainted with my little friends."

"Where have you been? Are you safe?" Charlotte said.

"Oh, we're all right. We're with Colonel Thompson down around Bloomfield. He's a horseman, so us infantry boys mainly sit and wait while he and his cavalry ride around and get into scrapes. We're supposed to march up to Fredericktown and wait for them. They rode off way up north somewhere, God only knows where."

"But Fredericktown is occupied," Turner said.

"Yeah, I expect we'll have to fight," Prentice said.

The thought made them all silent. "Well, be careful," Turner said.

"I always am." Prentice kissed his wife and gave each of the children a hug. "I hear that Pap Price is planning another big run north again. But that might just be a camp canard."

Then he was gone, and Mrs. Prentice turned to hide her tears.

Now it was nearly evening, and Turner thought he would tie up one last shock of corn before heading up the mountain. The idea of two thousand men heading north, just a few miles away, amazed him. Those two thousand would be met by thousands more somewhere, who knows where. For all he knew it could happen here. He looked out over the cornfield and tried to imagine four, five, six thousand men, battling across the valley. The little community they had worked these years to create would be swept away in such a clash.

It was impossible. He couldn't imagine it. There was no point in trying.

He started up the mountain after the cattle, but stopped at the barn beforehand and dug one of the rifles from under the hay, the bolt-action Greene. All the talk of troops and raids had given him an uneasy feeling.

Halfway up the mountain, his uneasiness deepened. He couldn't say why, but something made him slow down and pick his way quietly up the path. All he knew was that something felt wrong. Another few steps, and he realized what it was—it was the smell of cooking meat.

Turner squatted behind a tree for a few minutes and pondered what to do.

It could be a straggler of one sort or another, someone who could be scared off with a show of force. It could be some of the Indians from across the river, although that seemed unlikely. Or it could be an entire regiment, for all he knew. In any case, that smell meant that at least one of their cows had met its end. He couldn't stand not to know.

He put a cartridge into the breech of his rifle and crept up the hillside. In the quiet evening every step he made through the fallen leaves sounded loud to him, like the crashing of a child. But the cattle had made a well-trodden path by now, so he could move quietly.

When he reached the place where the slope began to round out to ridgetop, he paused again. The cooking smell was stronger. He could hear men's voices, but it was hard to tell how many there were. He could see the glimmer of a fire through the woods and crept closer. Then he heard the voice of a man behind him.

"Should I shoot you now, or take you to see the captain?" the man said.

"Take me to see the captain," Turner said through clenched teeth. He should have known they would post guards.

"Set your rifle against that tree and walk on, then," the man said. Turner did as he was told.

Around two small fires sat twenty men, lounging against their saddles. None of them were wearing uniforms. They had fixed up a spit from some saplings, and a rear haunch of one of the Daybreak milk cows was roasting over one of the fires. At the sound of their approaching footsteps, all heads turned in their direction.

"Over to your right," said the man behind him.

"Well, looky here," came a voice from the other side of the fire. "It's the town builder." Sam Hildebrand stood up and faced him across the flames. "What are you doing out here in the night?" he said. "Armed, too. That's dangerous play."

"Bringing the cattle home," Turner said.

Hildebrand's eyes flickered to the haunch of beef between them. "We confiscated one of 'em. May have to confiscate another one, too. Don't worry, we'll pay you for 'em." He turned to a man nearby in the circle. "Harp, write him out a scrip for me."

The man leaned forward and said nothing. It was Harp Webb.

"Hand me that rifle, Pony," Hildebrand said. He sighted down the barrel of Turner's Greene and then examined its breech-loading mechanism. "I've heard about these. How much time you think you gain on a reload?"

"I don't know," Turner said. "I've never had to reload in a hurry."

Hildebrand slid the bolt back and forth a few times. "That's right," he said. "You ain't joined up on either side, have you?"

"No."

He snicked the bolt in and out a few more times. "Little bit of practice, I'd say maybe twice as fast. That could serve a man well out in the field. Of course, for my kind of fighting, ain't nothing beats one of these." He pulled a revolver from his belt and hefted it in his hand.

Turner did not reply.

"Harp here wants to join up with me," Hildebrand continued. "What do you think, Mr. Turner? Would old Harp make a good guerrilla?"

"I couldn't say," Turner said.

"Oh, come on, now. A man like you has an opinion on everything."

"Yes, I'd say he has what it takes."

"Only thing is, Harp here has never killed a fella. I'm not sure that whiskey-making and squirrel hunting qualify a man to ride with me. What do you think?"

Turner spoke slowly. "From my experience, the right situation can make a man capable of almost anything. Almost."

"You wouldn't stoop to killing, eh?"

"I didn't say that," Turner said, looking him in the eye. Hildebrand held his gaze. "Now if you don't mind, I'll take the rest of my cows home. You can write me that scrip some other time."

"Can't do that," Hildebrand said. "We have some business to transact in the morning, and I'm afraid I can't trust your loyalty." He sighted down the barrel of the pistol at an imaginary enemy in the woods. "What do you think? Can I trust your loyalty?"

"No," Turner said. "You cannot."

Hildebrand put his pistol back in his belt. "Then you're going to have to spend the night with us."

"I'll kill him for you," Webb said.

Hildebrand chuckled. "I think Harp here wants to prove to me how blood-thirsty he is. Think so, Mr. Turner?"

"I don't want to get killed, if you don't mind."

"Hear that?" Hildebrand said to the men. "Mr. Turner doesn't want to get killed, if we don't mind." After their laughter had died down, he said, "I owe you for the cow. The least I could do is not kill you, too."

"People will be coming out to look for me. You know they won't just leave me out here."

"That is true," Hildebrand said with a shrug. He thought for a moment. "Well, boys, I guess we won't bed down here tonight after all. We need to ride down the mountain. Saddle up and follow me." He looked at Harp. "Don't shoot this man, at least not now," he said. "Maybe later. We'll see. Mr. Turner, you lead the way."

The men rode down the hillside at a slow walk. Turner thought about making a run for it but knew there was no chance. When they reached the pasture at the edge of the forest, the guerrillas spread out as if on cue, and Turner realized they had already planned what to do. Within a half hour they had rounded up everyone in the village and brought them to the Temple, hastily dressed in whatever clothes they could find.

Once everyone was gathered, Hildebrand and his men walked into the meeting hall and stood in front of the doors. He lit a lantern and raised his hand for quiet.

"I am sorry to disturb you tonight, but it cannot be helped," he said in his oddly soft voice. "You all just have to spend the night here, and with any luck we'll be gone by noon tomorrow." He paused. "And I have to tell you, if anyone—man, woman, or child—sets foot outside without my say-so, they will be killed. So just settle down and get some sleep."

Charlotte spoke up. "Mr. Hildebrand, some of these children need to go to the privy."

Hildebrand's eyes darted from side to side. After a pause, he said, "Take 'em." He looked at one of his men. "You go along."

When the children returned, Hildebrand looked around the Temple nervously. Holding a group this size overnight had clearly not been in his plans. Several of the children were crying.

"Can you calm this bunch?" he said to Charlotte.

"I can if you people leave," she said.

Hildebrand rubbed his chin. "All right," he said. "But we'll have a man outside each door."

The guerrillas filed out. By now it was full dark, and without a lantern the black quickly enveloped them. A few people tried to make places to sleep on the floor, using bundles of clothes or books from the library shelves for pillows. But for the most part, they sat huddled on the benches in the chilly room, the children whimpering or crying.

Charlotte stood at the dais, her figure little more than a shadow. She spoke: "Where there is inequality, let us bring balance." At "Where there is suspicion, let us bring trust," others joined in. They finished together.

Where there is exclusion, let us bring openness.
Where there is division, let us bring harmony.
Where there is darkness, let us bring Daybreak.

Then they repeated it again, twice. By then everyone had quieted down. More people settled on the floor to sleep.

Turner walked to the dais and took Charlotte's hand. She squeezed it in the dark, moving aside to let him speak.

"'It was a fine morning in June when I set out from New York harbor on my travels to Daybreak, although of course at the time I did not realize that Daybreak was to be my destination,'" he began, and in a flash of astonishment he realized that he remembered the whole thing, word for word, start to finish. He went on. "'My friend John Fletcher, first mate of a merchant vessel, had persuaded his captain to engage me as the medical officer for a long voyage in search of new sources of spice, a journey to which I, possessed by the spirit of adventure, readily consented. I was then an idle youth of twenty, the son of a wealthy family, and I fear much given to sloth and disregard of my fortunate condition.'" By the time he reached the end of the first chapter, the children were all asleep, but he continued to recite a little while longer, simply for the pleasure of hearing the words. It was, he thought, not a half bad story. But soon the recollection of the danger they were in returned. He stopped. Now was not the time for clever tales.

He found Charlotte lying on the floor with Newton using her thigh as a pillow. He lay perpendicular to her so that she could have his thigh for the same purpose, his boots behind his head for a pillow.

"What's going to happen?" Charlotte whispered.

"Some kind of attack, I guess. Beyond that, I don't know."

Adam Cabot lay on the floor on the other side of the room. It had been good to hear *Travels to Daybreak* again after so long. He had almost forgotten the story that had led them to this place, the imaginary tale of a young man transformed by experience into someone better, someone who learned to think of the community first. They recited the invocation every week, but the words had become mere sounds over time. Hearing them again in the darkness, in danger, with the children frightened and the adults trying not to transmit their fear any further, reminded him of their meaning. Replace suspicion with trust. Open whatever is closed. All those virtues seemed distant now, replaced by the old habits of thinking—suspicion, conflict, violence—that had kept the world in thrall for millennia. They all had bloody hands now, or would soon enough.

Would they survive the morning? It seemed likely. If Hildebrand and his men had wanted a massacre, they would have done it already. Still, that was how the Border Ruffians had done it at Marais des Cygnes—lure everyone into a sense of safety, then kill them all. And even if killing them was not the intention, once the shooting started there was no guarantee of anything. That would be the greatest irony, to end up shot down by Federals.

And if they did survive? What would happen to the colony? Slow destruction, the picking away of men one by one, until a ragged band of survivors had to make its way to safety, like those sorry Irish earlier in the year? Not a fate to crave.

Knowing they would still be awake, he crept to where Charlotte and Turner were lying in the dark. The faint light from the windows showed Newton asleep on the floor.

"Hey," Charlotte said softly.

"Thanks for the recitations," Cabot said.

"Did the trick," said Turner.

Around them the villagers were settling down. "Where's Emile?" Cabot said. "He shouldn't have been roused out like this. He's no danger."

"He's over in the corner," Charlotte said. "Marie and I fixed him up a pallet. He'll be all right."

The mention of Marie left them all silent. What was there left to say? Nothing. "If this is the end of us, I want you to know that I've loved you both," Cabot said.

"Oh, this isn't the end of us," said Charlotte. "Just you wait."

The quiet confidence of her voice cheered him. "What do you say, James? More ideas bubbling up from your fertile imagination?"

Turner was quiet. "I've loved you too, Adam. You've been a true friend. I'm just sorry I got you mixed up in, well, you know. And now this...."

"Don't be sorry. There's danger everywhere these days. And like King Henry says, those who are sleeping in their beds tonight will look back someday and wish they had been here."

"Well and good, but I'd rather have been given the choice."

"We don't get to choose our moments of testing. They're on us before we know them."

Charlotte stirred. "You men and your philosophizing! Will you go to sleep? Morning is what will be on us before we know it, and I need to think."

"About what?" Turner said.

"About how to get us through the next day alive, you silly," she said. "What else would I think about?"

Cabot tiptoed to his resting place, abashed. He lay on the floor with his head propped on a stack of books. Then there was nothing to do but wait, wait in the dark, and hope that the morning would bring less devastation upon them than what now seemed inevitable.

Chapter 26

Fog covered the valley at dawn, making the chilly air seem even chillier. Everyone stretched and ached. Hildebrand was at the door at first light. He removed his hat.

"You all can take your privy breaks, four at a time," he said. "Pony here will be your guard." Charlotte walked up to him.

"Mr. Hildebrand, those cattle on the mountain should have been milked last night," she said. "They'll be in agony this morning."

Hildebrand gave an imperceptible nod. "I'm a farm boy myself, ma'am," he said. "You go up and bring 'em down."

"I'll need help with the milking."

"All right, but no men." He scratched his chin. "Some of the boys was wondering if you all might have some breakfast?"

Charlotte nodded and called to Frances Wickman. "Mr. Hildebrand here would like some breakfast for his men. Could you and Marie meet me in the barn after you finish here? I'm going up to fetch the cows."

"This big a bunch, all we've got is biscuits and lard," Mrs. Wickman grumbled. "Or we could make hoecakes."

"Whatever you make is fine," Hildebrand said. "Beggars can't be choosers."

"Some beggars," Mrs. Wickman muttered, but Hildebrand pretended not to hear.

Charlotte walked up the mountain, her mind churning. These men hardly seemed intent on their destruction. If they had intended them harm, they would not have stayed to beg breakfast. Perhaps the safest thing was to stay quiet, do as they were told, and let the day happen. But there was harm headed for someone, there was no doubt.

The cattle were as she had thought they would be—restless and desperate to be milked and fed. They practically ran down the hill to the barn.

Inside the barn, Frances and Marie were waiting. The two of them immediately started milking, but Charlotte had other ideas. She dug the sack of rifles from under the hayloft and took out three Sharps carbines.

The two women had finished milking by now. Charlotte held out a rifle to each. "Let's see if we can get these under our skirts," she said. They tried several arrangements, finally ending with the rifles slung between their breasts on pieces of bridle strap, barrel end up. The cartridge boxes were too bulky, so they just took out as many as they could and put them in their dress pockets and bodices. "When you get to the Temple, go into the woodroom behind the speaking platform," she said. "There's half a cord of wood in there, and we can put them behind the woodpile."

"Are you sure about this?" Mrs. Wickman asked.

"No," Charlotte said.

They looked at each other. "Haven't been reading too many hero tales to the children?"

"Not a one!" Charlotte said, and the three of them laughed.

"All right then," said Mrs. Wickman. "Just so I know we're not doing something foolish."

They paused at the barn door and looked each other over. "All right," Charlotte said, taking the milk pails. "I'm stopping at the springhouse."

The three women walked with stiff haste. A rider came alongside them, a pistol in one hand. "Come on, ladies," he said. "We need everybody inside."

"You're not going to kill us, are you?" Marie said.

The man laughed. "We don't shoot women. What do you think we are, animals?"

Charlotte raised her milk pails. "I need to put these down in the spring water," she said. "I'll be right there. You all go on."

Inside the springhouse, she quickly set the milk pails into the cold water. The rifle hung like an anchor beneath her dress, and she felt hopelessly obvious. But it was the best she could do. She walked into the morning light and headed for the Temple, her head held high. The Temple had never seemed so far away.

Inside, Newton and Turner ran to embrace her, but she waved them off.

"One moment," she said. "I need to go over here first." She walked to the woodroom and shut the door behind her. Behind the wood rack, the other two Sharps rifles were lying on the floor. She undid her strap and placed hers on top of them, then looked around. There was nothing to cover them. She untied her apron and placed it over one end of the rifles, but decided it just called attention to the spot and tied it on again.

Charlotte slipped into the meeting hall and looked over the group. Families were clustered together, fearful and hushed, a few children whimpering. Adam Cabot stood alone, fully dressed as if prepared for a day's work. She walked over to him.

"May I borrow your coat?" she said. "I'm cold."

He gave her a questioning look, but handed her his overcoat. "Women and temperature," he said.

Charlotte said nothing, but put on the overcoat and joined her husband and Newton. She knelt in front of the boy. He was holding Turner's hand, and his lip was quivering.

"Don't be afraid," she said. "Your father will know what to do."

She stood up and pulled Turner close. "I love you," she said.

He held her for a moment. "Thank you. I love you too."

Then she whispered in his ear, "Father's rifles are behind the woodpile. Marie, Frances, and I have cartridges."

Turner's head jerked back in amazement, and he looked at her with a wondering smile. "My resourceful Charlotte. I should have known there was a good reason the people elected you."

She smiled back at him. "Can you stay with Newton for just another moment? I'll be right back." She walked to the woodroom, stepped inside quietly, and draped the coat over the rifles.

Hildebrand and his men were seated on the benches, finishing their breakfast, while a few others stood watch outside.

"You seem awfully calm for someone with killing on his mind," Charlotte said to him.

Hildebrand barely looked up. "You get used to it."

"You've joined the rebels then?" Turner said.

"I ain't exactly joined," Hildebrand said, squinting into the distance. "I'd say that my war and their war are running in the same general direction. I've never been a joiner." He opened his coat and drew a pistol, checking its chambers. "And now I'm going to have to get down to business. Boys."

At his word, the guerrillas jumped up from the tables and headed for the door. Hildebrand walked to the dais.

"Here's the thing," he said. "You people need to stay inside here until we're done. Stay away from the windows. I do not want you people hurt by stray bullets. Or aimed ones either, for that matter."

A man opened the door and put his head in. "Found some guns."

"What did you find?" Hildebrand said.

"Couple of muzzle-loaders, one old musket."

Hildebrand's eyes found Harp Webb standing beside the entrance. "Take a look, Harp."

Webb stepped outside and then back in. "They had some better ones. Breech-loaders."

Charlotte spoke up. "Those were my father's. He took them with him when he left."

"Could be," Webb said with a shrug.

"Search again," Hildebrand said to the man. He surveyed Charlotte. "Your father couldn't take the wilderness life?"

"My father was recalled to the service of his country."

Hildebrand sat down at a bench and wiped his face with his hand. "Union man, eh? I was a Union man myself. Brother William joined up, not sure where he is now." His face turned stony. "But that was before the Vigilance Committee up in St. Francois County hung Brother Frank, burned my house, and shot Brother Wash and Brother Henry. Boy of thirteen." He stood up. "Since then, if it's got a blue coat, I shoot it."

They could see the men gathering their horses on the side of the Temple that faced the mountain, away from the river. From there, no one on the road could see them. Their plan—and the reason for using Daybreak—came clear to Charlotte. Through the windows they saw a man climb from the rain barrel onto the roof, and soon there was the sound of scuffing and scraping as he crawled to the top.

The man returned. "No more guns. But we found this." He held the door open further and pushed Prentice inside. "Walking up the road like he was on a picnic outing."

"Step up here and let me see you," Hildebrand said. Prentice's captor handed Hildebrand his musket, which he examined with amusement. "What unit are you with?"

"State militia, first district."

"Those boys are a dozen miles away fighting Yankees. You're a damn deserter." He pulled a pistol from his belt and leveled it at Prentice's chest.

"Oh no, sir, they sent me out on a foraging party."

"A deserter and a liar. Too bad I can't kill you twice." He cocked the hammer of the pistol, but then stopped and cast a glance toward the roof. "Well, hell, don't want to perk up the Federals. If I had time I'd hang you. May yet." He lowered the pistol and looked at Turner. "That reminds me, I hear you make some fine rope."

"We do," Turner said.

"I am going to purchase some from you. We had to hang a fellow with hickory bark the other day, and it was damn hard going."

"I'm not going to sell you rope to hang one of our own people with."

"Guess I'll just confiscate it then." He put his hand on the door latch.

There was a soft knock at the door. "Chalmers says he sees something, Captain," said a voice.

"Ain't that something? I'm a captain," Hildebrand said, grinning. "If this goes well, maybe I'll make myself a major. Tell Chalmers to get down off of there." He stepped outside. The sun was full up now, and it was a beautiful morning. The fog had all burned away. Hildebrand took one of his pistols and gave it to Webb. "Harp, set yourself outside the door here. Kill anything that comes out, man, woman, child, or barn cat." He left, shutting the door behind him.

Prentice walked to one of the benches and sat down, his wife and children gathered around him. He put his head in his hands.

"I been almost killed now twice today," he said. "I got back to my company just in time for them to get throwed up against about twice as many Federals, just south of town, and artillery like I never seen. So I decided it was time to hoof it. And now here's this man going to shoot me right in the chest in front of my family, or hang me. I can't put up with this kind of thing."

Charlotte walked over and put her hand on his shoulder.

"Don't despair," she said. "You never know in the morning where you'll be by nightfall."

"Hanging from that tree yonder, is how it looks to me," Prentice moaned.

"Oh hush up, you fool," said his wife. "Is that any way to talk in front of the children? Now take hold of yourself."

Her words shamed him into stillness. He stood up and wiped his eyes, forcing a smile.

Through the windows behind them they could see the horsemen mounting up, hidden from the ford by the walls of the Temple. One man remained on foot, his reins in his hand, looking around the corner of the building.

"How many do you count?" Turner said quietly to Charlotte. She walked to one of the back windows and casually glanced out.

"Nineteen," she said. "Plus Harp at the door."

"And us with three rifles among us," he whispered to her. He looked around the room. "And fewer marksmen. Even counting you, and I know you're a better shot than most of these men. Maybe Prentice has had some practice." He raised his voice to a speaking level. "Prentice, how many battles did you get into?"

Prentice was still in a stupor, gazing out the window in contemplation of his future hanging. "A couple. Today was the first big one."

"Shoot anybody?"

"I shot in the direction of some people, don't know if I hit them. That old gun they gave me was like something from Colonial days. I didn't know you was supposed to bring your own weapon."

"Can you come here for a minute? There's something I want to ask you."

Prentice walked to where Turner and Charlotte were standing. They put their heads together.

"I don't need to tell you, if those men succeed, they will come back and hang you," Turner said in a low voice. "We have three quality rifles in the back room. Will you take one up when the time comes?"

"Sure," Prentice said, a look of surprise on his face. "Better than sitting here waiting to get killed."

Despite Hildebrand's warning, people crowded to the windows on the other side of the Temple, where they could see to the river. Before long they saw what the man on the roof had spotted: a troop of infantry, rifles shouldered, working their way down the hill across the river.

"Must have been sent to try to get behind the rebels," Cabot murmured.

"Either that, or they're just lost," said Charlotte.

From the other side of the Temple they could hear Hildebrand instructing his men. "Don't shoot till you're in among 'em," he said. "I'll lead the way. We'll take their uniforms once we've finished them all. They could come in handy."

"There must be forty men in that patrol," Charlotte whispered to Turner. "They're going to take on that big a group?"

"Looks that way," Turner whispered back.

The Union troops disappeared behind the trees after they had made it down the rocky slope. For several painful minutes nothing could be seen. Everyone waited in silence.

Then the first soldiers arrived at the ford. They stopped. Before long the whole troop was standing on the riverbank.

They could see someone, apparently an officer, striding up and down the ranks. Finally he pulled out a sword and waved it in the air, and then led the way into the river.

"Of course they don't want to go," Emile said. "Water's cold this time of year."

The men followed reluctantly, holding their rifles in the air above them.

"Okay, boys," Hildebrand said. "We start once the last one is halfway across."

From that distance, no sound could be heard from the soldiers crossing the river. Charlotte could imagine their mutterings of discomfort, their grumbling at the water in their boots and the blisters they would no doubt get from the soaking. The men went in the water by fours, trying their best to stay in ranks as they forded the river. Soon almost all of them were in.

Adam Cabot broke the silence. "Well, thunder," he said. "I don't think that old horse pistol of Hildebrand's has much range."

Without another word he threw open the door. Harp Webb was sitting on the step, watching the soldiers ford the river, and Cabot's exit caught him by surprise. Cabot kicked him to the bottom of the steps and ran for the river in a mad zigzag, waving his arms and shouting, "Look out! Look out! Look out!"

Harp Webb regained his balance and fired the pistol at him several times, missing each time. Cabot leaped the rail fence at the edge of the field and ran down the road, still shouting.

"Well, shit!" Hildebrand barked. He took his rifle from its saddle holster, drew a bead, and knocked Cabot down with one shot. "All right, let's go, boys!"

Charlotte covered her mouth to fight back a scream. Adam had been struck, but where? How badly was he hurt? The rattle of hooves, the neighs of the horses, sounded muffled and faraway in her ears compared to the sound of that single rifle shot. She watched the spot where he lay. There was motion. No, it was only her imagination. No, he moved for certain. He raised himself up, knelt, perhaps walked or crawled away a few feet. The fence and the weeds blocked her view.

The guerrillas rode around the corner of the Temple and were quickly at a gallop through the cornfield, leaping their horses over the rail fence at the other side of the field. But Cabot's warning cries had alerted the Union soldiers. The ones who had reached the near bank, including the officer, formed a thin line, but they fired much too soon and too high. Bullets spattered off the walls of the Temple, and one went through a window. Only one of the guerrillas was hit.

The soldiers on the bank tried to reload, but their weapons were old and had to be ramrodded. By the time they had gotten in the powder, shot, and wadding, Hildebrand's guerrillas were among them, firing at close range with their revolvers. Their officer made a saber swipe at one of the horsemen but was cut down by several shots.

The troops in the river ran for the opposite bank, and the ones who had not yet entered took cover behind trees. The riders galloped into the river after them, but the water slowed their progress, and even though they shot down several of the retreating soldiers in the river, the men on the other bank were able to get off a good volley. Three more horsemen went down.

Turner pulled himself away from the window and went into the woodroom. He took out the rifles and placed each one beside a window on the river side of the Temple. Marie and Frances saw what he was doing and moved to the windows, taking cartridges out of their hiding places. They didn't have many—maybe a dozen each—but it would have to do.

"Prop open all these windows," Turner said. "Prentice, get over there by Marie. She'll hand you cartridges as you fire. Children, get into the woodroom or up against these stone walls. There might be some flying glass. Boys, I'm sorry, but I think Charlotte's a better shot than you. Stay here behind the walls and be ready to pick up if someone gets disabled."

Charlotte heard him speak but didn't move. She couldn't take her eyes off the place where Cabot had fallen. She was sure she had seen something—had he waved? Was that a signal for help?

There was a gentle hand on her back, and Frances Wickman spoke in her ear.

"Here, dearie. We'll fetch him once it's safe." Frances pressed the carbine into her hands.

Charlotte looked at it a moment uncomprehendingly, then her thoughts snapped into place. Adam had leapt into action when he saw his moment, and so must she. She took the cartridges from her apron and laid them in a row on the windowsill. About half a box. Not enough for a sustained fight. If they ran out of cartridges, she didn't know what they would do. Throw rocks, she supposed. But the thick stone of the Temple walls felt reassuring.

The riders retreated to the near bank and began shooting the wounded, but one more volley from across the river made them retreat even farther. Then Hildebrand waved his arm. The men leaned from their saddles to pick up their dead and wounded, swung them up, and started back toward Daybreak.

"Shoot when they pass that last corn shock," Turner said. "Aim low." A moment later, he cried, "Now!"

Charlotte had not fired the Sharps in quite some time, and its recoil knocked her back. The side of the Temple was enveloped in smoke for a few seconds; when it cleared, she could see another rider down.

The guerrillas seemed to assume that the colonists were firing muzzle-loaders like the ones the soldiers had, for as soon as their volley had been fired they spurred their horses forward. But the speed of reloading the breechloaders paid off; another two horsemen hit the ground before any of them were even within good pistol range. Charlotte, Turner, and Prentice reloaded and shot as fast as they could.

Through it all, she kept an eye on the spot where Adam Cabot had fallen. For endless minutes he lay still, and Charlotte fought back cold dread at the thought that he had been killed. But she could not let this thought distract her in the smoke and confusion. There was no time for tender feeling. She had no idea whether she had shot anyone or not. Bodies were scattered through the cornfield, and she had aimed at some, but she felt a disconnection between her firing and the human beings lying in the field before her. The roar of the rifles firing from inside the Temple made her stunned and temporarily deaf.

She turned away from the windows, snapping open the breechblock on her rifle and blowing out the debris. She snapped another cartridge into place and thought about what might happen after Hildebrand regrouped his men. The front of the Temple was defended well enough; but if any of the horsemen made it to the back side, they could fire through the windows behind them, and that would be a quick end. Or they might come in from the back door through the woodroom.

Charlotte turned toward the front door just in time to see it open about a foot and the tip of a pistol barrel poke inside. She raised the rifle to her shoulder and fired through the door at where the holder of the pistol would be standing. The blast made a tremendous echo inside the Temple, the pistol fell away, and then all was quiet.

By now the remaining soldiers had recovered themselves and crossed the river. They took positions on the bank and fired into the backs of Hildebrand's men. Their aim was still not good—another window broke—but the shooting from behind had its desired effect, and the horsemen took off down the road at a gallop. Charlotte's ears were ringing so loudly that she wondered if the sound would ever go away.

She looked out the window again. Adam Cabot was no longer there.

They emerged into the October sunlight. Harp Webb lay writhing on the steps, but Charlotte paid him no mind. She walked past him. She could see the Federal soldiers gathering themselves at the ford and the last of Hildebrand's guerrillas disappearing around the bend past Webb's house. Everyone was coming out of the Temple, sooty and disheveled, into the cool morning air.

Charlotte began to walk, and then to run, through the cornfields to where Cabot had fallen. She threw the rifle aside and climbed over the rail fence by the main road.

"Adam?" she cried. "Adam!"

There was no reply.

She looked around, frantic. Perhaps she had come to the wrong place. Perhaps he had not been hurt as badly as she had imagined.

Then she saw him on the riverbank. He had crawled off the road and was struggling to prop himself up against the trunk of a cottonwood tree. His face was sweaty and covered with dust, and his eyes were open. Charlotte ducked under the ropemaking tables, scrambled down the bank to him, and wiped his dusty face with her apron. Her efforts only smeared the dust; she dipped the apron in the river and tried again. That was better.

"Here. Here," she said, helping him sit upright.

"Good," he murmured.

She placed her hand inside his shirt and felt his heart weakly beating. She felt lower. Hildebrand's bullet had caught him in the left side, a few inches below the armpit. With every breath Cabot took, she could hear a rattling gurgle from the wound. Cabot's gaze was unfocused, and his eyes wandered.

"Can you hear me?" she said.

Her voice brought his attention back. He looked at her with an expression of deep fatigue and nodded his head.

"You're badly hurt," she said.

He nodded again.

"Just stay still. We'll bring help."

Cabot's gaze searched her face. "Don't worry," she said. "I'm staying with you." That seemed to relieve him; he closed his eyes and took a deep breath.

Charlotte kept her hand on his chest, feeling it rise and fall in short, jagged bursts. He was gazing intently at the river; she reached with her other hand and dipped her apron in again, holding it to his face.

"Adam," she said. "I don't know what to say." He opened his eyes again and shook his head almost imperceptibly. "Oh, yes," she said in answer to his unspoken response. "There's always something more to say." His lips formed a thin smile.

She dipped her hand into the water and let a thin stream fall into his mouth. Cabot worked his lips, swallowing the water, and his face relaxed. "Good," he said again. His breath was shallow and wheezy.

From the shade of the cottonwood tree they could see the Temple of Community across the valley. Cabot's gaze drifted to it. "Long way," he said.

"Yes," said Charlotte. "It's a long way."

He looked at her with a vague expression on his face. "True," he said. She wasn't sure what he meant, but nodded anyway and held the damp end of her apron against his brow.

Then his eyes focused, and he seemed more intent. His face got the pugnacious expression it used to have when he was arguing with George Webb. "I meant to tell you."

He tried to draw a breath. His lips moved, but no more sound came out. His gaze drifted toward the river and settled there as Charlotte watched the light in them fade. And then he was still.

Chapter 27

Turner found her kneeling by Cabot's lifeless body. The agonized tenderness of her expression sent bolts of emotion through him—fear, doubt, sadness, jealousy, all in rapid succession—but he held his tongue and watched as she wiped the dirt from Cabot's face with her damp apron and murmured something that sounded like a prayer. She didn't look up, didn't acknowledge him. If soft feelings had existed there, he had only himself to reproach. He backed away into the road.

The troop of soldiers was at the ford, pulling bodies out of the river and lining them up on the bank. One by one, the people of Daybreak sifted out, some heading for their houses, some out in the fields, turning over the bodies of the guerrillas, and some just standing in front of the Temple.

One of the soldiers walked down the road toward Turner. He waved his hand at Cabot.

"That the fellow who ran out to warn us?"

"Yes," Turner said. They looked at him.

"Fine thing," said the soldier.

Turner looked away with a sudden taste of salt in his mouth and pressed his sleeve to his face, welcoming the reek of burnt powder that filled his nostrils and stung his eyes. He supposed they all stank of gunpowder now, gunpowder and blood, the living and the dead. So this was what became of dreamers and idealists, to be shot down in what would be recorded as a meaningless skirmish of an obscure battle—if it were recorded at all. He felt a pang of envious regret. At least Cabot was granted the honest tears of a good woman.

He turned back to the soldier. "Fine thing," he croaked. "Who's in charge over there?"

The man looked back at the group of soldiers. "Hell if I know. Lieutenant's dead, the rest of us are just greenhorns. There's four more gangs of us coming down the hill. Captain's up there somewhere." The soldier walked back to his group, leaving Turner behind. He returned to Charlotte, who had covered Cabot's face with her apron and was sitting motionless beside him.

"I'll go get the wagon," he said in the softest voice he could muster, resting his hand on her shoulder for a moment. She turned away.

He walked back to the Temple, where Harp Webb had been stretched out on a bench. He was still conscious, but his teeth were clenched and he drew his breath in short hisses. The rifle bullet had struck him in the lower abdomen. Turner pulled away his shirt and looked in at the smelly mess.

"Harp, we're going to have to flush out this wound," he said.

"What's the point?" said Webb.

"You never know. Men have recovered from worse. Looks like the door slowed down the ball. I'm surprised it didn't go right through you."

"Wish it had," Webb croaked out. "Saved me this shit." The Mercadiers had gathered around.

"Emile, why don't you get your shoemaker's kit and see what you can sew up in here," Turner said. "You could use some fine thread and needles. See if you can find the rifle ball."

Mercadier looked at him dubiously, but shrugged. "All right. I can give a try."

As Turner was about to leave, Webb reached out feebly and touched his sleeve. "Bury me next to my daddy," he said. "He's the only family I got."

"All right," Turner said. "If you die."

Marie followed Turner out of the Temple and took his arm. She took hold of his bloody hand. "Are you hurt?" she said.

Turner looked at his hand, noticing for the first time that it was covered in blood. "No," he said. "This is Harp's, not mine."

"And Mr. Cabot is—?"

He shook his head.

"Here." She drew a pan of water from the nearby well and bathed his hands in it. Her touch was urgent and gentle; he had almost forgotten how good the touch of her hand felt. One moment more, and then they released. She dumped the water on the ground and drew out another panful, turning toward the Temple.

"Wash him out good," Turner called after her. "Keep rinsing until everything's as clean as you can get it."

He brought a wagon out of the barn and drove it to the road, stopping beside Charlotte and Cabot. By now more soldiers had arrived. A group of them walked up to them, one man out in front. He was tall and slender, with wavy black hair flowing from under a broad-brimmed hat, and he walked with the air of someone who is used to having men follow him.

"I'm Captain Foutch," the man said. "These boys have been telling me about your battle."

"Oh, I don't know if it qualifies as a battle," said Turner.

"There was thirty or forty of them, Captain," said one of the men. "It sure felt like a battle to me."

"Thirty or forty, eh?" said the captain. "Regulars?"

"No," Turner said. "Guerrillas. Their leader has been through here before, but I've never seen him with this many men. He generally rides alone."

"We'll call it a battle, then. How many of them did we get?"

"Four dead out here in the cornfield, and one wounded," Turner said.

The soldier spoke up again. "They carried off a bunch of dead ones. I'd say another five or six. And Jacobs is missing."

"Missing!" Foutch said. "How the hell can he be missing?"

"I don't know, sir."

The captain looked at the man skeptically. "Well, keep looking. He's either run off or got killed. Boys, help get this man loaded onto the wagon, and then you can drive up and get ours. You got a cemetery around here?"

Turner pointed up the hill.

"Good," said the captain. "Hope you don't mind if we bury our boys here. We'll give you their names." He looked down at Cabot. "That was a damn fine thing he did. Civilian, too."

Charlotte stood up, her eyes wet. "In name only, sir," she said. "He's been fighting this war for us for half a dozen years."

Turner was about to add something, but the words he was getting ready to say—Cabot's character, his sense of honor and duty—sounded hollow by comparison. He squeezed Charlotte's hand as the soldiers loaded Cabot's body into the wagon.

The captain looked at the cemetery, and then his gaze traveled up the mountainside. "Those riders came down from there on you, did they?"

"Yes sir," said the soldier. "They used that churchhouse as a screen. We didn't see them till they was all the way into that cornfield."

"Hm," the captain said. "Your lieutenant should have detailed a half dozen men across the river first to set up a picket line before sending everybody. Remember that, soldier, because I'm putting you in charge of what's left of this section." He looked at the mountain again. "What's the name of that hill?"

Turner was about to say he didn't think it had a name, but Charlotte spoke up. "It's called Daybreak Mountain, captain. That's because when the sun rises in the morning, it catches those pine trees you can see there up on top, and they light up just like candles and stay that way for several minutes. It's a beautiful sight. And the town is called Daybreak, too."

"You have a good eye, ma'am," Captain Foutch said.

"Tell me, do you have news of Colonel Carr, in northern Virginia?"

The man shook his head. "None recent. Last I heard, they were creeping down the Peninsula about an inch a day. Kin of yours?"

"He is my father."

The captain removed his hat and held it over his heart.

At the river ford, seven men were stretched out in a row, each with his name on a piece of paper pinned to his coat. The missing soldier was found lodged in the water wheel. The force of the water was too strong for them to pull him out upstream, so they climbed on the wheel to make it turn; the dead man went under and then popped out like a cork on the downstream side. They loaded everyone into the wagon.

"We'll dig the graves if you'll do the burial service," Foutch said. "We had a chaplain but I sent him home, the reprobate. We need to move on down the road."

"Certainly," Turner said. "But you'll never catch those horsemen."

The captain laughed. "No, I expect they've rounded a few bends by now. But orders are orders. We're supposed to proceed down this road and engage with whoever we encounter. Where does this road go, anyway?"

A memory burst into Turner's mind, of the hillman he and Charlotte had encountered on their wagon trip back from town some years ago, and he said, "Anywhere you want it to, if you take it far enough, I reckon." But he laughed in response to the captain's puzzled look, and said, "It'll fork about fifteen miles down. Left takes you to Greenville, right takes you into Arkansas eventually."

Turner caught movement out of the corner of his eye and looked toward the village to see Prentice walking toward them. He was wearing his gray uniform coat and kepi, and he had the ancient musket on his shoulder. "What have we here?" the captain murmured. By then Prentice had reached them.

"I believe I need to surrender myself to you," Prentice said. He laid the musket on the ground.

"And why is that?" Foutch said, looking him over.

"Private Benjamin Prentice, Missouri State Militia," he replied, saluting. "I was on a foraging party and got kinda tied up here, then them guerrillas showed up and I never got back to my company."

"I see," said the captain. "So you just thought you'd surrender."

"Well, seeing as how you fellers have won the field here, I thought it was the proper thing."

"Very well." The captain spoke to the men behind him. "You four escort this prisoner up to town. We'll leave his weapon here. Ours aren't much better, but at least they're ours." He turned back to Prentice. "You'll have company, I venture. Things seemed to be going our way when my company was detailed down this direction. Well, I need to see to my men." Tipping his hat to Charlotte, he turned on his heel and walked away, leaving the two of them to walk back up the slope through the cornfield to Daybreak.

"You go ahead," Charlotte said. "I'll be up directly."

As Turner walked away, a wave of bitterness swept over Charlotte. She should just leave it all. The villagers could manage themselves. Nothing mattered, names of mountains, names of people—who cared? Carry off the dead, place them in the ground, just another layer of dead on top of the layers that had come before, like the Indian mounds they so blithely plowed through. Another layer of compost to fertilize the ground, that's all they were. Temples, houses, dreams, loves—everything would end up dead and buried, forgotten relics for some unthinking person to stumble across and ignorantly speculate upon someday, just as she had done when she found the arrowhead. And that if they were lucky. More likely, they would be forgotten entirely. Ignorance and foolishness were their inheritance, and destruction and waste were to be their legacy.

She turned her face to the village, where she could see Turner walking among the stunned townspeople. They were examining the damage, tending the wounded, consoling each other. The wagonload of human loss was creaking up the mountain to the graveyard, followed by a troop of soldiers who had fetched shovels from the barn. Life going on, ants on a hill treading around the bodies of their dead. And there was Newton, seeking his mother, struggling against the tight embrace of Frances Wickman as she tried to calm him.

Charlotte wiped her eyes, took a deep breath, and walked back toward the village.

They buried the soldiers that evening, four graves, two to a grave, with Wickman taking care to note which name went with which grave. "I'll carve out markers for them this winter," he said. The Federals had only dug graves for their own, so the Daybreak men spent the afternoon digging three more graves—two for the bushwhackers and one for Cabot.

"How should I mark these two?" Wickman asked.

"Just say 'Unknown Confederates,'" said Turner.

Cabot's burial was saved for the next day. "We should bury him at sunrise," Charlotte said. "It was his favorite time of day." So as the sun was slanting through the frost-tipped needles of the pine trees the next morning, Cabot's oak box was lowered into its hole. Turner had not prepared anything to say, but as they stood around the grave, it did not feel right just to start shoveling dirt. So he drew a deep breath, opened his mouth, and hoped some words would come out.

"This man could have lived anywhere in the world," he said. "He came from a fine old family, and he had a fine education. But he wasn't satisfied with living out the life his ancestors handed down to him. He wanted to live the life of his own choosing. So he came out here.

"He wanted to find out for himself what kind of light could be drawn from a human soul. And by God, the soul is a bright thing when you rub off the dirt that's on the surface. His was never much tarnished to begin with, for whatever reason. Those of you who came out here in fifty-seven will remember how he became a leader of the group, not because he had any great need to run things, but because whenever he saw a job that needed to be done, he just started doing it, no questions asked. And the next thing you knew, you were joining in and helping.

"He was no farmer. But once he learned the difference between a corn shoot and a grass blade, he was out there hoeing with the best. He was a fine man, and I'm glad I knew him. I'm glad we all knew him. He wasn't one of ours when he came here, but he's one of ours now. Goodbye, friend, you will be missed."

Turner stepped back from the grave opening. The sun was full up in the eastern sky now, warming their faces. He picked up a shovel and got ready to work along with everyone else. But in the moment before they started to fill the grave, Charlotte knelt down. She took a handful of bittersweet from her pocket and tossed in the bright orange berries.

"They'll not grow, buried so deep," Turner said to her gently.

"Those are for him," she said. "I'll plant some for the rest of us tomorrow." She walked away, her head bowed, her hair shining in the morning light.

Harp Webb had passed out when Emile began sewing up his intestines, but to everyone's surprise regained consciousness later that night. They gave him some water and broth, and by the next day, the day of Cabot's funeral, he was sitting up in bed, examining the stitches across his belly, and demanding to be moved back to his own home. But after two more days infection set in, and two days after that they were back at the cemetery, lowering one more body into a hole in the ground, into the universal forgiveness of the grave.

By that time the community had begun to recover from the shock of being rounded up and held in the Temple. The children were venturing out to play again, but they were nervous and stayed close to home. They repaired the shattered windows with oilcloth; there was no telling when they might get glass again.

But shattered spirits were harder to repair. The children's fearfulness did not go away with the passing of the weeks. Charlotte heard phantom hoofbeats in the night, and the knowledge that she was not alone in this apprehension gave her no comfort when she awoke, sweaty and startled, her muscles tense and her nerves straining. The bloodstained earth, the bullet fragments, the trampled fields, all forced the villagers into recognition that the war was real. It had come to them and would not go away for any amount of wishing and good will. Hildebrand and his men had ridden south for now, but they could return any day bringing more destruction—and this time it would be directed at Daybreak.

Charlotte tried to manage her grief at the loss of Adam, knowing it served the community no good to have her wrapped in mourning when so many weaker souls needed comfort. But she couldn't shake it. Every place in the village, every spot in the fields, was a place of memory for her. The place in the road where they had talked about politics. The doorway where she had stopped for a moment to watch him from a distance. The Temple where they had finally danced. Everywhere had meaning and everywhere had pain. In the night when Turner reached for her, she accepted his embrace, but the image of Adam would not go away, even if she had wanted it to.

November 1861 / January 1862

Chapter 28

Before they knew it, November had come. The harvest was over, and the days grew quiet. From time to time, companies of soldiers, troops of cavalry, would pass by on their way south; and from time to time more ragged groups would return, bearing their dead and wounded, or leading a clump of prisoners. Marie Mercadier organized the children to hand gourds of water to the men as they passed. The war energized her; with troubles at every hand that were greater than her own, she found release from the prison of scrutiny that had bound her and threw herself into soldiers' relief and sanitary associations.

A new garrison commander came to town and then disappeared, and then another. No one bothered to learn their names anymore. Holding an inconsequential Missouri town was no path to advancement; the only way up the ranks was to win a significant engagement. The guerrillas would not hold still long enough for that. They dodged the organized companies and took to raiding instead, picking off soldiers home on furlough, stopping trains to search for troops, killing informers and collaborators. It was worse out west, everyone said; the Federals and the irregulars had reached a state of total war, and you could night-ride from Lamar to Independence, navigating by the light of burning fields and farmhouses. The troops saw little point in chasing after these ghosts. They held the towns and tried to keep the railroads running, but beyond that—why trot out to an ambush whenever another farmer got hung?

Newton's fifth birthday came and went on a crisp day when the air was so bright it felt charged with energy. "Come walk with me," Charlotte told Turner in the afternoon. They walked past Harp Webb's empty house toward the narrow place along the riverbank where he had killed the one-armed man. Turner didn't like to visit this spot; even though he supposed he had killed others in the fight at the ford, that first killing remained vivid in his mind, and the place felt haunted to him. He supposed it always would. But before they reached the spot, Charlotte veered through the bushes down an overgrown trail. "This is where Adam always came in the mornings," she said.

She led him down the sloping rock to the water's edge. Together they sat and watched the river flow, its waters gently lapping near their feet. Turner thought for a moment to ask her how she knew this to be Cabot's private spot, but thought the better of it. The time for jealous questions, if ever there was such a time, had passed.

"Newton's going to have a baby brother or sister come springtime," she said.

The news took Turner by surprise, and even more to his surprise he found himself wiping tears from his cheeks with a trembling hand. "Almost makes you afraid to bring a child into a world like this," he said.

"Almost," she said.

"You're not afraid?"

She smiled. "What kind of madwoman would I be if I weren't? But you and I are not the sort to cower."

"If Sam Hildebrand shows up here, I may do some cowering," Turner said disconsolately.

"He's likely to, you know," she said, her expression serious. "Have you thought about that?"

Turner nodded.

"And?"

"As far as I can see, my choices are to wait here and let him kill me, or go out and find him first. Two can play the ambush game."

The rock was warm in the sun. Charlotte took off her shoes and put them beside her. Turner did the same.

"Murder or be murdered? Husband, is that the best you can come up with?" She flicked him playfully on his arm.

"Very well, Madam President, tell me what to do."

She paused, then spoke slowly, deliberately. "What do you think Adam would do?"

Turner didn't even have to think. "He was going to leave Daybreak for a while. He had written your father and asked him to take him on as an aide."

Charlotte nodded. "I'm not surprised. He always loved that sense of duty."

She leaned over and put her open hand, fingers spread, into the water, just at the surface, and watched it ripple over her fingers. "You may not have noticed, but he always admired you. Always. Even when you were—you know. In eclipse."

Turner reflected. "I suppose so."

"You know I'm right."

"I don't even admire myself sometimes."

"Who does? It's a good thing you don't." Charlotte pressed her hand, cold and wet, against his face. "You should take Adam's place. Go find my father, and enlist in the service."

"You can't be serious," Turner said. "This valley is dangerous enough as it is. But to leave you and Newton alone? With another baby coming?"

"I didn't say it would be easy," she said. "But to stay here and have Hildebrand show up some night, drag you out and hang you? That wouldn't be protecting us. And for you to stalk and kill him—even if you could, and don't forget, he's been ambushing people in the woods a lot longer than you have—what would that do? I didn't come out here to spend my life with a bushwhacker."

"Daybreak started out as a beautiful dream, and many have suffered to breathe life into it," Turner said. "I can't just leave."

"What was that dream, what did we believe in, really? People working together, putting aside competition in pursuit of equality. You're not giving that up. Daybreak will still be here when you return. And if it's not here, it'll be somewhere else."

Turner stood up. The river in front of him flowed on, north to south, always moving, always pushing, down out of the mountains, through the shut-ins, through the swamps to Arkansas and beyond. Now that he thought about it, why were they here, in this place? It was just chance. A good lecture in St. Louis, the meeting with George Webb. It all seemed so long ago. Maybe he should just load everything on another boat and float back downstream. But of course that was not possible. The river had flowed on. As he stood, he looked across to the other bank, and he recalled that the big cedar tree he was looking at, lit up with yellow light from the lowering sun, was the tree under which he and Adam had buried the one-armed man. It wasn't just the land that kept them here, or the loved ones they had buried in the cemetery; it was the killing as well, the body secretly buried in the sandy river bottom.

"Well," he said, "if the goal was to show how human nature could be perfected, we've certainly fallen short. That tree over there is where we buried him—you know, the man who killed Lysander Smith."

"Was that the goal? Perfection?"

"I thought so at one time. Maybe not." Turner reflected that he had always been prone to believing his own rhetoric—that human beings could rise above the endless cycle of work and spend, turning into gods. Instead, he had joined the monsters, a liar, a killer, a cheat. Some demigod he had become. Maybe the goal should simply have been to live a better life, or try to live a better life.

Charlotte tugged at the tail of his coat, and he sat back down on the sloping rock. "We're in a war," she said. None of us are innocent now. We aren't going to change the world for a while. All we can hope to do is keep things together and survive."

"I've been an idealistic fool, pretending I could remake humanity."

"I love the idealist. I married one. And if he ever gets realistic and starts accepting whatever the world hands him, I'll kick him in the shins."

It was getting dark. They put their shoes on and headed back from the river, hand in hand.

"Springtime, eh?" he said.

"Yes. May, I think."

"Shall we start talking about names?"

"Let's wait till springtime. Don't want to bring bad luck."

"All right. But if it's another boy—"

She read his mind. "Yes. That would be good. And when you return, we must think about how to keep this community on a sound footing. We know that farming won't support a town of any size, and I'm beginning to have my doubts about the rope mill."

"I haven't agreed with your idea about leaving," Turner said.

"Yet," said Charlotte.

When they emerged from the river woods, they could see a troop of Federal cavalry resting on their horses outside their house. Almost everyone else in the community was gathered around them. Sheriff Willingham was sitting in their front door, playing with Newton, making him guess which hand held a pebble. He stood up as they approached and removed his hat.

"Evening, folks. I have some bad news."

Turner felt Charlotte wobble on his arm, but she regained her strength. They walked the last few steps toward him.

"Yes, Sheriff? What is it?" Charlotte said. Her voice was husky.

He held out a piece of paper. "Evacuation order. Captain's issued it. This valley's had too much rebel activity, and we can't seem to stamp it out. So every man from fifteen to forty-five has to clear out. Women and children can stay or go as they please. I'm sorry."

"Is that all?" Charlotte exclaimed. "I was afraid ... well ... I was afraid someone had gotten killed."

"No, ma'am," he said. "But any man we find in the valley from now on is considered an outlaw. Orders are to shoot on sight."

"When does this start?" Turner said.

"Starts now," said Willingham. "These boys and me are riding on down the river. We're stopping at every settlement from here to Greenville. It'll take us another day or two, but when they come back, they'll be ready to shoot."

"Does the captain have that kind of authority?" Charlotte said.

"Well, ma'am, it's martial law. They can do anything they decide to do. Back when Frémont was the state commander, he freed all the slaves, till Old Abe went and un-freed 'em."

"Come on, Willingham," said one of the horsemen. "I want to make it to French Mills before full dark."

"Well, you've been served your notice," Willingham said, walking to his horse. He looked around the group and gestured toward Turner, Wickman, Schnack, and the others. "Don't know when I'll see you fellers again. Good luck to you." He scrutinized Emile Mercadier. "How old are you, mister?"

"I'm over forty-five, that's for sure," Mercadier said.

"All right then. Well, goodbye." He mounted his horse.

"How does it feel to be driving people from their homes?" Charlotte called to him.

"Better than it would feel to have these boys chasing after me and shooting at me," Willingham said. He rode off in the center of the troop.

The colonists were left standing in the packed dirt in front of the house. "What are we going to do, Mr. Turner?" Schnack said.

"Seeing that everybody on every side wants to shoot us, I guess we'd better do as the man says and leave," Turner said. "Like it or not."

"I go back to Cincinnati, I think," Schnack said. "After that, I don't know, enlist maybe."

"Not me," Wickman said. "Sleeping on the ground is not for me. We've still got Emile's shop in town. I'll just go up there and stay. Who knows, maybe I'll learn shoe repair. Missus, maybe you can bring the girls in now and then, whenever it's safe."

"How about you, Mr. Turner?" Schnack said. "Where are you going to go?"

Turner looked up at the ridge, which was now almost completely dark. "I'm going east. I'll try to find Charlotte's father and sign on with him. Do what I can to get this war over with as soon as possible and come back to Daybreak."

One by one, everyone went back to their homes. Turner and Charlotte stood in the yard and watched them go. Newton quietly slipped between them and took their hands.

"Your daddy has to go and fight in this war," Charlotte told him.

"Are you going to be a hero?" Newton asked with awe in his face.

"Only as much of a hero as I need to be to get back to you," said Turner.

That night they met at the Temple, then went out and dug up two fence posts from around Wickman's house to give the departing men their shares of the community treasury. "I may not have this much when I come back," Schnack said, embarrassed. "I hear you got to buy your own food and such."

"Don't worry," Charlotte said. "You're a citizen of Daybreak. You can come back without a penny if you have to."

"I give it to my mama back in Cincinnati," he said. "She'll hold it for me and send me what I need."

"Let's go out together tomorrow morning," Turner said. "We can leave the wagon in town with Wickman."

Emile Mercadier raised his hand as the group was about to leave. "One moment," he said. He tottered toward the front of the room; Emile's legs had been getting worse through the years, and his steps were slow and painful.

"We come a long way," he said. "Marie and I, we come all the way from France, and John Wesley and Frances there come from Baltimore, and Mr. Schnack from Ohio, and on and on it goes. But here we are today, together. I want you all to come back when this war is over, but we all know that war sometimes don't cooperate with what we want. So I ask you all, stop for a moment with me and accept my thanks. Thank you, my brothers and sisters, for laboring with me these years, and may we all meet here again soon." He reached out to Charlotte. "Take my hand, *cherie*."

Charlotte stepped up and took his hand, and with her other hand she grasped Turner's. One by one the members of the community joined hands, Marie last of all, taking the hand of Schnack and completing the circle by taking her father's. No one spoke. They stood in a great ring, hands clasped in the dim lamplight, for a long minute. Then Emile raised his hands, and they all followed.

"Where there is darkness," he said softly.

In bed that night, with Newton asleep, they made love, and Turner felt an intensity in Charlotte, as if she were making love to him for the last time in her life. Neither of them wanted the moment to end. But end it did, and afterward they lay together quietly, with her head resting on his chest.

"What kind of world will we see after all this is over?" Turner said into the night.

"The same world you left," Charlotte answered. "People love and are loved. You love and are loved. Men do horrible deeds and great deeds. Women wait and fear and hope and love. Children grow up and we try to smooth their way, but fail most of the time."

"Will Daybreak be here when I get back?"

She swatted his chest softly. "Of course, you silly man. Do you think Daybreak is just a place? That's only in the book. You'll take Daybreak with you, and I'll keep Daybreak here."

There was a silence for a time. Turner could tell she was working on what to say next. "In the morning," she said, "you must get up early. Go spend some time with your daughter, and her mother. Then come back to me." She rubbed her nose against his shoulder. "Now lie still," she said. "I want to listen to your heartbeat."

Charlotte lay there for a long time, her ear pressed against James' nightshirt, listening to the sounds of the dark. Newton stirring in his sleep. A cricket somewhere near the door. James' breathing in her ear as it grew slower and deeper.

How many nights had she lain here in just such a way, the one who stayed awake while the others slept? This was to be her task in life, it seemed, to be the watchful and strong one, the one who held everyone else together. Others could fall apart or indulge their failings, but not her. Where was the justice in that? Was there no room in the world for a moment's weakness for her? Giving James cheer as he marched off to war, when what she really wanted was to retreat from it all and hide away from the world. Her father far away, her husband leaving, and of course—

Her love gone.

She suddenly recalled her mother and understood what had happened to her during those final years. Someone she loved had been taken from her, taken without sense or cause, and her own life was hollowed out, a great emptiness inside her that could not be filled by anything else. It would remain forever empty.

Tomorrow she would try to be that strong person again. Tonight she lay in darkness. She turned her face away and rested her cheek on her forearm.

Charlotte realized that she had not truly mourned Adam yet. She had only experienced his loss in the same unthinking way of her mother, stunned by the blow into insensibility and mute gestures. She needed to do more to honor him than just feel sad and send her husband to fight in his place. She owed it to him—she owed it to herself—to ponder both his dying and his living, to make something of it. The qualities in her that had drawn him to her—those needed to be remembered and preserved, not like a flower between the pages of a book, but in life as she lived it, or else the woman he loved would be lost. And the things in him she had loved so much—

Those things were buried in the cemetery, at least in their true form. The best she could hope was to re-create them in the people around her, her children, the villagers, herself.

And a wall inside her broke and she began to cry, the tears she had been holding back all this time, let them run down her cheeks and over her arm without trying to wipe them away, tears for Adam and for herself. She let them flow. Perhaps there would be no end to them, but so be it. Surely there would be an end to tears someday. Let the flow begin, in the hope that someday they would wash out a clean channel from her heart into the brutal, brutal world.

November 1862

Chapter 29

C harlotte sat in the cemetery on the bench Wickman had carved, holding the Sharps rifle in her lap. The bittersweet she had planted on Adam's grave had grown a foot up the marker; in another year it would be reaching beyond its top. She would run a string from the grave to the overhanging tree branches to give it something to climb. Another year or two, and it would garland the edge of the forest with its bright berries, and then perhaps spread along the hillside. That would be good, autumn flashes of orange along the forest's verge to remember him by.

Charlotte recalled Harp's Webb's words about the power of watchful waiting; there had been turkey sign on the hillside across the hollow. She would have a couple of hours this afternoon to try to bag one while young Adam was napping; Marie had promised to come to her door and wave when he awoke. And if not a turkey, perhaps a deer would come out to graze among the corn stubble. Or a squirrel, or a rabbit. Anything would be fine.

She looked down at the village. She could see the river ford, the junction of the main road and the Daybreak road, the Temple of Community, the houses, her house, and all the way down to Webb's house. She could see Newton, no napper anymore, leading Angus Mercadier, who ought to have been napping, around the fields. From this distance she could not hear them, but she could tell they were talking as they played, a steady stream of kid-talk, Lord only knew about what. Now that the leaves were off the trees, she could see the water wheel in the river, turning slowly, its energy running to no purpose since the gear shaft was not engaged.

They had not put in any cash crops this year. There seemed no point to it, and besides, food was the first necessity. So the whole valley had been planted in row crops and hill crops—potatoes, beans, corn, sweet potatoes, greens, beets, turnips. Wheat took too much work for the flour it yielded, so this year there would be nothing but cornbread. There was one rangy hog they had been tolling down to the barn, and in a few more weeks they would kill it. Foraging parties and thieves—it was hard to tell the difference—had gotten all the cattle. At least the foraging parties stopped and gave them scrip.

She reflexively patted her apron pocket. The latest letter from Turner was still there. She always kept the newest one with her for a while before adding it to the packet in the bedroom. Turner was, as he always had been, a faithful correspondent, although the letters themselves were sometimes muddy or crumpled. She knew he was downplaying the hardships he and her father were enduring in Virginia; the newspapers were full of stories about the grind down the Peninsula, Lee's takeover of the rebel army and his dash into Maryland, and the horrific day at Antietam. But Turner wrote about people he had encountered, odd sights he had seen. If the weather was fine, he would mention it. If he didn't say anything, she knew they were pushing through knee-deep mud, or snow, or something.

Charlotte knew he sent letters addressed to Josephine as well, and no doubt there were words in them for Marie. She had made her peace with that fact. Frances Wickman liked to go into town after the mail; she took the children in once a week to see their father and spend the day. When Frances returned, there was usually a letter from Turner for Charlotte and one for Josephine. Charlotte could see the look in Marie's eyes as they waited for the mail and knew that Marie still loved him, probably as much as she herself did. There was nothing she could do about that. Life had its odd turns, and this was one of them.

Things had been quieter lately. The big military operations had moved south and east, to Tennessee and Mississippi, and Price's rebel army was somewhere in Arkansas. But the guerrilla war had gotten worse; it was dangerous to be a man, whatever the age. Earlier in the fall, the Federal commander up in Palmyra had taken ten prisoners out of the jail and had them shot, sitting atop their own coffins, as punishment for some rebel offense. And a week ago Frances had ridden to town and passed old Krummrich, at least sixty, hanging from a tree in front of his burning farmhouse. He had thought his advanced age would give him safety to talk up the Union, but he was wrong. So Emile stayed close to the colony and let the women make the town trips. So far, at least, a woman could still travel undisturbed.

The graves of Adam, Harp, and all the soldiers had grassed over a little; but there were three fresh mounds in the cemetery. Marie got the credit for that idea. Even the most desperate forager would not think to unearth such a site, so they had buried three tightly nailed boxes under about an inch of dirt, with potatoes and turnips for the winter. They would dig them out one by one as the need arose. It would be a lean winter, but they would manage.

As she sat and watched, a man on a horse crossed the river at the ford. He had to be a rebel—the Union soldiers always traveled in groups. And he was either supremely confident, or he had the carelessness of the desperate, to be traveling alone in broad daylight. When he reached the bank, he did not come down the road, but cut into the woods along the river. He followed the river-bank south through the underbrush, using the ropewalk as a path, riding slowly with his head bent over the neck of his horse. When he was across from the Webbs' old house, he turned out toward the road again. Charlotte watched him dismount, remove a couple of blankets from behind his saddle, and place them in a line across the road. Then he led the horse across, picking up the blankets behind himself. He rolled them up and tied them behind the saddle again, but when he tried to remount the horse, something seemed to be the matter. He couldn't lift his leg high enough to get his foot in the stirrup. He tried several times, his horse standing patiently, but with no success. Finally he led the horse to the porch of the house, climbed up a couple of steps, and tried to swing himself over its back from there. But the angle was wrong. He missed the saddle and fell on his face beside the horse. It stood beside him for a minute, the reins trailing on the ground, and then began to graze in the yard.

By now several of the villagers had noticed the activity and were standing in the street, watching, unwilling to go any closer. Charlotte came down through the fields. The thought passed through her mind that this upper pasture would make decent corn ground, and she made a mental note to set the children to picking up rocks out of it this winter.

She walked down the center street of Daybreak, the Sharps rifle cradled in her hands. Frances Wickman came out to meet her.

"What do you think?" Mrs. Wickman said.

"Let's go see," said Charlotte.

By the time they reached the house, Emile Mercadier and Mrs. Prentice had joined them, with Newton and Angus tagging along behind. They stood in a circle around the man as Emile rolled him onto his back. He let out a deep groan but made no other sound.

"Well," Mrs. Wickman said. "Sam Hildebrand."

Up close and helpless, with his eyes rolled back and his mouth gaping, Hildebrand lost all power to terrify. His left pants leg was caked and bloody from mid-thigh down. The horse nuzzled Charlotte's shoulder, as if it wanted to get a look too.

Mercadier gave Charlotte's rifle a significant glance. "Here's our chance," he said.

"I've not yet reached the spot where I'd shoot an unconscious man," Charlotte said. "Let's carry him back to my house."

They unsaddled the horse and used its blankets to make a pallet on the floor for Hildebrand. Charlotte took a knife and cut away the trouser leg. The thigh muscle had a deep bullet wound from side to side; it was stuffed with cloth and had stopped bleeding for the most part, but was still seeping moisture. The muscle had nearly been cut through.

"No broken bones, anyway," Charlotte said. She had watched the granny woman from French Mills often enough to have an idea what to do. She sent Mrs. Prentice to cut some strips of bark from the willow trees along the riverbank and Newton for water from Harp Webb's cave. She set the water boiling in two pans, one for willow bark tea and the other, just a small amount, simmering with some mashed slippery elm bark and coneflower root she kept in a jar in the rafters. She folded this mash into a clean cloth and packed it into the wound, wrapping it gently into place with more strips of cloth.

"Now we wait," she said. She looked at the group. "I'm going to go wash my hands. If he wakes up, soak a rag in that tea and give it to him to suck on."

She walked to the river and rinsed off her hands. The water was cold but felt good.

"Really, now," she said, surprising herself with the sound of her own voice. "What am I trying to prove?" She had no answer for her question and went on rinsing her hands and arms until all the blood was gone.

In turns, they watched him through the night, and in the morning Charlotte changed his dressing. By noon Hildebrand had roused. He made an ugly face as he drank the willow bark tea, but drank it nevertheless.

"You could put some honey in this," he croaked.

"If we had any," Charlotte said.

Hildebrand closed his eyes and laid his head back on the pillow. After a moment he spoke, looking at the ceiling. "I was figuring to get to Harp Webb's cave and rest up a few days," he said. "Either die there or get better and go on. My mama and wife are down in Arkansas."

"Run into some soldiers?"

Hildebrand peeked down at his leg and let out a soft chuckle. "No. I was staying with some friends up by Mineral Point, and some local boy thought he'd make his name by killing the notorious Hildebrand. Shot me as I was going to the privy in the morning, then run off." He looked down at the leg again. "Just so you know. You're not going to cut that off."

"Not planning to, Mr. Hildebrand." Charlotte picked little Adam out of his crib and went to the door. "If you're up to it tonight, I'll boil you an egg."

She stepped outside into the cool air, although she had nowhere to go. She could hardly imagine that she had been in there, talking with that killer, as if he were some casual passerby. Had she lost her senses? On the other hand, she couldn't see another path to take.

Newton came up to her as she sat under the tree. He leaned against her leg, which was his new way of keeping contact without performing the little-boy move of sitting on her lap. "Marie says that man is a very bad man," he said.

"He is, honey. He's a bad man."

"Is he going to hurt you?"

Charlotte put her arm around him. "No. He can't hurt me or anyone else."

"Why are we helping him?"

She squeezed him tighter. "I was just wondering that myself. I guess it's because he's hurt, and maybe helping a hurt man is more important than stopping a bad man. Even when they're the same person."

But she stayed away from the house the rest of the day and let Frances tend to Hildebrand. At night she went in to find him sitting in a chair at the table, drinking a glass of water with grave deliberation, while Newton sat across from him and watched his every move.

"Your boy looks like he's going to eat my liver," Hildebrand said.

"You needn't worry," Charlotte said. "He's a good boy, and we have already discussed you."

Hildebrand cocked an eye at her. "Glad to know it," he said. "That poultice you made is a fine thing. I can feel the healing already."

She boiled three eggs and placed them on the table. "Here you go," she said. They each took an egg, peeled it, and ate in silence.

"I came back here the night after that scrape," Hildebrand said at last. "I had figured to collect my boys. The Federals usually just let 'em lay. But I saw that you all had buried them, and for that I thank you. I sent word to their families, so if you have strangers wanting to visit your graveyard, that's probably who it will be."

"And you?" Charlotte said. "The ones you kill? Do you just let them lay?"

"Yes, ma'am, I suppose I do. I take your point." He chewed a bite of egg thoughtfully. "I heard about them running all the men out of here. I'm sorry for that. Your husband all right?"

"He's back East with my father, in the Army of the Potomac. He's all right as far as we know."

Hildebrand's glance sneaked over to the table by the stove, but it was clear that the egg was all any of them were getting that night. So he kept his peace.

"And that deserter?"

"When the Federals came through, they took him prisoner. He's confined up at Jefferson's Barracks. We don't hear as much out of him, but we're hoping he'll get paroled soon."

"What a world," he said. "If I had joined up when my brother William did, I might have been out east with the Federals myself. Instead, I'm here, getting shot by a sneak in the bushes." He took another drink of his water. "It's all right, though. I'm not cut out for warfare at a distance. If I'm going to kill someone, I'd prefer to know his name."

"Does that make it more moral?"

"Moral?" Hildebrand snorted. "I never made any such claim. I've got three brothers and an uncle dead, my house burnt out, and my wife and mother on the run. I'd hate to be the man who could see all that happen and not pick up a gun. I didn't want to be a sheep, so I chose to be a wolf instead."

"And after this war is over? Will you be able to put down the wolf and pick up the man?"

He looked at her in surprise. "Over? I haven't given a moment's thought to this war being over. I guess it will have to end someday, won't it."

"Of course it will. And when it does, we will all have to look at what we have become."

"What I would like to know," Hildebrand said, "is whether there is any spot on this earth where man is just. I can live with kill-and-be-killed. I didn't want to wait for divine justice, so I made my own. Put my thumb on the scales, you might say. And once your thumb is on the scales, you can't take it off. Now that I'm on this path, I have to walk down it to the end, and that's fine. But I'd like to know if somebody else somewhere has figured out another path, even though it's not for me. Just to know that it's there."

Charlotte gathered up the plates and put them on the counter. She could scour them in the morning.

"I'd like to know that too, Mr. Hildebrand," she said, with her back turned. "You killed a very dear friend of mine, I suppose you know that."

Hildebrand sat silent. "Yes," he said, after a while. "Good man, too. No reason at all for him to run out and warn those boys, except he thought it was the right thing to do. We weren't going to harm any of you people, just wanted you out of the way during the fighting and didn't want no alarms. Maybe help ourselves to some food."

She turned from the counter and looked at him across the room, her arms folded. "So if I were to want to put my thumb on a scale...."

"Yes, ma'am, I guess it would be me who would rise up on the other side. Well, if I may, I'd like to know where my horse and gear are. I will leave in the morning. Margaret and Mama will be worried down in Arkansas."

"They're in Webb's barn. Your horse is fine, a little underfed, I'm afraid, but that's all we can do. Newton, get ready for bed." The boy got up from the table, his eyes still on Hildebrand, and walked sideways to the back room.

"Ma'am, I need to tell you this," Hildebrand said. "I am not a man who forgets a slight, but I am also not one to forget a kindness either. If your husband comes back here, you can tell him that he is safe from me and mine. Normally, a man tries to shoot me, I'm not going to rest until I shoot him. But you, well...."

"Don't thank me," Charlotte said. "I was trying to shoot you, too."

This nonplussed him. He pushed his chair back from the table. Unable to walk, he lowered himself to the floor on his hands and scooted himself to his pallet, not speaking.

Charlotte was about to follow Newton into the bedroom but stopped at the door. "That one-armed man who was with you back in fifty-nine, the one who tried to hang Lysander Smith—"

"I remember him. Lost that arm in a flour mill, or so he told me."

"What was his name?"

"Cunningham. Matty Cunningham. It was his daddy's flour mill, down in Bloomfield, where he lost that arm."

"His parents, they're still living?"

"Far as I know."

"All right. Thank you."

She went to bed then, got Adam in his cradle and Newton tucked in the trundle, but sometime in the night Newton crawled into the big bed with her and she let him stay. She awoke in the wee hours to hear Hildebrand scraping his way across the floor and out the door. She knew it would be the Christian thing to go out and help him, but couldn't find it in herself to do it. A half an hour later, she heard a horse go past the door. When it reached the road, its hoofbeats clattered away at a fast clip; she supposed Hildebrand had decided to forgo secrecy in favor of speed.

The next morning, once Adam was fed and safely in the hands of Frances for a couple of hours, she went to the barn and found a piece of board. There was a broken shovel handle leaning against the wall; she split the handle end with the axe and fixed the board into it, tying it into place with some pieces of rope. Then she laid it in the wagon, brought a pot of ink from the print shed, and drove across the river. She tied the horse to a tree at the side of the road and walked into the scrubland.

It wasn't hard to find the grave of the one-armed man. The ground across the river was sandy, brushy undergrowth; the big cedar tree was one of the few landmarks. She located the mound of dirt on the north side of the tree, as long as a man.

Charlotte laid the marker on the ground, cleaned off a stick, and painted the man's name on it with the printer's ink. Then she found a rock and drove the broken end of the shovel handle into the ground. It went in easily; the soil was not hard packed.

She looked around. It was a scrubby piece of ground, with greenbriar and blackberry bushes all over. The blackberries were probably what attracted the bear Adam had mentioned once, long ago. It was not a good place to be buried, but then again, what place was.

When the spring floods came, this marker would probably be washed away. She knew that. But tonight she would write the family, and at least they would know where their son was buried. Even a killer was someone's son, somebody's darling.

Charlotte untied the horse and took the wagon back to the barn. She returned the ink pot to the print shed; the Washington press and trays of type sat undisturbed, gathering dust. Perhaps she and Marie should start up *The Eagle* again; Marie could typeset, and between the two of them they could come up with ideas. But she discarded the notion as soon as it passed through her mind. Where would they get paper? What bits they could come by were precious for letter writing. And who would be their readers? Their subscriber list was probably as out-of-date as Harp Webb's old muzzle-loader.

No, she supposed, the time was not right for publishing, reaching out, trying to set an example. Now was the time for holding on. Another morning in Daybreak, a day in which to survive, to gather remnants, to act the part of the groundhog and burrow deep, to hold on to what is dear while storms present and future raged overhead. God willing, Turner would return someday, Turner and her father, and all the rest, and they would write new chapters to their lives. And for those who did not return, she could only hope that someone would mark their graves and write their families.

Charlotte looked at the sky and checked the angle of the sun. Adam would surely be awake by now, and hungry. It was time to get on with the day.

Book Club Questions

1. Is Adam Cabot too idealistic for his own good? How would you strike a balance between idealism and practicality in their world and in ours?

2. How harshly do you judge Turner for his failings? Should Charlotte have forgiven him?

3. How do you feel about Charlotte and Adam and their involvement?

4. Which of the secondary characters is the most memorable to you and why?

5. Although Sam Hildebrand's actions in the novel are fictional, he was a real-life Missouri bushwhacker. How did you feel about him, and did your feelings change over the course of the novel?

6. What is your understanding of a "utopian" community? What ones do you know about? What have been their successes and failures?

7. What's your sense of the Civil War in Missouri and how it differed from the war in the Eastern states?

8. How do you feel about Turner's attempt to maintain Daybreak's neutrality as the conflict escalated in the rest of the nation?

9. What future do you imagine for these people after the close of the book?

10. Did you like the title of the book? Why or why not? Can you think of passages in the book where the theme of seeing things in a certain "slant of light" was used?

About the Author

Steve Wiegenstein grew up in the eastern Missouri Ozarks and roams its back roads every chance he gets. The Black River and the Annapolis Branch Library were his two main haunts as a kid, and they remain his Mecca and Medina to this day. He is a longtime scholar of the 19th century Icarian movement in America, which provided the inspiration for *Slant of Light*. He particularly enjoyed weaving the real-life story of Sam Hildebrand—the notorious Confederate bushwhacker who murdered one of Steve's ancestors—into the novel. Steve and his wife, Sharon Buzzard, both academics, live in Columbia, Missouri. *Slant of Light*, the first book in his Daybreak series, is his first novel.

About Blank Slate Press

Blank Slate Press, formed in 2010, seeks to discover, nurture, publish and promote new literary voices from the greater Saint Louis region. To learn more, please visit www.blankslatepress.com. Our previous novels include:

The Samaritan by Fred Venturini (2011)
Dancing with Gravity by Anene Tressler (2011)